VIRGIL

WANDER

LEIF
ENGER

corsair

CORSAIR

First published in the US by Grove Atlantic, 2018
First published in Great Britain in 2018 by Corsair
This paperback edition published in 2019

1 3 5 7 9 10 8 6 4 2

A CIP catalogue record for this book
is available from the British Library.

ISBN: 978-1-4721-5448-4

Printed and bound in Great Britain by Clays Ltd, Elcograf S.p.A.

Papers used by Corsair are from well-managed forests
and other responsible sources.

Corsair
An imprint of
Little, Brown Book Group
Carmelite House
50 Victoria Embankment
London EC4Y 0DZ

An Hachette UK Company
www.hachette.co.uk

www.littlebrown.co.uk

Leif Enger was raised in Osakis, Minnesota, and worked as a reporter and producer for Minnesota Public Radio before writing his bestselling debut novel *Peace Like a River*, which won the Independent Publisher Book Award and was one of the *Los Angeles Times* and *Time Magazine*'s Best Books of the Year. His second novel, *So Brave, Young, and Handsome*, was also a bestseller and Number 8 on Amazon.com's Top 100 Editors' Picks. He and his wife Robin live in Minnesota.

Also by Leif Enger

Peace Like a River
So Brave, Young, and Handsome

Robin

Bird in the garden
Tail of the kite
Wind over water
Laughter at night

VIRGIL WANDER

the previous tenant

1

NOW I THINK THE PICTURE WAS UNSPOOLING ALL ALONG AND I JUST failed to notice. The obvious really isn't so—at least it wasn't to me, a Midwestern male cruising at medium altitude, aspiring vaguely to decency, contributing to PBS, moderate in all things including romantic forays, and doing unto others more or less reciprocally.

If I were to pinpoint when the world began reorganizing itself—that is, when my seeing of it began to shift—it would be the day a stranger named Rune blew into our bad luck town of Greenstone, Minnesota, like a spark from the boreal gloom. It was also the day of my release from St. Luke's Hospital down in Duluth, so I was concussed and more than a little adrift.

The previous week I'd driven up-shore to a popular lookout to photograph a distant storm approaching over Lake Superior. It was a beautiful storm, self-contained as storms often are, hunched far out over the vast water like a blob of blue ink, but it stalled in the middle distance and time just slipped away. There's a picnic table up there where I've napped more than once. What woke me this time was the mischievous gale delivering autumn's first snow. I leaped behind the wheel as it came down in armloads. Highway 61 quickly grew rutted and slick. Maybe I was driving too fast. U2 was on the radio—"Mysterious Ways," I seem to recall. Apparently my heartbroken Pontiac breached a safety barrier and made a long, lovely, some might say cinematic arc into the churning lake.

I say *apparently* since this particular memory is not crisp. The airbag deployed at the barricade, snapped my head back, and swaddled me in a whiplash haze that took a long time to shake off. I missed the lightning thoughts and impressions a person might expect in this situation—cold panic, clenching denial, a magician's bouquet of vibrant regrets.

I'd have sunk with the car if Marcus Jetty hadn't been doing a little late-season beachcombing. Marcus runs Greenstone Salvage & Tinker, a famous local eyesore of bike frames, tube amps, hula poppers, oil drums, and knobs of driftwood. He was picking along the jagged strand in his raincoat, eye on a fat cork from somebody's herring net, when a car approached on the highway above. He later described the sounds of a whining V6 and thumping bass line before the barrier burst to shrapnel and the world for a moment muffled itself.

In the silence Marcus looked up. A midsize American sedan sailed dreamlike through thickening snow.

I forgot to thank Marcus when he came to visit during my recovery. Actually I didn't recognize him. That happened a lot at first. He was reserved and shook my hand as though we were meeting for the first time. "Salvage man," he kindly explained. Eventually I asked him if he ever expected to salvage a middle-aged bachelor and film projectionist. Nope, no, he replied. The market for such specimens was in decline. Marcus is one of those weathered old reticent types whose rare comment tends to be on point.

The neurologist was a Finn named Koskinen with a broad decent face and a Teddy Roosevelt mustache. He diagnosed *mild traumatic brain injury*. This sounded paradoxical but so did everything else he said. For example, the damage was short-term but might last quite a while or possibly longer than that. I could expect within months to regain my balance as long as I didn't tip over; to experience fewer headaches or maybe just get used to them. He said over time I would remember the names of friends and the nearer relatives, that I would recover fine motor skills and pockets of personal history I didn't yet realize had vanished. Despite my confusion I liked Koskinen immediately. He had the heartening bulk of the aging athlete defeated by pastry. He delivered all news as though it were good.

Most welcome was his prediction that language would gradually return. Not that I couldn't speak, but I had to stick to basics. My storehouse of English had been pillaged. At first I thought common nouns were hardest hit, *coffee* and *doorway* and so on, but it soon became clear that the missing were mostly adjectives.

"Don't worry, everything will come back," said Dr. Koskinen. "Most things probably will. A good many of them might return. There will be at least a provisional rebound. How does this make you feel?" I wanted to say *relieved* or *encouraged* or at least *hopeful* but none of these were available. All I could muster was a mute grin at which the doctor nodded with his mouth open in a vaguely alarming smile.

He was correct about the language, though. Within weeks certain prodigal words started filtering home. They came one at a time or in shy small groups. I remember when *sea-kindly* showed up, a sentimental favorite, followed by *desiccated* and *massive*. *Brusque* appeared all by itself, which seemed apt; *merry* and *boisterous* arrived together. This would be a good time to ask for your patience if I use an adjective too many now and again—even now, some years on, they're still returning. I'm just so glad to see them.

Upon my release I wasn't allowed to drive right away. Even if I could, my car was sitting on its roof under ninety feet of water, so Tom Beeman delivered me home. Beeman's my oldest friend, a massive garrulous North Dakotan of Samoan ancestry—that I remembered him immediately was a relief to us both. He owns and edits the local weekly. He drives a minuscule Geo Metro—he claims to like the mileage, but what he really likes is to pull over and flabbergast onlookers just by climbing out. So little car and so much Beeman emerging from it. The Geo has ruinous shocks, so we went bounding up historic Highway 61 while he brought me up to speed. Genghis, the raccoon Beeman had rescued when its mother was killed in the road, had run off again. He was openly relieved. Nothing is sweeter than a baby raccoon or more wrathful than the baby grown. Beeman said he'd written a short article about my close call and been inundated with people asking after my welfare. Apparently I was popular. Avoiding my eyes he said a rumor had started that I didn't make it, that I died in the lake, so he drove out to where it happened and sure enough someone had hung a twist of flowers on the torn fence. Carnations and baby's breath. There was a white plastic cross and a laminated photo saying, "Virgil Wander RIP." While he poked around, a little scorched-haired lady arrived in a Chevy pickup and marched to the brink with a rosary. When Tom revealed I was alive she wrapped it around her fist in annoyance and sped off dragging a veil of smoke.

I listened to Tom as best I could—he has a naturally comforting voice—but a bad concussion jangles everything. My mind was not clear. His gentle baritone came at me like elbows. The Geo's elliptical progress plus the acute brightness of the world made me queasy. We developed a hand signal so Tom could pull over and allow me to puke. Resting on a swale of grass overlooking the lake, sweat cooling on my brow, I thought I saw a man out there. Not in a boat—just a man standing upright on the shimmery surface of Lake Superior. The lake was so calm it looked concave. The man stood at ease a hundred yards out. He turned his head to look at me. I seemed to shrink, or the world to expand.

"Do you see that?" I asked Beeman, who kept a civil distance. I pointed at the man on the lake. Beeman shrugged: "See what?"

I didn't elaborate. The man smiled—he was way out there, but I could see him smiling right at me. He had a black suit on. He looked like a keyhole or exclamation point standing on the water.

Beeman took me home and carried a paper sack up the seventeen steps to my rooms above the Empress Theater. The sack contained my clothes from the accident, laundered and wadded back up, a toothbrush and razor, and two pairs of throwaway hospital slippers with square toes. Beeman had also fetched my mail from the post office and run into the Citgo for bread and a half gallon of two-percent milk. It was his doing I could get into the apartment at all—my only key was in the Pontiac, down in the glimmery murk. During my stay at St. Luke's, Tom had hired a locksmith to change out the assembly. I stood blinking in front of the flashy new knob until he handed me the key.

I've lived at the Empress a long time—first because of a dire romantic impulse and second because in seven years of trying I haven't been able to sell it. Nevertheless you put your stamp on a home. It's nicer than you'd expect. I had the bachelor's discreet pride in my maple floors and built-in cabinets. My big sister Orry comes from Colorado once or twice a year and always brings some vintage item that suits the place—the bird clock and art deco mirror, the Bakelite wall sconce. Orry walks the tightrope between irony and genuine zeal. She is fond of seafoam green.

For more than twenty years I'd felt at home, in my home. Now I stood weirdly slack in the middle of my kitchen. Everything was off. The fall of light from the wall fixture, the pressboard ceiling tiles mimicking ornamental tin. My skin prickled. What might seem to you only the webby neglect of a week's absence felt to me ominous and elemental. The scene felt staged for my benefit, down to the smallest details: a dead ladybug legs-up on the counter, fingerprint whorls on the chrome toaster.

The evidence of my life lay before me, and I was unconvinced.

After Beeman left I walked through the rooms, turned the TV on and off, flicked through shirts in the closet. The unease would not dissipate. I went through my mail. In the most recent issue of the *Observer* was Beeman's short article about my accident—I started it four or five times but couldn't stay interested. There was coverage of last week's city council meeting, a fluff piece on a local retiree whose antique wrench collection filled two boxcars, and a disturbing paragraph in the police blotter about a young woman found dead of exposure in the woods a few miles north of town.

I cracked open some windows. Even the views were askew. They had an inert stereoscopic quality: EMPRESS in vertical blue neon out front, with Main Street below and the water tower two blocks inland. Out back the pea-gravel roof of the auditorium and past it the moody old sea. I might've been clicking through with a View-Master.

I couldn't nail down what had changed in the apartment.

To begin with, it seemed to belong to someone else.

This made a kind of sense—my perceptions had shifted, just as Dr. Koskinen said. Still, I hadn't expected my hanging shirts to seem like somebody else's shirts, or my framed map of the Spanish Virgin Islands to seem like somebody else's daydream. The candle I light every week for my parents was reduced to a meaningless blue pillar. I wandered into my bedroom and lay down. I had made it to late afternoon. The doctor had said I should sleep as much as possible and try not to think too hard.

But as my bones settled on the mattress, a notion crept in. A short sentence appeared in my mind implying I could go ahead and wear those shirts. I could paint the walls, sell the furniture, throw out the candle. I could do whatever I liked with the building, for one simple reason.

The previous tenant was dead.

Poor Virgil didn't actually make it.

I popped off the mattress and pulled on shoes. They didn't seem like my shoes exactly. They resisted my hands and feet. I pulled them on anyway and got away from there.

I ended up at the waterfront. It's not as though there's any other destination in Greenstone. The truth is that I moved here largely because of the inland sea. I'd always felt peaceful around it—a naïve response given its fearsome temper, but who could resist that wide throw of horizon, the columns of morning steam? And the sound of a continual tectonic bass line. In a northeast gale this pounding adds a layer of friction to every conversation in town.

At the foot of the city pier stood a threadbare stranger. He had eight-day whiskers and fisherman hands, a pipe in his mouth like a mariner in a fable, and a question in his eyes. A rolled-up paper kite was tucked under his arm—I could see bold swatches of paint on it.

There was always a kite in the picture with Rune, as it turned out.

He watched me. He carried an atmosphere of dispersing confusion, as though he were coming awake. "Do you live in this place?" he inquired.

I nodded.

"Is there a motor hotel? There used to be a motor hotel. I don't remember where."

His voice was high, with a rhythmic inflection like short smooth waves. For some reason it gave me a lift. He had a hundred merry crinkles at his eyes and a long-haul sadness in his shoulders.

"Not anymore—not exactly." If I'd had more words, I'd have described Greenstone's last operational motel, the Voyageur, a peeling L-shaped heap with scraggy whirlwinds of litter roaming the parking lot. Though technically "open," the Voyageur is always full, its rooms permanently occupied by the owner's grown children who failed to rise on the outside.

"Oh well," he said, shaking himself like a terrier. He peered round at the Slake International taconite plant, a looming vast trapezoid which had signified bustling growth in the 1950s and lingering decline ever since. Its few tiny windows were whitewashed or broken; its majestic ore dock rose out of the water on eighty-foot pilings and cast a black-boned reflection across the harbor. No ship had loaded here in so long that saplings and ferns grew wild on the planking. We had a little forest up there. I looked at the kite scrolled under his arm. He'd picked the wrong day for that, but then he looked like a man who could wait.

He said, "You are here a long time?"

"Twenty-five years."

At this something changed in him. He acquired an edge. Before I'd have said he looked like many a good-natured pensioner making do without much pension. Now in front of my eyes he seemed to intensify.

"Twenty-five years? Perhaps you knew my son. He lived here. Right in this town," he added, looking round himself, as though giving structure to a still-new idea.

"Is that right. What's his name?"

The old man ignored the question. He pulled a kitchen match from his pocket, thumbnailed it, and relit his pipe, which let me tell you held the most fragrant tobacco—brisk autumn cedar and coffee and orange peel. A few sharp puffs brought it crackling and he held it up to watch smoke drift off the bowl. The smoke ghosted straight up and hung there undecided.

"Who's your boy then?" I inquired again, in part to disguise my shakiness; I was only hours out of the hospital. "Maybe I know him—it's a small town."

Again he ignored me. In fact he began to hum, an awkward surprise. First conversations are clumsy enough without the other person humming. It isn't Midwestern behavior. It isn't even really adult behavior. Later Orry would call it Winnie-the-Pooh behavior and that's as close as I can come. He hummed and he puffed and he did something miniature with his feet, like a blackbird keeping its balance on a tin roof, then turned and asked in a tone of courteous pleasure whether I'd care to stay and launch the kite he had brought, a kite of his own design he had carried a great long distance to fly over Lake Superior, the mightiest freshwater sea in the world.

"No wind," I pointed out.

"Not yet," he agreed in a tone of mild irritation, as though the wind were being delivered by UPS. He took the kite from under his arm and shook it out. I hadn't flown one in thirty years and was ambushed by a sneaky sense of longing.

"It's good in the air, this one," Rune mused. "Not that it behaves. No no! Its manners are very terrible! But what a flyer!"

As if hearing its name, the kite woke riffling in his hands. A wild sort of face was painted on it. He soothed it in the crook of his elbow like an anxious pet. My fingertips fairly trembled—it seemed as if flying a kite on a string was precisely what I'd wanted forever to do, yet somehow had forgotten.

He held out the kite. I reached for it, a mistake. Everything whirled. Colors blurred, my ear canals fizzed.

"I'm not so well at the moment," I said, then asked—a third time—"What was the name of your son?"

He turned to me. For an instant his whole face seemed to rise. He looked as though he might lift off like a kite himself.

"Alec Sandstrom," he said. I can't forget how he watched my eyes, saying it. Or how I looked away.

Did I remember Alec?

Good luck finding someone in Greenstone who didn't.

2

WHAT MOST PEOPLE KNEW ABOUT ALEC SANDSTROM, OR THOUGHT they knew, could be traced to a silken *Sports Illustrated* piece published on the anniversary of his disappearance.

The magazine's expenditure of four thousand words on a failed minor-league pitcher testifies to Alec's peculiar magnetism. In two seasons of small-time baseball, Alec was often compared to eccentric Detroit phenom Mark Fidrych, who is remembered for speaking aloud to the ball itself as though recommending a flight path. Alec didn't talk to baseballs—his quirk, adored by fans of the Duluth-Superior Dukes, was to break out laughing during games. Anything could set him off: an elegant nab by the second baseman, a plastic bag wobbling like a jellyfish across the diamond, a clever heckle directed at himself. His merriment was unhitched from his success. Sometimes he laughed softly while leaning in for the sign. His fastball was a blur, its location rarely predictable even to himself. Sprinting on-field to start the game, limbs flailing inelegantly, Alec always seemed sure his time had finally arrived.

"Reality wasn't strictly his deal," Beeman recalled. "My God he was fun to watch."

Engaging as Alec could be, he'd never have received the elegiac *Sports Illustrated* treatment had he not strapped himself into a small plane at dawn, lifted off in a light westerly, and banked out over Lake Superior never to return.

The few who witnessed his departure saw nothing unusual. The aircraft was a 1946 Taylorcraft, flimsy and graceful, owned by the fastidious proprietor of Alec's favorite tavern. The plane had few instruments; Alec, a licensed amateur, navigated by sight. It was a clear morning. He circled Greenstone twice as was his habit, waggled the wingtips for anyone watching, then up the coast he went. North was his favorite direction.

Like his vanishment, the *SI* piece was stylish. Forthrightly sentimental about its subject, it began with a tender recollection of Alec's live arm—his fastball had its own nickname, the Mad Mouse, after the twisting roller coaster that made you wish you were somewhere else. The article detailed his struggles with sporadic depression, with off-season jobs (bartender, stump grinder), with his inability to "get serious" on the field of play. A good deal of ink went to the "immaculate moment" that resulted in his feverish blip as a prospect courted by major-league scouts. At last the story followed him right out of baseball and up-shore to Greenstone. I remember clearly the splash of his arrival. He was charming and goofy, imprudent with money, adored equally in this hapless village for his brush with greatness and for never achieving it. We were proud to have him and we mourned his loss. A year later we were not above enjoying a bit of reflected glory when the *Sports Illustrated* reporter showed up, a young woman named Eunjin Park who interviewed the town to exhaustion. When her story appeared, we griped at our depiction as rubes and bought extra copies for friends and relatives. I appear briefly as "a sun-deprived projectionist" with "a degree of forbearance approaching perpetual defeat." As if proving the point, I could make no quarrel with this.

In any case the story was widely consumed, won some awards, got anthologized in a collection of literary sportswriting, and propelled Eunjin to a commentator gig on *All Things Considered*.

There were aftereffects locally, too. Occasional pilgrims began appearing at the Agate Café (Alec's favorite for its hot beef sandwich) or having beers at the Wise Old, or parking in front of the shaded bungalow where Alec's widow, the tempestuous Nadine, still lived with their young son Bjorn. It happened enough that Nadine began striding out to intercept snoops. "What are you waiting for? The resurrection?" Once she jerked open the door of a Ford Ranger which had surveilled the house for two hours and dragged its surprised occupant into the street.

Maybe it was inevitable that Alec began to crop up again.

Some months after Eunjin's piece, the owner of a hardware store up in Marathon, Ontario, claimed to have spied the "absent American pitcher" trying on work gloves before leaving without a purchase. The hardware man boldly took a picture, which got picked up by the Associated Press and shown on cable news. It's blurry but looks like Alec. The lanky build is right, the corners of the mouth evoke the familiar grin, and Alec did in fact own a pair of those iridescent wraparound sunglasses, though as Nadine pointed out, so did everybody else. While the so-called Marathon Man was never positively identified, there followed a number of sightings. Photos were snapped in northern California, in darkest Idaho, in Killarney up on the snow-goose plains. Most of the entries in this weird little parade bore small resemblance to Alec. Only that first one, in the hardware store, ever gained any traction—it had what Beeman called "an echo of authenticity."

It's worth mentioning there were no mysterious Alec sightings in Greenstone. We'd made our peace, it seemed.

I heard a cough and rustle of paper—the old kite flyer was watching me attentively.

"I'm very sorry about your son," I said. "I liked him awfully well." Which was true, of course—besides being a friend, Alec did some sign work for me at the Empress: repaired the marquee and built a fine original neon of his own design, a green Bogart silhouette. It burns clean and quiet to this day.

"Call me Rune," said the old visitor. "Would you please describe him a little?"

His request took me aback. "Describe your son?"

"Please, yes. You were friends, I think."

"We were, yes we were. All right then, Alec was funny, pleasant, popular," I said, only to run dry of adjectives. Rune stood waiting. He watched like a boy who hopes the answer is yes. In fact he seemed like a boy, bobbing gently on his toes, his fingertips tapping the rolled paper of the kite. His sea-green eyes were clear. I felt silly and mute. Finally I resorted to the classic evasion of turning the question back on him. "Wait," I said, in a lighthearted tone, "You're his dad, after all—why don't you describe him to me?"

At this Rune looked away. "I wish I could, but we didn't know each other," he said in his faraway lilt. "I am quite foolish, you see. Look—he was my son. Alec Sandstrom of Greenstone, Minnesota. But until a few weeks ago, I didn't know there was any such man."

When he turned back to me he had faded. It was a jolt—for a few minutes he'd seemed an intriguing old wizard with his kite and his pipe smoke, a beaten-down angel or holy fool. Now he just looked ancient and beleaguered. The left side of his face was oddly crumpled—how had I not noticed before? It was half an inch lower than the right, as if it had slid downhill.

I felt terrible to have been so glib—all he asked was a detail or two about his tragic son. I longed to make up for it by describing poor Alec in strong honest words—if they'd been within reach I'd have gone with *impulsive, comedic, sarcastic, droll*. In fact the longer I looked at Rune and his tumbledown face, the more clearly I remembered the baseline decency of Alec: the apologetic way he told jokes, knowing he would botch the punch line; his relief at being done with baseball and the expectations that went with it; and his intervals of anxiety, which he described as "narrowing," times when he felt like the Mad Mouse himself, whistling through life at precarious speed, hoping not to hurt anyone in his passage. I remembered these things but couldn't describe them. My ears rang and my mouth was empty. The moment stretched out. At length I managed to ask, "What is it you're looking for, Rune?"

"Only to know who the man was," he replied. His voice slumped into a croak. "*Fy*, listen to me. I am not even used to saying *my son*. Of course he is old news here, yes, I realize. An old story with a sad end. But my son all the same. I will have to be"—he idled a moment—"a detective."

It occurred to me that the kindest thing for this fraying pilgrim would be a ticket back home.

"Do you think," he asked, "do you suppose people will talk to me?"

"Oh, I suspect so," I said, warily—it wasn't going to take much to resurrect Alec Sandstrom, a favorite local topic. People were probably more than ready to hash through the old business again.

Rune now seemed to rouse himself. His gaze fell on the kite in his hands, and when he looked up I saw humor again in his glittery eye.

"Are you sure you don't want to fly?" he asked, nodding at the kite. "The wind is nearly here."

"Another day," I replied, then wished him good luck and headed slowly up the street, steadying myself first against buildings and then with a cracked hockey stick I spied behind the bowling alley.

Before I reached Main the wind arrived. A scatter of sparrows surfed along in the torrent, dipped and spun, and were gone. At the intersection where left leads to the failing hardware store, the padlocked union local, Amy's Grocery, and the storefront evangelicals, and right to the Empress Theater and World's Best Donuts, I turned and looked back.

Rune stood at the end of the pier. At this distance all his boyishness was back. He bobbed on his toes and reached back and forth in the air before him. Already he had that kite in the sky.

3

TWO YEARS BEFORE MOVING TO GREENSTONE—AND EIGHT BEFORE igniting a fruitless and profligate manhunt—Alec Sandstrom pitched the only perfect game in the history of the Duluth Dukes of the Northern League.

It was May 1994. I had season tickets that year, nice seats down the first-base line. I'd hired a capable high-school senior to operate the Empress just so I could take in those games, usually in the company of Kate Wilsey. Meticulous Kate! After all these miles my memories of her are more tender than specific, though she did have access to an offhand cruelty that mitigated my grief at her departure. Baseball made her impatient, as did cold weather. She also disliked Wade Stadium hot dogs, despite their low price and all-beef components.

As for the Dukes, they were mostly on the ropes. Eventually the franchise would say *enough* and depart for Kansas City. Poor lost Dukes—they never had another pitcher like Alec, the laughing southpaw with the precarious fastball. And poor lost Alec! For he never pitched another game like that perfecto down at Wade with the bitter fog tumbling in off Lake Superior. Typical cheery night in the old town, temp in the high wet forties—*fans* is too dismissive a term for that tiny tribe of loyalists crouched in ponchos and lumpy blankets. Later would come freezing mist and cars slipping sideways through traffic to reach the park, but here's what I remember early on: Alec Sandstrom out on the knob with his elbows and shanks, throwing a brand of magic even he could not believe. Oh, his speed was no shock—speed was never Alec's problem. It was his precision that astonished. Because listen: How many pitchers in any league have a fastball with its own nickname? And what kind of fastball earns the name Mad Mouse? I will tell you: the kind that twists in crackling without one notion where it's going. The kind you don't see but hear hissing to itself like the bottle rocket before the bang. People liked Alec Sandstrom but everyone knew the Mad Mouse made its own decisions. There were hitters in the Northern League who wouldn't approach the plate with Alec on the hill. Young men with ambition, benching themselves. The pay did not merit the risk.

For one night in May, that changed utterly. For one game, the Mouse did precisely what it was told.

The catcher that night was Ron Jenks, the rare Northern Leaguer with history in the bigs (fifty-eight games with the Royals across two disconsolate seasons). Later he said he'd never caught pitches thrown that hard. Saberhagen threw hard but these fastballs of Alec's were smears, they were lit ghosts. Hitters blinked and waved. Alec was no sophisticate, you understand; the Mad Mouse was his only pitch. So Ron propped his mitt where he would—at this or that corner of the strike zone, or straight over the plate. That night it hardly mattered. Alec would nod and reach back, right leg rising up like a pump handle, knuckles grazing the sand—then arm-blur and launch, a carbonated hiss, and Jenks would flinch awake to the smoky pop of the ball in his mitt.

It happened that way all night.

Alec's practice was to grin over at his wife Nadine, in her spot behind the home dugout, after every strikeout. Sometimes he also winked. This attention embarrassed her, but especially that night because there were so *many* strikeouts, and also because she was gigantically pregnant. Beautiful, absolutely—but eight months is a lot of pregnant, and Bjorn was a lot of baby. Of course staunch Dukes partisans, the all-weather tribe, knew Nadine by sight—the with-child darling of that handsome, daffy, terrifying Sandstrom boy.

Around the fifth inning, people began to understand a singular game was in progress. I mean to say they started watching it. At their best the Dukes were rarely compelling and a night game at Wade was more than half social occasion—a sportswriter for the *Duluth News Tribune* described the season ticket as "a standing invitation to freeze in company." But as Alec kept firing home, as hitter after hitter flailed at strike three or stood in rooted disbelief, the men in camo and women in quilts and even the half-dozen Italian sailors off the grain ship in the harbor began to sit upright in the sparse old grandstands and look at one another. A hush descended. We leaned in when Alec pitched, leaned back at the end of innings. Even the play-by-play man, Ivan Maitlin, broadcasting the game on a Twin Ports radio station, did not specify what was happening. A shambling poet and diesel mechanic, Ivan had come out of retirement for the privilege of describing baseball on the air. He guarded his tongue until the Dukes finally scored three times in the bottom of the seventh. This uncommon event Ivan took for a sign, and he joyfully relented and explained how it was: history afoot in the port city, a feat heroic, a wondrous groove. Ivan stood up in the tiny press booth and preached it: *Can I get a witness!* Forthwith people began spilling down the skinny streets to the ballpark, arriving in vans and the backs of pickups, pushing through icy fog with their parkas and thermoses and video cameras. By now the ticket window had closed and you could just walk in. It seemed, and still does seem, like good news to me that the final innings of the best game of base-ball ever pitched in Duluth were witnessed by two hundred and eight deserving customers, plus Ivan Maitlin and another two thousand or so who got in by grace alone.

Hours after the perfect game, Alec Sandstrom hustled a gasping Nadine down the hill to St. Luke's. The delivery was so sudden it nearly happened on the midnight sidewalk under the glowing EMERGENCY sign. Bjorn was a month from due but, as Alec said, maybe he was tired of the dark. Ready for action! That's what he told the *News Trib* sportswriter who got wind of the birth and placed the phone call.

"He's robust, amigo," Alec said. "He's been ready for a while. Whoever knew? You should see his shoulders. We got a little Viking."

"Middle name?" asked the sportswriter.

"Don't know yet," Alec said, affecting a pause. "He was only *Bjorn* an hour ago." And he laughed—Alec was never a man to forgo the easy pun.

The sportswriter was Tom Beeman. Of the people who knew Alec in those gold-rush days, I suspect Tom saw him most clearly. The perfect game resulted in Alec's being scouted by at least four big-league teams—the Twins, Brewers, Red Sox, and Giants. An *elbowing cadre* of scouts, Beeman called them. But sparks aside, a scout needs to see a little consistency. And God knows Alec did his best—he slept with the window open, worked with a guru, pursued reproducible motion. After that lone, tantalizing perfecto, the Mad Mouse refused to be tamed. Alec walked batters; he hit batters. One night at Wade Stadium a greenhorn catcher missed a high hard one and it glanced off the poor umpire's ear. The ump soon recovered, but the scouts were gone forever.

Beeman, by then a good friend to Alec, suggested other careers—in sales, real estate. Careers enhanced by Alec's affable nature. Beeman also warned him against moving to Greenstone. It wasn't a lucky town, he said. Alec pointed out the cheap housing and low taxes, the profuse beauty of the North Shore—its rock battlements, bald eagles, the lights of wheelhouse freighters gliding past like enchanted cities at twilight. Beeman would himself eventually succumb to these dreamlike attractions, but he was firm with Alec: Greenstone was cheap and beautiful, but awfully out of the way. And not lucky.

"Well, *I'm* lucky," said Alec—and he completely believed it, notwithstanding his loss of a baseball career. And who could argue? He may not have got to the majors, but a lot of people thought of Alec Sandstrom as lucky. The fastball, the seeming weightlessness, the healthy kid, and the incandescent wife: no doubt a lot of men looked at Alec, looked at Nadine, and felt themselves diminished.

So Greenstone it was. They bought a gilded button of a house— the kind called a tract home when Slake International built it in 1952, along with two hundred identicals, but veneered and replumbed and reroofed since then. They rented an office above the hardware store where Alec pursued what he optimistically termed "graphic design."

He wasn't a designer. He had an eye. *Knack* would be a better word. He painted some signs. I'm afraid Sign Me Up! was the name of the business. He got into some vinyl, some plasticized magnets. Nadine helped with layout and drawing—she stood back from his drawings and squinted her eyes. She rescued him is what she did. She understood color and the rule of thirds and other laws of proportion. She knew what lines meant. She put a lot of stock in fonts. They did all right—drove to Gooseberry Falls on summer nights and bought bakery rolls on Saturday mornings. And Bjorn, the baby Viking, turned into the gladdest sort of little kid, the tall-for-his-age sort who laughs with his whole body and goes outside a lot because it's interesting out there, and attracts other little kids, and becomes their roguish captain.

And their luck?

It held pretty well. They got some sign commissions. They made friends and stayed healthy and worked hard and hoped for the best. Their luck did last for a while.

It lasted—this is my read, anyway—until the summer evening a charcoal-colored sports sedan rolled up quietly behind them. Nadine recalls this clearly. They were out for a twilight stroll, counting the swallows emerging in the blue hour to fill up on gnats and mosquitoes. The sedan—not the usual indigenous bucket but low and exotically rounded, a Porsche or BMW— accelerated onto Ladder Street, then slowed abruptly and kept pace just behind them, as though the driver knew them, or thought he knew them, or were seeing a sight he wished to prolong.

"Did you know that man?" Nadine asked, when the car finally passed and turned at the next corner. "Ooh, Alec"—I imagine her winking here—"do you suppose it was the scandalous filmmaker?"

There *was* a scandalous filmmaker in town just then, a libertine son of Greenstone on R&R at his wuthering manse, but Alec shook his head. He wasn't interested in filmmakers, or scandals, or European sedans. He was ahead in the bird count and didn't want to lose out to Bjorn, who at five was his dad's sharp-eyed impersonator. Alec was also used to being married to Nadine. This was not the first time a passing motorist had slowed down for the view.

"Just a stranger enjoying the local attractions, I expect," Alec said. He had a guileless smile she loved. "I guess it's the price of beauty. Whoever knew?"

Alec said that a lot—"Whoever knew?" You couldn't be around him long without hearing it.

Nadine says he maintained a state of wonder as a refuge from unease.

The first time I heard about the swallows and the sports car I thought it simple rhapsody. When I heard the story again, years on, it seemed to me the shadows were deeper, that Alec's optimism was forced, that only little Bjorn was immune. By her third telling—to me alone, more recently—the birds were fewer. Bjorn was pale and silent. And the charcoal exotic creeping at a growl indicated, not the price of beauty, but instead the very moment when their luck began to slide.

4

IN THE MORNING I WOKE FEELING LESS LIKE MY OWN SAD GHOST. I'D taken two painkiller tablets the night before, something the doctor said I should do only if the headache made sleep impossible. The headache was manageable but I took the pills anyway. It was wonderful and gauzy, going to sleep that way, like drifting in a small boat over a rippling sea. Two or three times I woke in the night, but instead of worrying about my brain or the Empress or my soaring deductible I would remember I was still in a gently bobbing boat, a boat built for the single purpose of allowing me to sleep, and fade out again with enormous satisfaction.

Getting dressed in a shaft of maple sunlight, I still had the sense of borrowing clothes from my former self, but decided to push through. I put bread in the toaster, got out the brick of white cheddar and an over-ripe tomato from the vegetable drawer. While the toast browned I sliced tomato and shingles of cheddar. This was all muscle memory requiring no thought. I didn't have to apply any adjectives to the toast, only plenty of butter, followed by cheese and finally the slices of beefsteak tomato, over which I rained a bit of salt and some coarse black pepper.

I pulled on the blue wool sweater my sister Orry gave me during her brief intense knitting addiction and went downstairs to Main. People vacationing on the North Shore claim shock at our brisk weather, but it's hardly a secret. Duluth in ancient days advertised itself as the Air-Conditioned City and it is well south of Greenstone. Even now, bus drivers from steaming Minneapolis and office managers from the airless burbs, plus a good many melting Iowa farmers, head north during heat waves to poke their feet into our icy Great Lake—they're a common sight, sitting stunned in plastic lawn chairs carried into the shallows. Not everyone wants to see his breath in the summer but this is the bargain you strike up here.

Julie at the Agate Café brought me two coffees to go—one black, one cream—then while I stood peering into my billfold she came around the counter and wrapped me in her nice soft arms and kissed my cheek. It was very agreeable. I never really knew Julie—her sister Margaret owned the Agate and Julie moved here to help after they both got divorced the same year. Margaret slams your food down in front of you like an outrage, but Julie can set out your bacon and eggs with no more sound than the kiss I had just received. There is nothing wrong with being kissed on the cheek by a sweet round woman in a café after you have nearly died. She said it was briefly rumored I didn't make it, people were sad, I was a fixture in Greenstone—*endearment* was the word that she chose.

I expected she would pause there and ask me some questions I would lack the descriptive power to answer, but no. Julie gripped my arm with her very strong fingers and said coffee was on the house. Moreover, she said Marcus Jetty would never pay for another meal at the Agate as long as he lived. Later Margaret would fine-tune that policy, but it still strikes me as a fitting reward for a deed as brave as Marcus's—jumping into cold stormy waters to yank a man out of a sinking Pontiac. Marcus was a citizen at the edge of penury, the Agate was a good café. Now he could go in there anytime and have a first-rate hot beef sandwich. He could have the chicken and dumplings, or the peach-and-blueberry pie. I was glad for Marcus. I would not have minded for Julie to kiss my cheek again.

I took the two coffees and went on my way. Full sun is rare in October and when it happens everything shines—the streets shine up through their layers of grit, the cottonwoods and jack pines and silver maples shine, the darting flycatchers shine around picking off the last sluggish deerflies before heading south to Mexico. It was beautiful but too intense for my eyes. A headache flared at the edge of sight. At

Citgo I set the coffees down on the sidewalk and went in and bought a pair of Panama Jack sunglasses. They had black rims and dark fake tortoiseshell temples, like Nicholson's. The instant I tried them on my headache shrank away. I'd never paid more than ten dollars for sunglasses but when the girl said, "Forty-two eighty-five," I handed her my Visa without a moment's shilly-shallying. A lavish bargain, that's how it seemed. I'd have paid a thousand if she asked. My habits are frugal but my joggled brain informed me it was only money.

I smiled at the girl—sixteen or so, glossy black nails, black hooded sweatshirt with a Mexican skull painted on it in joyful colors. I knew her from the Empress. She and her friends spent whole screenings tapping at their phones, but then a ticket is a ticket. She said, shyly, "Hi, Mr. Wander."

"I'm sorry, I should remember your name."

"Lanie Plume. I heard what happened. What a deal! I'm happy you're okay."

"Thanks, me too."

"Somebody said you were dead—well, it was my boyfriend Kyle—that you went through that fence and sank in your car all the way to the bottom. He said you banged on the window but couldn't get out! He said there would be air bubbles coming up from the car for months, and the bubbles would pop and smell like dead person—I'm sorry to be ghastly," she added.

"It's okay. Marcus Jetty happened to be down on the shore. He pulled me out before the car sank."

"I heard that, too."

The headache was approaching—I could feel it getting nearer. I was anxious to put the new sunglasses over my eyes, but the girl hung onto them, swinging them back and forth in her fingers, a pensive set to her chin. "Mr. Wander, can I ask what was it like, going over the edge?"

The question was so direct it took me by surprise. She mistook my silence for confusion and clarified: "The edge of the road, I mean."

"Right, got it. I don't really remember. I remember driving along, listening to the radio, and snow coming down, but not the going-over part."

"Oh." She couldn't hide her disappointment. "Did you get knocked out then, I guess?"

"I got concussed. The whole thing is ..." I wanted *foggy* or *misty* or better yet *shrouded* but instead trailed off with a shrug.

She finished ringing me up. I took the tags off and put the glasses on. I felt better immediately and wondered what else a person could buy for forty-two dollars that would bring such immediate joy. As I went out the door Lanie said, "It would be super rad if you remembered, you know?"

"Remembered what?"

She laughed. "Flying off the cliff that way—I mean, everybody's seen it in a hundred movies, but no one actually does it."

"Didn't I actually do it?"

"Sure, but you don't *remember*," she said. "I mean, you were almost dead. Like briefly virtually dead. You went right up to it. My mom said you maybe got a peek at whatever. She thinks heaven or hell. I don't really, I think you're just here and then it gets dark, but if there *is* a whatever, you maybe saw it. How cool would it be if you remembered?"

"I could write a book."

"Do some podcasts," she said.

"Doctor Phil."

"Maybe it'll come back to you after a while."

"Maybe."

"You know what I think," Lanie said. "I think now you have to go on a quest. That's what this sort of thing means. Carpa deem," she said, with a precocious smile. "That means *seize the day*."

"Maybe after I seize a nap."

"Bye, Mr. Wander."

The two coffees were still on the sidewalk. Bending down I saw my two pale ankles sticking out of my shoes. I'd forgotten socks. Dr. Koskinen said I might forget to turn off the faucet, might gas myself somehow, set my sleeves on fire. He wasn't thrilled that I lived alone. He suggested I ask a relative or friend to stay with me the first week or two. I did borrow Beeman's phone and try Orry, but she was out of the country—I'd forgotten that too. Orry's husband Dinesh is a star surgeon, a holder of patents and doctor without borders. Whenever Dinesh flies off to heal the sick, Orry goes to Prague or Paris or New Orleans. A connoisseur and gourmet, my sister. She has three handsome tattoos that I know of, including one of a literate bar menu encountered in Florence. *Vino Allegro!* She says it is necessary to offset a little of Dinesh's overwhelming decency, which at times is more than she can bear.

My ankles were cold, so I kept walking. For the first time I tried to recall how it was to burst through the barrier and fly off the cliff. Nothing came. Marcus had described with hand motions the Pontiac's sweeping twist into the lake, so I had an approximate visual, but that was all Marcus. Where was my own memory? What if I'd seen the lit hillsides of glory? Maybe even glimpsed my parents, who died serving Jesus when I was seventeen. I will say more later about their departure in a train derailment in a Mexican canyon while I stayed at home—a dawdling, reeking junior in high school. After the derailment I wondered obsessively about the great *whatever*. Much seemed to ride on the character of the whatever, including the degree and tenacity of my guilt in the matter. But miles pass, years climb up your shoulders. My insistence on Mom's and Dad's joyous afterlife gradually dimmed.

It was disconcerting to think it might've shown itself at last, only to be swaddled in the bubble-wrap of concussion.

On the plus side, it was nice to be noticed. Everything looked warm and auburn through the new sunglasses. I did feel vertiginous, a word then unattainable to me, but also grateful and friendly toward the world.

A block past Citgo I arrived at a squat rectangle with ribbed steel siding and exposed rivets. Often mistaken for a welding shop, this is Greenstone City Hall. It was built to replace the lavish oak-and-sandstone hall that was constructed during the taconite boom of the 1950s and that burned down twenty years later. Arson was never proved but the town was careful to replace the stately edifice with one impossible to mourn should such a thing happen again. I set the coffee with cream on the desk of Ann Fandeen, who raised her plucked brows and covered her phone with her hand.

"As I live and breathe," she said.

"Hi, Ann," I replied, suspecting I was about to receive more of the fond affection granted the recently dead. But Ann said, "You look real stupid in those sunglasses. I guess going over the cliff that way turned you into some sort of a big shot."

"Clearly not." I took them off, squinting at the slightly meaner world.

"Well, you're late. Your appointment was here twenty minutes ago."

I didn't remember an appointment, but then I didn't remember my socks. Ann took a sip of the coffee, gave it a quick stare of disapproval, and returned to the phone. I proceeded down the short hall with its jaundiced paint to my office. I was glad to see the door, which had V. WANDER on it in gold hardware-store lettering, right above the title CITY CLERK.

Did you think I made a living at the Empress?

It's part-time work, of course—a city like Greenstone requires scant clerical effort. I keep the minutes and write the checks; there are usually papers to be filed or contracts to let. This morning it was a meeting with the Pea Brothers who are annually lone bidders on the city's request for snowplow services. Since my early years here the striving Peas have cleared snow and ice from the hall lot and various city properties—the park, the skating rink, the municipal liquor store. Shad Pea was actually the last surviving brother since Marty died of a heart attack brought on by televised hockey, but Shad's daughter Lily had grown up in the business and it was Lily who was seated at my desk when I entered. She didn't get up but paid me the compliment of a grin. "Hey, it's the ghost of Virgil Wander—and look, he brought me coffee."

"Good morning, Lily—how do you take it?" I asked.

"Black."

I handed her my coffee. She said, "I was kidding," while accepting the cup with both hands.

"Your dad along today?"

"Hangover. He said to go ahead and sign the papers."

"Which you are welcome to do, if I can find them."

I went round the desk and knelt at a bottom drawer to look. Lily was twenty-one—a slight blonde with wide-set eyes and arresting dimples, plus an impish wit. As a junior in high school she sang the lead in *Annie Get Your Gun* which had all Greenstone fired up about her Hollywood future even though Lily herself disliked entertaining. She never performed again unless you count posing for a calendar that appeared on the walls of automotive garages in the five-state area. Looking at her you don't automatically think *snow removal professional*, but you should see her navigate the hairpin corners at the base of the Greenstone water tower.

"Here they are," I said.

She stayed at my desk casting a dubious eye over the contract, hardly windfall money for the Peas. They also landscaped for summer people, tapped a few hundred maple trees for syrup in the spring, and ran an occasional fishing guide service during the autumn season. Lily said, "Have you ever noticed nobody in this town has only one job? Not even you, and you run the city."

"I take notes and ask for favors."

"I was teasing about the hangover," she said. "Dad got a fishing call last night. He's out with a client."

"Shad doing okay?"

"I stopped in last night to drop off the groceries, and he was sitting on the kitchen floor making a kite out of dowels and butcher paper."

"What is it with kites right now?"

"I don't know. He met some old dude flying one off the end of the pier and couldn't stop thinking about it."

I didn't mention my similar enchantment. Lily grimaced at the contract, then signed it. "So Dad's retiring next year, has he told you that?"

"He hasn't, unless he has and I've forgotten. Good for him."

"Not retiring like in the commercials. Old friend of his runs an RV park in Florida. He's been after Dad for years to move down and be his handyman. Dad laughs at Florida until the middle of January, then he gets quiet about it."

"Why, he'll thrive down there." It was nice to picture Shad, an obsessive fisherman, beach-casting into the sunset. "What will you do, Lily?"

"Probably stay. Dad thinks I'll be ready to *take the reins* by then. He talks about reins a lot now. He's evolved from *hold your horses*. But Virgil, just so you know"—she smiled and tapped the contract with the tip of the pen—"when Dad leaves? We're renegotiating this baby."

Lily left without further acknowledgment of my wondrous survival—she didn't kiss my cheek or call me an endearment, and she didn't ask for eyewitness testimony of the icy plummet or a description of the place where let's hope the good people go. But it's true while I knelt at the desk drawer, shuffling through files for her contract, she rested her hand on my shoulder. I felt its warmth through my knitted sweater. If I were younger I would have fallen in love with Lily Pea. Maybe I did fall in love with her, for a minute or two. Probably I did. Who wouldn't? Besides being pretty and smart, Lily was reliably kind.

5

TAKING NOTES AND ASKING FAVORS WAS ACTUALLY THE JOB DESCRIP-
tion offered me years before by Greenstone's mayor Lydia Fatz—she'll
want you to know it rhymes with *pots*. After Lily departed I spied one
of Lydia's own vigorous notes on lined tablet paper sitting on my desk.
I remembered the note with a pang of guilt. It had been there since
before I went over the cliff.

> *Virgil*
> *If you have time please accost Mr. Leer about speaking at*
> *Festival—*
> *Guess he's in town but who really knows?*
> *Absolutely a long shot!*
> *Leer no hometown fan.*
> *If he did make an appearance it would be to burn something down.*
> *Let's try anyway!*
> *Lydia*

Among my de facto burdens as clerk of a shriveling town
was to organize cheap galas, jubilees, and hoo-has celebrating past
glories like taconite, the smelt run, and prosperity itself. Nobody
really shows up, but you have to try. Lydia was intent on having
Adam Leer—our scandalous filmmaker and malcontent, son of

Greenstone's venerated founder Spurlock Leer—give a speech at next spring's city fiesta.

It wasn't a bad idea. Leer's first and only film success (*Herselves*, 1980) had endured scattered boycotts in the Midwest and throughout the Bible Belt. Critics called it fresh or frank or repugnant. Obviously this was decades ago, but given the tedium of most city events, Leer was a peppery choice. I remembered now having delayed out of timidity my visit to the Leer compound.

For a moment I looked over the note with dread.

Then a strange thing happened. Maybe certain fears had been disabled in the accident, or maybe it occurred to me that even the worst result—a profane improvisation, a slammed door—would be more interesting than whatever procrastination I devised. Whatever the reason, the dread leached out of Lydia's note. What remained was only a request from my boss—my boss, Lydia, whom I'd always liked. It carried no freight but was simply a thing that was mine to do.

"Where do you think you're going, Lazarus?" asked Ann Fandeen. I'd closed up my office and was striding past her desk. I thought I was striding, anyway—given my tentative equilibrium it's more likely I was listing along like a wearisome TV zombie.

"To see Adam Leer," I said, my spirits on the upswing. "Go pin him down for the festival."

"Reborn as a hard charger, you."

I smiled—Ann used to put me on edge, but now I wanted to laugh. Maybe the injury had left me impervious to sarcasm. I'd have to ask Dr. Koskinen about it.

"And where are you meeting the great one?" she asked.

"No one seems to know his cell number," I said. "Since he's back in town, I'll just be heading up to his house."

"Is that what you'll be doing? What will you be driving, then?"

Ann had me there. My unexpected gust of mojo had blown clean away the fact that I was still under orders not to drive. Also I was carless, though technically I still owned the Pontiac.

"Maybe you'd drive me," I said, and was struck with quiet surprise—like my shoes and the apartment earlier, my voice seemed to be someone else's. Yet it sounded appropriate to the moment: a simple voice, adjective-free, unapologetic, and satisfyingly deep.

Ann rolled her eyes. She had a marvelous eye roll, refined through long discipline, precise as acupuncture.

"Right now?" she inquired, when I failed to backpedal and stood expectantly at her desk.

"Why not?" said my upgraded voice. "Let's go."

When it came to Adam Leer, hearsay definitely routed our poor supply of facts.

He was vaguely thought to be a pampered silver-spooner ashamed of his Midwestern backstory. Following his initial success, his profile diminished—gossip had Adam laboring in the lesser cinematic environs of South Africa, Indonesia, Denmark. Nobody seemed sure whether this was the case, but if Leer was really the truculent brat of legend, then how nice to imagine him suffering botfly attacks in the fever swamps of Malaysia. Over pints at the Shipwreck, Beeman had neatly summarized what locals were pleased to believe—"Fifty percent practicing wastrel, forty percent seducer, ten percent expatriate film whiz."

The few certainties are these: Adam Leer was the second and last child of the geologist Spurlock Leer, who discovered minable concentrations of taconite after World War II and is considered the founder of Greenstone. Spurlock's firstborn, Richard, died in the Blizzard of '64. Popular Richard and his girlfriend, Madeline, were driving back from a basketball tournament in Duluth when the storm rose up off the lake. This was one of those record weather events that dwarf current experience, a violent, smothering, intensely local storm that dropped eight feet of snow in some places on its narrow and serpentine passage. Roofs buckled, trees lost crown and limb. People who were there describe a resounding deafness in which the sharpest cracks and bursts came wrapped in muffled thumps. So much snow fell that things simply vanished, including Richard and Maddie. They made it nearly home only to skid off into a steep ditch. It took six days to find them, entombed in Richard's Camaro, indigo-lipped and frozen to antiquity.

The stunned Leer family was further beset by a story that wound through Greenstone in the weeks and months after the tragedy. The tale, supposedly delivered in boasting fashion by Adam to his second-grade classmates, was that his father enlisted him to ride shotgun when they drove through the blizzard looking for Richard's car. Adam didn't want to go. Richard, he claimed, was a rotten brother—made fun of Adam all the time, made him look stupid in front of people. Let Richard find his own way home. But Spurlock needed extra eyes and made him go. Mrs. Leer sent them out with blankets and a thermos of coffee while she waited by the phone. The poisonous detail is that Adam, watching the precipitous ditch as they crept through near-whiteout conditions, spied the faint glow of a taillight shining up through deepening snow. Adam was seven. He saw the glow and knew what it was. He didn't say anything. The glow receded as Spurlock, eyeing the opposite ditch, drove on.

Adam's school photo shows none of the dead-eyed gaze we associate with tragic children. In fact his eyes are narrowed and focused slightly up and to the left, as though on something looming up behind you. Later he scoffed at the notion that he would let his brother die, or tell such a grisly story. But the photo works against him. There's a spark in his face. An ignition. You can't look away, or else you have to.

Suspicion shadowed him thereafter. People thought him allied with malignant energies. At thirteen he was humiliated at a pep rally when two spirited seniors hauled him up front and yanked down his pants during "The Minnesota Rouser." Within weeks one of the seniors went blind overnight; the other got dizzy in wood shop and neatly sawed off his own hand.

At sixteen Adam left Greenstone and vanished like a sylph. There's a black hole in the ledger until he pops up in California seven years later, directing *Herselves* which brought him notoriety and accolades. It also brought him his first wife—the ethereal wisp Simone Blaise, who played the titular schizophrenic. Many continue to believe that he murdered poor Simone, although the hospital record shows it was he who rushed the girl to the ER after she swallowed more than sixty quaaludes from her mother's limitless reserve.

His father died at the wheel of Adam's car, which he often used while Adam was off ravaging his inheritance. Spurlock had loaded several cases of heavy core samples into the German sedan for delivery to a geologist at the University of Minnesota. Somehow while he drove a fire broke out and in confusion he mashed the accelerator instead of the brake. The state patrol estimated Spurlock was going eighty or so there at the end, bouncing across the median and under the wheels of an onrushing logging truck. The trucker said the car was so full of smoke he didn't see the driver until moments before impact, when Spurlock unfortunately poked his head out the window.

Adam inherited his father's house and the six hundred forty acres surrounding it, including a musical stretch of the Pentecost River with its cutbanks and riffles and shimmering trout. He occupied the place only sporadically, a year here, six months there. He was said to despise his origins, to prefer his house in Sweden or Spain or Mozambique, depending on who said it.

It's also said he wrote two more screenplays which were never produced because, as one film agent drily observed, "the nihilist market is shrinking all the time," and that he composed a long essay entitled *My Radiant Death* so venomous yet enthralling that the few who read it died themselves within hours. At some point folklore takes over.

Besides these few facts, there's a notable lack of proof around the life of Adam Leer. Two marriage licenses are on record, but no ex-wives survive—neither Simone nor the subsequent Christine. No children exist that we know of; no high-school diploma, no college degree. There is of course the usual bureaucratic stream of tax records, passports, DMV receipts, social security documents, but what could they truly explain? There aren't even many photos of Adam. There's the grade-school picture mentioned above, the boy of seven already with *something* going on; another taken on a sidewalk in LA moments after the civil ceremony in which he married Simone—they're laughing, Simone in an achingly humble white dress and himself in a paisley jacket and mountaineering sunglasses with side-leathers. There's a sort of nasty mouth-open portrait from a 1982 profile published in *Esquire*, with the oddly memorable first line, "Adam Leer oscillates faster than you."

And then there's the widespread snapshot from a mid-eighties Cannes Film Festival in which Leer and enigmatic playwright Sam Shepard slouch on stools inside what looks like a white canvas tent. Shepard is laughing hard at something; Leer has a smirk on his lips and that same brash ignition in his eye. What completes the photo is that the tent flap is open and famed Minnesota escapee Bob Dylan has just stuck his head in. Dylan looks dismayed at being left out. What's he missed? Adam isn't saying—you can tell by the smirk. The picture always makes me feel a little melancholy on Dylan's behalf. Being your generation's cherished poet doesn't mean you're in on all the jokes.

"It's not what he's done or hasn't done that irks me," Ann said. "What do I care? I just abhor the looks of his yard."

She was driving a Nissan pickup that made sighing noises and pulled hard to the left. The pickup belonged to her husband Jerry. Her own car had quit working. It needed a serpentine belt. She couldn't afford a serpentine belt because Jerry had also quit working.

Ann said, "Just look around, when we get there. He doesn't mow. He doesn't trim. The yard is full of rocks."

"He rarely comes back, Ann. His house stands empty most of the time. Fastidious lawn care might be asking too much."

I was proud of *fastidious*, which had returned without fanfare, but Ann didn't notice. She said, "If he's not going to mow, he ought to sell the place." She thought it over. "Or rent it out to people who mow." Then the Nissan sighed round a bend and we came upon Galen Pea fishing illegally off the Green Street Bridge.

"Looks like my day for Peas," I told Ann. "Stop here if you would. I want to talk to Galen."

Galen Pea was Lily's little brother—he was ten, wearing what looked like his sister's flip-flops, pants rolled up to his knees, fishing pole in one hand and a flathead chub in the other. His salvage-yard bike lay in the tall grass. Ann rolled to a stop on the narrow bridge, next to the NO FISHING sign.

"Morning, Galen."

"Mr. Wander," was his wary hello. Suddenly he stepped close and poked my forearm, which was resting on the car door. "You're still alive," he said.

"And you're still playing hooky."

Galen glanced past me at Ann, clearly sensing her disapproval—not only was he playing hooky, but his hair, actually his entire appearance, could be described as unmowed.

"Nope," he said, "I'm sick today," meeting my eyes straight on.

"Your dad got a client this morning?"

"Hangover."

"Your sister Lily just paid me a visit. She failed to mention your illness."

The boy said nothing but tilted his head slightly left. Like his father Shad, Galen Pea was devoted to the pursuit of big fish and to whatever truancy might further that pursuit. He haunted waters like a fish hawk, and in fact resembled a young raptor—large eyes steady in a small round head shifting this way and that across his shoulders.

"You know where's good to fish from? Right—down—there," I said, pointing out my window to a grassy cutbank where the river slowed curling on its way to the lake.

"If I go down there the fish will see me. If they see you they don't bite."

I'd fished from that grassy spot myself. Never caught anything, so Galen was probably right. "All the same, you remember about Curtis."

Curtis Menlow was Galen's age when he got hit by a car almost exactly where Galen was standing, call it twelve years ago. Curtis wasn't fishing, he was playing Pooh Sticks, but the sign went up anyway and no kids had died on the Green Street Bridge since then.

"It's useless to fish down there," Galen complained. "Put a worm in front of 'em they still won't take it. Last summer, was a giant fish, fins moving like this—he didn't bite because he *saw*." He gave me a dark look. "They're not dumb, like people think."

"But don't they see you up here just as well?"

"They'd have to look straight up to see me here," said Galen, incredulous. "A fish can't look straight up—they can't bend their necks," he explained, as though I were the record idiot.

"Even so."

He stood holding the despondent chub in his fist. I waited to see whether he'd head down off the bridge or change the subject.

"Where you going this morning, Mr. Wander?"

I kept the smile off my face. "Up to talk to Mr. Leer."

Something moved inside his eyes. "Don't do it, Mr. Wander."

"It's okay, Galen. I'm just going to ask him something."

"Don't go up there, no."

"What are you talking about? Galen, what is it?"

He shook his head. "Don't astim for nothin. Just don't go up there."

I said, "Have you been bothering Mr. Leer? Did you go up to his place?"

"No I dint."

"You can talk to me," I began, but he just stood there with his head jutting forward, those fierce shiny eyes fixed.

Maybe I could've worked Galen a little harder, but if he'd had an issue with Leer I suspected I'd hear about it soon enough. Meantime a car was coming up the road. I wanted the boy off that bridge.

"That minnow's going to die in your hand, Galen Pea. You go down there right now and catch a big fish. Don't wait. We'll be back this way in an hour—you catch one big enough, I'll give you something for it."

He nodded morosely. As Ann eased forward I turned and watched Galen pick his way down through the high ditch grass, holding the rod up over his head. There weren't many kids his age in Greenstone. The others all had Xboxes. Galen fished alone.

6

I DON'T PUT MUCH STOCK IN A PERSON'S YARD WORK, BUT ANN HAD a point about the Leer place. Grasses and wild daisies had bolted up through the narrow drive's crumbly asphalt. It was October so the daisies were dead. Ann eased forward through dry foliage scraping the sides of the truck. The sky had crowded up with tiny, hard, tumorous-looking clouds. The driveway wound through a field of boulders big as Volkswagens strewn at random over the general scraggle. It was disorienting.

Ann said, "So he's got a house in Mozambique? Let him *stay* in Mozambique. Mozambique doesn't care about long grass. All kinds of tawdry business goes on in Mozambique." Then she went quiet as Leer's house peeked into view behind a stand of quaking aspen.

It was nothing extraordinary, the house—an aging foursquare with narrow clapboard, buttercream paint going chalky, roomy old porch with a slant floor to shed the rain. Not an unfriendly house, and the sight of it reminded me it used to be visible from the county road, long ago. Kind of a landmark actually, the Leer place. Then the aspen took hold. I don't know if Adam planted them there or they just saw their chance and moved in.

We parked in the front yard. The place looked deserted, no car visible, shades drawn. Even the birds had departed—despite the healthy aspens and poplars there was no sound of any kind save the whisper of desiccated leaves.

A scorched smell hung in the air. It was so trenchant we didn't even approach the front door but followed the reek to the backyard. There stood Adam Leer beside a sizzling dark pile. I'd never actually met him and was surprised at his average height. His back was to us and he swayed as though asleep standing up.

At my hello he turned. He had a smooth face for a man that age and it glimmered with what looked like amusement. He had black leather boots on his feet, a long-handled rake in his hand.

"Sorry to intrude, Mr. Leer," I said, introducing myself and Ann.

"It's all right—I'm nearly done." A tilted pyramid of flagging cardboard boxes stood to one side and he was disposing of their contents, pushing flames about with the rake and coaxing moist rags to catch fire. He moved with a precision and strength unexpected in a professional wastrel.

"What's this you're burning?" Ann inquired, as if that weren't clear—it was a heap of old clothing. Shirts and pants, neckties, at least one pair of satin-striped tuxedo trousers, wide-lapel jackets, what might've been a cravat, a top hat haloed in woolly blue smoke. It was a heavy, nasty, humid fire which even up close resembled a pile of bodies.

"Why, it's evidence," Leer said, looking sideways at Ann. He had a close, curious way of observing people. You could mistake it for admiration.

"Oh?" Ann was watching, not the flames, but Leer's kinetic form. Despite the cold he was sweating from the work, his light denim shirt clinging to limber back muscles. She said, "Evidence of what?"

"My own negligence, I'm afraid. Two years ago I stored some things in the basement. Now I return to sixteen boxes of black mold. Everything burns at last. Don't stand downwind."

It seemed good advice. Tendrils of tea-colored smoke uncurled to explore the immediate region. I felt a sudden wave of dizziness.

Leer turned from the fire. He took a rag from his pocket, wiped his face and hands, and gave us an honest look at him. *Mortal after all* was my thought, just a man with thinning silvery hair, a well-maintained smile, and the lengthening ears old men gradually obtain. He had a plain solid handshake and there was nothing to mark him as a person of standing except his eyes, which flickered and probed like someone trying the door.

Instinctively I looked away.

Leer however, our famed conundrum, seemed expansive, even friendly.

"My father's house," he mused, in dry lament. "Mold in the cellar, shingles turning to compost, squirrels in the eaves." He shook his head, eyes fastened on Ann. "Poor stewardship, that's what I call it."

Ann said, "Oh, now—nobody thinks that, Mr. Leer," and I shot her a look she ignored.

"That's extremely tolerant of you," he replied. "It's what I appreciate about Greenstone. No one's sitting in judgment. Not like on the coasts! Listen, Ann, I'm looking to do some sprucing up. Nothing ostentatious. Clean and simple, that's what I'm after. Trim back those aspens, do a little asphalt repair. Manage the yard. If you know anyone who could help with some late season cleanup, I'd be more than gratified."

"My husband's a fine landscaper," Ann right away declared.

Jerry wasn't a landscaper of any kind, never had been that I knew of—the Fandeen place was in fact a model of chaotic vegetation and topographical dismay. That no doubt accounted for at least some of Ann's strong feelings on the subject of tall grass.

"I *knew* this would be a good time to come home," Leer said. "Synchronicity! Maybe you'd mention me to him."

"I will," Ann said, then added shrewdly: "Of course, it's the end of the season, as you say—Jerry's in high demand."

"The good ones always are. Tell him I'll compensate for any rearranging he may have to do. May I give you my number?"

Ann unsnapped her purse and began to rummage.

"No need," Leer said, for a pen had appeared in his fingers. He took her hand and gently wrote some numbers on her palm, still watching her closely—so entire was his focus I half expected her to levitate. He said, "Ann? Ann. I hope you'll keep this between us and us alone."

"Oh!" she said, and blinked. While they went on in this way, Ann saying *Count on me* with a disquieting blush, Leer noting the blush and appearing somehow to perpetuate it, a shade at the edge of the yard caught my eye. A clutch of dead ferns parted and a fat raccoon bumbled blinking into our company.

"Why, it's Genghis," I said cautiously, for it was Tom's prodigal coon.

"So you know him," Leer said. "He's been lurking here ever since I arrived."

Genghis approached and circled us without fear. He was used to people and kind of a bully. Tom had tried returning Genghis to nature several times including once driving him sixty miles up-shore and releasing him in a campground fragrant with bratwurst and Doritos. Genghis always returned. When Leer squatted and offered his hand to the raccoon, I said, "Whoop, careful there," but Genghis went to him like an affable pup, ducking under Leer's hand and rolling at his ankles.

"Good animal." Leer rested a palm on Genghis's head as if imparting a blessing, then stood, turning to me. "Now Virgil—Virgil Wander—from what I hear, you've had a near escape. Good thing Mr. Jetty was on hand. Have you always been lucky, or is this new?"

I was surprised by his question and thought it over. "It feels new."

"Excellent. May it continue." Down in the whickering flames a moldy pants leg caught the wind and flopped end over end as if making a break for it. Leer gracefully snared it with the rake and moved it back onto the coals. "I imagine some city business is on your mind. Some deal you want to close."

He wore the relaxed expression of an old friend, leaned in like a confidant. My lips assumed an ingratiating smile. Not that I liked Leer— no—but I found, against my will, that I very much wanted him to like *me*. Marshaling my wits I laid before him the upcoming Founder's Day event, the community's ongoing respect for his father, and so on. My truncated vocabulary rendered me concise. I used no more than twenty seconds laying out the city's request.

"No indeed," he simply replied.

Just like that! After all his talk of negligence and stewardship, his eagerness to hire local sprucer Jerry Fandeen, I'd expected he might be amenable.

"It would display your public spirit," I said, experimentally.

There was a dim flash as something rose in his eyes—his shoulders shifted with a fluidity that made me think of the sea. The flash faded and he said, "I'm honored you would ask, Virgil. Truly I am. But speechmaking is a phobia of mine. After all these miles what I come back for is quiet. I'm sure you understand."

I said of course I did.

"I'll just stay here and watch the fire if it's all right with you," he said, by way of dismissal.

"Thanks again," Ann sang out.

"Go on," Leer said to the raccoon, who stirred himself and came with us. Leer turned back to the flames. Genghis trotted along making small chirring sounds. When I opened the truck door he climbed in as though he were tame and settled himself between the seats.

I was glad to leave—once again I'd overdone. Out we jounced over Leer's pitted blacktop, Genghis alert between us, me woozy and weightless as a head on a pole. The truck sighed and sagged. I wondered how long it would take to quit smelling those smoldering clothes.

Ann on the other hand was still blushing.

"I think he might do it," she said. "Speak at the festival."

"He made it pretty clear he won't," I replied, shutting my eyes against the overall twirl. I didn't care whether Leer spoke or not. For that matter I didn't want to hear Ann speak for a while. If things could only be still and quiet and aroma-neutral for a minute or two, I might yet avoid a depressing road puke.

"He might, though," Ann said, craning back for one last look at the house before it went behind the aspens. "He might speak, Virgil, if I asked him for you."

We delivered Genghis to the newspaper office where Beeman was not glad to see him, then Ann let me off at the Empress. I passed the afternoon as a kind of sentient vapor, wafting through rooms listening to NPR, napping, blinking, and drifting to the roof-deck where I watched weather systems gather and disperse above the indifferent waves. Attempting to focus I lit the blue candle and thought about Mom and Dad.

A word about the candle. I'm not Catholic, but there was a girl in high school I sure liked being next to and when her grandma died I went with her to church. Beth had a quiet voice and tremendous thick dark hair which turned auburn when she struck the flame. She was a very reverent girl. She was reverent about Mass, popes, martyrs, saints (especially Isidore, patron saint of farmers), the working poor, the idle poor, and Jesus; and she was most determined to light candles for her grandma, whom she never liked—I met the grandma once at a picnic and remember only black eyebrows and a disquieting Frank Zappa soul patch. Beth felt guilty because she had feared and avoided the old woman, who was now dead. Beth was steadfast about the candles. She said they made her feel calm.

After the derailment I started lighting candles too.

All Orry and I ever learned for certain was that the train had failed to slow properly for a stretch of bad track. Eleven people died including all six in their car. There were fractured bones and sun and flies and water befouled by diesel and everything was hot. My imagination filled in moans and smells, inadequate last words. What made me light the candle was the fact I was supposed to be along. Mom and Dad were not trained missionaries but laypeople wanting to be of use. Kind and mostly patient believers, across my high-school years they became steadily more fervent. The prevalence of lost souls became unendurable to Mom in particular. She dreamed of people weeping in darkness. With growing excitement and a sense of destiny they plotted a six-month tour in Mexico at an ecumenical mission in the Sonoran foothills, where they would plant fruit trees and the Word of God, reaping an eternal harvest. They learned Spanish from cassettes and how to cook with peppers. Pitching the trip to me as a lifetime adventure, they assumed I would happily go, but by then I was seventeen, with school and a job and a hundred entirely temporal ambitions. In the end after long deliberation and what seemed to me an embarrassing amount of out-loud prayer on the matter, they allowed me to stay home by myself.

When they drove off I vaulted into the backyard howling *Libre al fin*. Four days later I got a call from the American consulate in Hermosillo. I've been lighting candles ever since.

Now the blue candle flickered in a draft from the window—I'd fallen asleep. Blowing it out I found myself thinking of Lanie Plume, the Citgo girl. As she pointed out, I'd been "briefly virtually dead." The message was that I should've died, but hadn't. That was the sense I kept getting. Everyone was nice about it, but I was a living mistake. The notion that I'd somehow put one over on mortality was exhausting.

Was a quest really necessary? Did I have to *seize the day*? In the circumstances, I wasn't even sure what the phrase meant. I could barely walk straight. My eyes were unreliable and cognition did not feel definitive. Only that morning I'd thrown out most of my clothes, convinced they'd been smuggled into my closet by devious Salvation Army volunteers. *Seize the day* suggests the day has a handle or a set of lapels. I distrust epiphanies. During my brief theological misery, Orry sent me a Western Union telegram saying, "Existence is great but don't read so much into it."

Yet this much couldn't be argued: I'd gone to the edge, and got back alive by the slenderest chance. Maybe I was "here for a reason," as the optimists continually insist.

You'd think there might be comfort in the idea, but no. I remained sick. My stomach lurched, my head was sore, and my muscles were tired. In fact I'll confess to recurring ingratitude and even annoyance toward Marcus Jetty, who'd pulled me to safety. What was he *doing* outside in that filthy weather? Was he so desperate for one more shabby herring float? Was there no one else's beeswax he could mind?

Given my attitude, you may think what happened next was purposeful. It wasn't. I made toast, watched some *Deadliest Catch*, rinsed knife and plate. I scrubbed my face and brushed my teeth and called that sucker a day.

Apparently I got up later.

Apparently I couldn't sleep, swallowed two tablets, and lit a burner under a pan of milk.

It seems I then just cruised on back to bed.

Of this I can assure you: despite my grumpy existential stance, I was glad to be alive. Glad for my friends, for the strident dizzying world, for my beat-up equilibrium and plundered lexicon—all of it. I was also grateful in no small measure for the Empress. Carp as I might she was my own, my sweet ball and chain, my museum and mistress. God in heaven, I loved the Empress. I promise you I didn't mean to burn the old girl down.

7

I HADN'T SEEN KATE WILSEY SINCE SHE FLED TOWN FOR A CATTLE
rancher in deepest heartland. It seemed strange that a woman who sup-
ported Greenpeace and made wishes on sea glass would uproot without
notice to Tulsa, Oklahoma, but she was a bright hungry woman and I
suppose local beeves were inadequate. Now she was back, standing on
the sidewalk in the morning when I let myself out.

"Why, Kate," I said.

She didn't reply but stood there fetchingly in a dappled sarong
rippling in the very slight breeze.

"It's good to see you, Kate," I said. "You are lovely and diaphanous."

Unmoved by the adjective she looked past me with a blank expression as though at unfurling disaster. There was a rank smell like Adam
Leer's pyre except more industrial. I looked northeast toward massive
Slake International displacing its acres of sky. No smoke there. Turning
back to Kate I watched her mouth open real big—it just kept opening,
like a sinkhole. A noise came out of it—*eeee*—a scream with no bottom.
It went on and on. She screamed as though the body snatchers were in
there. The horror was such I was almost relieved to wake to a house fire.
I snapped on the light and brown smoke stung my eyes. I leaped out of
bed, caught the doorframe with my shoulder, and fell into the hall. Flames
explored the square yard of ceiling above the stove. The pan of milk was a
black clot throwing sparks. Bits of pressboard dropped hissing on counter

and floor. I skidded forward on my knees and whipped a fire extinguisher from under the sink. A practically new dry-chemical model. Pulling the pin I blasted the ceiling and blew tiles all over the kitchen. The burning ones I hit again. The sparking milk pan skidded off the stove and I twisted the gas knob, blistering finger and thumb. A slim vine of smoke curled from the ceiling. The extinguisher was empty but I'd kept the old one. I climbed onto the table and pulled down every tile in reach. Squinting at warrens of insulation and wiring I saw no flames but stuck the nozzle up there and pummeled each opening with foam.

My head roared, my stomach trembled.

I threw open the windows, silenced the alarm, and leaned out over the marquee with my elbows on the sill. It wasn't yet six in the morning. The streetlamps were still on. Only the bakery across Main was lit—Betsy Shane would be trundling around behind the counter. A distant storm door opened and thumped, a semi jaked on the highway. A few geese flew overhead in the dark blue—I couldn't see them but heard their fanning wings.

My head soon cleared but my fingers shook. The courteous doctor had warned of lapses. Again I owed my life to luck, or providence, or, now I think of it, my own cautious nature—a fresh nine-volt in the smoke alarm, not one but *two* extinguishers at hand. "Just think," Beeman later cheerfully remarked, "if you weren't such a sensible bastard you'd be seared like a nice fillet."

I slid to the floor. Foam dripped from the ceiling in irregular blobs that spread when they hit. The electricity was intact, though. Ceiling tiles are simple to replace. I got to my feet. When you live above a movie theater, mops are never far away.

At ten a.m. I carried the last ruined tiles to the roof-deck and dropped them on a blue tarp. My fingers had quit shaking and my thoughts were in order. I'd half-convinced myself the whole event was no more than an embarrassing fluke. When I stepped back inside, the Empress landline was ringing. I answered and was informed by a woman named Rita I had missed my follow-up with Dr. Koskinen.

"I didn't know about this follow-up."

"You did know," Rita said. "Your appointment was this morning at nine. We set it up with you in person before your release. We left a confirmation voice mail on your cell. We sent two text messages, one yesterday and one this morning." Rita paused. "Therefore you knew."

"I'm sorry ... hmm, gosh." I did feel bad about missing the follow-up, but less so the longer I knew Rita.

She said, "Dr. Koskinen asked me to reschedule. Would you like me to do that now?"

"Sure."

"If we make another appointment, Mr. Wander, will you go to the trouble of keeping it?"

I could've explained, of course. My cell was in the lake and I'd forgot to buy a new one. The appointment was on the wall calendar, which I had forgot to check. Then last night I'd forgot to shut off the burner, which resulted in a busy morning. I could've explained but instead just hung up.

It was rude, absolutely. The previous tenant wouldn't have done it. The previous tenant would have groveled and then held a grudge.

The phone rang again. Rita said, "We were cut off."

"We weren't, no. I hung up because of your tenor."

"My tenor?" she repeated. "Excuse me—do you have an issue with my tenor?"

"Well, I do, yes. It's tremendously hostile, Rita."

I experienced an unspooling sense of freedom—genuine antagonism is something I've rarely encountered, and it felt good to respond with honesty instead of obsequious scraping. There was also enormous linguistic relief. How could Rita know what a triumph *tremendously hostile* represented?

She hung up.

After a few minutes the phone rang again. "Virgil, it's Paul Koskinen. How are you?"

We didn't talk long. I expected to be lectured or at least handled with care and instead he was nothing but kind. He inquired whether I could walk without tripping, or read normal print, whether meat and potatoes had begun to taste faintly of aluminum. He asked about limb tremors and headaches and impossible visions. Did I own any firearms? If so were they stored in appropriate fashion? He asked how my memory functioned and I said it was fine—I tried to say *runs like a top* but couldn't remember the spinning toy so the phrase petered out. This may have alerted him to something. I don't remember how he got to the truth about the kitchen fire, but he got there. There came a long silence in which I anticipated rebuke.

At last he said, "Find someone to stay with you, Virgil."

"I'd really rather not."

"Only for a few days. Maybe a week. You can do this, I think."

I said, "You know, doctor, it's okay. I put the fire out and I won't start another. Alone is all right with me."

A stymied silence on the other end. I could hear the moist wheeze of a heavy man in deep concern.

"Humor me," he said at last. "Otherwise, I'm going to worry about you."

I opened my mouth to object, but then the doctor coughed softly—he wheezed, and I faltered. He was a patient old Finn, this Koskinen. He had called me back himself, the rarest of physicians. He spoke in a tone of forbearance. He was going to worry if I was alone! Suddenly I had a lump in my throat as hard as a buckeye. Blinking fast I promised the doctor I would find myself a houseguest before the day was through.

It was true what I said—alone was all right with me, and had been for a long time. Orry comes every year for a week and while she's terrific mordant company there's no denying the lift I feel at her receding taillights. Beeman is the best friend I've had since grade school, but I couldn't imagine him settling in for more than a few hours, ducking his bison head under the archways, knocking around in the guest bedroom with its lopsided futon. Of course because of the dream I thought of Kate Wilsey—she'd settled in once for quite a while and seemed to like it, but Kate was in Tulsa with her sinewy stockman.

It's odd to realize you know everyone in town—you're a fixture, an endearment for God's sake—yet can no more ask for help than sprint in the Naked Olympics.

Out on the roof I gathered the edges of the tarp. Ninety pounds or so of tiles and rags, the blackened pan, also the retro chrome toaster Orry had given me, now ruined with chemical foam. I tied the whole business in a corpselike bundle and dragged it to the cornice overlooking the alley. Earlier I'd gone down and opened the lid of the rusty green dumpster. Now I heaved the bundle atop the cornice, balanced it there, and let it go like a burial at sea. Straight into the dumpster it dropped, crinkly-whack, the weight rocking the unit forward so the lid fell neatly shut. The perfect shot gave me a sensation of lift, of unseemly liberation, as when I had been impolite to Rita. I looked out over the waterfront, the marina with its few bobbing sailboats, the Shipwreck Tavern's trashy lakeside veranda, the city pier and swimming beach, and the tall black ore-loading dock like the last of all permanent things.

The breeze picked up. Halyards sang against their spars. The broad water surged along, deep blue with chevron whitecaps angling up-shore.

For a moment the world made its welcome old sense.

Then from behind the ore dock rose an improbable shape—through the October haze it came into focus. It was a dog. A massive, jowly, sad-eyed dog. The dog was low in the sky, ears up, nose down, scouting the horizon. At first I was spooked. Hallucinations aren't necessarily a disaster but are rarely propitious. Where was it going to end?

Then the dog hesitated in midair. While I watched it shook itself, and the sound gave it away—a shivery rattle, like blown newspaper.

I didn't know the dog—not yet—but I knew its master.

I laughed on the rooftop as the dog loped out over the waves.

8

RUNE'S SECOND KITE (WHAT I THOUGHT OF AS HIS SECOND, THOUGH he'd been building kites for decades) was a tribute to his favorite animal, a short-haired mutt given him by a friend. The mutt had bloodhound genes and a keen nose—too keen for the friend, Espen, a renowned Casanova in his wind-scrubbed Arctic village. Espen simply couldn't get away from the dog, which slipped all leads and followed him everywhere. Anyone wondering where Espen was had only to see at whose doorway the dog was lying any given afternoon. As the trumpeter declares in *The Commitments* (1991), it *ruffled his savoir faire*.

"A loyal soul—we had him twelve years, Sofie and me," Rune said, clearly pleased both by the dog and its hovering look-alike. He was in good humor, standing on the cobbly rocks north of the pier, wearing a pair of cowhide gloves so new you could smell the leather. A cluster of sparrows worked the nearby grasses for seed. The kite, more lifelike the closer you got, hunted to and fro over the water. It was at least nine feet from nose to tail and a hard puller. The heavy string whistled in the wind—those gloves were a good idea.

"Whereabouts do you live?" I asked.

"Tromsø," he said. "We, I, live in Tromsø. Not Espen—these days he spends most of his time in Svolvær." He paused. "There are some charitable women in Svolvær."

"Ah—Norwegian." I wouldn't have guessed from the accent, which had to me the weathered consonants of not just a distant place but an ancient time.

Rune said, "Tromsø, Norway. You've heard of it, hmm? The Paris of the North?"

"I've not heard *that* exactly."

Already low over the lake, the trusting dog began sinking tail-first toward the steaming waves. Rune let a few feet of line off a wooden reel, gave a quick tug, and it stabilized; like an actual dog, the kite demanded attention.

"And your project here? Your detective work, I mean. I hope you're finding what you wanted."

He nodded. Today his face appeared level right across, not like the downhill slide of our last meeting. "I went to their house—Nadine and Bjorn's. How gracious she is. We had roast beef, some very good potatoes. She showed me photographs. Fishing, picnics, the neon signs. I don't know many things about baseball."

He looked out toward the water, keeping his voice level and his eyes away from me to veil his palpable melancholy. It was impossible not to imagine him in Nadine's living room, facing proof of a life for which he was directly responsible, yet had missed from beginning to end. Had he seen eyes like his own looking up at him from the photos?

In a subdued tone he said, "They have no reason to show me kindness, yet they do."

"Alec was kind as well. You should be pleased he was yours."

"*Takk*," he said softly.

I thought he would now bring up the matter of Alec's disappearance, his amended and suspect reputation, the obvious axis on which his name revolved. But he didn't. He allowed the dog to sink within inches of the wave tops, then walked it slowly forward, a neat trick.

"How do you get on with Bjorn?" I asked.

Rune didn't reply. The question seemed to demarcate a zone of caution, and why not? Bjorn was a spirited small boy, impetuous and sociable, but that changed after Alec's departure. He fell sick in fact—developed a recurrent fever and cough, a reedy elongated wheeze that made you want to draw your coat over his ever-bonier shoulders. His lucent pallor outlasted the fever and became his permanent shade. He lost his ability to imagine the future. Maps were as fiction to him; as his friends took up soccer or resolute truancy, Bjorn just fell away. He was counseled, exhorted, and drugged. He could no longer lay the plans boys lay. His taciturn gaze attracted aggressors. Reassured by her friends that Bjorn would in time recover himself, Nadine instead witnessed the flowering of an ominous quirk. As though the father's abrupt disappearance were genetically ordained, like gray eyes or long fingers, Bjorn too began vanishing at chance moments. He and Nadine might be watching a movie, she would glance over to find him gone. He wasn't "running away" or demanding attention; often he was only upstairs, perched on his bunk or peering outside. He began to sleepwalk. Waking to the impression of an empty house Nadine would throw on a jacket and retrieve him down the block in his stocking feet, or adrift in the leaf-blown alley behind the bakery. She found him once in a willow swamp on the edge of town, once climbing the abandoned ore dock under the moon. Now he was seventeen. A dreamy boy can get in deep. This past summer he had taken up surfing, always alone, a dicey endeavor on North America's coldest water.

A southerly gust caught the big kite and sent it overhead with clattering ribs. Rune leaned back against it, the tails of his coat whipping forward. "Bjorn is uncommon," he said. "He is careful with words. It is a good quality." Rune's understated manner in no way disguised his pride in his grandson, though he admitted the feeling was not reciprocated.

"It would be easier if I looked like Alec. For example, tall," Rune conjectured, as a clutch of sparrows spooked up out of the grass and circled him tightly a moment. Distractedly he held out a gloved hand and two of the birds landed on it while he talked. "If I were lanky, yes? If I had my son's nice face, instead of this damaged edition. It might be easier for Bjorn if he looked at me and saw a man he could almost remember."

"He'll adjust."

Rune looked at me searchingly, as though I had been dismissive of his grandson. And maybe I had. Maybe I was recalling my own hard adjustment at seventeen; maybe I was also thinking of Nadine, who for a long decade had raised that boy alone.

"What a patient woman she is," Rune said, as though reading my mind, sadness stealing into his voice.

"Nadine is resilient," I said, grateful that a circumspect word was the one to surface. What if I'd said *appealing* or, worse, *bewitching*?

I had long guarded my speech where Nadine was concerned.

"She is a beauty," Rune said, observing the sparrows at ease on his hand, then gently flicking them off. "Why did she not remarry?"

This was a subject I could scarcely talk about, and not just because of my withered terminology. After Alec vanished any number of men came knocking—loud entrepreneurs from Duluth; a Twin Cities surgeon in a Mercedes convertible; not one but two track coaches from farther up-shore, both weirdly fond of polyester shorts. Beeman took his shot, as did the local school superintendent who'd been disciplined but not fired for goosing cheerleaders in his office. Even old Adam Leer took a run at Nadine during one of his hometown sabbaticals. Through it all I watched Nadine discourage, deflect, delay. Of course some were more persistent than others. One of the coaches went so far as to secure a purchase agreement on a house in Greenstone, as though this somehow sealed the deal. Yet like the others he soon hit the road, moaning about vain pursuit. It made me think of Penelope waiting for Odysseus—Penelope at her loom, not missing a trick, lumpen suitors everywhere.

I said, "Maybe she believes he is still alive."

Rune watched the kite, moonwalking it backward with rattly precision. "Is that what you believe?" he asked.

"I believe if he were alive he would have come back to her."

Rune reached into his back pocket and tossed me a pair of leather gloves.

What a winning kite, that big dog, with perky ear and downcast eye— so much care had plainly gone into its fashioning, the previous tenant would've been terrified to fly it lest it dive straight into the lake. Rune showed me how to hold the wooden reel in my left hand and adjust the string with my right. If I paid out line, the dog backed toward the water; if I tugged, it bounded joyfully into the air.

Flying had immediate effects. The wind seemed a clarifying agent. My dizziness, severe after last night's fever, disappeared. The headache smoldered far away. A pleasant tension traveled down the string. The whir entered my fingers and went up my arms. It hummed in my brainstem, shaking up vowels. My face ached from grinning. The dog hunted gleefully over the harbor and I was out there with it, land far behind, wind in my ribs, waves shooting along below. Nothing seemed out of reach or even unlikely. It was like entering a whirlwind where ambition and disappointment are flung off, yet you remain calm in its eye. Rune asked a question about Alec, and the whirring line gave wings to my memory.

When I was still seeing Kate, she cooked up an idea. Often she spent the evening with me up in the booth, the old Simplex projector spinning along while she got cozy at my side, riffing on noxious real-estate clients or designing in the air the splendid pile she expected to attain. What a promising couple we briefly made! In this connubial spirit she one night said: Hang on, boy—ain't we young professionals? At her happiest Kate violated grammar just for the joy of it. Ain't life splendid, and ain't we got this vintage theater at our fingertips? Yes yes and yes, I said, my eyes on her generous wide smile. Ain't it a shame then to shut things down at the fogy hour of ten p.m. and shoo out the crowd and lock up? It was indeed, said I, not pointing out that the "crowd" that night was seven adults and three children. What was on her mind, I asked. And she leaned in whispering: *after-party*.

I reached for her but she swatted me away—No, you big nast, I mean a party. Like with pizza! She had a dauntless practicality, Kate. I was quite in love with her. It's never been hard for me to fall in love, a quality that has yet to simplify one single day of my life.

So we concocted an after-party, even though the primary event was only a seven p.m. screening of the latest Pixar, and even though *after-party* suggests a coastal hipness that not a soul of us possessed. The guest list was minimal. Alec and Nadine, little Bjorn too, Don Lean who sold insurance then and later ran for sheriff, Beeman with whichever wife he had at the time—Darla, I think it was. When the last customer left we extinguished the marquee and I laced up an illegal print of the old Marlon Brando–David Niven comedy, *Bedtime Story* (1964). We played it with the lights half-dimmed, kidding each other through the slow parts, enjoying gas-station pepperoni and substandard beer, becoming, of all things, friends. Alec was at his disarming best that night—checking on Bjorn who was asleep on a blanket, ribbing Tom and me about our respective empires in media and entertainment, ribbing himself about *making it big in neon*, when really none of us were making it, all of us just bleeding wherewithal, week in and week out, except of course Kate who was selling swampland hand over fist to hard-shell Y2Kers hoping for the worst.

So pleasant was this after-party, such a tight little club were we, that a month later we threw another, with lasagna and box cabernet and another unauthorized print from the vault (*Ensign Pulver*, also '64). Soon it was our regular deal. Your own theater with art deco lighting and unlawful film stash is not a bad venue for personal whimsy.

Rune may have asked another question. It seemed to come from far away. Without really hearing it I answered at length—even minus adjectives I babbled along, and the more I babbled the more I remembered. The dog romped hither and yon, the kite string hummed like a prayer in my head, I had access to stories not remembered in years. When the high school biology department was getting rid of old taxidermy, Alec snagged the moldering Great Horned Owl and one evening hid in the shrubbery outside Beeman's house. Beeman was delayed at the Shipwreck so Alec crouched in the junipers humming to himself for *two hours* before finally scaring the actual bejeebers out of Beeman coming up the walk. Alec really was funny. The owl story reminded me of a few more, and when I finally looked over, Rune seemed fatigued. He'd taken a seat on a large rock and was resting elbows on knees like a man out of breath. One of the sparrows had lit on his shoulder and regarded him now with a concerned tilt of its tiny round head. Rune's face had again the tumbledown appearance of rockslide scree.

"Oh—sorry," I said.

He gave a patient, preoccupied nod. Several people had arrived on the waterfront and hung shyly about. Shad Pea was among them. I recalled Lily saying he'd met the old kite flyer and now here he was, boots untied and his hair stuck down, a pencil tucked back of his ear. Rune put on his gloves and motioned for the reel. I hated to give it up—I very nearly couldn't—with that beautiful hum in my veins. As I handed it over an idea came to me. I'd thought of it earlier, but forgot.

"Rune, where are you staying? Did you find a motel?"

He turned to point inland. There's a small grassy lot just up from the water, with swing set and drinking fountain and a former tennis court turned desolate skateboard park. At the curb was an orange VW camper van, its canvas top propped at an angle. I'd walked right past it on my way to the waterfront—even at a distance, the van smelled like corned beef.

"Pretty cold for camping," I said.

"Goose down bag."

"Good, but it's supposed to freeze tonight. If you want to get out of the weather, there's an extra room up at the Empress. That's the movie theater up on Main. It's warm and it's private. You won't be bothered." He looked indecisive so I added, "The truth is you'd be doing me a favor."

Relief crossed his tired old face. I knew I should warn him my brain was on sick leave, I might puke without warning or fall to the floor, but before I could do so Shad Pea stepped in and seized Rune's hand, the hand not holding the string. "Remember me?" Shad asked in a loud voice—he had roaring tinnitus from decades of snowplows and outboard motors and had to shout to hear himself. "Shad Pea! We talked last night, or the night before!"

"Of course," Rune kindly replied. "How are you, my friend?"

"Pretty okay!" Shad said, though he looked awful—sallow and rank, fingers twisting a bandanna into a greasy snake. He had a hungry, dark-eyed expression. "Look, I brought you something." Hiking up his jacket, Shad pulled a flask-shaped bottle from his hip pocket. "Maple syrup, from last spring—me and Galen made it."

"Shad, *takk*, how thoughtful." Rune held the bottle up to the light. A ghost of sediment slid along the bottom. "Would you care to take a spin?" Rune asked him.

Shad said nothing but reached for the string with both shaky hands.

9

I WAS VACUUMING THE HALLWAY BETWEEN THE TWO AUDITORIUM doors. The ceiling kept dropping tiny motes of dust. I'd painted and textured and painted again, but nothing kept the streams of dust from dribbling down. Sometimes in the proper light you could see tiny iridescent threads descending to the carpet. If I didn't vacuum several times a week, there would be dime-size cones on the floor. Through a magnifying glass they looked like a chain of volcanoes.

A motion drew my eye—a man at the door. I thought it might be Rune and had a moment of lift, but it wasn't him. It was Jerry Fandeen.

I was nearly done vacuuming, so held up a hand and Jerry nodded while I cruised back and forth, sucking up the last of the dust volcanoes. The thought of having to talk to Jerry Fandeen made me tired. I had never talked with him all that much, but when I did it was heavy lifting—he was a hearty one, a big bluff beefsteak tomato, a man who shook hands and held on a long time. For some reason it was harder work than talking to Ann. Still, there was nothing for it—there he stood looking mournfully in through the glass, his nose deep purple, his fingers white. He had a long red steel toolbox tucked under his arm.

I unlocked and he came right in.

"What can I do for you, Jerry?"

"Hi, Virgil, I'm glad you're all right, you know, with the accident."

"Thank you."

He set the toolbox on the floor and blew into his fingers. "It's eerie—I drove up and had a look where you went over. It's a long drop."

"It sure is."

"I said to Ann, Poor Virge. What a thing! The dude upstairs stepped in for sure. Tell you something, though," Jerry said, in a confessional tone, "In all these years I never drove past that spot without thinking what it would be like to do what you did. Floor it, man. Over the edge. Get it done with. Lights out—not that you were trying to do that!" he added hurriedly. "Not saying that! A guy thinks about it, though, is all I'm saying."

"What can I help you with, Jerry?"

He eyed me uneasily. The white of his left eye was shot with scarlet. It was hard to look at. He said, "You went out to Adam Leer's place, right? With Ann?"

"She drove me there, yes. I understand Mr. Leer wants to hire you."

"Did you hear him say so?"

"Yes."

"Okay," Jerry said. "That's what Ann told me, but I wasn't sure. Ann's always saying this person or that person wants to hire me, then it never turns out to be true. I told her I wasn't about to go see Mr. Leer about a job and embarrass myself, but she said to ask you if I didn't believe her. I tried your cell phone but you didn't answer."

"The offer is real as far as I know. He has some yard work in mind, if you can get to it before the snow. Maybe some other jobs too."

"Like mechanical jobs?"

"He wasn't specific. He mentioned taking out that stand of aspens. And the driveway's in pretty rough shape."

Jerry walked over to my concession stand and set the toolbox on the counter. With his back to me he said, "I just came by to collect my socket set."

"Your socket set."

He opened the big box. It was a nest of cords, screwdrivers, ball-peen hammers, loose washers, and other bits. "Remember a couple of years ago? I lent you my set."

I didn't remember. Jerry said, "You were working on something and needed some sockets. I brought you mine. Now I need them back." At my doubtful expression he added, "Ann warned me you wouldn't recall. She said you're pretty forgetful right now, because of your brain thing." He sighed, pawed through his toolbox a few moments as if making absolutely sure, then held it open for my inspection. "You see— they're missing," he said, as though his jumbly toolbox were proof that I was hoarding his sockets.

"Jerry, I don't have your socket set."

"How do you know that?" he asked, startled. Then, with deep concern, "How *could* you know it, for sure, old friend?"

I laughed. I couldn't help it. My brain wasn't at full power—just then it felt less like a brain than a barely sentient dumpling—yet I was sure Jerry was inventing. In fact I was reasonably sure this was the longest conversation Jerry and I had ever had.

"Ann said you wouldn't recall," he said, sorrowfully. He looked up from the chaotic toolbox to me. I held his gaze. He didn't look away and neither did I. Eventually something crept into his eyes. It was slight, but it was there—the rash nerve of the boy thief, sticking to his story. Jerry didn't blink. I felt admiration and enormous sadness. Greenstone was full of people who could make you sad just by strolling into view. Jerry was one of them. Shad was another. I realized I was one of them too—maybe always had been. He said, "Ann feels real bad how forgetful you've become."

I asked what he needed the sockets for and he replied simply, "Work." Any work Leer had for him would require tools. He couldn't just show up unprepared. Ever since Ann told him about this opportunity he'd been out in his garage, sorting through tools.

It was clear to me this part of his story was true. I watched his moist and mottled brow. Talking about Adam Leer made him anxious. "The guy is not regular," he said. "Guy killed his own brother when they were just kids, I don't know if you're aware."

"That's just a story, Jerry. And a pretty mean one."

Jerry said he didn't know about that. He said Leer was never even sorry, not about the dead brother, not about anything he did—he sure went through the wives, too. Not to even mention making dirty movies, and then letting his decent old parents' house fall apart. Now he, Jerry, was supposed to go fix what Leer hadn't cared enough to keep in shape. The whole thing made Jerry nervous. He needed the work, but it was hard to work when you were nervous, and had lent out half your tools.

His face had gone red and patchy while he talked. "Come on downstairs," I said. "Maybe you're right about the sockets."

Descending into chilly gloom I tried to recall what I knew of Jerry Fandeen. He was way older than Ann. He'd worked one time or another for most of the taconite outfits on the Mesabi Range—driving trucks, welding, keeping equipment in trim. Eventually he became something of a specialist at setting the sequential explosive charges that pulverize taconite ore into rubble for processing. When I moved in there were still a few former blasters in Greenstone, decent old deaf union men who described the years in cubic tons. In 1987 I sold a ticket for *Peggy Sue Got Married* to a bald man with a grin and a stout handshake—"You owe me your basement," he said, an inscrutable remark until he explained he'd been on a municipal blasting crew back in '53. Lots of us owed him our basements. Mine is smooth and vertical, the cool square walls interrupted every two feet with the half-pipe tracks of drill bits. I wondered what Jerry thought of the workmanship. He'd lost his job because of a work-related calamity, details of which I could not remember. Afterward, Jerry's employment was haphazard. He washed dishes, cut grass, collected government assistance. It seemed likely Ann rolled her eyes whenever Jerry spoke. In fact it seemed certain. By the time we reached the basement I had accrued a large fund of sympathy for Jerry.

"Nice down here," he remarked. The rock walls are the color of graphite. Lights bob from the massive old joists. A few small rooms are cobbled up from pallet boards. It looks like a mine in a Howard Hawks western.

"Nice," Jerry repeated.

The storage room is lined with shelving attached to clean bedrock with spikes. The shelves hold boxes, Rubbermaid bins, fruit crates. A tray of tubular maps like scrolls. Every tool I own is down there, in more or less decent arrangement.

"Aw, nice," he said in wonder, and I pretty much agreed. There's a rack of Tarzan paperbacks, a pint of schnapps in a sliding drawer, a cork dartboard I rarely use but like to see hanging in its place. Summer and winter it's fifty-eight degrees. Kate never liked it down here but this gloomy old room has always lifted my spirits.

I pulled out an ancient fruit crate with a peeling label. The label said *Claudio's* with an orange painted on it like a sun. The crate contained three socket sets. I heaved it onto the big workbench which is also spiked to the rock.

Jerry opened the cases, laid them on the bench, and ran his fingers over the shiny sockets as if playing scales. He was a big specimen with translucent fuzz on his cheeks and Christmas yearning in his eyes. It began to seem foolish that I owned a giant box of redundant sockets I never used, while Jerry, who needed sockets, had none. Finally I reached out and tapped the biggest set. "I remember now. These are yours."

His wariness returned. He thought I was setting a trap. It was a comprehensive socket set in a chromium case with both metric and standard components. Like most of my tools it was here when I arrived. A lovely bit of conflict came into Jerry's face. He was torn between the joy of good tools and the guilt of ripping me off. It was impossible to guess which way he would go. He watched me a moment, then shut the case and started fast toward the stairs with the sockets under his arm.

"Hang on, Jerry," I called after him.

He turned at the foot of the steps.

"I think there was something else," I said. "Didn't you lend me a few other things?"

"Electric drill," he instantly declared.

I had two. The previous owner had left one behind, a hefty antique with a pewter-like sheen; then my brother-in-law Dinesh gave me a birthday Black and Decker. Jerry got that one, still in the box. He looked pleased and confused. We moved on to shop clamps and claw hammers and wood chisels, where he helped himself more freely. Soon he began telling me about his professional descent. He'd got off track somehow, back in his blast-technician days. He didn't know how exactly. He used to be sharp and self-directed. A leader. He told his crew what to do and they did it, setting up rolling charges in a series of holes so on detonation the ground rose rippling and it was like shaking out a blanket. His voice grew poignant at the image. But time passed, his edges got dull. He did not mind a drink in those days. One afternoon on the mine floor he fell asleep driving a dump truck in low gear. The truck moved forward at a slow rate of speed. It rolled over a generator so things came unplugged, and still Jerry didn't wake up. The truck clipped the edge of a portable toilet, then flattened a Ford Fiesta that shouldn't have been parked where it was. There wasn't much to those Fiestas. Flimsy cars. The trouble was that another man on Jerry's crew was sleeping inside the Fiesta. It was a bad day at the mine. A lot of people yelled at Jerry because of it. He tried to answer them but couldn't. No answer came to him that would explain how such a thing had occurred. He simply fell asleep—he forgot himself, somehow. Ann took his side, but not for long. She soon turned a corner. She didn't accuse him, but no longer defended him either. She didn't really even talk to him, unless it was to tell him about some work he should do. It seemed to Jerry that after he forgot himself, Ann forgot him as well. She forgot he was her husband, or that they had been happy. Eventually she forgot everything she had liked him for in the first place. Thus Jerry's determination to collect his tools and go to work for Mr. Leer; he felt if he could complete some jobs correctly, really knock them out of the park, even just mowing the grass, he might start to remember himself. If he remembered himself soon enough, maybe Ann would remember him too.

Looking over my shelves he abruptly recalled lending me a circular saw and a set of screwdrivers. Flat-head or Phillips, I asked. Probably both, he replied. We filled a few crates with tools and hauled them up the steps to his pickup.

10

JERRY HADN'T BEEN GONE HALF AN HOUR WHEN SNOW STARTED TO fall, accumulating in the gutters and putting his mowing plans in jeopardy. It was one of those deep, drenching, autumn snows, six miserable inches that clung to twigs and windowsills and reminded summer holdouts to bolt while they could. I cruised through the concessions, took a quick inventory of popcorn oil and Hot Tamales and Junior Mints. I hadn't shown a film since the accident but planned to reopen next week. When I turned on the lights a filament flashed in a lobby fixture, so I was standing on a stepladder with a replacement bulb when Rune appeared at the glass door under the marquee—it gave me a jolt, him standing there, peering inside through cupped hands.

I unlocked and in he came with a satchel and two cylindrical fishing-rod cases. Snow stuck to his shoulders and slid off the brim of his hat. He stamped it off his shoes in clumps. His eyes were lit, his handshake was cold, he looked disheveled and happy.

"Would you like me to change that bulb?" he said.

He'd been watching several minutes, it turned out—watching me paralyzed on the second step of the ladder, looking up, dreading the vertigo that became inevitable as I came close to the ceiling.

I handed him the bulb. He went up like a Narnian elf—out with the old glass, in with the new—and in a blink he was back on the floor. "Look," he said, "I've brought supper."

He reached into the pockets of his long-tailed coat and pulled out a square tin of corned beef, raised a finger to stop my protest, then bobbled up a handful of redskin potatoes, a yellow onion, a head of garlic.

By now I was laughing. He said, "Is something the matter? What is the matter? Do you not care about hash?"

"I care deeply about hash," I said. "Let's get this stuff upstairs."

In my kitchen Rune rustled about, locating dishes and forks, unearthing pans I failed to remember, starting a kettle of water and shooing me into a chair. I would later learn Marcus Jetty was among those who'd wandered down to the harbor and ended up flying the dog. It was Marcus who told Rune about the soaring Pontiac, my mighty splashdown, my unsettled mind. With a grunt Rune hoisted his heavy satchel to the tabletop, zipped it open, and pawed down through, exclaiming *Ha ha!* as he pulled out a jar of coarse mustard and set it aside. The mustard was followed by Worcestershire, pickles and peppercorns, sausages, cheese, a sturdy tomato, two brown speckled eggs—it was bottomless, that satchel; if he'd contrived to pull a friendly bear cub out of its depths I'd have been delighted but not all that surprised. He hummed and murmured as the goods kept coming: crackers, fruit cocktail, coffee and cream, black bread and black beer, the flask of Shad's maple syrup, a tiny bright city of bottles and tins. *Ha ha!* Chopping onions on a plank, Rune advised me to check the bag and see "what's below," and reaching down I lifted out half a berry pie still in its foil, a bar of Freia chocolate, and a flask of *akevitt* which Rune forthrightly allowed was terrible unless poured at the end of a strenuous day, when it was more than a little bit good. Behind the fry hiss I became aware of an aggressive snapping sound—fat wet snowflakes striking the window. Rune rubbed steam from the panes with his hand and EMPRESS became a dozen blue rivers as snow ran melting down the glass. He stood at the stovetop turning the hash a long time, then slid it crackling onto plates and laid a bright fried egg over each.

It turns out there's little better than corned beef hash, if you are exhausted, with popping ears and wayward balance. The hash vanished in near silence, but during the coffee afterward, with the berry pie and chocolate, Rune leaned back on two chair legs and began to hold forth. He claimed his English was rudimentary yet he held forth ably, and the day must've been strenuous enough for us both, since the akevitt was as mellow as cream.

Six weeks earlier Rune Eliassen was a retired widower feeding the juncos and accepting the conclusion of his lineage. He lived in a white house with a steep red roof in Tromsø, two hundred miles above the Arctic Circle, with a small sailboat resting on blocks in the yard and a high round window through which he could watch sturdy Hurtigruten ferries plying to and fro under the soaring bridge. His wife Sofie, a piano teacher and baker of profound loaves at a local café, had died the winter before; his sister Gretchen, a sparkling poet, two winters before that. Neither Sofie nor Gretchen ever had children. As his sister cheerfully told him, "On the day I tip over, you will be the final post in the fence."

He'd gotten used to being the final post.

Oh, he and Sofie had wanted children—wanted them badly. When the early years passed without a baby they'd seen one doctor, then another. A kind of panic took hold, Rune said; they became conversant with schedules and temperatures, they worked the mapped tides of fertility. You might not think so, but a reluctant bachelor understands a little of this. The passing bullet train of years, I mean. The quiet bowl of soup at six. Yet sitting in my kitchen Rune held off sorrow and became if anything more sprightly. He waxed a bit enthusiastic about the spirit and disposition required of a final post. It wasn't for everyone but a man could get through. He said certain fecund neighbors would always suspect you had brought it on yourself through transgression or frivolity. You might even believe this yourself for a time. There was a period of adjustment while you gave up blood legacy.

"Sofie recovered first," he admitted. "A practical one, my wife. A good hard head on those soft shoulders. On the other hand I am fairly slow. I had to wallow. A capable wallower, she called me. Sofie was patient until she couldn't be anymore. Then it had to be all right."

"Why didn't you adopt a child?"

"We pursued it, certainly. And twice came close—people gave us baby clothes, the bed with sides, we bought *den lille* shoes. But both times fell to pieces. A mother can change her mind, you see? But to come so near—and then not. The disappointment is extravagant." This he stated in a flattened voice like a wall built hastily to conceal ruins.

The akevitt warmed my eardrums and fingertips. "But then," I said, "you weren't the last post after all."

"No. How about that?" Rune pointed at the flask which I handed over.

Six weeks ago today—only six weeks!— he'd gone as usual to Sofie's grave. She was buried in a churchyard uphill from the water. The hill was covered with stone markers and sparse yellow grasses. The wind rarely stopped up there; it was a beguiling place to fly. That day Rune flew a kite modeled on the darting sloop he and Sofie sailed weekends for almost thirty years.

When he got home there was mail in the box. In the mail was a letter from an attorney in South Dakota, United States. The attorney named a woman who had died in Watertown. Per her instructions he was giving Rune the news—delayed and bedazzling, like light from an extinguished star—that long ago he'd fathered a son in America.

"You see," Rune said, in a tone of pleased apology, "when I was young, before I ever knew my Sofie, I came to the States for a bit."

The whole tale was so unlikely, and so plainly described—the stone markers and yellow grasses, the tidings on a strange letterhead—it began to play in my head like a film. If I shut my eyes I could watch it all. I knew its look and genre, a genial romance in oversaturated hues, with snow falling on eyelashes and little doubt of the outcome. A transatlantic romance of the early sixties. I imagined Rune as a brooding young Terence Stamp—for the girl, say, Tuesday Weld.

Her name was Roberta. *Nimble* is the word Rune liked for her—a lively Duluth girl from St. Scholastica, teaching *småbarn* in Greenstone that year of 1964. Rune was twenty-three and had come to the States to drive through the prairie, a dream of his, and to recover from what he nebulously termed a *prøvelse*, or affliction. From this I took it he'd been ill or suffered some brute trauma. He was not an explainer of dark areas unless the mood took him. He was happier narrating times of light, and what arrested him that day on the streets of Duluth was a copper-haired girl in a white beret. She stood on the walk outside a downtown bookshop. It was snowing and she held a brand-new book behind crossed arms to protect it from the flakes. Rune still remembered how he squared himself walking and hoped she would look his way. She didn't, instead peering wistfully into the shop window. As Rune passed on the sidewalk he slowed and looked too.

There in the window glass she caught his eye.

He stopped, of course. He meant to say *Hi* or perhaps *Good morning* but instead said, How do you do? A formal English phrase in his looping Arctic cadence. The girl smiled. In a rush she explained she had just bought this novel and was nervous about reading it. A Japanese story known for its ruthless view of the world. Her mother had borrowed a library copy and proclaimed it ghastly. She'd never read a book so fast before. The girl opened her arms. The book was *The Sailor Who Fell from Grace with the Sea*. Rune hadn't heard of it. He was already half in love with the copper-haired girl. He said, I am recently off the sea myself.

Actually he'd come off the sea eight weeks ago in Florida, glad to leave the moaning freighter after twelve rough days on the Atlantic. He traded kroner for dollars, then dollars for a wood-paneled Ford De Luxe from a fibrous old woman in Live Oak. Standing on her porch he asked how to register the automobile. She replied that America was cash only. She sized him up through the smoke of her hand-rolled cigarette. He tried to show only the right side of his face. The left side slouched badly. The sagging eyelid was the worst of it—he felt it gave him a degenerate appearance. But the woman would not be put off. She took his chin in her parchment fingers and turned his head as if gauging its worth in currency. Ducking inside she returned with half a loaf of bread, a Ball jar of water, a Pure Oil road map.

So Rune drove west—on gravel, macadam, on bone-dust tracks past Aermotor windmills and sharecropper huts. The De Luxe smelled like leaf tobacco and rattled badly. At fuel stations he acquired more maps and over the weeks he traced an oval through the browning, desiccated, snapping-turtle South and upward across the Great Plains.

Sleep was evasive. The back seat was cozy but the flat North American dark gave him tremors. Station attendants avoided his eyes. At night he perceived things watching in the dark. His face was numb. Blood thumped headlong through his veins. Day by day he thinned. The trip seemed a mistake except when he was watching the sun fall through columns of ocher and yellow dust, colors not seen in boreal Norway.

As autumn declined he hit more familiar latitudes. Frost napped his fenders in the morning. One evening with the sun at his back he crested a rise and beheld an inland sea. He'd heard of Lake Superior and now here it was. Far to the east the sky was already dark and night sped toward him over the water. Duluth smoked and blinked as the lights came on. The air was wet as a lung, with the spiky smells of nails and fire. The forest leaned in over the city. A steely-looking river twisted fjord-like into the steep-sided hills.

He asked for the YMCA where he ate a bowl of ham broth and slept in the sheltering reek of an Army blanket. The other mattress was occupied by a renegade prophet, a haunted man with trembling limbs. The prophet's head was bald and scabbed. He wore an eye patch which he flipped up and down while delivering his monologue of complaint. God Almighty was after him. Fearsome was Jehovah, but irritating too. His petulant silences! His demands for attention! The prophet wore hook-laced boots spattered with cryptic effluent. He left them on to sleep.

Rune dozed guardedly and tiptoed out early. He bought coffee and carried it past redbrick warehouses to the waterfront, crossed the Lift Bridge into shoreline dunes covered with saw grass and willow. Two boys about ten had a driftwood fire at the water's edge. They'd killed a fat bullfrog gone torpid from cold. They were trying to cook its legs over the fire but kept scorching their fingers. Without a word Rune produced a small jackknife and shaved down a pair of willow-twig skewers which he handed to the boys, then walked on while they roasted the frog legs and ate them smacking and boasting. He walked another mile down the strand. The cold sand shifted underfoot, the dying grasses moaned in the offshore breeze. The wind blew strength into his frame. It cleared his mind and raised his vision. Walking back he developed the conviction that his travels were finished—*ikke mer av dette!* No more of this! He became convinced that here his affliction could be erased. As he hiked back toward the city the boys waved him over. A third boy had joined them, smaller with thin reddish hair. The others deferred to him because he carried a diamond-shaped kite they wanted to fly. The kite was made of a Texaco road map. Tied to a fist-size ball of twine it went up ducking in the breeze, pulling its scrappy tail. While the frog-eaters fought over the string, the red-haired kid picked up a burning twig and lit a cigarette with practiced poise. Rune smiled because his uncle Arne had taught him to roll cigarettes at this age. The tobacco smelled pure in the cold lake air. The kid took a puff and handed the cigarette to Rune who puffed lightly and handed it back. Then the frog-eaters wanted to smoke and shoved the kite string into Rune's hands. Grasping it he began to laugh, a quiet laugh he could neither explain nor squelch. The kite clattered and roamed about. Rune experienced sudden forgetfulness and expectation, a sense of things widening.

And then, when he was walking back to the YMCA, this nimble girl met his eyes in a bookshop window.

So Rune fell in love—*like rolling downhill* was his tender confession. So did Roberta, just as you please. A pale-cheeked foreign boy with an inner burden and a face that broke in two when he was tired. He believed Roberta was part of his cure.

A decent first act, wouldn't you say? I'd say so—in fact I did. "Why, that's a perfect first act," I declared, but Rune put his elbows on the table amid plates and crumpled foil, his hands over his face. Blithe as he'd been earlier, when the food was hot and the flask inviting, he was that defeated now. Somewhat belatedly I realized it was all still new for my guest—the realization that this long-ago girl had walked all over the city with him, held his hand, showed him off to her family, got so close to him she was carrying his son, which is close by any measure, and yet she never told him. Instead she chose to break his heart, and back he went to Tromsø. Not until her death did she send this old fact into the light. Think of being told *You have a child*, and a moment later *Your child is dead*. The knowledge was still new, and I saw that it harrowed him.

"I would have married her without hesitation," said he. "Without regret. I thought she knew it. Whatever she asked, that is what I would have done."

"But you did, Rune. As I understand it, you did."

"Did what?"

"Did as she asked. She asked you to go home. You went."

Rune looked at me over the table, the skin papery under his eyes. "You're saying she meant to spare me something."

I hadn't been saying that, not exactly.

"She spared me—what?—an unfairness," he ventured. He made scales with his two hands, tipping right and left. "A disparity."

"It's possible."

Rune resettled, swirled the flask. "Maybe she saw how it was. I loved her more than she could ever love me."

It wasn't an idea I wished to muse on. *Unrequited* is an adjective I'd have happily lost in the accident but of course that one clung like a tick.

"Even if this were so," he said, "I would have stayed and raised my son. Everything would have been other than it was. Alec might be living now. I would badger him to come around and help me paint my house."

I said, "What about Sofie?"

Surely he was heading that way before I even asked. His face lifted as I said her name.

"Yes—yes, you are right. Virgil Wander, my rare friend! I would have missed Sofie if I stayed. And I wouldn't miss Sofie for this world." On reflection he added, "Or any other," as though this were a bargain a person might be offered.

It was late—we were both, I think, at the end of ourselves, the end of the evening, the end of the akevitt. But there was one more thread I meant to pull.

"What was the affliction, Rune? What happened? Why did you come here, of all places, to recover?"

But I'd waited too long to ask. His face had slid back downhill. He got to his feet and was instantly winded, as creaky and stooped as November. "Why don't we just set these dishes in the sink," he said. "I will wash them in the morning. Is that all right, Virgil? Maybe the morning would be all right."

11

AT THREE A.M. I POPPED AWAKE, GASPING, FROM DREAMS OF RAIN. Sometimes I hunched in the shivery rain, sometimes I watched a girl lean into the wind while the rain slicked her cotton dress against her skin. In one extremely satisfactory dream I *was* the rain and fell with merry violence on streets and asphalt rooftops, on foam-specked waves, on the deck of a tiny ship where a slickered helmsman squinted uneasily at the sky.

I switched on the lamp. Close at hand were reliables from my rotating stock—*Lucky Jim* if I wanted a laugh, *Copperfield* for under-dogs and vigor, a few razor-faced Zane Grey saddle tramps, *Aunt Julia and the Scriptwriter* if miracles were required. Also a Brontë novel or two, as if Greenstone were not dark enough. Insomniacs have a leg up in the reading game, but in the end I just turned off the light and lay fretful under the gray square window. All I wanted was to get back to that dream—the one about being rain. It brought an ache but I didn't wish to fade. It felt recent and familiar. I shut my eyes and fished for the dream, the heeling ship in the winey sea, teak hatches glowing under the foredeck lamp, the anxious upturned eyes of the helmsman. What finally answered was not image but sound, the sound of rain soughing across the waves. That or something close to it I remembered—not from any actual rain or boat ride, but from Rune's soaring kite. Scouting the heights it had produced and sent down through the string a kind of rolling arterial whir, like crowd noise on the radio, like a description of the heavens I could nearly transcribe. I don't know how else to explain it. The wind pervades your cells blood and bone. Your fingertips tingle, the brain quickens. Off the ground come your heels. Pants and shirtsleeves snap like pennants as you rise.

On second waking I was greeted by a muscular hangover that adjusted its claws for a better grip whenever I turned my head. Beeman's cheerful hypothesis that hangovers exist for our benefit didn't sweeten the noise of my doleful groans while lurching toward the kitchen for coffee.

It was a slight jolt to remember I had a houseguest—his depleted satchel hung on a ladder-back chair. The greater jolt was how the kitchen looked. We'd given it up for lost, I now recalled, table and countertops smeared and despoiled by wrappers and grease and bottles and tins. Yet now the table was cleared, the sink emptied, the floor swept. The drawer-pulls and chrome faucet shone. Except for the fire damage—ceiling tiles missing, a few black craters on the countertop—the kitchen gleamed as though polished by elves. Somehow Rune had gathered the leavings, bagged the trash, washed and dried things and stowed them away, mostly in the wrong places, it transpired. Either he made no sound or I'd slept the sturdiest sleep of my grown-up life.

I found him on the roof-deck, smoking his fragrant blend and studying the clouds. He said, "What would Alec do, if he were here today?"

"He'd go buy lunch," I replied. "Give me an hour to let the coffee work, and I'll show you where."

The Wise Old didn't get much of a lunch rush, which worked to our benefit—mine because my head hurt and the quiet was medicinal, and Rune's because the Wise Old was Alec's favorite, and the last place people saw him alive.

Lou Chandler called out and emerged from behind the bar when we entered the dusky room. He was in his eighties and starting to run low, though he still had the beef-roast forearms acquired during his years laying block, and he must have heard of my accident, for he looked carefully at my face and gave my shoulder a squeeze.

"You are different now," he told me, quietly, adding, "it isn't bad."

When I introduced Rune, Lou smiled with real delight and asked to join us a while. He told how Alec came in one day to sell him a neon sign. The tavern had once been called the Wise Old Owl, but the word *Owl* blew down in a storm, after which it became the Wise Old, because it was cheaper not to fix the sign. Alec wanted to build him a replacement. Lou did not have the money.

"We stood over there," Lou said, indicating the broad set of windows along the west wall. Looking out, the two men could see Lou's grass airstrip, the metal-sheathed pole barn he used for a hangar, and the sprightly aircraft, half a century old, that was Lou's dedicated passion.

Alec had inquired, "Are you a good pilot then?"

Certified flight instructor, Lou replied.

"Always wanted to learn," Alec said.

"See, I knew," Lou told us. "He was a little wild—the usual things didn't frighten him. Failure and such. People liked that about him then, though now I guess some resent it. But he wanted what all of us want."

"What's that?" Rune asked.

Lou gave a rumpled smile. "The sky, you know? The broad reach. The great wide open."

Standing at the westerly windows Alec had said, "Teach me to fly and I'll build you your sign."

And that was how it went. Lou gave Alec a short stack of books, flight theory, the mechanics of stick and rudder, heavy-weather manuals, followed by instructional flights in the Taylorcraft until Alec soloed. In return, Alec built a sturdy neon owl five feet tall with blinking yellow eyes and mounted it on the roof. When Alec wanted to keep flying, Lou bartered flight time for more signage; over the course of three years Alec built a foaming pitcher; a woman in a red dress, peering through a spyglass; and a second owl, this one in full glide, with subtly upswept wing tips, which still hung over the bar. Observing Rune watching the owl Lou said, "People put up with my lousy beer selection just so they can look at it." Lou rose from the table, announcing a round on the house. To Rune he said, "I didn't really need all those neons. Alec was just nice company."

Rune blinked and turned away, just as Shad Pea came through the door squinting into the gloom.

"Over here, Shad," said Lou kindly.

His eyes still adjusting, Shad seemed to swim toward us. He said he couldn't stay but had noticed the camper van outside. "Rune, I wondered if you want to catch fish," he said.

"Yes, when?" Rune said.

"Tomorrow," Shad said, "or the next day. The bite improves after dark. Virgil knows where I live. Virgil, you are welcome too."

I was about to ask what time when Lou, trundling back to the kitchen, gave a deep bark. "Ho! You gave me a start—didn't see you come in. What can I get you?"

"Whatever the house round is, Lou," said a voice I knew.

Adam Leer rose from the booth directly behind us.

"I got to blow," Shad said, but he didn't blow right away—Leer's pull was strong, his eyes and teeth alight, his glance including us all.

"Shad, Shad Pea," he said, grasping his hand. "After all this time! I see you're just leaving and I'd never delay you."

Shad said nothing but seemed to retreat without moving his legs.

"Are we good, Shad, you and I?" Leer asked, reeling him in an inch. In a low confident tone he said, "Bygones?"

"Bygones," Shad mumbled.

"Good!"

Shad was released to hurry away. Leer stood at our table as though expecting an invitation, then joined us anyway when none was offered. He made a vague remark or two about Shad, to the effect he was a fisherman unequaled in zeal and imagination; toward Rune he was curious, toward me jaunty and familiar. Again I had the sense of someone trying the door, a quiet insistent presence outside, testing locks and hinges. Again I looked away; but as he spoke, Leer's own eyes began troubling him—he rubbed them with his thumb, then tried blinking them clear, as if they refused to focus, or were painfully dry, or as if the soft glow of the neon owl was to him a piercing glare. When Lou arrived with pints Leer rose to accept his, tipped his forehead, and returned to his dark booth. We fell quiet. The Wise Old became unstayable. When we left our money on the table, Adam Leer remained silently in place, swaying, I thought, with his eyes fast shut; the last thing we heard was Lou, behind the bar, beginning to cough as though his lungs would split.

That night Rune, organizing a tackle box full of paint, fabric, scissors, and thread, asked why Shad had fled at the sight of Adam Leer—what was the old feud between them?

I told him what I could recall. Leer's acreage contained a stand of pristine sugar maples. One spring while Leer was overseas Shad hauled in his taps and lidded buckets and harvested sap for twenty days. No one would have known but he failed to leave no trace and Leer returned in early summer to find a maple trunk healing around a galvanized spile. Suspecting Shad, to whom he'd refused permission more than once, Leer approached with a pretense of friendliness. He teased out Shad's confession and accepted his apology, then, still smiling, offered to buy all the syrup Shad had produced that season—several thousand dollars' worth, easily a quarter of Shad's yearly income. Leer laughed, gripped Shad's shoulder, and declared him a man of spine, further promising a bonus if Shad delivered the syrup in his pickup truck. Shad promptly did so and went immediately to the bank, where he learned Leer's check had been stopped. Redress was impossible. He applied to conciliation court but had no case. He'd trespassed on Leer's property every day for weeks, had drilled holes in Leer's trees, and had stolen Leer's sap. He was advised to be grateful he wasn't a defendant himself.

Rune muttered a word that sounded like *gruesome* and is Norwegian for cruel.

The incident had at the time sent Shad on a monstrous bender, which cost him a lot, including custody of his young children for a while. Even now, with his feet mostly under him, he was apt to slander Leer recklessly at a specific inebriate phase. "Shad's never forgot it," I said.

Rune sat a moment in indignation. "I think Leer never did either."

12

RUNE WAS UP AND OUT EARLY NEXT MORNING—HE WASN'T ON THE roof-deck this time, though from there it was plain where he'd gone. Standing in the air above the Greenstone cliff was a rising speck. A spot of cinnamon in the milky scrim. The speck moved west and hesitated, darted east, then climbed with a flourish.

I'd planned to go in to work, but that fled my mind straight off. It's strange, and again I plead brain damage, but those days I couldn't see a kite without wanting to fly it. As a kid I'd enjoyed kites, but only in the usual way of kids, losing interest once they were airborne and manageable. Now I thought of flying daily, hourly. I didn't hold the string so much as climb it, and once flying I felt small and unencumbered, as if the moving sky were home and I'd been misplaced down here. Maybe I wanted the broad reach, as Lou Chandler had said. That great wide open.

On the landing I found the cracked hockey stick which had made a helpful staff earlier. The crack was worse from the weight of me leaning on it. I wrapped it with silver duct tape I tore off with my teeth.

By the time I reached Rune a little throng was gathered. Well, twelve people. Still quite a few to accumulate around a shabby kite-flying eccentric. Most were local and some passing through—a trio of blaze-orange deer hunters, the bread-truck lady en route to Grand Marais, a frowsty ancient couple in a Buick Regal fleeing interventionist children. Marcus Jetty was on hand with his windswept daughter. Julie from the Agate had got off shift and waved to me. Also back for more was Shad Pea—he couldn't seem to stay away from Rune. Maybe kites had joined big fish in Shad's realm of fascinations. Galen circled his dad like a border collie, as though to keep him together.

In the midst of this loose crowd stood Rune, untidy and jubilant, coat unbuttoned, hat brim flexing in the peppy breeze, fingers bare against the blue-white day. He bent down to a blonde pixie in a pink stocking cap. She might have been six. The pixie told him something with extravagant drama. She clapped her mittened hands.

Rune was flying the dog. It dipped down as if noting our presence, then shot away.

A restless mender and fixer of trifles, Rune had got out his paints and retouched its eye and body. The edits were small but significant. Yesterday the kite was any old hound, easygoing and set on cruise. Overnight it had matured, its brown gaze deepened. So here's what you saw as you came spinning uphill on Highway 61: the long snowy slope with tall tan grasses, white-robed monks of jutting stone, the milky sky scrolling overhead—then up it bounded, the last thing you'd expect, this marvelous animal, this rippling big cinnamon hound. To see it was to laugh aloud, to sense that it liked you already.

How could you not pull over?

The pixie shed her mittens, jammed them into her coat pockets, and pulled on the big stiff gloves Rune offered. What a game creature! Her whole self hardly ballast enough yet on she clamped, leaning against the pull with tiny backpedaling steps. It still stands out to me, that morning—that scatter of people, together by accident, as if they'd all been called to the place with no idea why. There was a current of solidarity, expectancy, a knock-wood perception of something bound to happen. The pixie flew until she tired, gave Rune the string, and ran skipping to her dad who lounged against his tailgate eating buttered bread. Rune hummed and flew, handing the string to all who approached. People talked and nodded, stretched out their arms, scratched and smoked, and watched the dog in the sky. A pickup arrived in a pod of exhaust and a tetchy old lady emerged. Another car pulled in, the driver toothless and lesioned, then another, a man fifty and a woman thirty he sucked in his gut to impress. A man in a navy peacoat bowed to Marcus's daughter who smiled and twirled away. Rune was delighted at this orbital spin, but not surprised, I think. He had a little Pied Piper in him. There was even a tatty big raven who landed on a stone near his elbow. It rubbed its beak on its wing with proud tuts, shifting from one foot to the other.

As for me I held back. I confess to a jealous twinge on reaching the lookout to find him so surrounded. It's childish, but I probably took for granted a kind of exclusivity. Didn't I greet him on his first day in town? Wasn't I first to fly the big kite, and didn't I see that he slept in a bed, instead of that manky VW? He'd called me his rare friend—now here were all these other people, the lot of them hopeful and hungry and greedy to take the string.

I couldn't stay grumpy, however—the sociable mood was infectious. The smiling Julie now opened her trunk and produced a box of raised glazed. Someone turned up a radio playing a Chopin waltz. Hand to hand went the kite string. *Did you know my son?* Rune asked all who flew, and quite a few of them did. A small town like Greenstone is thoughtful and nosy. It had got around fast that Alec's father was here. Rune wrote with a pencil in a pocket-size notebook while the dog clattered high in the gusts. He hummed sometimes, he whistled through his teeth. He wrote as fast as he could.

Because of what happened I have this etched memory. Shad Pea and Galen were there, as I said, Shad staying out on the fringe. His limbs were shaking and his knitted stocking cap kept falling off, revealing his purply bald spot. He seemed the worse for yesterday's encounter with Leer.

Then Rune handed him the kite string, and Shad relaxed. He moved it back and forth, speaking easily without shouting. He laughed aloud and Rune laughed with him; his tremors subsided, and his cap stayed on.

13

RUNE FLEW UNTIL SUNDOWN—HE'D HAVE STAYED TO THE LAST HOLD-out, but I was abruptly exhausted and frozen, my voice dissolving in shivers. On getting back to the Empress he was distracted, rubbing his hands and then blowing into them as though keeping embers alive.

"I spoke with Shad," he said, in an exploratory tone; while I filled a kettle and lit a burner he went on, "I have been asking, and people think one of two things about Alec. He perished in the sea when his plane went down—that is the main one. Or he simply—hmm—"

"Absconded?"

"Yes—abscond. That he started over elsewhere." He paused. "Shad Pea thinks neither of these is correct."

I busied myself with mugs and brown sugar and cloves and butter and rum.

"He believes the airplane was spoiled, tinkered. Sabotaged? In fact," he said, pretending not to watch my reaction, "he thinks my son's death was a murder."

At the word his voice fell off into grief. He'd read about the so-called Alec sightings—unlikely as they were, they allowed him to imagine his boy alive, working in a machine shop, or spraying crops, or bending neon, still striving somewhere under a name we didn't know.

On the other hand, the notion that his son had abandoned Nadine and Bjorn for some unspecified life haunted Rune terribly.

He'd got to know them now. Already they were his own and had no imperfections.

"Maybe Shad is onto something," he said.

I was quiet. Rune had cruised all afternoon on currents of good-will. The last thing I wanted was to cut his string and see him tumble to earth.

"Ah—you don't credit him, I see."

"Rune, I just think you want to be careful."

He caught my eye and held it. "Your friend is not honest?" Rune wasn't angry or defensive but was losing altitude all the same; there he stood declining. "Shad is not genuine? Is that your hesitation?"

"I wouldn't say that. Shad's a good man. Better than most of us, maybe. But he's . . ." I shut my eyes, looked for adjectives, and could come up only with "not reliable," a choice I instantly regretted. Shad had plowed snow twenty years, in dangerous weather, for embarrassing pay. Reliable is exactly what he was. Yet it was also true he had a headful of spiders which woke now and then and altered his personal scenery. Somehow I'd managed to disappoint one friend and rat on another at once. "Don't listen to me, Rune—honestly don't. I spoke out of turn about Shad."

But he'd crumpled, his face half slack and his color all fled.

I passed him a mug of hot buttered rum. He didn't reach for it.

"Well, I'm going out to Shad's anyway," he finally said. "He invited me to fish with him—tomorrow maybe. Soon. But don't worry—if he explains how my son was murdered, I'll be careful not to believe him."

I was taken somewhat aback, and not just by Rune's sad taunt, which I had coming. I'd known Shad Pea most of my tour in Green-stone, watched his daughter graduate, helped him with paperwork when his wife moved to memory care. Until Rune showed up, he never asked me to go fishing.

At last taking a sip of the rum, Rune seemed to change gears. "Maybe I am doing this wrong."

"What do you mean?"

"You see how it is. Everyone has a story about Alec. A baseball game, a neon sign, a funny thing he said. I like that Lou Chandler, very much," he said. "But none of it gets me close to Alec," he added, with an intensity of sorrow that kept me quiet. "With Sofie, I know how much lemon in the tea, I know the songs she sang while stirring up the bread. She became vain for a while after a man at the café mistook her for Grete Nordrå. She was proud of her nice long hands. When arthritis came, she hated the disfigurement more than the pain. If I could know Alec this way, none of the rest would matter."

"You understand this is the sort of thing you can only begin to get from Nadine and from Bjorn."

He nodded.

"You worry you're being a bother. That it's painful for them, having you around."

"Not Nadine so much. It's hard on Bjorn."

"I could talk to him."

"No."

What else to say? Rune wanted the impossible. Regardless of bloodline, how can you know the absent ones you never got to meet?

It made me rethink my own memories of Alec. He had many friends, but friends drift. Even friends who still live down the street. Over time I had drifted into thinking of Alec as most people did, as a likable man who had some bad luck or succumbed to his singular darkness. In fact, until Rune appeared and reminded me, I'd begun to forget I *was* his friend.

I was, though not the kind of friend who could supply what Rune was seeking. I didn't know Alec's vanities, or his weaknesses, or what songs he hummed when cooking.

Rune sipped and sighed and tapped his fingers on the table. He was so downcast it began to infect me. My back ached, a thumb came to rest against my heart. My gaze moved past Rune to the lakeside windows, the small blackened fireplace rimmed with tin plating, the door to the north closet. The sight of this door with its faux-crystal knob reminded me I was not without resources. I *was* Alec's friend—moreover, I owned the Empress.

"I do know one thing," I stated, "and that's what Alec's favorite movie was. And it's here. You want to see it?"

He looked at me listlessly without understanding.

"Well come on—I can't describe his aftershave for you, or what made him come over all misty, but I've got his favorite picture. I'll show you the same print I showed him. Shoot, I can probably put you in the same seat."

I'd never been grouchy with Rune before. He perked up and grinned, which for some reason made me grouchier. "Take it or leave it," I said.

The picture, one of the few actual classics in my vault of illegals, was *Butch Cassidy and the Sundance Kid*—Newman and Redford, 1969. Though he was from the remotest of climes, I assumed Rune had seen it; this was the film that made Redford as common as hamburgers. But Rune *hadn't* seen it—when I told him the title, he only shrugged. It was as if I'd mentioned a pair of local roustabouts.

While Rune washed out the cups, I retrieved the reels from the closet and carried them down to projection. A feature film contains over two miles of celluloid so is quite heavy, properly so since it contains the labor of hundreds of people over many months to produce your two-hour vacation. How good it felt to be in there again! My booth is a low-ceilinged rectangle with blue carpeted walls and analog dials. I switched on the power and opened the flat tins with their golden-age Eastman Kodak smell and spun the reels one at a time onto the massive horizontal platter until the whole feature lay spliced up dense as a manhole cover. I get a little chill at this point in the proceedings, a chill of expectation.

I looked down and saw Rune settle into the seat I'd pointed out—center section, third from the aisle—then rise and search out another more comfortable. Fair enough. Finding a better seat he looked around, trying to locate me. I started the film, lowered the volume to allow for the empty auditorium and my own newly sensitive ears, and went down to join my friend.

As for *Butch Cassidy*—well, the picture still thrives. I credit Newman. There's barely a frame where he isn't laughing, at least with his eyes and often with his entire face. Redford mainly broods but that's his job here and he holds to the brief. Best for me was watching how it played for Rune. At first he leaned forward, visibly edgy during the long sepia opening. He later acknowledged straining to "watch like Alec watched." But the pressure was lifted from him early, at the comic scene where Butch puts a boot in Harvey Logan's crotch and establishes cred with the gang. Rune hooted like a chimp, and after that the movie picked him up and carried him along. He smiled at the benign train robberies and paled like the boys themselves when things got tight in Bolivia. I believe he also appreciated Katharine Ross—to this day a glimpse of certain bicycle handlebars can lure me into sun-drenched sadness.

As the picture went on I perceived that the more Rune forgot Alec, the more like Alec he became—he had Alec's high laugh, a similar melancholy at the eyes. Although saying this, I realize it may have been illusory. Memory's oldest trick is convincing us of its accuracy.

When the credits rolled I went up to the booth. I switched off the lamp to save the expensive bulb and let the film run through, then ran it back, desplicing the celluloid onto the original reels. With the digital coup all but accomplished, film-handling gets labeled a "dying art." Soon I'll have to show movies from a hard drive like everyone else, a disturbing idea. I would say projectionists aren't more sentimental than blacksmiths except that we probably are.

When I came back down Rune hadn't moved. Though it was quite late, he was reluctant to leave the auditorium. "All this is wonderful," he said, looking at the faded paint, the faraway ceiling. "*Magisk*," he added. The Empress does look fairly magical at that hour, golden and dim, the ratty seats lining up in the gloom, the screen retaining a remnant of light much as your mind retains the fading pleasure of the story. I was pleased. I got into the business for *magisk*. Once in a while it's not indefensible.

"How is it you have this film?" he inquired, as we went up the aisle. "Do you keep them all?"

I explained that I rented and returned the films, but also had a few old prints in a closet, like *Butch*, though these were not actually mine.

His confusion was evident so I added, "I came into them by accident. It's not the most legal situation."

He absorbed this ambiguity before asking, "If they aren't yours, whose?"

"They are the property of the studios who made them. And no, they don't know I have the prints."

"And this bothers you," he observed.

"I don't screen them for profit," I replied, sounding lame—it was tempting to add that I'd rarely screened *any* movie for profit, but why confuse matters?

"What would happen," Rune mused, "if these studios found out you had some of their movies?"

As you might expect I'd looked into this question. I told Rune about an amateur collector in Memphis with a print of a popular biblical epic. This man wrote a warm letter to the studio head in 1996, praising the film as an artifact akin to the gold of Ramses himself. He assured the executive he'd kept it pristine and offered to ship the print to the studio at his own expense. Days later this fellow was frog-marched into court, tried for wrongful possession, fined five thousand dollars, and given six months in jail. This news item from *Cinematique* alarmed me so much I telephoned the collector. Money aside, what he regretted was his naïveté. He'd bought the print—from an unnamed citizen—because he loved movies. For the same reason, he'd written that letter to the studio in the convivial tone you might use with a revered but distant uncle. His reward for this overture was a brisk mugging. The collector had his jail time commuted but the story subdued my confessional urge. If my conscience took a hard right I'd have to admit I had not only *Butch Cassidy* but dozens more films, all of which I'd wrongfully possessed for twenty-five years.

"No leniency, then," Rune said sadly. He thanked me for the movie and I said there were more he might like.

It was after eleven. Rune went upstairs while I doused the auditorium lights and performed a dispiriting lobby check. Enchanting the Empress might be, yet more sawdust volcanoes had risen. The carpeting smelled like a seedy hotel. Some kids had nosewiped both front doors.

*　*　*

Back upstairs the landline phone was flashing.

The message was from Lily Pea, sounding ragged. Shad had gone fishing and hadn't returned. She checked the usual places: the public pier, the Green Street Bridge, a backwater known as the Pasture for its grassy weeds. Around ten thirty she found him. He was rotating facedown in an eddy of the Pentecost River, near the mouth where it empties into Superior.

I crouched, leaning against the wall. Rune lowered himself to a chair. After a long silence Lily continued. It appeared a fish had taken Shad's lure. It looked like he'd slipped and his waders filled. Maybe a big fish pulled him off balance, or maybe he was that way already. Please could I call, she wanted to talk. She said her dad's face didn't look scared. More like exasperated. Lily's voice was like something left out in the weather. I looked over at Rune just as a bright tear slid down his face. The last thing Lily said on the message was that nothing went right for her dad for as long as she could remember.

14

A STRAIGHTENED-OUT HOOK—THAT'S WHAT WE SAW THE NEXT morning. A heavy-gauge hook pulled straight as a nail.

Shad's house was half a mile north of the Pentecost under some spindly jack pine. He was proud of the house, having built it himself from a shipping container acquired from Marcus the tinker. He did the plumbing and insulation, installed a woodstove and some rattly windows retrieved from a demolition in Hibbing. He painted it a pleasant celery color. It still looked like a shipping container and got very loud in a rain.

By the time Lily had answered her phone, at nearly midnight, her first shock had dimmed and she asked me to come in the morning and bring Rune if he was willing. Lily had an apartment in town but had stayed the night with Galen at Shad's. She emerged from the house as we drove up. The sun was out and the snow in retreat. She kicked through the slush in a pair of green wellies, leaned into the passenger window, and put her forehead against my neck.

"What can I do, Lily? What do you need right now?"

"Two hours' sleep," she said. "And the brain of Solomon when I wake up. Thanks for coming. Are you Rune?"

He smiled—his cheeks were pale and bruised.

"Dad talked about you a lot," she said. "Alec Sandstrom's father."

Despite the grim circumstances Rune shifted and brightened. I was to see many times the alteration this description worked on him.

"Come in, I made coffee," said Lily. "It's a cyclone in there, so excuse that, and Galen."

Cyclone was right although no more than usual. Shad had filled his home with tools, toasters, dorm fridges, folding chairs, fishing tackle, leaning towers of *Field & Stream*, and dishes clean and filthy. There was a framed Charlie Chaplin poster on the wall next to a wedding photo of Shad and Maria back at the outset. It was an outdoor wedding. They were laughing, the sun in their faces.

The sink brimmed with suds and there was a foot or so of clear countertop where Lily had made a dent. Galen was at the table with his dad's tackle box open in front of him. A swampy smell came from the box. Galen looked sallow and pinched. Rune set down a box of Danish pastry we had brought and pulled up a chair.

"You okay, Galen?" I said, as though he might be.

He nodded.

"Lot of people will miss your dad."

Galen had a ziplock bag in his hands. It was full of garish blue and violet worms. They resembled the gummy candies kids enjoy, but these were fishing bait. Galen looked the worms over as if they were evidence.

"Galen, you remember Rune?"

The boy gave him a glance, set the worm bag in the tackle box, and picked out a jar of brined pork frogs.

"Give it a break now, Galen. Have a Danish." Lily put some on a washed plate and poured coffee into mismatched cups. Galen ignored the Danish and handed me what looked like a barbed finishing nail.

"That was on the end of his line," Galen said.

It took me a moment but then Rune said, "That is a very big fish," and I understood.

Shad had been working a favorite spot. Usually Galen went along but last night he'd been coughing and Lily came and made him hot lemonade. They watched some TV. Shad set up his gear on a mudbank and waded down in. It was shallow but soft-bottomed. You had to be careful in those conditions. The paramedics had made note of an empty Don Q bottle in Shad's tackle box.

"It wasn't the rum," Galen said. "They're going to say it was, but it wasn't. It was the fish."

While the paramedics loaded Shad into the ambulance, the sheriff's deputy located his fishing rod. It was caught on a submerged aspen branch, the reel end sticking up like a mortified hand. Deputy Stumbo got hold of the heavy braided line which stretched down through the riffles into the lake and pulled it in, two hundred feet of it culminating in a few split-shot weights and a steel leader attached to the ruined hook.

"I seen the fish before," Galen said. "A bunch of times. Big old sturgeon—we know that fish."

I glanced up at Lily whose look said *See what I'm up against?* Galen caught the look and bridled, but Rune said, "My dad was a fisherman too." He peered into the tackle box. "What have you tried before, on this sturgeon? You must remember, if you can."

While they talked Lily caught my eye and we retreated to a far corner. Her hair was pushed into matted escarpments. It smelled like sweat and looked like panic. Lily's everyday competence made you forget how young she was but now she was both anguished and cornered. Grief aside it's expensive to die. So far as she could tell, Shad kept no papers. What if there was debt? How to get him buried? What to do with a painted shipping container on two acres of mud with seven pine trees?

I could do little except try to be useful, a man who'd lost some relatives and knew who to call. She wasn't a church person but I wrote down the name of a woman in Duluth whose lifework is leading unprepared survivors past funeral directors and other death-industry vampires. I said, "At least Shad went doing what he loved."

"Shut up, geez," Lily said.

Over at the table Rune and Galen were eating Danish. They had their heads together, both of them drinking coffee, nodding like accomplices. I heard mention of nine-aught hooks, the allure of beef liver or poultry in steep decay, the hours when a monster might let down his guard and swallow whatever horrifying baitgob.

I was proud of Rune—he made himself Galen's ally and encourager. Lose your dad at that age, you want a scapegoat. What better than a giant fish? Soon enough—in days or weeks, maybe longer but finally certain as winter—the mundane facts would come forward. Shad polishing off the Don Q, taking one step too many, the late stab for balance as the freeze flooded in. The world always comes for you. Let Galen chase fish for a while.

As we drove out of the yard the tires spun in what remained of the slush. Lily stood in the sopping yard, her fingers white on Galen's shoulder. She'd thanked me for coming and Rune for connecting with her little brother. You want to offer a person relief, but there was no relief on her face. In the house she had whispered with quickening despair, *Virgil, Jesus, Galen's up to me now*. As for Galen he had no expression. He could've been a boy from some hopeless wartime photograph—mud to his boot tops, arms crossed, black around the eyes.

the bottle imps

the noble imp

1

WHEN I CAME TO GREENSTONE AS A GROWN ORPHAN AND FAILED theology student, the town was already past—the mines finished, the Slake plant padlocked. Kids would shout on Main Street and listen for the echo. The silent ore docks on their stilts had an impenetrable air, as though constructed by aliens or, why not, Egyptians.

For me—as for Tom Beeman later, as for Alec and Nadine—ruin was part of the draw.

In 1987 you could buy a house a block off the lake for nine thousand dollars, or a movie theater with an art deco marquee and catastrophic upholstery for thirty. I was fresh out of God but had adequate cash. I did both.

"Another," said Orry, "in your long succession of brilliant choices."

I told her to stuff the sarcasm, but she was right. We were a mining and shipping town from which mining and shipping had vanished with no hope of return. Unlike those in the nearby Mesabi Range, which supplied the iron for two world wars plus millions of Bel Airs, Hudsons, Eldorados, and Mustangs, the Greenstone deposits were smaller than first believed. To this day the Mesabi produces ore, if not at historic levels; the Greenstone mines waned after a decade. By the mid-seventies most local miners, engineers, blasters, and mechanics went elsewhere. A few decided to sit tight, pick up a few hours at the gas station or grocery, coach a little football, and wait for things to turn around. No one's waiting anymore. The photogenic waterfront once featured in a *Life* write-up titled "Surprising Villages of Rural Charm" now hosts a barren swimming beach, a tilty pier where old men cast unsuccessfully for trout, and a quiet marina with a few aluminum skiffs and ragtag sailboats bobbing in it. Every so often a gang of earnest sailors will lobby the state to upgrade our disused port into a "harbor of refuge," where pleasure boats can shelter from the frequent gales, but that would require constructing a breakwater. Breakwaters are expensive—as the state contends, there simply aren't that many boaters looking for pleasure off the remote coast of Greenstone.

All this gloom and money sorrow has been accompanied by surreal ongoing juju. Maybe you've heard of our frog monsoon, a true story. It wasn't just a frog here and there tumbling out of the sky—this was *thousands* of frogs, raining down from a dense black cloud. I'd just wrapped up a matinee and was cruising over to World's Best Donuts when the frogs started hitting the pavement, mostly small brown specimens and a few greens. Some atomized on contact, others bounced and lay still. A few survivors hopped blindly in circles while overjoyed seagulls picked them off. The frogs received a neat riff on Letterman but were no joke on Main Street where they hydroplaned vehicles.

That same summer our archaic hillside water tower slid off its footings with a hundred thousand gallons inside. Dishes rattled across town as it rolled through a residential block. Luckily most residents had moved away. The cylindrical tank flattened four vacant bungalows and a city councilman in his Buick who saw it coming but froze at the wheel.

We made headlines in 1995 after Arnold Markey woke up with an eastern pipistrelle stuck to his arm—these are the smallest bats native to Minnesota. Arnold was a retired school bus driver famed for toughness, a man who confiscated water pistols and drove over them to combat recidivism. He killed the pipistrelle and threw it into the trash. A few weeks later Arnold complained of neck pain, then limb weakness, a fear of light, and a horror of water. At last he lurched out of his house, two doors from mine at the time. He shrieked and chattered and roamed the street. When the police came there was a dreadful standoff in which Arnold lunged at an officer who'd ridden his bus as a child. *Please Mr.*

Markey the officer said. Eventually Arnold Markey was raced to the hospital where he died of rabies days later. The sympathetic officer got a bad scratch and twenty-one shots in the midsection with a long needle.

Before my time there was even a high-profile kidnapping, when Las Vegas comedian Marvin Booley brought his wife and baby daughter to a local resort and the Booley child was instantly abducted. No ransom, no phone call, the infant gone like breath. After months of pleading and public frustration Booley left Las Vegas forever and wrote a book called *Sorrow* which revealed him as a philosopher of disquieting clarity, the last thing anyone expected. He was briefly the celebrated face of bereaved parenthood. He sat for *60 Minutes*. He met Mr. Reagan. He went to Nepal and tried summiting Everest but strayed off the path and froze himself to death. He is still up there if you know where to look.

All this and frankly much more connected to one tattered city of two dozen short streets, a new water tower already rusting at the seams, a few spires, an exhausted block of brick façades, and of course our mightiest edifice, the shuttered monolith of a taconite plant. I saw it all once from the seat of Alec's plane. It was late April and the town was circumscribed with litter and plywood and discarded couches revealed by melting snow. Alec handed me a pair of those vintage binoculars that fold into a little tin box. They didn't work very well. My eyes stung and filled. The airplane was noisy and delicate. We circled Greenstone twice not saying a word, then Alec pulled back on the stick and pointed us north. His voice crackled like an astronaut's over the headset. "Great wide open, amigo," he said, and we rose out following the coast.

The Empress when I got here was what you'd expect—the single screen, the porous roof, the faint ammonia scent old theaters acquire. Why was I interested? Because I was young, with a tragic inheritance I was determined to spend. Youth and folly aren't inseparable, yet it's true that at twenty-one I had no grip on economics, no means of sizing up the cost of repairing a water-stained ceiling or the neon of a lifeless marquee.

What I had was the doltish conviction that romance finally wins.

Not even the theater's owner could dissuade me, though he bravely tried. I street-parked my coughing Dodge beside a shaggy giant slumped in the posture of apology. He was an old Australian who came to work in the mines, became a bouncer at several iron range establishments, and ended up showing movies. His name was Edgar Poe—a gift from his dad, "equally given to books and bad jokes, he were a frosty one," Edgar revealed in a mournful tone. I doubt he in any way resembled the unhinged literary master. This Poe was bear-like, with the demeanor and syntax of tender confusion and hair too thick for combs and massive hands that didn't know where to land. He led me upstairs to a dusty apartment with a view from atop the marquee. Down in the middle of Main a small black dog with a white muzzle decided to curl up for a nap; behind me Mr. Poe dropped an armload of ledgers on the kitchen counter. It would've been easy for him, faced with a credulous youngster, to conceal that he'd not had a paycheck in eight years. Instead he was honest. He said the Empress was less a business than a fading public service. There were nights he sold five or six tickets, nights he sold none at all. He frankly wasn't sure whether to sell the place or just turn off the lights.

I have an unclear memory of speaking up at this juncture. No doubt I declaimed the ageless wonder of cinema, the power of stories to surmount market forces, demographics, VCRs, and ever more facile demons roosting up the sleeve of technology. In those days I was a proud campaigner for the impossible. Eventually the old proprietor closed his books, shook his head slowly—very much the flummoxed bruin at that moment—and offered me his hand.

The Empress was mine.

When I told Orry about it she said I had been Tom Sawyered for sure. It's easy to see why she'd think so, but then Edgar started appearing weekday afternoons and Saturday mornings before matinees, explaining in his melancholy fashion the quirks and beauties of the Empress, its tricks of plumbing, the moods of the clanky Simplex projector. He stayed for hours expecting nothing. Sometimes I caught him looking at me sideways as though awaiting a signal. One evening he cleared his throat and asked my opinion of the north closet upstairs, the one next to the bank of windows overlooking the harbor.

"Good you asked," I replied, "I tried all the keys but none of them work. It's locked up tight."

His eyes widened. "You've not peeked in the closet."

"Locked," I repeated.

"Never," said he. "The door sticks but it weren't locked. There were never a key. You go up there tonight, your two hands on the knob, you give her a pull."

"Why? Come on then—what's in there?" I demanded, but Edgar wouldn't say or even meet my eyes. Had he dangled this ten minutes earlier there'd have been time to run up, but it was seven o'clock, a Friday night, a dozen teenagers flirting in their gaudy big shoes underneath the marquee—the picture was *Robocop* as I recall. You can believe it was a long evening for me, conjuring whatever skeletons or hidden kingdoms or casks of amontillado Edgar Poe had left behind in that closet, while the auditorium rocked and Peter Weller heaped bodies on-screen and I laid my palm on the brow of the trembling projector every few minutes like a nurse checking for fever.

When I finally did take hold and yank, the door opened so easily I fell backward.

A tomb smell, a light switch, a bulb that whined when lit. Before me was a wide shallow closet. Its shelves were stacked with movie reels in silver metal canisters. A distant frying sound started in my brain. The cans were labeled in Magic Marker on white cloth tape peeling at the edges. I reached for one labeled *Hombre*. Hefted it in my hands. The tin had a dull shine and was stamped EASTMAN KODAK USA.

I lifted off the cover. It was Reel One of the Paul Newman western from 1967.

Holding my breath I opened more canisters. *Hound of the Bask-ervilles* (Rathbone edition). *The Hanging Tree* with Gary Cooper. My fingers shook. I wanted to call Edgar and ask about this trove, its provenance and value and dubious legality, but it was past midnight. Finally I tried anyway. The number was out of service. I went to the kitchen and made a toasted cheese sandwich and ate it standing at the rear windows looking over the lake.

The final tally? Thirty-two movies, each composed of five or six reels. One hundred seventy reels in all. The newest was *Bring Me the Head of Alfredo Garcia*, from 1974; the best-preserved, *Death of a Salesman*. That one shows virtually no wear because it's depressing as graves—that's my theory, anyway.

In the morning I went to see Poe. He lived in a gray paperboard rooming house on a block otherwise abandoned. He didn't answer my knock that day or the next. His landlady said he'd stopped his mail but she didn't know for how long.

What could I do but settle into a life showing movies in a fading town? No doubt it sounds dismal, but I loved it and felt made for it. The north closet was an entrancing distraction. I examined the reels and laced some of them up and watched them in solitude. Who had collected these artifacts? How did they end up here, at the whistling edge of the earth?

After a month Edgar showed up. He was thinner and quite tan, with the solemnity of a reformed addict. He'd been staying with a friend in San Diego, which had easy winters and a nice zoo—he especially liked the seals. When I asked about the north closet his eyes widened in apology.

"The films are on my conscience," he said. He described buying the Empress from a local grump named Bill Plate who feared the apocalypse and thought about it constantly. Plate had renounced women and stylish clothing and the concept of private ownership. He sold Edgar the theater and took the cash to Chicago to propagate the Krishna.

"He never explained about the reels?"

"No, and I didn't stumble on them until my second week. Then I wrote him two letters. Sent one to a William Plate of La Crosse—his papa I think. The other to Bill Plate care of the Lunt Avenue Krishnas. The first one got no answer, the second got returned."

Edgar walked through the lobby as he talked, admiring the cheap area rugs I'd thrown over the threadbare carpet. He ran his fingers wistfully over the COMING SOON poster display. He grew pensive, then said, "Listen to me, Virgil. I should've told you about those films, before we made the deal."

"It's okay," I said.

"It isn't. I put you in a spot. I needed a buyer and here you came. A young person. A true believer. I let myself be swayed. But now I wake up nights. It isn't just that I sold you a failing business." He leaned in with pale and fiery eyes. "Those old films are trouble. Imps in a bottle is what they are. I wonder at the mischief they might cause."

"They're a few old movies—they're hardly imps," I said, though a draft stroked my neck at his description.

"Nevertheless, they are in your closet." His face grew small and lonely. "Do you know I miss them, Virgil. I dream about them, sometimes. I used to lace them up and watch them by myself. All alone. It wasn't healthy, no."

I didn't mention I was already some distance down that road.

He said, "I was wrong not to disclose. If I'm ever to sleep, I must make the offer."

"What offer is that?" I was suddenly alert—defensive, even.

He looked briefly away. "If you now believe the purchase were a vital error, say the word. I've hardly spent a dollar—say the word, is all, and I will forgo my San Diego, and buy the Empress back."

He met my eyes and there I stood dumbfounded. It's true by this point I was eating my inheritance. How many mornings had I sweated at the calculator learning black from red? Already it was plain a second job was necessary, and I'd begun to consider selling my pleasant bungalow and moving to the Empress apartment. Here was a chance to recoup. I was young. I could go to school, adjust my course. Investigate a sequence of less permanent mistakes.

Edgar watched me think it out, his left hand on the ticket counter, pinkie finger quivering. To this day I can't tell you whether he hoped I'd turn him down—freeing him to go watch seals in San Diego—or accept his offer, and return to him the life he seemed to miss.

I really did think it over. True, I was jumpy about the north closet. Yet in a devilish paradox, the cache itself made me loath to give it up. *Thrall* is too strong a word, then one day it isn't. Only that morning I'd brushed against the closet door and felt a scatter of life inside. Maybe the films were imps at that. In some undeclared sense Edgar seemed to want them back—but now, God help me, I wanted them too.

I said, "Actually, Mr. Poe, I think we're on good terms. It's a gracious offer but there are ways to make the business work. You're a good man. I wish you well in California."

He pulled back, forlorn yet still somehow expectant, as though my decision came too fast. I took a breath, caught his eye, and made it not just formal but a little grandiose: "As for the imps, they are with me now. I forthwith take possession of their stewardship."

His face seemed to collapse, then refill; his old melancholy kindness returned. "Well then," he said, "no doubt it's for the best. However," he added, unable to help himself, "I fear you'll lose your shirt at this. It's not an easy road. In two years you will be shirtless, and then it's me you'll blame."

"Ha," I said to this grim prophecy, then shook his hand and watched him go down the street. The triumph in my gut had an apprehensive shade but it was triumph all the same. It was Saturday, a few kids were lining up. I had a matinee to screen.

2

WE BURIED SHAD PEA ON A COLD SATURDAY WITH SNOW CLOUDS AND brittle sun. The cemetery overlooks the lake and a late October easterly was stacking up waves and pounding them over the fetch. Folding chairs flanked a small mound of dirt beside a round hole eight inches across. A posthole digger lay on the grass. An old man wearing a military flight cap and a shrunken Army jacket told me some of Shad's friends from the service were "stepping in to provide the honors." Moments later the shudder of motorcycles came up through the ground. The old man had tears in his eyes. He touched my shoulder as the men rode in on their Harleys and Indians and Hondas. They were led by a graybeard on an olive-drab Triumph. In they rolled, gloves on, black helmets squeezing faces red from the wind, a pack of paunchy old centaurs come to bury their own.

I didn't even know Shad was a veteran. He would talk as long as you stood there about his deceased brother or whipsmart kids or his wife Maria whom he adored even after she forgot his face and his name and their tale of burning love—a generous talker, Shad, but his Army time never came up.

The riders lined up their bikes and shut them off and stood beside them. They outnumbered the locals and came to shambling attention as Shad's family appeared and walked down the line of folding chairs. Lily then Galen then Shad's wife Maria, whom a group-home staffer had driven six hours north to tell Shad good-bye. Maria wore blue rubber boots and a black coat of nubbly wool. When she sat in the folding chair it dug into the earth at a tilt.

Rune raised his hand at Nadine wending her way through the gravestones. She saw him and altered course toward us.

I waved and prepared myself. I'd long found it difficult to speak with Nadine. It shouldn't have been. We were all friends. But early on—less than a year after Alec vanished—I made a key mistake.

We were both at the post office, waiting in line, not really talking but just idling while the creaky postmaster wafted around the back room hunting for somebody's mail. A sleepy malaise fell over the post office. An interval passed. Abruptly I realized I was holding Nadine's hand. What a thing to find yourself doing! When had I reached for her? What must she have thought? I don't remember what I said but am confident it was stupid. Maybe she laughed, maybe I should've laughed but didn't. Maybe I turned away and waited for the postmaster and finally sent whatever I was sending that day.

How did this happen? What did it mean? I would answer differently now but then, in my fraught solitude, it meant I'd lost track of myself. It meant I was no different from the hapless entrepreneurs and BMW owners and polyester track guys who thought the lovely widow should be that night's entertainment and maybe appear on next year's Christmas card. It meant in fact I was worse than them, and by quite a bit. They were only unworthy. As Alec's good friend, I was also disloyal.

Her hand, though—that capable hand, holding mine right there in the post office. I never forgot the cool strength of her fingers.

Nadine veered over and spoke to Lily a moment, Galen too. She knelt beside Maria and coaxed out the only smile we would see from her that day, then came and greeted Rune with a hug—you could tell from her shine and low laugh she was glad Alec's father had dropped into her life.

"Virgil," she said—whispering, because a chaplain had appeared and seemed about to start. "How are you?"

I nodded and smiled. To my surprise I felt no anxiety, no sense of impending futility. Except for immediate family it was a standing service and Nadine stood between Rune and me. "I came to see you in the hospital," she said in my ear. "Twice. Not that you'd remember—the nurse said you were *out like a mackerel*." She smiled at the breach of medical jargon and whispered, "Did you know there was a rumor about you? That you died in the lake?"

"So I'm told. It's good to see you, Nadine." Saying it made me remember her laughing once that she had a name made to be embroidered on bowling shirts.

"Lily used to sit for Bjorn sometimes. What a sweet girl."

"She is."

As we watched, the old man in the flight cap walked up through the cemetery holding a trumpet. He spoke to the chaplain who nodded at his notes and pointed toward a slight rise. The old trumpet moved slowly away through the tombstones and took a position near a leaning white pine. The music is supposed to float in from a distance. The chaplain stepped forward coughing into his fist.

He kept the talk short. After a few minutes the clouds parted briefly. Sunlight glittered off Lily's bright earrings and Shad's cylindrical urn which turned out to be a Hills Bros. coffee can painted with silver Rust-Oleum. In that sunny moment I glimpsed our shadows stretching forward on the ground—Nadine's skirt blowing toward me a little, her hair and scarf likewise. Rune's shadow was oddly lanky and big-handed, as though Alec were making a brief return.

Then clouds took over, the chaplain wrapped up, and the trumpeter, leaning back slightly, lifted taps into the air over the coastal pulse of the waves. Lily cried quietly and Maria, accepting the folded flag, let out a scratchy wail. One of the riders took her elbow and guided her out through the leaning stones. The rest of us followed. It was only when we were some distance away that the motorcycles started coming awake, coughing and clearing their throats, at last snaking out in a long southwest line on Highway 61.

Rune offered a lift, but I decided to walk. It felt good to be on my feet in the breeze coming off the water. I had on my charcoal Men's Wearhouse suit from Orry's wedding all those years ago—it was quite baggy now, plus I forgot my wing tips and wore ruinous Nike trainers. At least I could walk the stony shoreline in comfort back to town.

"Virgil. Ride?" Nadine rolled up in her tired Wagoneer.

"Thanks, I'll walk."

She nodded. The Jeep rolled on a few feet, then stopped and reversed so Nadine came back into view. The window slid down. "I'm glad you lived, Virgil."

"Me too."

I tapped a light good-bye on the roof of the Jeep and started down to the water.

It's a demanding route home—that part of the shore is all oval rocks that shift underfoot like turtles. I picked carefully through and still fell four times, nailing my shin once but doing no real harm. A gang of seagulls joined me along the way, making covetous cries, sometimes hovering a yard or two off my lakeward shoulder. When they suddenly dispersed I looked up.

The man on the water stood forty yards out.

He was facing away, dark coat on like the one I wore except better tailored, standing in the troughs so the waves struck his knees and flew into spray. It was my second glimpse of him. I shouted *Hey* but got no response. He took his hands from his pockets and clasped them behind his back. The hands were very white. The wind shivered his trouser legs. You can know it's not real and still be spooked. To shake it off I picked up a couple of small rocks and heaved them out there. One got within three feet of him but he paid no mind. After a minute I turned and kept picking my way home over the turtley stones, now and then glancing over my shoulder. To my relief the man stayed where he was—relaxed, evidently unconcerned, as if watching for rain, or waiting for a light to change.

3

MONDAY MORNING I WALKED TO CITY HALL WHERE THE MAYOR, evidently euphoric, had left this note on my desk.

> *Virgil—Bob Dylan!*
> *the Greenstone Retrospective*
> *See me Lydia.*

"You want me to book Dylan," I said, poking my head into her office.

Lydia beamed. "Wouldn't it be so nice? Come in and shut the door."

Her fondness for Dylan was no secret—the *Blood on the Tracks* album cover was framed on her office wall—but until that day I had no idea Lydia had seen him perform twenty-seven times, or that she'd written him a Christmas letter every year since 1965, when he went electric, or that sometimes he wrote funny disjointed cards back. She showed me one that said, *Sorry for the penmanship John Wayne shook my hand and man did he bust it*.

"Dylan on the Empress stage," she sighed.

I thought about it. Sometimes I still think about it, right down to the lighting, as though it had actually happened. Lydia asked me to reach out to Dylan's booking agent and "start a dialogue." She said he'd grown up nearby so he couldn't fail to remember Greenstone—maybe he'd enjoy coming back.

"We might have a better chance if you start the dialogue," I ventured. "On account of being his longtime correspondent."

"I would, but I am too tired," she said—she did look worn thin. "Please do it for me, Virgil."

I said of course I would.

When I got home Bjorn was just climbing the steps to my landing. He carried a six-foot length of driftwood. It was light gray with a gentle curve and looked like a great old crackly rib plucked from the desert floor.

"This washed up on the beach," he said. "It's light but real strong. I thought you might want it for a . . ." I could see him struggling not to say *cane*, since canes are for ancients. Would he go with *stick*? *Walking stick*? *Staff*?

"Stout quarterstaff," he said at last, and I remembered one afterparty he actually may have stayed awake for, the MGM *Robin Hood* with Errol Flynn. Who wants a cane if you can get a stout quarterstaff? It was smooth and sturdy with a few tiny knots like sparrow eyes, a tight coil in the grain. It felt cool and eternal in my grasp. Bjorn had drilled a hole two inches from the thick end and tied a loop of leather through it.

"Why Bjorn, thank you." Another effect of the accident—I choked up easily. "Come in if you like. Rune made bread."

Bjorn looked past me. "Is he here?"

"No, out flying."

"Okay." Bjorn stepped in peering around the apartment, which he'd never seen. "Hey, this view is all right. You got a little porch out there."

"Have a look if you want."

He stepped across and went out on the deck. While he stood in the cold, blowing rings with his breath, I got out Rune's bread and tore off a couple of lumps and set them on a plate. It was the simplest possible loaf, just flour and water and yeast and salt. It was the best I ever tasted. Many days it was all I ate.

When Bjorn came back in he said, "Is that where he sleeps?" nodding at the open door of the guest room where Rune's rod cylinders and satchel were stacked in a corner.

"Yeah."

"Mom's pleased he's got a place for now. She invited him to stay with us, but he wouldn't."

"I'm sure he didn't want to intrude. Besides, I can use the company. I just about burned it all down, you know."

"Because of the brain damage," Bjorn said, looking away.

"Yeah."

He didn't know where to go after *brain damage* so buttered a piece of bread and took a bite. Through the mouthful he said, "Geez Louise."

"I know. I'm wrecked for store bread. Now you are too."

He sat down at the table and ate both chunks with butter and then tore off a third and ate that too. I poured us coffee. It was lukewarm and on the strong side but Bjorn drank it up and helped himself to more.

I said, "Tell me about your face." A crescent-shaped abrasion curved from his left cheekbone to the corner of his eye.

I could see he was proud of the injury. I called him brave and he laughed, said brave had nothing to do with it, he just stumbled on some YouTube surfers and wanted to try. How many people live a block from the sea? He nicked a sweet board for only two hundo, then a scabby old wetsuit. He was a poor swimmer but liked the cool solitude, sitting alone in the swells. At first there were two or three concerned citizens who would see him floating in the distance and call 911, but he kept at it. You had to keep at it. They can't make you stay on land if you want to go in the water.

What I suddenly missed, as Bjorn talked away, was the easy arrival of interests. Of obsessions. I remembered stumbling onto things I loved, almost by accident—it used to happen a lot. I admired Bjorn's courage, his sense of why-not, his easy appropriation of language— nicked a sweet board, only two hundo.

"It looks easy if you're doing it right," he said. "I'm still pretty bad but I won't always be. It's like with guitar: shredders think of a riff and it comes out their fingers. That's how I'll surf pretty soon."

The hungry way he talked made me realize he had no one else, no local tribe. He'd bought *The History of Surfing* for a dollar plus shipping, along with titles like *Stoked Wisdom* and *West of Jesus*. The literature made it sound like a sport full of monks, but Bjorn said it was practice like anything else. It took him a full floundering afternoon to ride his first wave, lying prone on the board with his elbows tucked in. The next day he got up kneeling. Then came days of calm, weeks with no ridable swell. All he could do was read and watch YouTube. When at last a storm kicked up the sea, he locked the Citgo station where he was working then and left. That was the day he rode upright at last, a waist-high comber into the shallows. Citgo fired him. The ride was worth it.

"It's not magic, you know? Just physics," he said. "But it's nice physics. Nothing else picks you up and carries you that way."

When he talked about being picked up and carried I thought of him at five or six riding into the Empress on his dad's shoulders, the way he ducked laughing to get in the door. Who doesn't want to be carried sometimes? Come to think of it, it sounded a little like how I felt flying Rune's kites.

"So you got a new grandpa out of the blue."

Bjorn got up and poured a glass of water at the sink. He drank the whole glassful and leaned against the counter wiping his mouth. "First night he came, Mom went upstairs during supper and cried for an hour. We couldn't hear her crying but that's what she did. Me and the old man sat there eating potatoes. The whole time he kept looking at me. No idea what he expected. Then Mom came down finally. None of us knew what to do. The two of them ended up looking at pictures. I got out of there—hey, geez."

He had spotted Rune's latest kite, propped against the opposite wall. It was modeled on the old-school English three-speed bicycle and that's what you'd think it was if you just walked casually past. In fact it was a kite with a split bamboo frame and spoked wheels that spun independently.

Bjorn crouched in front of it, reached out, but didn't touch. Rune had spent three evenings on this project, humming small rhymes to himself, re-creating from memory a bike he'd borrowed once decades ago—he even took a fine-line Sharpie and lettered *Sturmey Archer* on its fat rear hub.

"Can this thing possibly fly?" Bjorn asked.

"I wouldn't bet against it."

Now he did lay his hand on the kite—cautiously, just his fingertips, as though expecting voltage. He took his hand away.

"What's he doing here, Mr. Wander?"

"It's pretty straightforward, I think—he wants to know what he missed."

Bjorn gave an agitated laugh. "Well *that's* an easy one. Everything until now, that's what he missed. Dad's whole life. What's weird is thinking you can go back and retrieve it. The store's closed. If I can understand that, why can't he?"

"Is it so terrible, Bjorn, having him around? He's strange but he's generous, and he's interested in you. You're his grandson."

Bjorn looked weary. "I barely remember Dad. He's been gone since I was seven. I was just starting to think about what's next. Get out of Greenstone, find some work. Drive someplace. Then this old guy pops up. Goes to the lookout every day, flying his weirdass kites. No one can walk past him without saying hi—you know the way he is. So now Dad's on everyone's mind again, and what Dad did—or didn't do, depending how wishful you feel."

He spoke with grown forbearance.

"How does your mom see it?" I asked.

"Not like me," he replied. He almost said more—you could see the currents moving behind his eyes—but thought better of it and opened the fridge. "Could I have some milk, Mr. Wander?"

"Help yourself."

He filled a glass, drank half of it, and topped it off before putting the gallon back in the fridge. Watching him drain the milk, all elbows and limbs and skinny neck, I had the melancholy thought that what Bjorn needed in managing the loss of his dad was, in fact, a dad—not a kite-flying stranger, and certainly not an underachieving film projectionist. Yet it was me he'd approached with this business on his mind. I felt a responsibility to convey some wisdom. No doubt the previous tenant would've reached down and found a little Gregory Peck, yet I seemed unable to do so.

"You asked what it cost," Bjorn reminded me.

I said, "You understand Rune means nothing but well."

"Right, but so what?"

I looked at Bjorn's abraded face, the scarlet patch fading as new skin formed beneath it. His eyes were gray-green and reserved as the sea. He shrugged into his jacket by the door. "Mom thinks I ought to go stand on the hillside with him, fly the kite, whatever. But what for? I've been decent to him. Told him everything I could remember. Say I do it—hold the string, let him pat my shoulder. Will he go away then?"

He started down the stairs. Halfway to the bottom he turned and said, "I'm heading out to the break, see if there's a swell. Thanks for the bread."

I held up the driftwood quarterstaff. Already I felt more stable on my feet. I touched my forehead with it in salute. "Thanks yourself, Bjorn. Stay upright out there."

"Stay upright yourself," he replied.

Rune dropped me off at Dr. Koskinen's. He had some business in Duluth and said he'd come back in an hour.

A nurse weighed me on a scale, then pointed to an exam room where I avoided the usual stack of happy-oldster magazines and sat playing with a model knee joint. It was pretty convincing, the yellowish bone with gummy pink menisci, ropy ligaments, and a fragile patella which kept sliding off and spinning across the floor. For comparison I took hold of my own left knee and checked its motion. It seemed less gritty—maybe all my walking was smoothing down the edges. Presently the door opened and in came the neurologist. He was older than I remembered. His eye bags and heavy white mustache made him look beaten down. He shook my hand and asked about my dizziness.

"Getting better."

"From your weight I'd say you're doing some walking," he said. "Nice lumber," noting the driftwood. It had drawn stares in the waiting room—a cane or walker is fine but a quarterstaff in confined spaces makes people nervous. When I mentioned this later to Orry she said, "Nobody trusts a junior wizard."

I told the doctor a surfer friend had found it on the shore.

"Where's he surfing?"

"Greenstone."

"That's brash. I admire these cold-water guys." Koskinen's eyes drifted and he rubbed his beefy cheek. "When I was young and not as you see me now, I went to California and surfed for five months. A friend let me sleep under his van. I've made three good decisions in life and that was the first. Marrying Celeste was another."

"What was the third?"

"Paying off the house early."

"What about becoming a doctor?"

"It's all right, but would I do it again? Not sure. Whereas the surfing I would repeat tomorrow. The fever was upon me. There was a guy named Soc, a great surfer and epigram king. We all loved him. Soc went around saying things like *Life is more than the next sandwich*, but what did I go and do?" The doctor glanced fondly at his stomach. "Are you getting stray memories back?"

I said yes, but admitted it was disconcerting. It was enormous fun to hear a Blondie song for the very first time, only to realize I knew every word. On the other hand, utter strangers kept greeting me on the street as though we'd known each other forever. Sometimes it turned out we had.

"But your friends, colleagues, your everyday lineup—these you remember?"

"Mostly."

"Mistaken anyone for a hat?"

"Not yet."

His eyes sharpened slightly. "Are you tempted by speeding trains and open windows?"

"Not yet."

He asked whether language was returning, and I said yes but slowly. Seeing my frustration, he said if a person were to lose any grammar then let it be adjectives. You could get by minus adjectives. In fact you appeared more decisive without them. He asked politely after my nouns, which were mostly intact, then declared with sudden intensity it was verbs you must truly not lose. Without verbs nothing got done. He peered at my eyes with a penlight. He tested my reflexes with a tap under my own patella. My bones were more prominent, he remarked. I had new hollows and ridges. I had "picked up a smidgen of vagabond."

This was true. Except when shaving, an autopilot maneuver, I forgot to look into mirrors. My clothes hung weirdly around my joints and my hair was long and snarly. Rune cooked most nights and I didn't eat much else. After Beeman observed that Guinness tastes like burnt toast with cream, I resolved to try it for breakfast. Rune joined me and agreed it was bready and likable, if not ultimately sustaining.

"Anything else? Emotional potholes?"

At this stage the previous tenant would've nailed a polite off-ramp and been out the door with a blessing. Instead I said I had lost an old friend who drowned while fishing. It didn't occur to me to weep at his grave, yet a driftwood gift turned me into a swamp. I didn't miss driving. My houseguest was an Arctic kite flyer who called up the wind like a take-out pizza. On and on I went. I talked like a man waiting for sunrise. It was unpardonable. There was a woman I loved and never told, a contraband hoard in my north closet, a man of bedlam standing on the water.

Up went Koskinen's eyebrows. "Tell me about himself on the water."

I said he was my height or slightly taller, dressed in a suit of conservative cut. His face was dark or mottled and his hands were white like boiled eggs. He seemed at ease out on the surface, even in reasonably high winds. He wasn't the usual hooded reaper but if he knocked you'd leave the chain on.

"This isn't your surfing friend, by any chance."

"It's not Bjorn, and he's not on a board—he's standing on his feet on the water." I thought a moment, calmed myself, and added, "Probably other people can't see him."

He considered this while I wondered if I'd said too much. Physicians are busy people. Empathy is a lot to assume. Imagine my relief when Dr. Koskinen, wheezing lightly, face patchy with rosacea, said, "For now I think you shouldn't worry. You are less dizzy, your words are coming back. Don't fear occasional ghosts. Every day my mind suggests two or three impossible things. Tell me if the man comes back, though. Will you do that?"

"I will."

He leaned in. "Tell me if he gets close."

This seemed so unexpectedly sensible I bounded up and seized his hand in both of mine, and he laughed with surprise.

I left the office happy and went down to the coffee shop adjacent to the lobby. It's an unassuming place, tan walls, nondescript really, though the woman behind the counter was bright-eyed and inked from neck to elbows. The ink told a seafaring tale of ships and mermaids, and she'd knotted a vivid Mexican scarf around her middle. She made two or three jokes I didn't understand while conjuring the best cappuccino in my experience. Duluth is a world port. The drink was a storm cloud with coffee thundering around inside it. It made me laugh at first sip. I was already glad from my visit with Koskinen and became immeasurably gladder from the espresso and the cheerful barista. It's taken me a while to understand tattoos but now I think I do.

From my booth I could watch people going into and out of businesses across the street: a brewery, a record store, an AT&T, the woolly Army-Navy with its rows of backpacks and rubber Mickey boots. Next door a pawnshop had a window full of Gibson and Strat knockoffs plus assorted taxidermy, and a counter where you could sell your gold and silver if it came to that. I wanted to go see the guitars. I don't play, but the sight of those lustrous instruments always lifts my spirits. Beeman used to play his Telecaster in a North Shore country band called Angus Beef, he said to meet women but also for an excuse to say *humbucker* all the time.

The door of the pawnshop swung open and a man stepped out shielding his eyes. It was Adam Leer. He'd bought something, a picture frame which he held under his arm while looking up-street and down. Right away he spotted me through the window and crossed over and came in, settling opposite me as if we'd planned this all along.

"Hello Virgil—what's brought you to Duluth?"

"Doctor's appointment. My ride will be here in a moment."

"The old kite flyer," he said, amused. Turning toward the counter he held up a hand to the barista who nodded and busied herself.

"Yes."

"Excellent. I won't keep you but it's good we bumped into each other. I see the Empress is for sale."

"Yes," I said carefully, wondering how he found out. Most of Greenstone didn't know. I'd advertised in the trade press both in print and online, but never locally, nor in Duluth nor the Twin Cities. This discretion sometimes prompted Beeman to suggest I didn't really want to sell. In fact I didn't want to sell to anyone who didn't read the trades. In a business plodding toward extinction you'd better know the landscape.

"I'd like to make an offer," Leer said. He appeared entirely serious.

"You want the theater."

"I do."

I took my time with this confounding news. He said, "I can't promise how long I'd continue to show actual *movies*. But it's a very decent location, you know. Center of everything."

"Such as it is. You wouldn't show movies?"

"Virgil. You're getting eight people a night."

"What would you do with it, then?" I attempted to sound curious instead of defensive. Small-town theaters have been transformed into every sort of establishment—cafés and bookstores, bars, museums.

Leer said, "Do I need a plan this moment? It's potential that intrigues me. What a thing might become."

He leaned toward me across the table. I remember him talking about the nature of risk, the cost of inspiration. I looked away—not that his voice was unpleasant or sinister; if anything it was nearly smug and savored the tidy phrase. Yet it set me on edge, that voice of his. It seemed deftly persistent, as if it carried not only words but a sub-frequency, an inaudible current describing unspeakable things. Despite my resistance I felt something give. I heard him as if through a layer of water. The coffee shop dimmed at the edges.

"My point is," he said from far away, "you need the vacancy and then something can fill it. My offer is genuine, and cash." And he named a figure—I don't remember how much.

"Speculators make me nervous," I managed to say in a slow soggy tone.

"What needless suspicion," he said. "To speculate is to imagine. To wonder."

At least I think that's what he said, before a shape sank past in my murky sight—a watery shape, a descending turtle—and then I knew where I seemed to be, in my honest old Pontiac, ninety feet deep. There sure enough was the ovoid speedometer, there my drifting blue hand. A bit of my brain believed I was dead, believed in the peace, knew the wavery coffee shop was only the weak invention it turns out a corpse can summon. Relief rinsed through me, followed by a chiding phrase from the past—*fight the good fight*. Someone important had said that. Had I fought well? I didn't know, but what did it matter? The fight appeared to be over.

Then a merry laugh punctured the shadows. Yellow and orange got in and peeled the dark away: the barista arriving with Leer's coffee and a large cinnamon roll. She was laughing hard, and Leer laughed too. He leaned back in his chair; his attention slid off me. I was weak and spooked and grateful, watching Leer take the barista's hand and coax her down and whisper in her ear. She laughed again, a sunlit sound, and went on her way.

He tore into the roll and swallowed a chunk, licking icing off his fingers. "You've done magnificently in your turn at the Empress," he said, resuming our talk as though nothing had passed. "That wild man Poe had some fun there, but let it go downhill. And the previous guy ran off to the Moonies! You're easily the best of the bunch, Virgil. But the wheel spins. You know it does. What if your next work awaits?"

"My ride," I said with infinite relief, for Rune was parking the camper van on the street, feeding the meter, and looking at the sky. I gathered myself and stood.

"Off with you, then," said Leer, in an upbeat careless voice. "Think over my proposal. Or *brood* on it, if you'd rather," he added pleasantly. "I suspect that's more your style."

4

THREE DAYS LATER RUNE AND I PUT THAT BICYCLE IN THE AIR, AND I reopened the Empress.

Rune's notion was, the best kites looked like things unlikely to fly—not that he had anything against the common designs based on birds, bats, airplanes, and so forth. He just felt there was extra delight in the rise of things typically earthbound. "Every day you see an airplane up there," he explained. "Every day many birds."

Dogs on the other hand you didn't. Or steamships, bass violins, grandfather clocks, men in bowler hats. For a short time there, you never knew what you would look up and see in the volatile Greenstone sky.

The bicycle still looked as unlikely to fly as it had when Bjorn visited—spindly and distinctly terrestrial with its painted blue frame and upright handlebars fashioned from tagboard. A closer look showed it was backed with clear Mylar. Its spokes were angled paper blades which spun the wheels freely on their axles.

Rune was proud of it and tutted importantly while rigging a complicated flight bridle consisting of at least eight different lines which attached to the kite and led back to a snap swivel tied to the main string. He wouldn't let me near it.

"Isn't quite ready," he said, not daring to take his eyes off it. The breeze was gusty. He made a slight flicking motion and the bike popped into the air, shivering and rattling on the climb. "Stand back a little, now. Be patient, Virgil!"

"Okay," I said, feeling anxious. I shouldn't have been there at all—I had a problem to solve back at the Empress—but somehow this launch seemed like something I couldn't miss. So far I hadn't articulated even to myself the attraction these kites exerted; they were beautiful, but beauty is everywhere. They had some devious sentience. They seemed at play, and wanting company. When a new one went up I needed to be there.

"Look now, it won't answer," Rune said. He had the bicycle on a short line, less than a hundred feet. It refused stability. It climbed and dived in spirals, screeching to and fro inverted as if ridden by poltergeists. Rune slacked and pulled without effect. The wind sizzled in the intricate bridle. Without warning the bike folded in two and shuddered to earth.

"Fy," said Rune in disgust.

We were not at the overlook this time, but in a vacant lot downtown. Rune had a small tool kit with him and set about repairing the bicycle with needle-nose pliers and split bamboo. I wished he would hurry but not a chance. He had to examine the joints for strength. He had to spin both wheels, in both directions, and refer to implicit design challenges, and make miffed little vowel sounds about the kite's spasmodic performance. Finally he said, pleasantly, "Am I annoying you? You seem rushed."

Well, I was rushed. I wanted to fly but needed to get back. Since I arrived in Greenstone, the Empress had never been closed. Among small operators there is the superstition, often true, that to shut your doors for even a single night is to invite the end. Therefore, on this first public showing since my accident, I wished to reopen with moderate panache. I'd ordered what the trades were calling a smart poignant comedy about an aging burglar with a robot accomplice: PG-13, the robot, for the kids; and Frank Langella for their grandparents. I had also spent two mornings repainting the lobby a vintage green—very stylish, but an overreach given my brain injury. The fumes put me on edge and the paint rippling off the roller sounded like bacon frying.

When the burglar picture arrived I laced it up, dimmed the lights, and went down to experience the opening scene.

This is a thing I always do. A movie can get all the high marks but that first two minutes is a trusty forecast.

I stood in the left aisle two-thirds back. The screen brightened slowly, then *bam*—a swirling oval graphic appeared with the sound of a thunderclap. It was just a production credit, the shiny work of a studio nerd, but that noise! My sternum contracted. I curled like a shrimp, hugging my ears, but kept my eyes on the screen.

I wasn't entirely surprised. When showing Rune *Butch Cassidy*, I'd been careful to set the volume low. It worked well enough for the two of us in an empty house, but wouldn't fly with paying customers. Cautiously I removed my hands from my ears, on-screen someone rang a doorbell, and the noise knocked me on my backside right there in the aisle. When dialogue ensued, the voices were bird screams in my head. I crabbed away and went flapping up the steps to halt the projector. Blinking back sweat, I checked the sound console. The slider was set per usual. Normal volume—if anything, a little on the low side.

Just to be sure, I tried it again—backed up the film and ran it, this time staying up in the booth. The credit boomed, the doorbell rang. Nausea answered. In a drawer I found a pair of foam earplugs employed by machinists and skeet shooters—I pinched them in, waited for them to expand. I rewound and went for a third try, even though my stomach had issued a warning about what was certain to happen. It did.

So I'd done all I could to bring off a comeback, and now couldn't project the movie. I needed a plan, and here I was goofing around, hoping to fly a kite.

About this time Rune, still tinkering, switched gears and began musing about what it was like to suddenly acquire a grandson.

"I'm a large disappointment," he said. "An old man never understands what a large disappointment he is going to be."

"Why's that?"

"Bjorn must have hoped I would be like his dad. Of course he would hope this! And I would, if I knew how. Do you know I have filled two notebooks with nothing but stories of Alec? Yet I can't find enough of him to matter. I am unable to be some different way."

"I doubt Bjorn wants you to be Alec," I told him, cautiously.

"I embarrassed him the other day," Rune said. "Flying on the shore, some kids along. Everyone wanted the string. We went around a point of land and there was Bjorn out in the water. Sitting on his surfboard in the small waves. I knew he did this but hadn't seen it. I wasn't sure it was him. The hood shows only his eyes. I shouted, 'Bjorn, Bjorn, is that you?' And this group of kids thought it was funny. Extremely hilarious. They started yelling, 'Bjorn, is that you? Is that you?'"

"Oh, boy."

"I made them stop, but Bjorn was humiliated. He turned around and put his chest on the board. He paddled out a long way." Rune sighed, his face slumped.

"Maybe you should give Bjorn more credit," I suggested.

"I have the wrong approach," Rune said in a tone of resignation.

He looked at me to speak, but I kept quiet. What I couldn't say was that Bjorn wanted a future as something besides the son of an unsolved problem, and that meant the best thing might be for Rune to forsake his inquiry and go home to the Arctic Circle. Maybe he was meant to be the final post, after all.

But I couldn't say that to Rune—I couldn't. Therefore I took sanctuary in my ravaged vocabulary, and watched him work on the bicycle kite. He repaired its broken spars, retied its cat's cradle of a flight harness; he wrapped a final splice with thread, then bit it off and asked, "Do you want to try this now?"

He must've made several adjustments, because it wasn't the chaos machine of earlier. It was hardly domesticated, but I paid out some line, maybe two hundred feet, and the bicycle didn't crash or break in midair. Flying it I felt my panic about the Empress subside. Hither and yon it zipped across the bright cold sky, wheels spinning with a lively purr that came down into my fingers. I let out more line. A buoyancy expanded in my chest and I seemed to rise toward a small cumulus cloud scudding toward the province of Ontario. The cloud misted me with a greeting and went on its way. A brace of late snow geese moved south along the shoreline; their black wing tips whistled as they passed. Far below Bjorn rested on his board, suited up and waiting for a wave. I saw the modest rooftop of the Empress.

"What are you laughing about?" Rune said, a little time later.

"Was I laughing?"

"You were."

"It's a fine flyer. I don't know how you did it."

"Any adjustments I should make?" He beamed at my praise—he already knew it was a brilliant kite.

All I could do was shake my head. Any kite that pulls you up and makes you laugh shouldn't be tinkered with further.

I never did explain to Rune the effect of his painted wings—the lift, the ease, the entrance into something else. The flights had a dream-like fragility. What if they were ruined by talk? Likewise Rune never elucidated his discipline or theory of flight. He was more practitioner than advocate, in the way of believers whose religion is so intimate they keep it to themselves.

Flying the bicycle gave me an idea, though. I knew what to do, and handed Rune the string.

Bjorn met me at the Empress. He was curious and quick to understand the machinery. He did a lot of vaguely acerbic smiling, saying *Sure thing boss*, with cryptic remarks about analog gear, calling it "steampunk" as though it were all cogs and coal shovels. I showed him how to lace up a movie from several reels onto the single platter, keeping heads and tails in proper order; how to run the primitive Mackie soundboard; how to perform a quick splice if the projector stalled and the hot bulb melted through the print.

"Actual buttons," was his deadpan observation. "Razor blades. Sticky tape."

Old-school as it was, he caught on fast. When I learned the ropes from Edgar I was a slow study, clumsy with celluloid and wary of gear—every splice seemed a victory, every screening without a melt-through or a print jumping the tracks was me squeaking past on grace and good fortune. By contrast, Bjorn in the booth seemed inherently poised. He flourished two spools on the flats of his hands, threaded the old machine as though buttering up a favorite aunt. He stretched out his long fingers and rotated dials that seemed to have called to him from former times.

I'd bought a yellow legal notebook and written down each step of my process. He gave this finicky list a once-over, eyed me indulgently, and proceeded on his own. When the red bulb lit above the door, letting me know the landline was ringing, I quite comfortably left him and went down to answer the phone.

Normally in the afternoon I let it ring through to the recording, which gives the current movie and showtimes. Today I didn't. Tom Beeman had run a short item in the *Observer* about the reopening, which might lead to some curiosity or even other media showing up—years earlier Duluth TV had profiled the Empress during the summer news vacuum, and for two weeks we averaged thirty-five tickets per night. Feeble numbers for your metro screens but a world-shifting deluge for my dissipating palace. That fall I renovated four rows of seats and had the screen professionally cleaned; it made a bright and beautiful difference. Therefore I picked up the phone and with what I imagined was forthright energy said, "It's the Empress Theater, good day."

"Virgil? Jerry Fandeen."

"Ah, Jerry." I won't deny my vocal élan took a hit, but Jerry didn't notice. His own voice sounded stressed and oddly hollow.

"In a small little bind here," he said. "I wonder if I could just tap into your knowledge of plumbing."

I pleaded ignorance but he shook this off. After seeing my organized tool storage, Jerry had begun to imagine I was a capable handyman. I told him I knew nothing of plumbing, but he was sure it was only something else I had clean forgot, like adjectives, and balance, and the many useful tools he had lent me. At the moment he was fixing Adam Leer's main-floor toilet. Something was jammed way down there and wouldn't come loose. Leer was out on mysterious errands. Jerry was desperate to get it fixed before he returned.

"Try one of those flexible snake deals," I suggested.

"I did. No luck."

"Call a plumber," I recommended. "Call Benedict." Clarence Benedict was Greenstone's last remaining plumber, and a good one. He was eighty and wore striped coveralls everywhere he went. He kept trying to retire.

"I can't call Benedict. I'm supposed to be the one fixing things. If I can't unplug a toilet, Mr. Leer will find someone else to do his repairs."

"Up to you, Jerry. Benedict is fast and good. Or you could wait until Leer gets home and let him make the decision. All right? Good luck, Jerry," I said, and hung up.

Back in the booth I found Bjorn lacing up an old outtake reel I'd gotten down.

I'd planned to show it to Rune after *Butch Cassidy*, but he was so reflective after the movie I forgot. The screen lit up. There were Newman and Redford in their western clothes.

Bjorn said, "Hey-o, what's this?"

They sat on a bench in a darkened room. They'd removed their hats and were gazing slightly upward, into the camera—Butch amused, Sundance guarded as usual. The seconds passed and there they sat. There was no repartee. Butch cleared his throat once.

"I remember this movie," Bjorn said. "I think Dad liked it."

I had to smile. In all my secret trove this was my rarest pearl, a clip from *Butch Cassidy* that didn't make the cut. Few living people know it exists—not that many would care, I fully understand.

The shot widened to include Katharine Ross, sitting next to Redford. Of the three she looked the most delighted. Behind them sat a few gauchos with sunburned faces and dirty kerchiefs. All sat quietly on creaking benches. Shadows played across their faces. Because of their silence and steady gaze there was the sensation they were watching us back.

"What are they doing?" Bjorn whispered.

"Same thing you are—hush."

We watched the clip to the end. It throws a spell. It's fifty-two seconds in which no one speaks, an edit, I suspect, from a rumored scene where the desperadoes visit a movie house in South America. There's no music, no suspense. For nearly a minute you simply relax in the company of three fine-looking people you feel you've always known. Moments before the end, Butch grins right at you—his grin spreads to Etta, but not to Sundance.

"It's like a window." The actors were no longer on-screen, but Bjorn kept his voice low, as if they might still be listening. "You look in and there are your friends, looking out."

He spun the film back and we watched it again.

"It feels like we all know each other."

"Like we have certain matters in common," I said.

"Which we maybe do," Bjorn said, with a cagey look. "We're all outlaws, for example."

"I don't follow."

"We're outlaws. Tell me this isn't a stolen clip."

I admitted it probably was.

"And all those movies, up in your secret vault? Are they *all* nicked?"

"It's the most likely scenario."

Bjorn was pleased. "It's all contraband! You're an outlaw and I'm your accomplice. Who else has seen this clip?"

"A few studio people, years ago. George Roy Hill, I imagine. An editor or two. Most of them would be dead now. And then yourself."

Bjorn liked that. "And how illegal is this stuff? Fine? Jail?"

"No one would care about most of it. It's a gray area. You don't really know until you turn the stuff in."

"It's just as well," he replied. "That clip is a holy relic. It belongs with you. You want to keep possession."

I was pleased he liked the outtake, but later I began to wonder. If something's a relic, what's your obligation? Is an attic with a sticky door really its best home?

What was I hanging onto?

We put the clip aside and I had Bjorn break down the Langella picture, then splice it back up—he had good solid process, almost right away.

The red bulb over the door lit up again. This time I took the call in the booth.

"Virgil? Jerry Fandeen."

"Did you sort that plumbing?"

In a dry voice he implied the job had gone badly.

"Still plugged?"

"Obstructed, yes. I tried Benedict but he's in Iowa. Can you come help with this?"

In the end, I didn't go help. For the record I didn't ask Bjorn to go either, but off he went anyway on his gangly pins, looking alarmingly pleased. Much later, Nadine would tell me that was a banner afternoon for Bjorn—he learned to thread a projector and splice film with a razor; he watched a rare lost clip from a classic movie. And he got to witness with his two eyes the matchless spectacle of a grown man employing a dynamite blasting cap to unplug a toilet.

That was also the afternoon Bjorn met Mr. Leer—or, more properly, met him again. I didn't remind Nadine of that fact, however. Acquaintance with Adam Leer seemed rarely to anyone's benefit, and I didn't want her to hold it against me.

5

NINETY.

There were ninety people at the Empress. I kept count while selling tickets. There hadn't been ninety since the last Harry Potter. Word had gone round about my splendid accident. Rune was sitting halfway back, Nadine beside him on the aisle; Tom Beeman was on hand with his camera and a woman I had never met or else did not remember; Marcus Jetty came, and Margaret from the Agate, and even Lanie Plume who sold me the sunglasses—Lanie, sitting with a row of friends, held up her phone and waited until I looked at her to turn it boldly off.

The speech is the other thing I always do. It starts, *The Empress welcomes you.*

Kids think this is deeply lame, adults think it self-indulgent. Both things are true, but standing up to introduce a film is one of the little pleasures of ownership—most of them are little, as you may well imagine.

I'd thought about what to say, of course I had. You want to be properly grateful. Those warm faces, those expectant smiles—you don't get many chances to return from the dead. I confess to a tightrope moment, a wobble in which I nearly tottered into some sort of maudlin spillover. But something reined me in. In the end I just said a few words about the movie, as always. I said it was good, with a wistful turn from Mr. Langella and a wily script by Christopher Ford. I had gone to the thesaurus earlier for *wistful* and *wily* and written both on the back of my hand. I hoped they all liked the picture and thanked them for coming out and supporting local cinema.

As the lights dimmed I walked up through surprising applause and climbed to projection. Bjorn was up there and had everything set. I gave him a redundant checklist and he gave me a dead stare, his version of Ann's eye roll, fitting many occasions. In this case it implied he had everything in hand. The projector hummed at the ready—God bless the old Simplex, I loved its enginey smell. "You got it from here?" I said.

"Got it, Virgil. Enjoy the night off."

I went down the steps and walked outside and down the street. Even out in the wind I could hear splashy credits, waggish voice-over, trailer bombast. I turned at the corner and went toward the lake, the sidewalk lightly spinning, until the movie music vanished in the waves against the seawall.

6

IN THE MORNING I ROSE AND MADE COFFEE. RUNE WAS OFF FLYING.
The sun was an inch off the lake.

I lit the blue candle.

After the derailment I spent a year living with Orry. She was
stunningly calm and let me shout. I shouted a lot that year, then enrolled
in a Bible college and studied with what now seems forensic intensity.
I wrote exegetical papers, absorbed apologetics and hermeneutics until
they pooled up and ran off. My professors were learned theologians, a
tight group, occasionally competitive about their publications—they
had crisp elocution and penetrating rhetoric, and best of all did not
seem haunted but were confident in their convictions. I admired their
pursuit of divine mysteries. It seemed to me that they, if anyone, might
understand why God wished my parents to die in a torn train car with
people shrieking around them. God's mercy was a popular theme in
their classes, even though the required texts suggested this mercy was
provisional. At bottom, what God seemed to want was affirmation. Basi-
cally praise in every circumstance. Without it he could turn menacing
in a hurry. Ask the Israelites. For that matter, ask Mom and Dad—
they praised God in every circumstance, then their train derailed and
smashed all their bones. Their deaths provided me with the spiritual
dudgeon to buttonhole professors. One said God usually kept his reasons to himself, only occasionally revealing them through his Word or

through special insight, or sometimes through other people, apparently not himself in this instance. Another believed that God allowed tragedy in order to draw us into closer communion with him. "Why not some easier way?" I suggested; which the professor received as impertinence. The third was a man with white hair and renowned decorum, a man you might see in a crowd of thousands and know for a theologian—the gravitas, the gaunt suit and ascetic nose. He saw me coming and became elusive but I caught him and stuck. He finally revealed that it took a long time to develop the "eternal perspective," from which things like this made sense or were in any way acceptable. I cautiously remarked that the eternal perspective was much to ask of creatures as temporary as ourselves. Snapping turtles live longer. The professor looked at his watch and wrote down the names of three books I should read. He spoke reverently of the books. He promised they would guide me correctly. At the library I discovered he had written all three.

In discouragement I headed to the nearby Benchmark Theater. It's gone now and was derelict then, screening second-run and classic and would-be classic movies, admission one dollar. It was showing *Ghostbusters*. In the row behind me slumped Rufus Delaney, another professor. He was in his fifties, dowdy and cardiganed, glasses atilt, a known disappointment to the faculty. A few years ago he'd stepped away from Bible courses and taught some English literature. In the lobby I told Rufus my story. His skewed bifocals amplified his eyes which to my astonishment brimmed with sorrow. We walked to a tavern where he asked about my parents, their ambitions, their burdens, and my own. The other profs had appeared to gauge their remarks for appropriate heft. Not Rufus. He asked what he could do. He bought us some french fries, a pitcher of beer. Eventually he confessed that while theology had infected him young, he'd recently come to prefer movies, where the questions posed were smaller and could actually be answered. What's making that noise in the forest? What do these strangers really want? Will he reach her in time? He wheezed when he laughed. He was a twinkly old failure and I'll never forget him. His favorite *Ghostbusters* bit was Bill Murray remarking of a demon-possessed refrigerator, "Generally you don't see that kind of behavior in a major appliance."

*   *   *

Orry called at last. I was drinking coffee on the roof in my bathrobe, savoring the successful Empress reopening as well as the startling sunshine—the morning was warm, after that early illustration of winter.

Orry had received my flood of voice mails at last. She'd been three weeks on a boat in the French canals, her friend Jeffrey along for conversation and gastronomy. Jeffrey is a New England chef whose hobby is auditioning for Food Network reality shows—he never gets called back.

"I'm sorry you couldn't reach me," Orry said.

"No problem. Where was Dinesh?"

"Someplace with burn victims. Listen, I went to your Empress page. There are seventy get-well notes, none of which mention your illness. Usually that means cancer. Do you have cancer, Virgil?"

"I left you messages, Orry."

"They were nonspecific."

"No cancer," I told her.

"Could you have said that on the message? It's two words."

I gave her an abbreviated version, punching it up a little. I kept the heavy snow and the dive off 61 but left out the vertigo and rumors of my expiry. My ransacked vocabulary also went unmentioned, though Orry sensed something amiss.

"You're editing," she said. "What gives? Short declaratives aren't like you."

"I'm told I sound decisive."

"Virgil, you had a near-death experience. You drove off a cliff and went in the hospital and got back out. Now you are home sounding strangely staccato. It makes me worry."

"I've decided to get rid of the film collection."

"Well *that's* abrupt," she said.

"You offered one time to put me in touch with an attorney. I'm hoping you still can."

This was a discussion we'd had long before, when in a weak late-night moment I fretted about the bottle imps. Orry was acquainted with a Hollywood lawyer whom she trusted because he so disliked the movie business. Sinatra had threatened him once, in the dim light of a hotel back entrance. He saw the entertainer's legendary knuckles up close. They were genuinely hairy. The lawyer said the only way to have a soul in Hollywood was to exasperate the thugs. The lawyer's wife was a surgeon who worked with Dinesh in his grueling medical excursions.

Orry said, "How did you come to this decision?"

"It's been on my mind."

"Be honest, Virgil—is this a lightning bolt thing, after peering at the void? Because it might not hurt to wait a little."

"Like I said, it's been simmering. Does your lawyer friend still practice?"

She thought so. She'd check into it, give the man my number. Again, she asked how I was.

"I'm right here, showing movies like always."

"I can be there tomorrow."

"Orry, don't. You just got home. Anyway, the guest room is full right now."

She was slightly affronted to hear about Rune, and this put me at ease. Orry is happiest when affronted on my behalf. Something in her needs to believe I am routinely taken advantage of.

"So you're recovering from a deadly accident while lodging gratis a bizarre stranger there to ease his conscience."

My laptop was open—I typed *bizarre* into the online thesaurus. "Let's go with eccentric. He flies kites and asks questions."

"How long does he plan to stay?"

"No idea."

"I suppose I could get a room at the Voyageur," she mused, then: "Hang on—this fellow is *whose* biological father?"

"Alec Sandstrom's."

"Friend of yours," she vaguely assayed. "Baseball player."

"That's the one."

"Wait . . ." she said. It clicked. "Wait, this is the vanished pitcher. And—oh Virgil!—he of the gorgeous wife! Nadine," she said, in triumph.

"Excellent recall." I felt wary—my sister had actually met Nadine during one of her visits. It was years past the post office incident, yet Orry claimed to detect some moony element in my behavior.

"Nadine," she repeated now, with surprising tenderness. "So, what about Nadine? Does the torch still smolder?"

"Getting another call, I'll have to ring you back."

"I'm your sister, ring *them* back. It's a plain enough question."

It was, so I attempted a plain answer. I told Orry I was done with torches. At least that torch. That torch was pointless, as a long succession of men had learned. Certainly some of the men were predatory or disingenuous but others were earnest, smart, even rich. A torchlight parade is what happened, but to no avail. Nadine raised her son and grew the neon business and added to herself the glow of lonely persistence. I admired her too much to appear on her doorstep, one more earnest moron carrying the predictable flame.

I didn't say all that in exactly that way, but Orry got the idea. "Nice, Virgil. You build an impressive pedestal. No wonder you can't just call her."

"She believes Alec is alive," I said.

"You're not serious."

"She believes he landed safely in Canada and evaded pursuit all these years."

At the time I had no idea whether that's what Nadine believed—I lobbed it out there only to distract Orry. She was quiet, wavering between romance and snark.

I said, "She believes he will walk in the door one morning and fall to his knees before her."

At this Orry took a large breath and let it out with a sigh. "I'm not a fool, Virgil, I know you're only dodging—but wouldn't that be a story?"

My sister comes on like a box of nails, but her devotion to the mythic is profound.

*   *   *

When I arrived at the lookout Beeman was already up there. He'd told me days earlier he wanted to interview Rune—he meant to write a ret-rospective about Alec as legendary absconder, pin it to the forthcoming ten-year mark, and add this new wrinkle of the wayward father showing up at last. He said, "One morning you open the mail, you got a family across the ocean you knew nothing about. If I don't write this story I might as well sell the paper."

"You tried selling the paper. Does Rune want to do it?"

"I'm still trying. Yeah he does. We're going to fly some of his kites."

But I didn't realize Beeman would pursue the idea so quickly. When I emerged onto the roof-deck after fencing with Orry, two kites were sailing around above the lookout—just specks at first, but through binoculars I made out the bicycle spinning its furious wheels and along-side it the ribby dog. Two figures were visible on the ground.

After my conversation with Bjorn, the thought of his illegitimate grandfather showing up on the front page of the *Observer*—in fact Bee-man's whole retrospective on Alec—seemed an untimely idea. Surely he could be persuaded to hold the story off.

It's a long walk to the lookout. I felt some urgency about getting there, so helped myself to an unlocked bike in a weed patch next to somebody's house. The bike was a Walmart disposable with rusty spokes and a big gear cluster making for clanky downshifts on steep climbs. My breath was short and my balance poor yet I felt a corporeal joy in both ride and theft. The joy was lessened when I noticed I was wearing a bathrobe and boxers instead of my clothes, but I was halfway there so too late. Eventually the two kites reappeared much closer and I came gasping over the final crest to the sight of Rune laughing.

"Here's Virgil," he said, as I dropped the bike and sat down quite forcefully on the gravel. Beeman greeted me with a wave but did not interrupt the story he was telling. It was about the time Alec was pitch-ing and a monkey bolted onto the field. The Dukes like many minor-league clubs sought to arouse their fans with offbeat promotions; in this case they'd hired a dinky warlike rhesus monkey to carry a cane and wear a top hat for on-field stunts. The monkey was a crude entertainer who pleased the crowd by strutting triumphantly, pointing at its own butt or, when the team was losing, emerging in late innings to whiz on the umpire. The Dukes had been fined repeatedly for its behavior, but kept trotting it out there anyway. Plain and simple, the monkey sold tickets. That night in the eighth, game on the line, the hitter laid down a standard bunt—Alec was nearly on it when the monkey flashed past and the ball was gone. The little beast zigzagged through the infield to the gap in right-center, hugging the ball to its scraggly chest while the hitter circled the bases laughing. You'd think the officials would call interference. Not a chance. The umpires were tired of the monkey. The Dukes lost. Alec refused to be angry. He subscribed to the vintage notion that monkeys are inherently funny.

By now I'd got my breath back and got to my feet. I took a nonchalant stance, narrowing my eyes ironically, as though the mint-green bathrobe were a deliberate choice. Beeman talked cheerfully on. He told about Alec finding a deer leg in the ditch at Christmas and making reindeer tracks on the roof so Bjorn would wake to proof of Santa. Rune's kite string was tied to the arm of a nearby bench. Beeman had gone up to interview Rune, but it was Rune jotting crisp notes while the bicycle flew itself overhead. This reversal strengthened my suspicion that these kites had the same effect on others as they had on me. The irresistible hum was not exclusive. It was disappointing but also reassuring. Beeman was enjoying himself. When Rune threw me a look of pure gladness I had the same feeling I'd had the day we met—that he was a variety new to me but very old, with the recklessness of innocence. I felt that anything at all might happen. Maybe it was happening already.

"Tom," Rune said, when Beeman paused for breath, "when did you move to Greenstone?"

"Bought the paper in ninety-nine."

"You wrote about it, then—when Alec disappeared."

Beeman started paying close attention to the kite, reeling in a bit of line and then letting it out. "I covered that story."

"Do you believe any of the sightings have merit?"

"No," Beeman said, gently. "But I do have some materials you might be interested in—bits and pieces about Alec from over the years.

I should have thought of giving them to you earlier. Come by the office and I'll see what there is."

"When?"

"Tomorrow. Not before noon, though."

Rune slipped his notebook into his pocket, then unwrapped his string from the bench and reeled in.

"Now hold on," Beeman complained. "You didn't give me any interview—I've talked the whole time and got nothing for the paper. You're a devious operator, is what I think." But Beeman wasn't truly upset. It was tough to be annoyed with Rune. He was a likable strange old man yearning to know his lost son. Who wouldn't try to help him?

7

THE BIKE I STOLE BELONGED TO A SEVENTH GRADER WHOSE MOTHER,
name of Mazy, worked a split shift at the Duluth paper mill. A friend
of hers observed the doofus bathrobed city clerk clattering uphill and
got hold of Mazy during her coffee break. Mazy finished her cigarette
and called the county sheriff.

I was dressed by the time he climbed the steps and knocked.

"Why Don," I said. "Come in, there's coffee."

Whatever you think when you hear the word *sheriff* our sheriff
is not that. He is not laconic or severe. His gaze does not pierce. He in
no way reminds you of Mr. Remington's paintings. His name is Lean,
which he is not, nor did he come to the office through police work or
investigative proficiency. He is a former banker and insurance salesman who failed as both. His calm demeanor suggests a native honesty
hazardous in those careers.

He said, "I wanted to come to the movie last night, welcome you
back, but I had a livestock call it took a while to sort."

I thanked him for his part in my survival—it seems he drove out
right behind the ambulance when Marcus called 911.

He said, "I feel terrible I didn't come back to the hospital and
check on you. I meant to. It just got away. Next thing I know you're
back showing movies again. Like it didn't even happen."

It didn't feel that way to me, but there was no need to explain this. I poured us both coffee which we carried onto the roof-deck in the wind. Don had put on weight. His shoulders were hunched as though in anticipation of some descending burden. He wanted to talk about Shad Pea, whom he'd treated like a friend instead of a habitual drunk—a mistake, he now believed. Maybe if he'd locked Shad up more often, Shad would've begun to consider the upshot. Maybe Shad would have moderated the intake. Maybe Galen would still have his dad. Don Lean's eyes were moist. "That Galen's a good kid. Every few weeks I used to haul him back to school. Lily keeps him on a shorter line. I sure like him."

"So do I. He holds the fish responsible."

"That's fair. Ever fish for sturgeon?"

"No."

"Friend of mine hooked one up on Rainy River. Eighteen-foot skiff, forty-horse Evinrude, himself in the boat plus two long oars and a cooler and live tank. Fish pulled the whole rig eleven miles *upriver* before the line broke. Eleven miles against a decent current. Think about this. Monster like that on the hook, a little rum in your bloodstream. Anyone would lose their balance."

Don finished his coffee and went back in and poured himself some more. He sat on the roof-deck with his shoulders up around his neck. He said, "Do you know if Beeman's raccoon is around?"

"No, he took off. If you want your raccoon to be docile, possibly don't name him Genghis."

Don said, "Was Genghis up to date on his vaccinations?"

"Do people vaccinate raccoons?"

"I wish they would. Last night while you were showing your movie I got calls about four separate animals in two hours. They all showed like rabies. Two raccoons, a dog, a cat."

"One of the raccoons was Genghis?"

"No. Both little skinny specimens. But the owners of one cat saw a blobby old raccoon fighting their cat in their front yard a few nights ago."

"Lot of fat raccoons out there."

"Fewer with collars."

The idea of rabies disturbed Don. He had a cat he was attached to—the cat often went with him on sheriff calls, amusing some people but not everyone. "I'll ask him all right," he said.

In the kitchen he rinsed his own cup and set it in the rack to dry. Out the door he went only to put his head back in. "I forgot to ask. Did you steal a bicycle this morning and go for a ride in your bathrobe?"

"I did, yes."

"Anything I should know about this?"

"I needed to get somewhere and don't have a car right now."

"It was the bathrobe part that got my attention," he said.

"Sorry about that. I returned the bicycle."

He nodded. "I stopped by Mazy's on the way here, saw it on the porch. Virgil, did you tape a twenty-dollar bill to the seat post?"

"I might have."

"Listen, I have five or six bikes in the garage. I'll bring you one. Tide you over till you're driving again."

I thanked him. He nodded and went clumping down the stairs. Watching him go it occurred to me Don was too empathetic for law enforcement. The cost showed. From youthful businessman and community optimist he'd progressed speedily to anguished authority. He was graying fast like a high school principal or US president. Down the steps he creaked, holding on to the rail.

That night I made popcorn and sold twenty-seven tickets and left Bjorn in charge while Rune and I drove out to the Pentecost River to check on Galen Pea. Sure enough Galen stood at the water's edge with Shad's tackle box in the tall grass beside him. When we stepped out of the camper van Galen lowered his head to glare at us in the twilight. I was glad to see he wasn't alone—Lily was there too, sitting in her blue Dodge Dart with engine running and heater on. She waved at us with what looked like relief.

Rune walked down to consult with Galen while I took the easier job.

"Get in," she said when I knocked at the window.

She had a wool blanket, her dad's red plaid thermos bottle, and a paperback romance. I asked how she was and she said sick of Galen.

"He's obsessed. It's awfully unpleasant. Last night I didn't want to come so he took off and walked here alone. Eleven p.m. I gave up and drove down and got him. It's a damn fish Virgil."

"Is he getting any nibbles?"

"No. If he doesn't catch the thing soon I'm putting him on a Greyhound bus."

"Where to?"

"I don't care—here, I brought cocoa."

She poured some into a Styrofoam cup. It was extraordinary—creamy and barely sweet at all. She said, "I met this guy from Norway who sends me chocolate bars. I melt them in milk with a cinnamon stick." With lovely defiance she declared, "I am not wasting one more minute on subpar cocoa."

"Is school all right for Galen?"

"Yeah. Wouldn't you know it I'm a better enforcer than Dad. His teacher says he's a good reader. She's playing up the positive."

"He have friends?"

"Not that I can tell. Maybe Rune." She nodded at the old man and the boy becoming silhouettes in front of the darkening river. "What do you suppose they're talking about?"

It was all sturgeon talk—so Rune told me later. Galen was an expert. Sturgeon lived two hundred years and grew as big as dump trucks. In 1940 a sturgeon swam up this very river and died in a flooded hayfield where a farmer and two spooked horses loaded it onto a wagon. The wagon sank in the mud and people came from all over with knives to butcher the great fish. They lit fires and ate for three days. When only the skeleton remained, the farmer hoisted it on a scale and it still weighed two hundred pounds. Another time an American Indian got swallowed whole right out on Lake Superior. He was fishing in his birch canoe and the sturgeon rose up out of the dark and took him down canoe and all. "Like Pinocchio and the whale," Rune said, thinking of the old animation, but Galen glared at him. This Indian was an actual guy who got swallowed by a sturgeon and waded around inside its guts until he found the beating heart. He stabbed the heart with his knife. The sturgeon died and washed ashore. The Indian cut his way out. That's how you had to deal with these bastards.

"He needs to catch that fish," Rune said. We were back at the Empress, cleaning up. Bjorn had done the screening and rewound the film and put the booth in order, but in the aisle someone had dumped a large Coke which ran down front and made a nasty pool.

"Well, he isn't going to," I said. It was late, I was out of momentum. The auditorium lights browned and flared. The back seats were full of man-shaped shadows.

"Why would you say that?" Rune asked.

"Because I don't think it's easy to catch any sturgeon, let alone the precise specimen you have a grudge against. Plus, Galen's a boy. He doesn't weigh a hundred pounds. If the fish is so big, how is he going to haul it in?"

"Pessimist," Rune said.

"That's me," I replied, but Rune was alight somehow. Clearly his talk with Galen had given him something to ponder, something that pleased him and set him on edge. In absent fashion he rolled a whitecap of popcorn in front of the broom, then finally asked whether I'd heard anything else about this fisherman the boy had mentioned, the American Indian. How long ago was the sturgeon adventure? Was the Indian still around? If so, would he talk to us? Could we maybe go see him?

There were times Rune was so foreign as to seem Martian. And yes, this would've been a good time to remain lighthearted—to roll with it, make a joke. But I was shaky with vertigo, my ears rang, confusion crowded the margins. I shut my eyes and squeezed the mop handle. "It isn't a real story, Rune. It's a tedious poem by a nineteenth-century American. It's called 'The Song of Hiawatha.' It has nothing to do with actual Indians. Sturgeon don't get that big."

This nickel rant pulled him down for a time. He swept up the last of the popcorn in silence while I rinsed Coke out of the mop and shoved the bucket on its rattly casters up the now tidy aisle. Soon, however, Rune was back to smiling, uttering strange words to himself. Weeks later, during one of our late-night akevitt sessions, he declared that just because a thing was poetry didn't mean it never happened in the actual world, or that it couldn't happen still.

8

THE NEXT AFTERNOON ANN FANDEEN CAME INTO MY OFFICE. "DID
you see my car when you came in this morning?"

"No—did you get that serpentine belt fixed?"

"Serpentine belt! Just come over here a minute, you, come on!"

She beckoned me to the window, where I peered out not at Ann's
old ride or Jerry's weary pickup but at a late-model Buick LeSabre,
maroon, with glinting wax and a white vinyl steering-wheel cover. She
said, "Look what I found last night down in Duluth."

"It's beautiful."

"I looked at a Jeep Cherokee and a little blue Mazda, but you
know me," Ann said. "I've always been partial to Buicks."

"Congratulations," I said. She stood real close to me. Her skin
was pink and shining.

"It's all because of you," she exclaimed, and went on to clarify: because
I had forced her to drive to the Leer property, and because she had deftly
worked her intuitive connection with Adam, Jerry now had employment
again. After the early snow melted, Jerry had started with a "fall cleanup
special," which meant mowing the grass and then mowing the thick parts
again, after which Adam asked him to re-spline a couple of screens where
the squirrels got in. Now he'd tackled Adam's encroachment of aspen, ren-
dering small logs and slash piles he would burn once there was more snow.

"Sounds like he's been up to a spot of plumbing, as well."

"I don't know anything about that," she replied, then continued with the news that it appeared Adam was back in Greenstone to stay. He had lots more work for Jerry—installing bat excluders, repainting the guest quarters over the garage. Adam had certainly taken Jerry under his wing, Ann divulged—often the two men ate lunch together, sandwiches accompanied by posh brown ales out of Adam's own fridge. During these sociable pauses Adam relaxed his guard, even expressed regret about his high-octane past. The pretensions, the eyeliner and pharmaceuticals, the faceless desperado sex marathons. People back then thought cocaine was good for you. Jerry was actually *counseling* Adam, when you thought about it. Guiding him by example back to the wholesome small-town life from which he'd come. Adam was receptive and curious. He asked Jerry's advice about community matters, the value of downtown locations. Closing my office door Ann took a less upbeat tone, confiding she'd divined Leer's motive for the sprucing up. He expected a visitor in the near future. A woman. Jerry didn't know who, but Ann suspected somebody famous.

"Like who?"

"Somebody from the movies, that's what I think. Didn't he have a thing once with Andie MacDowell?"

"I wouldn't know."

It occurred to me that Ann Fandeen had not said this many words to me in our six years working together. I noticed too that besides the LeSabre, she had new earrings. They looked like gold dangly feathers. She said, "Do you want me to talk to Adam again? About the festival? Now that he's come back to his hometown? Think what this could mean to Greenstone," she added in a coaxing tone.

"Don't do it," I said.

"Oh no—did you find somebody else?"

"Working on it." I wasn't. I just didn't want Leer to speak. When I thought of him in front of a crowd, it never went the way it should. In my imagination his voice spread slowly overhead like a cloud of infectious mosquitoes.

Patting my shoulder Ann formed the sly smile of she who will have her way at last. "I know you're not driving yet, Virgil. Just ask, if you need a ride someplace."

9

ADAM LEER'S FAMOUS VISITOR SWIRLED INTO GREENSTONE ON A hard-core North Shore day—twigs snatching in the gale, black filth at the storm drains, the sea hissing in dismay. It was a better day for leaving than arriving, so Lucy DuFrayne got noticed, waltzing up Main in a vivid yellow coat that went to her ankles. *Sashaying*, as the oldsters say. Only an ingrate could fail to admire it. The coat billowed, it misbehaved, it was the brightest thing in forty miles. Lucy went straight to the Agate to see who was still around.

"Always such a big wheel," Margaret told me later. "Even as a kid she'd show up smeary and breathless. Like she was kissing somebody ten seconds ago."

Of course with me Margaret was her normal disapproving self but seeing Lucy she'd flown out of the kitchen and they hugged like sisters. Lucy was not local but had visited every summer with her parents, back in the days of high employment, days when the beach had a lifeguard. Lucy's nickname then was Bangles. It still seemed to fit.

"You've come back to see Adam," Margaret guessed. "Oh, you'll be surprised at the house! He's just been working so hard!"

They talked a little—"Longer than I wanted to," Margaret later declared—long enough apparently for Lucy to decline Margaret's offer of a sit-down visit, and to glaze over at Margaret's segue into pressing local matters. Margaret was gathering talent for a community production of *Oklahoma!* Lucy smiled and was out the door with her yellow tails wheeling in the wind.

Lucy DuFrayne wasn't as famous as Andie MacDowell, but she had in fact been a little famous for several minutes among a post-beatnik splinter of jazz freaks. She made a successful record for Columbia, which I tracked down—standards and forgotten near misses in a sultry contralto. Lucy DuFrayne was Leer's first cousin and the first girl he ever fell in love with.

While this same Lucy accelerated north through the chilly gray scale of Main Street, Rune and I were up at the lookout. He'd launched a new kite in the shape of an ambiguously European car, with a dissipated-looking fellow at the wheel and a small white dog poking its head out the rear window. Rune let me fly it until I got a desperate crick in my neck, at which point I stepped out of the bitter wind and sat in the camper van opening my mail. There was a check from the insurance company for twenty-five hundred, the value of my Pontiac; also a box from Orry containing a set of noise-canceling headphones, and a handwritten query about the Empress. The query came from a man in Des Moines who'd always wanted to run his own business and thought a movie theater "seemed like a fun way." He wrote in pencil on lined paper to prevent the government from reading his e-mails. He thought my price was high and wondered whether the theater would "comfortably support" his family of five. Fifteen hilarious responses popped into my head. A person should write these things down.

I was reading the headphone instructions when the sheriff's cruiser pulled into the overlook. Don Lean was driving, his tiger cat Roger in the passenger seat. Roger thought of himself as a dog and rode everywhere with Don, who bought a booster seat so Roger could more easily observe the passing world.

Don parked and got out, leaving the cruiser running so Roger would be warm. He waved to Rune, came over to the camper van, and climbed in. "I stopped by the Empress," he said. "Got a bike for you, but I wasn't sure where to leave it."

I could see its spoked wheels angling up in the car's back window. "Thanks, Don—if you leave it here, I'll ride it home."

"Great, I'll get it out for you and be on my way." But Don just sat there and didn't get out. He drummed a short rhythm on his knees. Over in the cruiser Roger was in motion. He had big shoulders for a cat and a massive square head that bobbed two or three times as though he were halting a mouse with his paw.

"What's Roger doing?"

"Hitting the down button," Don said. As he spoke the cruiser window lowered an inch or so at a time. Every time it went down, Roger tried to push his lion head outside. You could see from the way Don watched he was proud of his big smart cat.

"Is there something else?"

"There is. I understand you got Bjorn Sandstrom working for you."

"He's terrific. Right now I'd have a hard time running the place without him."

Don nodded. "Do me a favor. Convince him to give the surfing a rest. At least until the days start getting longer. I see him out there in this cold dark weather, it isn't normal."

"I'll talk to him, but he enjoys it out there. He says the waves are better, now that it's getting cold."

"If people just weren't so foolish," Don began, then his phone rang. He answered, "Sheriff—this is he. Wait, hang on." He took a notepad and pen from his jacket. "Go ahead."

From the questions Don asked I gathered someone was reporting a break-in. There was a greenhouse several miles up the shore that sold hanging flower baskets in the spring, garden gnomes, gazing balls, tomato cages, topsoil, and bags of manure. The place closed in October, reopened briefly after Thanksgiving to sell Christmas trees and pinecone wreaths and local cider, then closed again. It wasn't the sort of place you imagined getting robbed.

"One set of wind chimes," Don said. He was a slow and meticulous notetaker. While Don asked questions, Roger finally got the window down far enough to squeeze himself out. He leaped to the ground and trotted up to Rune, spooking the shaggy raven who had arrived again and was perched on a boulder. Sometimes it said things that were almost words.

"Well, look around," Don said into the phone. "Check the doors and the rest of the windows. I'll be there in twenty."

He hung up, shaking his head. "Marcie put up some wind chimes once, out on the screen porch. They tinkled in the slightest breeze. At first I really liked them, but they never stopped. Not for a minute. After a while all that tinkling started making me angry. I heard it all the time—in the car, in my office. I can hear it right now, if I try. If someone had stolen those wind chimes, I'd have shaken his hand."

Don got out of the van and whistled to Roger who trotted right over. I followed them to the cruiser where Don extracted the bicycle with considerable twisting and huffing. He snapped down the kickstand and set it in front of me.

"I pumped up the tires, but don't know how solid they are."

"It's really decent of you, Don."

"No problem. And no hurry. I have five more."

After he left I took the bike by the handlebars and gave it a lift. It was a ten-speed Schwinn from the '80s, narrow leather saddle, deep blue lacquer with gold metallic on the lugged joints. It had the dropped handlebars wrapped with padded black tape. Just seeing it buoyed me—I felt as excited as I would've in junior high. I began to imagine how nice it would be to coast downhill, cruise around town, make the late-night cheese run. Why had I been without a bike for so long? If it worked out, maybe I wouldn't need to replace the Pontiac. You can't buy much of a car for twenty-five hundo, but you can get an excellent bike.

While I mused on this, a blue Ford turned in off the highway and parked. I hadn't realized how dark the afternoon was becoming until its headlights went off. The car door opened and a startling stripe of yellow stepped out.

"Hello?" called the stripe. This woman had shoulder-length silvery hair that moved across her face in the wind, a coat bright as a honeybee belted at her waist.

I helloed in return. Rune looked at her over his shoulder and raised a hand.

"What a cute shiny car," she said, nodding at the kite with a laugh—an appealing laugh, slightly gritty and right there at the surface.

It would turn out she was another easy laugher. This is sometimes seen as a trait of the nonserious or inexperienced, the too easily satisfied. With Lucy DuFrayne I think it had to do with the fact that she went around all the time with her eyes open.

"Kind of a shiny one yourself, on a day like this," Rune observed, his voice somehow clearer than usual.

"I'm Lucy."

"Rune," he said—again I noticed how he seemed to condense, to gather light and substance. "This is Virgil Wander."

Lucy smiled. She stepped forward taking a hand from her deep coat pocket. "Wander—what a name. It's almost a calling. You've had some adventures, with a name like that."

"Not yet really," I confessed.

"No? Well, watch out then," she said, looking lightly up and around, as though a whole sky full of escapades were imminent and would soon gush down in a cloudburst of destiny justifying my audacious surname. She turned to Rune who stood guiding the kite this way and that, precise as you please. She seemed to belong here, though maybe she was the sort to belong wherever she was at the time. She was obviously taken by the lively kite, and by the old man flying it, and maybe also by the large raven which was still around. She had a soft rounded face that looked used to smiling. When she smiled, her eyes looked hopeful. She seemed to have a lot left.

"Easily the prettiest flyer I ever saw," she told him.

"How kind you are to say it," he replied. With a small jolt I realized the two of them were flirting. Rune would smile and look away, while Lucy leaned slightly in his direction. I was glad, though I also became aware of a hollow back behind my ribs. It wasn't dangerous or new, the hollow—it had been there a long time, so long it was just geography, the weedy depression or crater at the back of the property.

Lucy laughed her low laugh. The sun had dropped behind the hilltops and stripped the kite of most of its color. Its profile was still striking, though. She said, "It looks like a car I rode in a few times, just outside Berlin. It looks like a Citroën. Is it a Citroën, Rune?"

At this they shared a look like two strangers surprised to discover they are from the same town. Happily he explained the kite was indeed modeled on the '49 Citroën his uncle had owned back in Bergen. His uncle liked it because you could take the whole car apart panel by panel and replace whatever was broken. You needed only pliers and a crescent wrench and the sense of a common farm duck, "all of which," Rune said, "my uncle possessed."

Lucy's laugh was a *woe-ho-ho* that started small and opened outward until you wondered whether you'd got the whole joke.

Rune stood with his head slightly tilted. He said to Lucy, "You would maybe care to take it for a spin."

She stepped close to him. At this I recalled I was supposed to meet Bjorn down at the Empress. It was Friday, and there was a new film to lace up.

"I'm glad to know you, Virgil Wander," Lucy called—already she had the string in her fingers. The wind was in her hair. Rune shot me a stunned smile, then looked immediately away.

I swung a leg over Don Lean's bicycle and bumped away slowly over the grass. Reaching the pavement I bent low over the dropped handlebars and let gravity take hold. It was immensely pleasurable to coast down toward the lights of Greenstone. The wind felt icy with speed. Though I'd gone in a moment from loyal friend to third wheel, I wasn't unhappy. It was heartening to see two people roughly half a generation further along strike a few sparks. Besides, I liked very well this clear-eyed Lucy, and what she had said about my name. Of course I put no stock in it, but I liked it all the same, and liked her for saying it.

I let go the brakes and flew down Highway 61 with speed thumping in my ears. You see I'd forgotten my poor balance. The Schwinn sizzled down the painted line. I met a car coming uphill and waved at the driver with confidence, wondering how fast I was going, thinking of the great scene in *Breaking Away* where Dennis Christopher hits sixty. Then something small and solid came out of the grass on my right. My first thought was Roger but it wasn't a cat—maybe a large weasel or small mink, something with that humping mustelid trot. A mink traveling at dusk doesn't anticipate a grown man racing down on a silent machine. I tried to brake but couldn't reach the handles without losing control. Vertigo returned in a rush. The creature reared back. The bike veered and buckled. The road rose up to bounce me into the ditch.

I didn't black out that I know of but lay in the grass awaiting the pain. It soon arrived. I attempted to rise but something slipped inside my shoulder and I fell back yipping. I wondered where the bike had wound up. The wind was cold but I was mostly protected by the tall ditch grass obscuring my view. There was nothing to do but lie and wait. Highway 61 doesn't sleep for long. The sky darkened perceptibly and in ten or twelve minutes a car slowed and stopped. A door opened, a radio switched off, steps came seeking me out.

A lady peered down—she was older than me, with a kind, fearful face. She leaned tentatively away, in case I were faking and preparing to lunge. Seeing this made me feel shy and grateful. What makes a Samaritan good is the possibility of the lunge.

"Are you conscious?"

"Yes—thank you, I am."

"Are you hurt?"

"Yes, it feels that way."

"Should I call 911?"

She had her phone out. I said, "Actually, I'd rather you don't. I live just down the hill in Greenstone—if I could use your phone a moment, maybe I'll call a friend."

Calling 911 would've been the smart decision, but it also meant another ambulance ride all the way to Duluth. I'd taken that ride only a few weeks before, and my whole life had changed—right or wrong, I felt to call an ambulance now was to concede another serious hurt. I said, "I'm just too tired for 911." She knelt down and handed me her phone.

I tried Beeman first, but he didn't answer. I thought it through— Rune hadn't a phone; Lily Pea would be working; Ann Fandeen had offered, but who could face it?

Then I remembered Bjorn.

He happened not to be surfing. He said he'd get his mom's car and come right out; in the meantime, Mr. Wander, don't you move.

"I'll stay until he gets here," said the Samaritan—she really was a good one. She went back to her car and turned on its hazards, then opened the trunk and got out a thick quilt that was rolled up and tied with a ribbon. She covered me with it, a quilt all shades of blue and cream. It smelled like cinnamon and cardamom. I felt heavy and warm, drifting toward sleep.

"No, don't you do that. Open those eyes and look at me. If you have a concussion, you need to stay awake."

I nodded. She got up and dragged the Schwinn off the pavement. It had a bent front wheel and a cracked fork. "You ought not to ride after dark."

"Let me write that down."

"What's your name, smart guy?"

"Virgil Wander."

She sat down next to me in the grass. "I like that. A good unusual name."

Twice in an hour, women I didn't know had complimented my name. Whatever came next, my day was a success. I said, "Thank you. I figure it's like a calling."

"That's probably too much to put on it," said my practical Samaritan.

We didn't talk any more. The clouds had blown off and the stars were out. Orion chased the Seven Sisters. When I was a boy I could pick out all the sisters individually. Now they were a vague patch, like milkweed fuzz. When the fuzz began to rotate like a carousel I shut my eyes. I tried to imagine a center of gravity, something I could grip when things spun too fast, then wondered what would happen if I just let go. How far would I fly? Would it hurt to land, or would I be all right? Lying under the quilt I opened my hands. For a man named Wander I'd spent a long time in one place.

10

IT WAS ACTUALLY NADINE WHO SHOWED UP. BJORN STAYED BEHIND to run the Empress. Tickets, popcorn, projection, the whole buffet—I missed the evening but it seems he thrived, even traipsing down front to introduce the picture for twenty paying customers. When someone called out, Where's Virgil? Bjorn said, He went off the road again. They all roared and Bjorn said, No, really.

The Samaritan left when Nadine arrived. My left shoulder was dislocated, the arm dangling a foot below normal when I lurched up out of the grass. In the headlights my thrown shadow was more than half chimp. The sloped shoulder, the low-hanging knuckles—Nadine turned briskly away, I thought to spare herself the grotesquerie but really to spare my feelings. She helped me into the Wagoneer where I lowered my arm between the seats. The hand was palm-up and oddly distant. I moved the fingers and they waved back like homesick colonists. Nadine saw this and put her forehead against the steering wheel. She shook with laughter.

"I'm delighted this is great for you," I said. It was nice to hear her laugh, though. In fact she had difficulty stopping—she'd straighten, clear her throat, check the rearview, set foot on clutch, then glimpse my faraway dismal gorilla hand and go to pieces again.

"I'm sorry," she said, getting hold of herself. "That shoulder's going to tighten up. It'll be hard to set."

She was right. I could feel the bereft socket deliberating, consolidating its losses.

Still, I wished she would laugh some more.

"Why didn't you call an ambulance?"

"Because I am tired and stupid. I was hoping to avoid the ER."

Switching on the dome light she looked me over critically. There lay my hand down by the stick shift. She said, "I might be able to reconcile that joint of yours."

"Seriously."

"No guarantees, but yes. Maybe. Bjorn dislocated his shoulder when he was twelve. We were out West and he fell off a horse. After that it started happening every few months. I got pretty good at popping it back in."

"I'm game."

We got out of the car. I sat on the front bumper with my back against the grill. The headlights were blinding so she put on the fog lamps instead. Bending at the waist she took hold of my left wrist and straightened my arm at the elbow, shifting it experimentally.

"Can I ask what you were doing, racing downhill on an antique ten-speed at dusk?"

I told her about Rune, the scarlet Citroën, Lucy Yellowjacket walking out of the gloom.

"You're getting some language back," she smiled. "Sounds like you felt uncomfortable up there. Got on your bike and rode away."

"You're never too old to repeat junior high."

"And you hit, what, a pothole? Loose rock?"

I described the mink sliding out of the grass. Nadine sat beside me on the bumper. In the fog-lamp glow her years were visible. The shadowed crease between her brows, her scribed cheekbones, the faint veiny delta of her temple. *Drawn* is an adjective meaning careworn, but Nadine looked drawn in the verb sense too—as though the slight softening of her cheek, the swanlike parentheticals at her mouth were the careful work of pencils or charcoal. I'd long thought of her as an unfading Penelope, but that was the lazy eye of infatuation. In truth she'd aged more than the decade elapsed since Alec disappeared. Yet somehow the years revealed her strength. Like a willow she turned all weathers to advantage.

. While I mused on this she stood, took my arm, and made a simple firm upward motion. There was a moist pop in my shoulder. Radiant warmth eased through my whole arm, right down into the fingers.

Nadine said, "That'll be a thousand dollars."

I stood up carefully—you'd expect some residual pain, but no. She brushed her hands as if saying *Job done*. I said, "Can I buy you dinner?"

We went to the Wise Old because neither of us wanted the glaring lights of the Agate, or the regulars at the Shipwreck. Most of the tavern's lights were turned off but the kitchen was open and we took a booth by a latticed window looking out at the parking lot with its soft blue snow piling up. Lou brought out a loaf of sourdough and a plate of cheese. He mentioned the fisherman's stew, the hot spiced wine he brewed every winter with cloves and lemon peel. We ordered everything he suggested.

What we talked about I remember less than the atmosphere of promise. No one else was there, just Lou in the back, occasionally stepping out with refills and samples of dessert, pleased, it seemed, to see two people he liked smiling in each other's company. His surly charm made us laugh, though quietly, in keeping with the low lights and thickening snow; and while Nadine's auburn hair and pretty lines and low confident voice were right up front, what persisted for me was her equilibrium, her loyalty to Bjorn, her choice of words and expenditures of silence. It seemed significant to discover she'd lived a stormy girlhood about which I'd never heard a word, with parents neither more sensible nor less loving than my own. I think there was an interlude where we sat looking at the snow, instead of saying things, maybe for quite a while, and that Lou stayed back and let us have the place. At some point I craned around and noticed that the graceful sign Alec had made—the owl in flight—was no longer illuminated. It was lit as usual when we first came in. Lou must have switched it off.

When I looked back at Nadine she was leaning slightly forward, studying me as though I were absorbing, or disquieting, or tragic—that is, as though I were someone else entirely. I was happy then to have flown off the Schwinn.

"What's this you're turning into, Virgil? Come on—you're turning into something."

"I don't know. Some beat-up version, maybe. Whatever I say you should pay it no mind."

"That sounds like a disclaimer."

"It might be."

"I get the same deal, then. No judgment. Whatever I say, forget it immediately."

"Deal." I felt offhand and daring. What *was* I turning into? And what might she divulge that begged forgetting? Tingly questions at this hour, with snow purling at the window and spiced wine surging in my veins.

At this juncture, however, Nadine's cell phone rang—Bjorn was done at the Empress, how was Mr. Wander, when would she be home?—after which we seemed to have nothing worth disclaiming. Each of us settled back. I suppose we took stock. She fell into talk about the business—Alec's business, which she had stepped into and was good at but did not love. She asked did I love the Empress and I confessed I did. Despite the building's porous roof and inverse profits it remained a pleasure to spool up a tale for whatever handful of souls on a given night. It still felt useful. Frame by frame a hard moment could be endured because the next was always rolling in. The next might sweep you up.

She said, "Virgil, is there something you want to ask me?"

There very much was, but first there was a matter to address. "I invoke the disclaimer."

"Go ahead."

"Do you think Alec is alive?"

She sank back. "Well nobody knows, do they? I'm tired of it, though. Everything's unfinished. Nothing's ever done."

"I'm sorry about that, but the question is not unfair."

"No. The sightings threw me for a while. Journalists would phone me up. Alec's in Winnipeg, Alec's in Vancouver. After a while they passed the job along to an intern. You could hear how mortified they were."

I wanted to leave it there, but couldn't. "So you believe Alec is dead."

Her brows lifted.

I said, "What you think matters to me."

"I see that. Well, dead doesn't seem precisely the word, does it, for what he is." She looked away, then back to me. "But yes. Probably. He flew out over the water. Little plane made of plywood and cloth. I could lift the tail myself."

"All the same," I said. "Search turned up nothing. There's always the chance."

"Right, the chance." Nadine looked at me, a little unfocused. The day was wearing us down. An insistent ache returned to my shoulder, reminding me of the hour.

Lou ran my Visa card while Nadine went out to start the Jeep. Crossing into the city limits we saw Lily Pea in her snowplow surging toward the municipal lot. Other than that no cars were out. Main Street under the lights was an Arctic island chain. Nadine pulled up in front of the Empress to let me off.

"Thanks for dinner," she said.

"Thanks for mending the shoulder."

"You'll want to move carefully the next few days."

"Nadine, there's something I want to ask you."

"Nope," she said. "Nope, not now. It was a promising evening but I'm tired. The disclaimer is no longer in force."

"I'll ask another time."

"You should do that." As I stepped out of the car she said, "Virgil."

"Yes."

"Don't forget. Honestly, don't wait too long. It's possible to wait too long." She gave me a weary, lovely glance. "Maybe you know that already."

11

I LET MYSELF IN SLOWLY. RUNE, I'D LEARNED, WAS A LIGHT SLEEPER and fellow insomniac—more than once I'd risen in the small hours to find him standing at the window, watching stars or distant freighters. But he wasn't there now and his door was shut. The apartment was unlit save for the skewed Bakelite wall sconce which threw a drowsy corona. I went to the fridge, poured milk into a pan, lit a match, and got down vanilla and sugar.

I was past tired and wanted to think about Nadine, who'd smiled so easily and answered my intrusive questions and perhaps believed I was not a bore. I wanted to think about the way she said *Don't wait too long* and what this meant or did not mean.

The hot milk cooled and grew a skin. I poured it out, noticing now that the kitchen table was covered with Rune's kite-making tackle—usually fastidious, Rune had left things in a heap.

I looked for a completed kite but saw none. As though on cue the door to the roof-deck opened wide and Rune came gusting in.

"You are home! Come out on the roof, come on!"

He wore his straw hat and long-tailed coat with glistening buttons and snowcapped shoulders.

"Did you think I was sleeping? Did you think I would leave such a mess? But I'll get it later. Come on!" He plucked my coat from the chair and lobbed it my way.

"It's two in the morning," I said, but was glad to see him, glad for the disturbance and his startling energy. Out he went onto the roof. The lawn chair was covered with snow except for a dark blot like a large teakettle. The blot had a round shining eye. The raven rustled its feathers and gave a truculent tut.

My eyes adjusted slowly to the cobalt glow cast by signs and streetlamps. The snow came in smokelike squalls from the south. I saw a string tied to the deck rail rising out of sight.

"Here is a secret," Rune said. "To fly at night in the snow is the best of all. Have a spin."

I untied the string from the railing and held it tight. It's strange to fly a kite you can't see. Even more than usual it seems you've caught a living creature, sometimes fighting, sometimes singing. Soon I felt Greenstone fall away. The snow came in lighter and lighter plumes. The string buzzed sleepily. I was quiet and happy and aloft. Rune scratched up a flame and pulled it down into his pipe. I said, "What is it?"

"What's what?"

"The kite. I can't see it. What's the design?"

He was distracted and didn't answer the question, instead remarking, "Lucy DuFrayne is a splendid woman."

"In what way?"

He told me some things he had learned in a few hours of kite flying with Lucy—her jazz career ended when nobody bought her second album; her first and only marriage had yielded triplets, two girls and a boy, now scattered down the West Coast in assorted nonprofits and lost causes; her husband, a sound engineer and rash optimist, had succumbed to pancreatic cancer—it took him fast. Now Lucy was come to Greenstone for the first time in twenty years to visit her cousin, Adam Leer, whom she'd not seen in even longer.

"Lucy is sixty-four," Rune said. "Sixty-four, and Virgil, she believes her best years are still coming."

I admitted that was pretty splendid.

"Do you think the hour is late?" he mused.

"Late for what?"

"For me. Time is not the friend it was. You've seen what happens. I could dissolve any moment. Maybe the hour is late."

I looked him over. His face had not slid downhill—my own felt gravity pulling, yet his was smooth and lit by snow. "I suspect the hour is fine."

At this he took the reel from my numb fingers and played out a good bit of line. He meant to fly a while. The raven shook snow off its back. I plodded to the door and turned to say, "Nadine is splendid too."

He didn't answer. No doubt he was too caught up. I could hear the kite rattling above in the dark snowy puffs but still couldn't see it—in fact I never knew which kite I flew that night, and Rune refused to tell me, insisting it was a curious privilege, one he himself had never experienced, to fly without so much as a glimpse or perception of the wing.

maximum ceiling

1

THIS WAS EARLY IN RUNE'S PERIOD OF FEVERISH CREATION. HE DROVE
to Duluth and returned with dowels and epoxies, brushes and rice paper,
ten shades of ripstop, a wild carousel of paints. The shortening days
made him sunny and voluble, framing up his wings while admiring the
icy squalls speeding to and fro over Superior. The apartment's broad
field of east-facing windows made the Empress as good for watching
weather as movies. Like most Greenstonians I took pride in our grim
conditions, but Rune good-heartedly mocked them.

"This is nothing—you still have light," he pointed out. "It still
gets light in the morning, and stays light until late afternoon."

I hadn't thought about that. Except for lovestruck '64, Rune had
spent every winter above the Arctic Circle. In his boyhood village north
of Tromsø, the sun fell into bed in November and didn't crawl out again
until February. "Twelve weeks lit only by stars," he said, with grim
frivolity. "And the moon, of course, two or three planets, the borealis.
There is a small twilight at midday, but really it is night for two months."

"It sounds magnificent," I admitted—I knew about the dark
far-north winters, but only from tenth-grade science, the Discovery
Channel, and my hazy reading. It's hard to explain, but the very fact of
a two-month night made me long to endure one myself.

Rune smiled. He said at first you scarcely noticed the sun was
gone, the days were so short by then. Further in, it got strange. Dogs

normally friendly frothed at your passing. It was said by children that empty houses became occupied by minor devils and that big fish patrolled the shoreline, beguiling the friendless. There were quarrels and disappearances. Rune remembered a pair of American university researchers, a married couple studying the psychological weight of the long dark. They carried notebooks and were overly friendly. By spring the husband had fled for the dusty sunlight of Spain and the wife was ensconced with a Nordic sculptor who'd lost half a hand in the cannery.

If many of Rune's stories had a fable-like atmosphere, the kites he constructed during these weeks were also fabulous. One looked like a stained-glass window, another a cloudberry pie. One had the body and motion of a sixteen-foot catfish—low over the water it grazed, as though it had lately evolved levitational properties, long barbels streaming down into the lake. He built a fireplace kite with a crooked brick chimney and flames of loose orange that flapped in the wind; its flying companion was an overstuffed armchair, its winged back looming oddly forward, as if having just tipped an unwary sitter into the fire.

All this building and talking and flying made me homesick. It wasn't logical, since I was at home, but that's what I came to perceive—a fulminant ache high in the rib cage, a sense of time's shortening fuse. After the first accident, it had felt as though my apartment belonged to someone else; after the second, I began to feel as though there *was* a home I belonged to, and this one, though pleasant and likable, wasn't it. The previous tenant would've rejected such nonsense, but then the previous tenant never had an eccentric foreign houseguest, sewing up artworks to hang in the sky, talking to ravens, spinning twilit Arctic stories. My weary old ground was broken and watered, and what sprang up was a generalized longing. I began to feel like a character myself, well-meaning but secondary, a man introduced late in the picture. I wished to spool back and watch earlier scenes, to scout for hints and shadows, clues as to what might be required of a secondary actor when the closing reel began.

Lydia was right—it turned out Bob Dylan did remember Greenstone. So said his West Coast booking agent the day she finally called back.

The first time we spoke I'd told her about the singer's personal connection with our mayor, which made her laugh in a way that made me think we had a shot. The agent had then contacted Dylan, whose curt reply was a memory of driving through en route to Thunder Bay in 1964—he got a flat tire on Main Street, unloaded guitars to reach the spare, jacked up the car, and made the switch only to blow another tire half a block later. While the service station fixed the second flat he went to a café and ordered a meat pasty. Inside the pasty was a thumb-size sliver of dark brown beer-bottle glass. That was his Greenstone story. Apparently he wrote a song about it. I don't know which one.

"So he won't come back?" I asked. "Surely we could expunge that old verse, and give him something glad to remember."

"I have to tell you," she said, sounding pained, "he'd really just rather not."

I went into Lydia's office. She stood at the window in a low frame of mind. An inch of snow had fallen overnight and it slithered around over the icy parking lot. "Dylan can't make it," I told her.

"Oh well," she said. Lydia wasn't someone to dwell on bummers, but her eyes turned glossy and large.

In the wake of this letdown we had an impromptu powwow. Lydia was determined to settle on a theme for the festival. She called in Ann Fandeen—a *concept gal,* she said—and also veteran councilman Barrett Becker whom she regarded as an ally. Ann entered the office with enormous energy—she wore a dress the shape and color of a chili pepper, and a fanlike gold necklace. Her ideas were appealing: she'd learned of a traveling accordion orchestra that played for twinkle-light dances; a retired ore-boat that could be hired to tie up at our dock and give tours; a former circus elephant that had learned to hold a paintbrush and now did freelance caricatures for twenty dollars a throw.

Barrett Becker listened in silence. He'd recently had a number of precancerous moles removed from his face and scalp. While Ann spoke, his fingers wandered from lesion to lesion, seeking out loosening scabs.

Ann said, "What's the problem, Barrett?"

"Liability," he replied. He swiveled his big pitted head to pin Ann with his eyes. "An elephant is no respecter of persons. Accordions draw lightning. This is Greenstone—your dance-hall ship will probably sink at the pier."

Lydia looked stricken. First we had lost her friend Dylan. Now Barrett Becker, for decades a reliable booster, showed up tossing grenades. She said, "Let's table this."

But something was coming to Ann Fandeen. You could see it happening. She said, "Hold up a minute."

"What now," said the dispirited mayor.

"Barrett, you're exactly right," Ann said. "Greenstone is cursed. We had mines, but they shut. Ships used to dock, now they sail past. Our water tower comes loose and rolls over people, our congressman gets leprosy, Bob Dylan drives through and gets two flat tires." Ann glowed as the idea coalesced—she couldn't have been more incandescent if she'd physically caught fire. "Hard luck! *That's* our legacy. You know it's true, Lydia. It's a dreadful one, but it's all we've got."

"It wasn't leprosy, Ernie got psoriasis," Lydia said. The former congressman was a longtime friend. "What are you suggesting, exactly?"

"Hard Luck Days," said Ann. "That's our festival. We take the one thing Greenstone is known for and ride it as hard as we can."

"What would this look like?" said Barrett, interested at last.

Ann threw out a few notions—a parade along the path of the rogue water tower, a submarine lowering tourists to the bones of a sunken ship. Excitement made Ann even shinier as Lydia paled at the cheekbones. I felt bad for her—Lydia had a strong utopian impulse. She didn't want to preside over an ironic three-day toast to our humiliations.

"Hard *Luck* Days," Barrett mused. His jaw made sideways ruminant motions. "Hard Luck *Days*! Hoo hoo!"

What chance did Lydia have? She never would have said so, but it seemed to me the awful luck of Greenstone had found her, reaching forward in time from a pair of flat tires in 1964.

Barrett took my elbow as we left. "The Sandstrom boy, working for you over at the movies."

"Yes."

"You keep a close eye. He's damaged. Goes out in the lake and straddles a plank in the waves. I do not approve."

"He's not damaged," I replied. "He's surfing."

"Don't you contradict me," Barrett said, squeezing my elbow as though I were a problem teenager and himself my petty tyrant. "His dad was unstable and so is the boy. He's trying to kill himself, is what I think."

Abruptly annoyed, I reached for a quick adjective or two in Bjorn's defense—*perceptive* would've filled the bill, or *solitary*, or even just *clever*. I took a breath and searched, trying to picture the word I wanted printed on a page, a trick that sometimes worked. The page stayed blank while Barrett glared. Finally I said, with the gruffness of defeat, "You just shouldn't *talk*, sometimes. Can't you see that, Barrett? When you talk, you sound ignorant."

Right away I knew it was bad form to call Barrett ignorant, and probably not without consequence—he stiffened when I said it, and Lydia drooped a little. Barrett wasn't my boss, but we talked at meetings and city events, especially since I started keeping the minutes several years earlier. Barrett was a stickler about the minutes. Things had always gone smoothly between us because I was good at the minutes, and probably also because I hadn't yet called him ignorant. His actual ignorance didn't excuse my bad form. It was my job to put us back on track.

With a clumsy smile I said, "Look—Bjorn made me a staff," offering it for inspection.

"Keep that stick away from me," he barked. "You know, I called the sheriff on that boy. Two different times. 'There's a boy in the lake,' I said. I don't even know what to think about a county sheriff who won't get off his giant butt to drag a disturbed boy out of a freezing lake. Don Lean—how did he get that job?"

"He got elected," I reminded him, "twice," but Barrett didn't hear me. We had just stepped out of the building. The setting sun got him right in the eyes. He swatted at it bitterly.

2

WHATEVER ELSE HE MIGHT BE, BJORN SANDSTROM WAS GOOD FOR business.

Besides being a natural projectionist, he gave movie introductions that were funnier than mine—when he stood onstage gaunt and pallid it was impossible not to smile along. The girls in particular liked him, Lanie Plume and her friends, and there was another girl, with lank hair and passerine eyes, who sat by herself a row or two back of the others and seemed not to breathe while he spoke. Going over the books I saw we averaged almost five more tickets per night than in the same month a year earlier. It was marvelous timing—between fuel costs and the autumn doldrums, November is stark for the Empress.

Still, I had to admit old Councilman Barrett wasn't entirely wrong. There *was* something damaged about Bjorn. Increasingly he seemed distracted. His shoulders folded in upon each other; you could see his slow pulse in his temples. I say this as a damaged man—so often adrift myself, I could see him drifting away.

On our first night of truly dangerous wintertime cold, Bjorn abruptly went missing.

He'd just screened a little Jack Black comedy about amateur bird-watchers. He'd rewound the film, put the booth in order, then come down and tallied receipts while I swept the auditorium. Attendance was light so there wasn't much to sweep, although someone did squirm around for two hours on an unwrapped Baby Ruth, so that took a bit of time. When I reentered the lobby Bjorn was gone. He'd left nothing undone, even turned off all the lights except the Bogart neon, which I always douse last.

Still, the lobby felt wrong. It wasn't like Bjorn to leave without letting me know.

I killed the Bogart and marquee, checked the locks, and climbed upstairs. It was almost eleven. My disturbance wasn't logical—a young man needn't say good night to his boss. Yet I was edgy. Rune had turned in and fallen asleep, his light snores emerging from the guest room. I stood at the window watching a fast scrim of clouds obscure the stars, then took my Army-surplus parka from the closet. Back downstairs I wheeled the Schwinn out the alley entrance. Marcus Jetty had welded the burst fork and found me a new front wheel.

The alley was a wind tunnel. Later the talk was all about the freakish cold pouring down out of Alberta, engulfing the unwary; all I knew was that my eyes watered and lips numbed as I stood in the alley. I zipped up the fox-fur hood. A cardboard box bounded past like sagebrush in the gloom. I strapped the quarterstaff to the bike so it stuck out in front like a lance. Streetlamps quivered on their poles, my tires skidded this way and that. I turned out of the alley and rode up to Main and didn't see Bjorn or anything else alive.

Surely he just went home.

Three blocks north I turned left into residential Greenstone. Bjorn and Nadine lived in a neat squat bungalow with a wide Russian olive tree in front. The leafless tree flailed. The porch flood and lights inside were on. Nadine stood looking out the picture window. She wore a heavy knitted sweater and had a coffee cup in her left hand. You could tell from its angle the cup was empty.

She had the door open before I got up the porch. By the time I said, "He's not here?" she was getting her coat on.

I'm not sure how long we drove around. The Wagoneer got warm, so long enough. I suggested we call Don Lean but Nadine said not yet. First we tried places where she'd hunted down Bjorn before—the ore dock; two of Bjorn's favorite surf haunts; the giant abandoned Slake edifice, where he'd broken in once and been fetched by a lecturing deputy. We came close at the bowling alley. The owner, Vera Ness, said he'd come in ninety minutes ago but didn't stay. It was glow-in-the-dark-bowling night and the place was full of church youth groups, the last hope of small-town operators. "He took a seat over there." Vera pointed. "Under the pizza sign—his dad built that sign, you know," she added to me in a whisper.

This gave Nadine an idea. We got back in the car and drove to the Shipwreck. The tavern had two signs of Alec's—the seascape he'd repaired, and a handsome blue rowboat with a white-bearded fisherman in it. Inside we quickly ascertained Bjorn wasn't there. "Shoot, no," said the proprietor, Lester Billings. "And you can't find him? I'm all yours, Nadine."

While she spoke to Lester I went outside. Wind went up the back of my coat. I tucked in my hands and walked round to the back.

There sat Bjorn on an overturned recycling bin. He held a lit cigarette in bare fingers and was leaning against the siding. Pale light fell on him from a window above. I hadn't seen him smoke before. It made him look younger and awfully sad.

"Hey," I said.

"Hey, Mr. Wander." He looked surprised to see me, but not unhappy.

"You doing okay?"

"Sure."

Nothing seemed like the right thing to say, so that's what I said for a while.

"I would've gone home pretty soon," he told me.

"We got a little worried with the dirty weather."

"Is Mom with you?"

"She is."

He sat there looking regretfully at the cigarette. The clouds had layered up over the moon. You could just make out waves racing parallel to the shore—their crests rushed forward like blown yellow paper, subsided, gathered up, and rushed again.

I started for the parking lot but Bjorn stayed put. Turning I saw he was sitting in the glow of the sign his dad had built—the neon fisherman in the rowboat was visible through the window. Bjorn said, "Hey, you're using the staff."

"I take it everywhere. People fear it. There are restaurants that won't let me in." Bjorn grinned at this. It was a relief to see.

He got up and walked down to the water. Moving away from the window he seemed to lose form. His arms and legs became part of the night. Not much was left of him except the sound of his shoes on the loose round stones, the glowing dot of tobacco at the edge of his wavery shape. He seemed to dissipate like a note of music. The thought occurred that Nadine might come round the corner of the Shipwreck, only to see Bjorn recede altogether from hearing and sight.

Then he must've bent for a rock and flung it—the rock briefly shone before plunking into the face of a rolling wave.

Watching him there, immaterial at moments, made me think of his dad—he wasn't as tall as Alec, but seemed taller from being so thin. Like the cigarette, his gangly limbs rendered him younger; there was so much play in his joints they barely held him together. In fact the longer we stayed the less he reminded me of Alec and the more of Galen Pea, another boy who seemed stranded somehow. I was no one's protector nor ever had been, yet standing behind the Wreck, peering out from my furry hood at Bjorn's hovering self, an unfamiliar burden settled on my shoulders. I shifted on my feet; there was actual weight. An adjective bloomed and it was *answerable*. The yellow-crested waves surged past under the clotted sky. The lake looked cold and violent. I gripped the quarterstaff. It was nice to have but it was only a stick. Anything could happen and I was small security.

The orange speck arced from Bjorn's hand and was gone. A moment later Nadine's voice called, very distant behind the waves. "Bjorn? Are you here?"

His shoes scuffed on the rocks—he assumed form again as he neared. I offered him a pack of breath mints from my pocket. He shook one into his palm and passed them back.

"Virgil?" Nadine called, coming around the corner.

Seeing him she ran lightly over the stones. Bjorn went to meet her—he seemed glad, a little sheepish even, bending down to let her hug him. She kissed his neck and looked at me over his shoulder. I remember that look, that bright liquid smile. I smiled back. Solid and self-possessed is how I felt, like a man with work to do—in other words, useful for once.

After this I began to keep closer tabs on Bjorn. I gave him more jobs at the Empress—had him repaint the auditorium in a two-toned scheme, seafoam and mahogany, which took nine afternoons and attenuated my budget. I showed him the tiny dust pyramids that kept growing on the carpet and asked him to discover their origins. Whatever I requested he was happy to do, and yet he was distracted. He flickered and blinked. When a person is gripped by a fugue or idea you can't just busy him out of it, not for long anyway. What I wanted was something to engage him.

In the end he came up with an idea himself.

It was a Friday afternoon and he'd just laced up the next week's film, which was *Midnight in Paris*. Everyone has their favorite Woody Allens and mine are the ones without Woody in them. With time on his hands, Bjorn had previewed a good chunk of *Midnight*—it has a wistful allure.

"I know you're about to give up your stash of old movies," he said, coming down into the lobby where I stood at the window with a cotton rag, wiping out a late hatch of slow-moving flies.

"That's the idea."

He nodded. "I wonder if we could screen a few. Just a few of the good ones, right? Before they go forever."

That's how we reinvented the after-parties. We started small. The first night Nadine brought a lasagna in a quilted bag. Rune arrived with his windburned face, and Bjorn took projection as though the job were his all along. He'd picked out *The Ladykillers*, from 1955. Alec Guinness is a con man with mule teeth, leaning in the shadows. His nemesis is everyone's snowy grandma whose wily innocence is her sword and shield. You could fret all day and not choose a better picture—with its music-box opening and EALING STUDIOS in jiggly letters you don't expect much. What you get is sly as Bergman but with less freight, and more fun to think about later.

Honestly, if Bjorn had pulled out a dog—and there were plenty of those in the vault—the whole thing might've derailed. I like a terrible movie as well as anyone, but people need to know going in if you're cuing up *Muscle Beach Party*. On the other hand, *Ladykillers* filled us first with relief and then with mushrooming joy. Nadine seized my shoulder whenever Mrs. Wilberforce thwarted the robbers; Rune unleashed a gusty chuckle. Bjorn said later he "didn't buy in right away" but by the end was bobbing and quaking in his seat.

After that the old band more or less reconstituted, with several new faces of course. Lucy DuFrayne, now flying with Rune almost every day, appeared in a fedora and turned-up collar she seemed born to wear, kissing Rune who blushed happily, pretending it was nothing. Don Lean showed up with an anxious expression and his ex-wife Marcie whom he was trying to win back. Tom Beeman appeared laughing as though this whole business had never stopped—he even landed a new girlfriend for the occasion, Connie Swale, a displaced hippie from a cannabis ranch outside Beaver Bay. In the old days I used to worry over the number of people who knew of the vault and its contents. This time around it didn't matter. Soon Bjorn invited someone, a girl named Ellen Tripp whom I recognized as the waif sitting behind Lanie Plume's posse at the Empress. Just a kid of fifteen, Nadine told me—got pregnant last year and had an abortion, lost all her friends and her folks kicked her out, although she was back with them now. Ellen was working things through. One week she'd show up plain as a hymnal, eyes cast down and her hair yanked back; the next she arrived in glitter and paint, short and bright as a puffin. Regardless of dress her most piercing weapon was a smile that burst out when least expected, as though too much to contain. Inside of five minutes we all adored her.

In fact Ellen ended up choosing most of our movies. Bjorn wanted to show her the vault and I couldn't think why not. Ellen was no cinephile and didn't need to be one. She loved the clandestine trea-sure-cave vibe, the tarnished gleam of the canisters under the humming bulb. Falling hard for poetic titles, she selected accordingly—bypassing *Spartacus*, for example, in favor of *Splendor in the Grass*. There are better movies but if you're choosing by title that one's hard to beat.

Conscious as we were—a few of us, at least—that the after-parties constituted an epilogue of sorts, we did our best to make them count. They grew rapidly into prodigal feasts. We laid a painted door across two saw-horses for a table. Regular lasagnas were accompanied by loaves of Rune's bread—he brought them down so hot from the oven they sat crackling as they cooled. Tom bought pies from Betsy Shane, usually three, one being raisin which Tom would devour himself. Don's former wife Marcie went full-on with quiches and tarts and one time a whole chicken braised in red wine, which changes the common bird forever. We ate before the show or during it; stood up or sat down in the ruinous seats; talked through the pictures or gave in to their spell. Ellen often climbed up to sit with Bjorn in projection, but the crux of her orbit was Nadine, who treated her like Bjorn's provisional girlfriend. Certainly Bjorn was alert around Ellen, attentive and funny, doubtful with his hands, but it was also clear she spooked him, herself seeming thirty one minute and twelve the next but rarely the fifteen she was. Sometimes she took his arm and held tight while not talking, not even glancing at his face.

Meantime our undisclosed parties became ever more disclosed. There isn't much to do in Greenstone—word was bound to get out. One night after the regular show a woman in a puffy down jacket skulked under the neon Bogart. "Why, Julie," I said—outside her usual context, the Agate Café, I didn't know her at first.

"I heard you're showing classics in secret," she said in a rush.

"When the urge strikes, and for a limited time. You're welcome to join us. Most of them aren't really classics, though."

Next to inquire was Lily Pea, who came to my office asking about the "midnight showings" and why she hadn't been invited. A week or two later Nadine sent her a text, and that night she arrived with a chocolate cake for a screening of *I, the Jury*. Galen came too—he seemed to enjoy the lurid vigilante plot.

In this way people poked and stumbled and demanded their way in. What does it say about Greenstone's social famine that goofy unadvertised cinema could rouse any interest at all? Sometimes we got a bigger crowd at the after-parties than at the legitimate screenings beforehand.

Maybe they sensed that beyond the films and feasts, the Empress had begun to feel like a shelter, even an ark. Rain and sleet fell throughout the autumn, sometimes clearing for an hour so Rune could fly. Greenstone was inundated with water and distressed animals. We had a vole explosion when the rodents left flooded warrens for high ground. On their scrabbling heels came weasels and mink. I had a near miss with an unhinged raccoon—Genghis, I'm fairly sure. I'd seized a lull in the weather and got out the Schwinn. The raccoon was turning half circles under a streetlight, clawing the air without conviction. As I neared we made eye contact. Out came his bright little fangs. I swerved in a wide arc but Genghis led me and made a close play of it. I'll never forget the sound of those clickety teeth. Day after day the lake rose up. Fish gasped in the storm drains. The black rain throbbed on the Empress roof and seeped in to zigzag down fresh-painted walls. Drops gathered on the tin ceiling and fell with pebble velocity—Beeman took a big one on his bald spot and it sounded like cracking a whip. We set out buckets and wastebaskets and kept the ark mainly dry while the world outside, like Noah's, got more savage by the day.

You can imagine how good it felt to welcome a loosely joined crew into the warm old Empress.

One night Galen Pea, not much intrigued with the Rock Hudson movie whose title had beguiled Ellen (*Pretty Maids All in a Row*), leaned forward from the seat behind and whispered to me. The dark days and rising waters had Greenstone on edge, and lately Galen had been repeating whoppers picked up from his nine-year-old classmates—an alligator on the loose, a human hand in the gutter. This time he said he had seen the big sturgeon again. In fact he'd seen it three nights running, down at the river's mouth. The great murdering fish wouldn't take his bait but still it kept coming and showing itself, ten minutes or so before sundown.

"Come down tomorrow," he said. "Bet you anything it'll be there. Come down and see it yourself."

I told him I would.

One night, with a picture spooled up and the back table loaded like an Italian kitchen, somebody rapped hard at the lobby glass. It was Jerry Fandeen.

I unlocked and waved him in. "Jerry, it's your lucky night. We're showing *Cobra Woman*."

"That sounds terrible," Jerry said forthrightly.

I was still getting used to the sight of him. He'd dropped at least twenty pounds. He'd got some new clothes and they fitted. His face had the lines and hollows of a sobriety not associated with Jerry Fandeen.

"It isn't as bad as you think. You're welcome to join us if you like—otherwise, how can I help you?"

"What are those spices?" Jerry said. I couldn't help noticing the neutrality of his voice. Even out here in the lobby the aroma was alluring, my own mouth watered, but Jerry inquired after spices as if asking the day of the week.

"It's lasagna," I said. "Come in, you're among friends—when is the last time you had a proper lasagna?"

"No thanks, no," he said. "I just came to tell you that Mr. Leer, I work for him now, he's purchased the building across the street."

"Really? Which building?" It won't surprise you that several of them were for sale.

"Hoshaver's." Jerry pointed and I stepped to the door. Sure enough the lights were on in the crumbly brownstone's upstairs apartment. No one had occupied the Hoshaver Building in at least five years.

"That'll be some work then."

"It will," Jerry agreed. "And I'll be doing it. The work."

"What are his plans for the place?" I was remembering Leer's offer to buy the Empress, his easy assumption I would leap at the money, his hardening skin when I didn't.

"I don't know," Jerry said. "I guess we'll both see. He got a good deal on the building."

Jerry stood in the lobby clothed in his strange new dignity. His shoulders were straight, hands clasped at his belt, and he looked at my face without blinking. There was a long moment during which he seemed a vacancy himself. Then a plaintive light came into his eyes and he said, "If it's all right I'll stop by this week. I might need to borrow a few more tools. Would that be all right, Virgil? If I borrowed some tools? Now that we're going to be neighbors?"

3

NEXT MORNING THE PHONE RANG AND A MAN INTRODUCED HIMSELF as Fergus Flint. He had a deep, tired, hoarse voice—not my image of the Hollywood lawyer. He sounded honest and weary. Orry trusted him. I decided to trust him, too.

"Thanks for calling. Orry speaks well of you."

"Your sister's one of a kind," Fergus said. "I'm told you have a stack of old films to repatriate."

"One hundred seventy reels."

He let the number pass without comment. "Up front let me say I will represent your interests without fee in this matter if that is what you'd like."

"Without fee? Does Orry have something enormous on you?"

"In fact yes. Dinesh got my wife Celia out of a sickening mess a few years ago in Somalia. This one is on me."

"I appreciate it."

"Obviously I can't promise a particular outcome. It would be my intent to see you relieved of the materials with no penalty to yourself. Whatever you say to me would be confidential. I would rely on you for similar discretion. Do you accept my representation or do you wish to think about it further?"

"I accept."

"Start at the beginning."

I did. It didn't take long. Fergus himself was no fan of movies but excused this saying he'd worked in some capacity for most major studios and was steeped in "the culture," which meant you took what was said and expected its opposite.

"Your caution sounds Midwestern," I told him.

"I aspire to the Midwest."

"Don't be fooled by our modest dress, we're surprisingly devious."

"Even I have seen *Fargo*, and it isn't your modesty I admire. It's your solitude. I never imagined such luxury, then one time instead of flying I rented a car and drove to New York. Everybody said I'd hate the northern plains, but I never wanted them to end. An old man fishing in a drainage ditch in North Dakota—catching big pike, ten or twelve pounds, sleeping in a tin camper, can of beans for lunch. What a life. I told Ceci when we retire it's off to North Dakota. She doesn't think I mean it. I probably don't. I'll need a complete list of the films along with any documentation you have."

We didn't talk much longer. He knew people in the legal departments of most of the studios; he was "dialed in" at the universities and the American Film Institute. It was going to take some time. He assumed I was nervous about showing my hand and reassured me that my worries were most likely groundless. He said, "No one's going to jail here, my friend." Studios had become more forgiving. Sometimes they even thanked the person who had kept whatever artifact safe these many years. I mentioned the collector in *Cinematique* who'd got in touch with the studio about his stolen epic, a story Fergus knew well.

"That's the thing about the business. It can go either way or no way. Nobody knows anything," he said, a theory of Hollywood I had encountered before.

Before hanging up he asked how the films had ended up at the Empress in the first place. I gave him the name Edgar Poe gave me— Bill Plate, William Plate, who had run the theater in the 1960s before moving to Chicago. "William Plate," he said, typing it slowly. "Let's throw this in the pond and see what nibbles."

*   *   *

I stayed away from City Hall that afternoon. There wasn't much to do there, and I didn't feel up for Lydia's notes about the festival. I didn't feel, either, like enduring Ann, who the previous day had left an ecstatic note of her own—she'd "seized the initiative," driven the LeSabre out to Leer's where he agreed after "extremely vigorous" haggling to "keynote our springtime event."

I didn't want Leer to keynote anything. On the other hand, I admired Ann for bagging a speaker—one less duty for me.

The lights were on in the Hoshaver Building, so I crossed the street for a look. I always liked the Hoshaver—it has a grandiose brownstone façade, inlaid turquoise ceramics, and Greenstone's only gargoyles. Jerry Fandeen was inside spreading drop cloths in what had been the main retail space. He saw me at the window and beckoned.

"I got straight to work," he said, offering a look around.

I hadn't been inside for a decade. Jerry pointed out where plaster was cracked or water had seeped. Light swam in through the large foggy windows and stayed low in the room. There's no real color in that kind of light—a big red fire extinguisher stood in one corner and I knew it was red only because it was the shape of a fire extinguisher. The room induced a mild unearthly vertigo. My staff echoed as I thumped around.

"I remember when this was a dime store," Jerry said. "They had baby turtles."

That was before my time but even so it was easy to picture the Hoshaver as a Woolworths or Ben Franklin, crammed with socks and toys, a soda fountain, Big Chief tablets, parakeets, goldfish. In the late sixties Chevy came in and made it a dealership with wide showroom windows, but by the time I arrived the building had cycled through lives as a cut-rate department store, used-clothing outlet, and realty office, and was at that moment losing its pulse as an antique co-op selling Depression glass and Mylar-sleeved comics. Later an audacious coffee shop opened, but it was 1988 and Greenstone wasn't buying. I was there one morning when a soft-spoken gentleman sipped his first espresso and politely requested a refund, whispering *It's real strong* to the sunken-eyed proprietor. After that the Hoshaver stood empty except for a brief occupation by rapture cultists who drove up in a bus from

Missouri and moved in with their futons and slow-cookers. I was curious because the bus had a battered "I Found It!" bumper sticker similar to the one on my parents' car long ago. The cult people were anxious to tell you what they had found, which was the news, somehow blissful, that the world was soon to end. They were friendly and lonesome. To make money they sold homemade soap and pencil drawings of Jesus high-fiving plumbers and Indian chiefs and other American regulars. They painted a sign saying EVERYONE WELCOME. They seemed at loose ends. When you poked your head in it didn't smell nice. One night in January, thirty below, the whole group vanished, poof. Nobody saw them leave. It was joked they got raptured along with their bus and their futons.

On Jerry's request I'd gone to the basement that morning and retrieved a few chisels and a sander he seemed likely to need. But he never brought it up. Walking the perimeter of the echoing room he said very little. He seemed isolated and terribly somber. His brown Audi wagon with rusted-out wheel wells crouched in the center of the floor, as if mocking the Hoshaver's dealership days. Propped on the hood was Jerry's to-do list written carefully in wide-tip marker.

1. ~~SERVICE BOILER~~
2. ~~FUEL OIL~~
3. COVER UP THE FLOOR
4. ASSERTAIN LOOSE PLASTER
5. WATER DAMAGE
6. MOVE IN

I said, "What's number six? What are you moving in?"

"Myself," he said. "Just me. You know what, I'm already in—hang on, let me cross that off."

"Why move in here, Jerry?"

His face bobbed slightly.

"Are things not okay with Ann?"

He didn't look at me but took the marker from the pocket of his neat chambray shirt and drew a line through the item. He said, "We made it quite a while, really."

"What happened?"

"A lot, I guess. A lot happened. But it's okay. What she says is, I'm not for her anymore, and so she isn't for me either. She said I ought to move out." Jerry capped the marker and put it in his pocket. His face was turned away. "I've tried to get us back together. I find her things I know she likes. Got her a concrete birdbath, one of those shiny gazing balls for the garden. She likes all that gardening apparatus. She still isn't for me, though."

Rather than say something feeble I stayed quiet. The building was used to quiet. In the gloom above us something took flight—I heard its papery wings. It seemed very hard that Ann wanted Jerry out just as he seemed to be rebooting at last. He looked tremendously sad in the heavy brown Hoshaver shadows. He stood up straighter than usual, which added to his air of sadness. I had never seen him so low before, though I suppose he'd been pretty low after losing hold of himself and driving an earthmoving vehicle over his sleeping friend. His face had dark pockets and troughs which looked like empty places. There were absences in Jerry, things that used to be there but weren't anymore. It was almost as if Jerry were not there at all, as if he'd gone away and been replaced by a sadness that assumed his general shape. His hands hung at his thighs, his breath was deep and steady. There was a sense of him idling as though waiting to be put in gear.

"Where are you sleeping, Jerry?"

He nodded at a door at the rear of the large room. I went and leaned in. It had once been a stockroom or work closet. A twin mattress lay on the floor beside a cast-iron radiator. Two big crates full of rusted bolts and hinges and screws were stacked in a corner. Blankets were heaped on the mattress and a hot plate sat on a metal shelf next to cans of mushroom soup. I became conscious of a caustic rodent smell. There was a scatter of tiny brown pods along the wall.

I asked Jerry if he would join us for supper later. He had such sadness and absence inside, I couldn't think what else to do. He turned me down gracefully. He was pulling long hours and glad for the work. The subject seemed to cheer him. He liked Mr. Leer. Mr. Leer liked him, too. Mr. Leer was nice, and asked his opinion, and wasn't critical of his work. "Never even tells me what to do next," Jerry said. "I just show up, and it's like my head clears. Finish one thing and on to the next. He jokes like I'm reading his mind." Jerry confided that one day Leer took him aside and told him he had "maximum ceiling." Jerry was pleased. He'd never considered his ceiling especially high. Maybe it was once, before his edges got dull and the mine event happened. Still, if Mr. Leer thought his ceiling was high, then maybe it was. A man of Mr. Leer's experience knew a high ceiling when he saw one. Why not? Maybe it was way up there.

I nodded along but was imagining the unbearable picture of Jerry alone in the mouse closet later, heating up mushroom soup. "You sure you won't join us tonight?"

He shook his head. The light was getting dim. The sun backed off earlier every day. Jerry said, "I know you mean well, Virgil."

I did, but so what? When I was growing up in Minnesota's dairy country, we had a neighbor who talked about "old farmer's lung" which many old farmers developed after years breathing hay in the mow. The neighbor's uncle had this condition. It poisoned him bit by bit and he never saw it coming. One day he expired with his lips all blue. The stockroom made my eyes run. I said, "If you're going to sleep in here, at least run an air purifier."

"How come?"

I nodded at the trail of rodent sign along the wall.

"I don't even smell it, no. It's fine."

"I have one I'm not using. A purifier. I'll bring it over."

"Don't, I'm good." Jerry was suddenly distracted by something out the front window. "Hey Virgil, somebody's busting into your place."

I squinted out the window. A figure was indeed trying to jimmy open the door to my stairwell, probably with a credit card. The figure wore heeled boots and a long woolen coat that flared at the bottom. "That's no robber," I said. "It's a mayor."

"Oh, right," Jerry said. He seemed relieved I wasn't being robbed, and also that I was leaving. "Thanks for coming, Virgil, good-bye."

4

LYDIA WASN'T BREAKING IN—SHE WAS ONLY LEAVING A NOTE. IT WAS tucked in an envelope she'd folded twice and was jamming into the door crack.

"Why not just come in?" I asked, startling her as I walked up.

"Virgil! But I don't have much time." She followed me upstairs anyway and stepped in stamping snow off her boots.

"Ann says she talked Adam Leer into speaking at the festival next spring—you must be pleased," I said.

"She surely did," Lydia replied in a subdued tone. "Now I want you to go talk him out of it."

"Out of it? He just got in."

She started to say something but stopped herself. She was strangely skittish. "I want you to rescind the invitation."

"Okay," I said. "I'm going to need a reason."

She didn't want to give one. She stood twisting a pair of black driving gloves in her hands.

"It feels like we're in another bad stretch," she finally allowed.

This was so vague I let the silence go on. When her gloves were a knotted rope she said, "Shad Pea drowned in that dismal river. You almost died too. Even the animals are out of whack. A squirrel got into my furnace, it was horrible. Voles have been reading my mail. Beeman's dumb old raccoon is still out there, biting everything he can catch."

"Why disinvite Leer?"

"Oh God." She scrunched her face together. "You'll say I'm super-stitious. You'll think my hold is slipping."

"I doubt your hold is more tenuous than my own."

"Remember the frog monsoon?" she said.

"In detail."

"Me too," she said, and told about driving home from her daugh-ter's place in Hibbing. Nearing Greenstone she saw a man at the edge of a hayfield, standing still as a column of rocks. As she passed it began to rain. The first frogs struck her roof and windshield with ugly wet thumps. The wipers smeared, a yellow haze came off the earth. Rec-ognizing the man as Leer she slowed, meaning to offer him a ride, but he stayed where he was. In fact he produced an umbrella and popped it open, watching the car with an amused expression while dead and stupefied frogs trampolined in all directions. The image was so indelible she kept it to herself and eventually began to believe it never happened.

"But now that he's agreed to speak I can't get it out of my head," she said. "There we were in the midst of plagues, and he just looked at home."

"Can I ask why you were so anxious to invite him in the first place?"

She looked at me with regret. "Because of his father Spurlock, of course. Finder of iron ore, founder of Greenstone. And Adam *is* a famous director. Or was. And don't we all moderate, with time?"

"Do we?"

"I always thought so, before. So he moved back and I figured, Why not?"

"I'll tell him we're going a different direction."

She sighed. "Am I being foolish? People say he's single-handedly repaired poor Jerry Fandeen. They say he's in touch with a brewing magnate who could bring in two hundred jobs. I heard he's even talked to Slake about retooling the taconite plant."

"Really? Retool it for what?"

"Chopsticks," she said. "Matches, pencils, cribbage boards—we've got the forests, you see." She sighed. "Maybe I'm just nervous right now.

My grandson Oliver is graduating from preschool in Minneapolis in the morning. I'm driving down to watch him get his degree."

"They get a degree?"

"Do this for me, Virgil."

"I'll talk to him tomorrow."

Lydia nodded. As the light declined I realized she needed to get on the road. Even in perfect weather it's a generous three hours to the Twin Cities. Lydia didn't like driving after dark.

"You better get going."

She hugged me and departed. I stood at the window and watched her appear on the sidewalk. Her white Lumina was parked out front. She circled it, peered at the tires, rubbed at the windshield. Clearly she was dreading the trip. The headlights threw a comet shape on the snowy street as she eased away from the curb.

Galen was at the river's mouth when I coasted in on the Schwinn. He'd been there a while—the snow was trampled and his tackle box lay open. His bike was thrown down next to the river where it shallowed nearing Superior. In that gray scene the lone color was a green Day-Glo float riding over the current. The float marked the location of a sturdy hook Galen had baited with venison liver. It was the last chunk of liver from a deer Shad had poached in the spring. As I approached, Galen held up his fingers at arm's length toward the horizon and declining sun. He was measuring daylight.

"We got forty minutes," he said. "Then twenty more before it's too dark to see."

"Anything yet?"

"He never comes early. He waits till just about dark." Galen spoke in low tones, however, in case the sturgeon broke protocol. As usual he was underdressed, baggy denim jacket, cotton gloves, no hat. His ears were white-tipped and his feet were somewhere inside roomy basketball shoes with two pairs of socks poking out. He'd propped his fishing rod in a forked twig and kept warm by walking up and down the path he'd trodden in the snow.

A wet easterly wind snaked in off the lake and slipped down my neck. I unstrapped a thermos of cocoa from the Schwinn—not as good as Lily's but Swiss Miss was what I had. I poured some into the lid and handed it to Galen. He downed it in four seconds, then pointed out the venison liver, a hovering dark gob in fourteen inches of moving water. It seemed very shallow but Galen said the fish liked that spot.

The Day-Glo cork went under, popped to the surface, and seemed to tug itself upstream. "Is that him now?" I asked.

Galen lifted the rod so that its thin tip bent slightly and the bait rose reluctantly to the surface. It was unmolested and surprisingly drained of color, a knob of liver the size of my fist.

"Just a sucker fish," he said, lowering the bait again.

Next time the float dipped and spun I saw what he was talking about—a tubby fish twenty inches or so was nosing the bait around on the bottom. The fish had pale brownish skin covered in overlapping scales like guitar picks. Again Galen lifted the rod and spooked the sucker away, but it was back in a minute prodding the liver. Galen trotted to his bicycle where he'd leaned an old BB rifle with a plastic stock. He pumped the stock a few times and shot down into the river. At his second shot the sucker moved left a few inches. The third time the light was just right and I actually saw the golden BB at the end of its strength touch the fish's side and bounce off. Galen said, "Lift the bait almost out," and when I did the fish followed it to the surface where Galen stung it again in the tail. We watched it fin away upriver, more annoyed than afraid.

"Dumb old suckers," Galen said, smiling. It was clear he liked the curious fish and probably appreciated their company while waiting for the murderous sturgeon to appear.

After this the action stopped. We walked up and down the riverbank as light leaked out of the sky and the world became a gray-blue wash. The luminous float didn't dance anymore. The darker it got the more Galen talked. His voice was hoarse and scratchy as always. He said he didn't mind living with Lily, Lily wasn't bad. It wasn't as good as living with his dad, though. His dad got him, and in fact got some other things a girl like Lily didn't get. He was sorry his dad would never move to Florida like he wanted, though Galen himself was glad not to go. Galen didn't want to be warm all the time. He liked the cold and never got sick. This reminded me that when Galen was a baby Shad brought him in to City Hall to show him off—it was December, below zero, a bitter day. Maria came too, still lively and sharp. Maria had made up a big plate of Christmas cookies and Shad carried Galen in a woven basket like the baby Moses. When they came in the door his bare feet stuck out in the wind, yet Galen was cheerful, he whistled and chirped. You could see he would grow up to be tough. When he got a cold his dad gave him blackberry brandy with a little hot water and that made it go away. "That's something *else* Lily'll never do," he said, in his hoarse low voice.

The sun was down, but strong twilight remained. The moon was just past full. Moonlight came up out of the snow and gleamed on the smooth milky stones of the river bottom. Galen quit talking. The river burbled along. The east wind slackened but was still cold enough that I started to think of the ride home. The ride would warm me up. It would be dark, though. If I planned to keep riding at night I would need a battery headlight. Galen had one, I'd noticed.

Quietly Galen said, "There he comes."

He pointed and I focused on the stippled tan rocks which seemed to shift and breathe under the flowing water. Then a long solid shape came down among the rocks and approached through the shallows with effortless sweeps of its tail. Galen squatted to reach for the rod. I could still make out the black fist of venison liver on the bottom. The sturgeon came close to the fist and hung there. A long heavy shadow like a sunken timber. It arrived quietly and hung in the current, playing it cool. If we hadn't been looking we'd never have seen it. I wondered then and still wonder what giants we miss by not looking.

The sturgeon backed off and re-approached, keeping the liver between us. In a low voice Galen confided he wanted to shoot it. His dad owned a lightweight Springfield .22, but Lily had thwarted him by locking the gun in a steel safe in her closet. Galen searched weeks without finding the key. She allowed him only the BB rifle. It was an insult to his manhood but he carried it to discourage suckers. Now the sturgeon was coming every night, hovering at the bait, giving Galen the stinkeye, yet still Lily refused him a firearm. I'll say again the fish was massive. There was no way Galen would ever reel it in. It held itself in place in the swift cold water. Now and then the surface parted around its knobbly spine which closely resembled the human backbone.

"Look at him watch us," Galen said. "Look at him, the bastard." As if to demonstrate the fish's brazenness he took from his pocket a small flashlight and shone a beam at its face. Its eyes caught the light and shone it back, two yellow insouciant moons.

"He's never gonna bite," Galen said. "Bait's right there, he'll never take it."

The sturgeon hung motionless. Galen switched off the flashlight. "You know what it wants now?"

"No."

"Me."

"Now, Galen—"

"Nope, nope, watch him now," Galen said. "He got Dad, and he wants me next. Because I know what he did. You see it as much as I do."

We looked down at the sturgeon which glided backward in the shallows, against the current, into deeper water away from the moonlit stones. Then we didn't see him anymore.

5

NEXT MORNING RUNE'S DUTIFUL RAVEN FRIEND PLUNKED ONTO THE window ledge and tapped the glass twice. It was a big raven with a beard of black feathers and a heavy scarred bill.

Rune ignored the bird—he was refining a kite. It was a box design that looked like an anvil with the horn coming forward. The very idea had him exclaiming and pleased with himself. An anvil! Up in the sky!

The raven tapped again. Rune sighed and went to the bread box, which Orry gave me years earlier and I never used until he arrived, and tore off a chunk of rye. He went to the window and opened it a few inches meaning to slide the bread out, but the raven simply ducked its head and stepped into the room, a civil and elegant gesture. It stood on the sill looking pleased and curious, then lifted its wings and jumped lightly to Rune's shoulder.

"Oh, now," Rune said to the bird. "I agree you are smart, but such bad manners." He held up the bit of rye and the raven pushed it aside, looking only at Rune. The bird rubbed his nose with its ample beak. "Fy, off you go," he said gently, and neat as you please it hopped back to the sill and stepped out. He handed the bread through the window and this time the raven took it and he slid the window shut. The bird settled itself there on the ledge. It ruffed up its feathers and made itself comfortable. A light snow began to fall.

* * *

I spent the morning hunting for cassette players. For days Rune had mined Beeman's paper files, stories, and notes on Alec's disappearance. Beeman had also handed over a box of Maxell cassettes—interviews conducted a decade ago as he covered the search. I used to have a cassette player but now couldn't find it; Beeman gave us his, but it smoked when we plugged it in. Finally I called Marcus Jetty who said he had a boxful, come on up.

Greenstone Salvage & Tinker is an exalted iteration of Shad Pea's shipping container. There are stacks of painted pine boards, crates of outboard motor parts, a wall of beer signs and taxidermied pike, record players, cigar boxes, a wardrobe stuffed with putrescent hardcovers by Horatio Alger and G. A. Henty, tables of bird's-eye maple and trash pine, bins of Gameboys and joysticks and leather-cased Argus cameras. The smell is of slow-moving organic rot and quite comforting. When I arrived Marcus was pulling boxes of loose electronics off the shelving along the back. He set the boxes in a makeshift wheelbarrow and pushed it up to the counter. The floor was uneven, which gave his progress a slow bounding motion—that barrow had a fat bouncy tire.

We piled cassette players on his glass countertop: Emersons and JVCs, Sonys, Technics, and one labeled Holiday sold by the gas station chain. Those with cords we plugged in. We tested them with a cassette copy of *Graceland*.

In the end only one of them worked. I pushed start and stop a few times. The speed was a little fast and wavery but high fidelity wasn't the mission. I said, "Would you look at this, it's just like my old Panasonic."

"It *is* your old Panasonic. You brought it in years ago with a load of crap." Marcus allowed himself a thin smile. "Now you need it and here it is. Rare service in these unfriendly days."

"How much," I said.

He waved me away. "It ain't in high demand."

We talked a few more minutes, then I nodded good-bye and left with the player under my arm. I did consider refusing to take it for nothing, but that felt silly—I already owed Marcus more than I could really repay.

* * *

I continued up 61 with northwesterly gusts nearly knocking the bike over. I didn't mind. My legs were stringy but becoming more powerful. My lungs worked better than they had in years; language itself seemed to fall into a nearer orbit; and my heart, which had beat at high speeds since my hospital stay, descended to normal range. Nearing the lookout, I saw Rune's newest kite aloft—there it squatted at five hundred feet, not even trembling, a solid, familiar, iron-black hole in the sky. The anvil was instantly one of my favorites—so stable as to seem immobile and therefore strangely at home. If anvils could fly they would fly like this anvil. Rune saw me coming and nodded. So cold was the wind we didn't speak. I handed him the cassette player and he gave the string into my fingers. It pulled hard and evenly with a different hum from previous kites—a deep one, down to the marrow. I flew a few minutes. Warmth came down the line through my fingertips into my veins and extremities. My heart slowed and my mind felt clear and sunlit.

"Where's Lucy?" I asked—she nearly always flew with him now.

He nodded at the camper van. Lucy sat behind the wheel with a book. I handed him back the string and went to say hello.

She had the heat on and a Brandenburg Concerto playing. The book was about small-scale goat farming. One of the things Rune admired about Lucy was her impractical curiosity. She was writing notes in the margins.

"Why Virgil," she said, pleasantly. "What can I do for you?"

"I'm on my way to visit your cousin. I'd appreciate any advice."

She asked about my errand with Leer. I struggled to describe it politely and used the word *disinvite*.

"Oh, oh—ho ho! Are you afraid he'll be offended, when you rescind the offer? Angry with you?" Lucy looked at me fondly as though Adam Leer were one of those lessons a person must learn from experience.

"Not really," I said.

"Then why ask me for advice?"

"He makes me nervous," I admitted, though it was of course unfair to blame my coffee-shop reverie of the deathly Pontiac on Adam Leer, just because he was there when it happened.

"That's reasonable," she said. "Be direct. State your business without apology. And Virgil, keep it brief."

"Brief."

She said, "No one seems to benefit from his direct attention."

"He makes you nervous too," I ventured.

"Me? Not a bit! Although," she added cheerfully, "I did choose not to stay at his charming little guest house."

"Ah." I wasn't sure how to proceed. On the long uphill climb I'd been ruminating on Lydia's story of Leer, grinning in a field under steep black clouds while frogs ricocheted off his umbrella.

"My cousin was never standard issue," Lucy said. "Fascinating, yes. But not normal or regular. That would've been Richard, you know?"

"The brother who died in the blizzard."

"Along with Maddie, what a sweetheart she was. Both of them were! But Adam, even as a boy—he had this velocity, even sitting still. You could almost hear it. Remember those toy buzz saws kids used to make, out of buttons and string?"

"Adam Leer oscillates faster than you," I recalled, from the *Esquire* piece.

"I guess," she said with an odd look, and described staying with her Leer cousins in the summer when she was small: how Adam would recite the alphabet backward at top speed to impress her, or lapse into a private pig Latin of his own invention in order to make fun of Richard. "Adam could never stand his brother."

"How come?"

"I think he hated how Spurlock loved him," she said. "Everyone loved Richard, really— so charming and hardworking and funny. Only Adam could resist him, but then he had an advanced capacity for hatred. It came to him easily and fully formed." She gave a sad half-joking smile. "He was a prodigy that way."

*   *   *

The turnoff to Leer's was a mile farther through gusts of pellet-like snow. The place had noticeably changed. While pocks and humps of snow covered the yard, Jerry Fandeen's work was apparent. The aspens had been cut and dragged to a slash pile away from the house. The guest cottage had been retrimmed and fitted with new gutters. It was dark-windowed, and I wondered how Lucy had sidestepped Leer's wish that she stay. He'd gone to some trouble and expense, hiring Jerry to fix the place up.

"Come in," Leer said, opening the door before I could knock.

"Thank you."

"Still not driving," he observed—he was slightly flushed, his hair damp.

"No."

"Good for you. I like the bike. A bold winter choice." Leer seemed amused.

I told him the place looked improved. Jerry Fandeen had done fine work.

"He had no idea he was up to it. Daily he surprises himself."

"Does he? His ceiling is high, then?"

Leer smiled. "I'm always on the lookout for lofty ceilings."

I followed him in. His kitchen was mostly barren with a box of oranges on the counter and a pair of plucked game birds laid out on a long wooden table. The birds smelled fresh and slightly bloody. He had coffee ready in a French press and water ticking in a kettle.

"I've come at a bad time," I said.

"Not at all. What can I do for you?" He nodded me into a kind of parlor with built-in bookshelves and a globe on a stand.

"The event in the spring," I said. "The city's decided to go a different way. I hope you aren't let down."

"Ah! You're sacking me," he said. "Thank God. I didn't come willingly in the first place, you'll recall." The pot whistled and he said, "Hang on."

I heard him pour and set a timer and lay cups on the countertop. "Just be a few minutes," he called. "Look around if you like."

I did. It was an impressive bookshelf, full of Plutarch and Ovid, Tacitus, Pliny, others in this vein, books I haven't read. They bunched up on the shelves in twos and threes, some standing with heads together, others propped open on cracking spines. Many had pages folded cornerwise in lieu of bookmarks, as with any drugstore beach read. There were biographies, volumes of botany, oceanography, astronomy, calligraphy. I took down an architectural treatise on cathedrals that smelled like a shovelful of earth. Scattered among these antiquities were what I took to be Leer's own mementos, small framed photos of his parents; his long-dead brother Richard; the waiflike wife of his youth, Simone. There was a badge from an old Camaro, a cracked teacup like those brought up from the *Titanic*, and what looked like a metacarpal bone from a human hand leaning casually against a tarnished Union Carbide belt buckle.

Leer came in with the coffee and cups, setting them on a sideboard. Lucy's advice *Keep it brief* came to mind. I should've obeyed it. Instead I said, "Why did you change your mind in the first place, if I may ask? Why agree to speak?"

"Ms. Fandeen is persuasive," he said with a smile, filling both cups and handing me one. "Beyond that, a simple change of heart. That's allowed, correct? We are all changing into something else, wouldn't you agree?"

His words emerged kindly enough yet put me at odds with myself. I experienced again a servile longing for Leer's approval. Compensating with an air of hostility, I ignored the coffee and met his gaze. He pulled back, adjusting his tone.

"I only mean that a man deserves a second act. Maybe even a third." He nodded toward the window. "Look at Jerry. Once a steady hand, then a lost stray, now shifting yet again before our eyes—into what, would you say? A man of substance?"

"Of sadness, I would say."

Leer watched me, sipping his coffee, the fingers of his free hand making a habitual cigarette motion although there was no cigarette in them. "He is anyway transformed, at least transforming." He seemed to want to expand on his point. "Look at yourself. A keeper of Green-stone all these years, doing the city's thankless jobs, maintaining your nostalgic theater—I mean that in the best sense. Head down, mouth shut, yes? Until at last you drive"—his face brightened—"literally *drive off a cliff*. Honestly, I talked to Marcus, what a spectacle you made, the car in the air, drifting through the snow. What a declaration! Yet you survive, and *now* look at you—"

"Declaration? You think I went over on purpose?"

"Does it matter? Into the dark you went, like Orpheus! And *lived*. And here you sit today—to my point, hardly the same man."

"You know nothing of it. We never even met before Ann and I came out that day," I said, but not with much mojo. The truth is, I *wasn't* the same man. For better or worse, who could tell? The jury was in recess. Abruptly I felt distant and sodden. Leer's voice retreated. A shadowy coolness passed overhead like a great fish swimming between me and the sun.

"Nonsense," he said. "Obviously we met. I bought tickets from your own hand more than once—I've eaten your popcorn, sat in your derelict seats. Congenial, that's what you were. The man at the Empress. A little soft if you don't mind my saying, a little eager to please. But that's all finished, isn't it?"

He watched me over the rim of his cup.

"What's finished?"

"Soft old heads-down Virgil. That version is gone, that's what I believe." He leaned forward. "You're changing rapidly into the next. Some rangy ascetic if I had to guess. Lasering in on what's *important* in life, now that you've nearly died. Why not? Everyone wants to start again. Rebuild with new bones and fresh skin. Why are we here if not to grow! Plus, aren't you discovering it's attractive?"

"I don't follow."

"Attractive to others. Keep up with me Virgil! People are drawn to rebirth." He leaned forward. His breath was cool and his teeth were perfect. "People notice you now—Nadine is a package, isn't it true? And Bjorn is special, that's what I think. Out on his board in the freezing rollers! Bjorn will always bear watching."

"I'm done here," I said, and stood. I wanted to say more but couldn't. My insides twitched—I seemed to have caught a bug in rapid progression. My head whirled and he pointed to the bathroom. I just made it, sweating at the temples and the soles of my feet. I barked and rinsed. When I came out Leer offered me a ride home which I did not accept. He handed me my coat.

The cold wind cleared my head straight off. The bicycle leaned against the porch rail. I carried it down the steps, swung a leg over, and rested a moment before setting off. The wind was whacking the treetops around. Then I was distracted by movement in an upper window.

A hand was wiping steam from the glass. The hand belonged to a woman who came into view as the glass cleared. Her dark blonde hair was wet as if from a shower. She wore a man's light-blue dress shirt and a pair of cat-eye glasses. Intent on the window she didn't notice me right away but then peered down and caught me looking up. I felt abashed but she seemed unbothered by my boorish manners. After a moment's hesitation she smiled, then offered a good-natured wave.

What could I do but wave in return? It was Ann Fandeen.

6

IT WAS SO GUSTY ON THE HIGHWAY THAT I GOT OFF THE SCHWINN and walked it home. I was trying to make sense of things, Ann Fandeen for starters, in the upstairs window, an image that returned in high-def. If nothing else it gave me some understanding of Jerry's devotion—her unguarded smile, her guileless wave. I had to wonder if Ann was okay, yet she looked pleased to be there.

More than anything else I felt bad for Jerry, who was still for Ann, though she wasn't for him, and who felt so honored when Mr. Leer took an interest in him, and gave him work to do.

As I neared home, still walking the bike, a coyote trotted out of someone's backyard—I admire coyotes, they persevere smiling, but this one carried a gigantic turkey carcass, which reminded me of Thanksgiving, which made me realize I had *missed* Thanksgiving. My favorite holiday. It was over already, we were into December. I watched the coyote recede in the gloom.

I had not been thankful enough—I, who should be a corpse in a sunken sedan. I was dizzy again and slowed way down. The last few blocks were hard going. I kept my eyes on the ground, looking up only when cars passed. Above all I took care not to glance out at Superior. It was exactly the sort of day when the man would appear, standing on the waves, long pale hands at his sides. I sure didn't want to see him.

* * *

Bjorn showed that night's movie, a bad one; I remember the dazed look of exiting patrons. He vacuumed the lobby, put the machine away, and came out rubbing his neck. When he stood for a moment in the open door there was the illusion of looking through him at the street beyond.

He said, "I forgot to say earlier, Mom wants you to call."

One sentence, a crack of light.

"What about?"

He shrugged and blinked out.

It was much too late to call Nadine—it took her six rings to answer, in a sleepy voice. "It's Virgil," I said and she didn't mind. She'd thought of something earlier but forgot it, then got tired and fell into bed. The rustle of shifting covers tightened my throat. I offered to call back in the morning but she said, "Now I remember," and her voice came close to the phone. "Do you have a minute?"

She'd been working in her studio, creating her first neon in months. A bookstore in Wisconsin, a small independent, had acquired a liquor license and the owners wanted a sense of coziness. She designed a neon hardcover, an open book of blue and white, with a page curling back as though turning itself. The curling page was key, she said—if you got it right, the whole sign gave an impression of magic. It should look like a book that would open each time to the words you needed that moment. She was nearly done with the sign and thought it the best she had made. Sophisticated, a little sexy, fit for a dimly lit bookstore or literary tavern. She was happy. Her voice was softer than I'd ever heard it and right there inside my ear. "I wanted to tell you because of what I said at the Wise Old, that I'm good at the work but don't love it. I need to amend that. Sometimes I do love it. I loved it today." She shifted in the covers. "I didn't want you to think of me as joyless."

I laughed. The day had not shattered records for gladness. Yet a small thing had gone right for Nadine—she bent a glass tube, and it pleased her. I'd lived years without a woman to tell me small things. Her work went well and she wanted to say so, and I was the man who was listening. That fact swung open and light came in.

"When you have a chance," she said, "come over and see it."

"I will."

"Call first," she said, then, "I hear the door—Bjorn's home."

"I'll let you go." I didn't want to let her go, of course—what I wanted was to hold her tight, to keep hearing her soft, near, barely-awake voice. There is no better sound than whom you adore when they are sleepy and pleased. I wanted to hear about many small things, the smaller the better. I wanted to tell her small things in return. It came to me that you can't retrieve a lost holiday but you can pick up the next one and honor it well. I said, "What are you and Bjorn doing for Christmas?"

"Not really sure."

"Spend it with us. Here at the Empress. Not for a movie," I clarified, "just come for dinner, for Christmas dinner." She didn't reply. "Or anytime really—doesn't have to be dinner—you could come by early, or late if that's better, just come knock at the door. Don't do anything else, Nadine." You'll notice my run-on technique but there was no way around it. I had a sudden horror that she might, after all, *do* something else—she might have other plans, might've committed to being with other people on Christmas Day, instead of being with me. The previous tenant would've borne this bravely, would've expected it, embraced it, shouldered up under it. A proper stoic, him—me, I couldn't stand it.

"All right, Virgil," she said, laughing. "Yes to Christmas Day, all right, yes."

I floated upstairs like a man in space.

7

RUNE SPENT THE NEXT MORNING LISTENING TO BEEMAN'S cassettes—interviews with the police, with a missing-persons specialist from Minneapolis, with the Coast Guard during the early search. These were tough on Rune because of their impersonal tone, as though Alec were only an unsatisfying job, or at best a challenging riddle. But tougher still were the personal interviews—those with Alec's friends and neighbors, his longtime people, with whom Beeman spoke in order to write a eulogistic story once it seemed he wouldn't be found. Among these were Lou Chandler, a few former Dukes, Shad Pea, and yours truly—I happened to walk in on Rune and was relieved to hear myself sounding suitably regretful. Not as regretful as Shad, though—Shad was in a terrible way, alternately angry and crying, obviously quite drunk. What broke him up was the idea he'd been last to see Alec alive. He and Maria had fought the previous night and she suggested he sleep elsewhere, so he drove out to a spot on the bank of the Burnt River, half a mile from the Wise Old and Lou's grass airstrip. At first light he woke to the strange sight of a naked man emerging from the rushes on the far bank—it was Adam Leer, he said. "Walked down into the water and saw me and smiled, the big turd," Shad said. "Then he ducked under and swam away." An hour or so later Alec flew out, jiggling his wingtips when he saw Shad. Shad waved back, and that was the last time he ever saw his friend.

At City Hall that afternoon Lily came in and set a white bakery box on my desk. There was snow on her shoulders, and her knuckles were red. She looked older, with a careworn expression. When I stood and came around the desk to shake hands she hugged me instead and kissed my cheek.

"Are you well, Virgil?"

"Yes."

"Getting your meals?"

"You're pretty young to be mothering me."

"Open the box."

It contained half a dozen chocolate croissants. I thanked her—I'd often seen these deep-brown beauties in the bakery window, but never tried one.

"Go ahead," Lily said.

"Join me." I offered her the box.

"Not a chance, those are for you." Seeing I was about to flag down Lydia, who was passing my door peering in, Lily hissed, "Not for *them*. For you. I'm not leaving until you have one."

"What's on your mind, Lily?"

"Nothing, except there's less of you every time I look. You totter around with that stick, I can hear all your joints, clickety-clack. Please have a croissant now."

I smiled and took a bite, making a show of it. It really was delectable. "Sometimes I forget to eat, that's all. I'm actually fine."

She watched me eat the rest of the pastry. I must've been hungry because without thinking I launched into another—that made her smile.

"Galen told me you saw the fish," she said.

"It's really big."

"I thought he was making it up. Now he wants me to let him shoot it, which wouldn't be legal. Anyway he's too young for a gun."

"What are you hoping will happen, Lily?"

"I was hoping he could let this go. Instead he's down there every night. I don't want to be paranoid but what if something goes wrong? It's freezing, and what if he falls in? What if that fish takes the bait and *pulls* him in?"

"Make him wear a life jacket."

"He won't unless he's in a boat—it's against his manhood."

I didn't know what to say to this. Galen Pea was staunch about his manhood as only a ten-year-old can be.

Lily said, "I'm in Duluth three evenings a week. If someone could only check on him, you know? Like you did the other night. But I know you have the theater to run."

I sighed. Don't let anyone tell you that looking out for your vulnerable is less than a full-time deal.

"I got to run," she said, squeezing my arm. "If you decide to cut your hair I am good at it. And buy some new pants, honestly, yours are falling off. Good-bye now." She kissed me awkwardly on the ear.

As Lily left, Lydia came in. Council members had been calling her about Hard Luck Days—they loved the idea, thought Ann Fandeen was a genius. "Now it's inevitable," she said, sadly. "Barrett's pushing 'Hard Luck Days,' oof. Do you think anything can be done?"

"I doubt it, Lydia."

She sat down on my desk and considered the open box of croissants. "I'm old," she said. "I didn't see it coming, I'm old and tired of irony. What's the matter with people? Hard Luck Days. Irony isn't going to save us."

"Maybe it won't kill us, either," I suggested. "Maybe it can do us good." I felt gentle toward Lydia. She was probably the kindest mayor in the history of mayors. Across her long tenure she'd done ever more with ever less and always without complaint. I said, "Irony doesn't seem to have hurt Bob Dylan, and he's a longtime practitioner."

Lydia sighed. I offered her a chocolate croissant and took another myself. She chewed with her eyes closed. When she opened them Ann Fandeen was standing in front of her, which seemed to make Lydia uncomfortable. She said, "Well, then, anyway."

"Sorry, Lydia," Ann said, "I didn't mean to interrupt."

"You haven't. We're finished, I guess," Lydia said. She thanked me for the croissant and marched away with a civil nod to Ann.

Ann looked at me with a grave expression. She came in and shut the door.

I'd been curious how this encounter would go.

Ann looked away and said, "Lydia hates my idea."

"You aren't enemies, Ann. She recruited you. She called you a *concept gal*."

"Do *you* hate my idea?"

"Not at all. Hard luck is the only mine still producing. Have a croissant—Lily Pea brought them."

Ann looked at the rolls, then back at me. "I'm sorry if I made you uncomfortable yesterday. I was visiting Adam." Her cheeks flushed lightly; her dangly earrings came forward, along with a perfume like dried apples; her hair had been cut and she pushed it behind one ear. She said, "Do you think I am terrible now?"

"Ann. Of course not."

She was clad in a yellow cashmere sweater which seemed to make her self-conscious. She crossed her arms over her chest and looked away.

"Are you all right?"

"Oh, sure I'm all right." If she were going to roll her eyes it would be now, but she didn't. "You're afraid Adam's taking advantage, only he really isn't. I'm a tough one, Virgil. You wouldn't think so, but I'm sort of unbelievably tough." She said so in a tone of wonder, as though this knowledge had only recently landed.

"Can I ask you about Jerry?"

She gave me a blank look.

"I went and saw him at the Hoshaver. It isn't ideal over there. He's sleeping in a closet with mice."

"Jerry's at the Hoshaver?" Ann was startled. "I didn't know, Virgil—he hasn't lived with me in a year."

Now I must've looked blank.

"Fifteen months ago," she explained. "We didn't throw things or make a lot of noise. He just left. It isn't official but will be someday. Do you know until he started working for Adam I was still buying his groceries and gas? Jerry is always broke."

"Where did he move to fifteen months ago?"

"Little dumpy hunting shack on his brother Owen's piece of swampland. One day he went out there and just stayed. He said I was bossy and a damn schemer—okay, but somebody better make plans or what ever gets done? He comes over Sunday afternoons, we have a meal together, and he begs me to take him back, but I can't. I can't do it, Virgil. Life is improved without Jerry around."

I was sorry to hear this news. Ann blinked a few times. She didn't cry but commenced listing regrets. She regretted marrying Jerry instead of finishing her business degree years ago. She regretted Jerry's deep sadness, though it did not persuade her to reconcile. She regretted that Lydia, whom she admired, now thought of her as a damn schemer, the way Jerry did. It wasn't her fault she was goal-oriented. If Barrett hadn't glommed onto Hard Luck Days she had twenty other ideas, most of them better. Ann talked quite a while, there in my office. Why am I still surprised when it turns out there is more to the story? There were still two croissants left so I slid the box toward her and she took one. Eventually she thanked me for listening and opened the door and went to her desk. Her phone rang and she answered politely. A person never knows what is next—I don't, anyway. The surface of everything is thinner than we know. A person can fall right through, without any warning at all.

8

AFTER BJORN ARRIVED AT THE EMPRESS I CALLED NADINE AND SLIPPED over there for a visit. It was a cold night with damp wind rising off the lake, shaking the yellowed plastic lamppost angels. Every year the city considers new holiday decorations but never follows through. Even the cheesiest snowflakes, stars, or reindeer are a big investment for a town like Greenstone. Those angels remember Dick Nixon.

The last time I was in Nadine's house it still felt like Alec's house too. He'd been gone half a year then, but his stuff remained everywhere—his blue flannel shirt on the doorknob, his Barbasol cream on the sink, and his moccasins in the carpeted hallway. It was as if he'd just popped out to the post office.

A decade later much was changed. Nadine met me at the door and rushed me through the living room which was no longer dark-paneled but open and white as a canvas. Alec was absent except in a framed wedding photo on a side table and a family snapshot from when Bjorn was five or six, standing on a dock with a lake in the background.

"Come on in the basement," she called—she'd already disappeared through the kitchen and was heading downstairs. Alec had set up his neon equipment down there, I remembered, while the sign-painting and vinyl repairs were done in a chilly downtown garret rented from a florist named Bleeck. After Nadine decided to carry on the business, she told Bleeck farewell and worked from home.

"Thanks for coming," Nadine said, as I arrived downstairs. "I have to ship tomorrow, so you're my only chance to brag."

The workshop was simple and small; the walls were whitewashed bedrock with gas lines running to torches and ribbon burners and home-built racks stacked with phosphor-coated glass tubes. I'd been down there when Alec repaired my marquee. Back then it was a vaguely ominous scene, with low buzzing fluorescents and an alleyway smell. Nadine by contrast liked a clean dry shop. It was crisp and lit up; she'd installed an egress window with a grass-level view of the backyard and a rectangle of sky framing the water tower two blocks away. Instead of an alley it smelled of drywall and paint. It wasn't a scene but a work-place. On a tall bench were propped two neons in stages of repair—one a rocket ship with fins and round portholes, the other a sign saying *breakfast* in appealing handscript. Nadine's bookstore creation was tem-porarily mounted above the bench. It looked like a ropy gray rectangle. No corpse is as dead as unlit neon.

"Hang on." She snapped off the overhead. In the darkness a mild vertigo made itself known, also the sound of my own breathing, a sense of space. Nadine stepped forward and threw a switch, and the sign smoldered up before us.

Imagine a volume of bold proportions, a book you would struggle to lift—a Gutenberg Bible, an unabridged Webster's lying open on its stand. It was outlined in blue that flared at the corners and glowed with subdued intensity. Its leaves were indicated by a strand of white neon, plump and curvaceous on top, the lower corner of the right-hand page curling upward as though caught by a breeze.

She took hold of my arm. Lit dust loitered in the gloom.

"Well?"

"It's beautiful," I told her.

"That's it? I'm dying for compliments here."

"Hang on, I'm just taking it in. It's balanced, you know? Bracing. Spare. But generous too—the way the pages curve at the top. Almost lavish."

She grinned at this contradictory and overblown description—she wanted some adjectives, after all. Still, she seemed to agree. She'd just received an order for eight neons from a barbecue chain headquartered in St. Paul. They'd called that afternoon.

"What kind of designs?"

"Pigs," she replied. "They asked for pigs. It's a rib joint. I went historical. A brave pig crossing the Delaware, a pig on the deck of Noah's Ark. They liked my drawings."

"They'd be idiots not to," I said, turning to face her. "You're awfully good, Nadine."

She looked away and back to me. "Maybe I am."

We fell into a slow sort of talk. When happy or pleased with herself Nadine became very deliberate. She spoke in short sentences and made self-mocking faces. Her eyes drifted as if she were detached or distracted, but really she was taking her time absorbing whatever the happy thing was. Some people are natural bubble machines. Not Nadine. Her gladness needs a little room.

So we went along slowly, standing in the soft radiance of the neon book. I felt more comfortable than I had since the accident. I forgot to wonder what Nadine thought of me and just enjoyed the rise and fall of her voice, her occasional glances, her agreeable laugh reaching in my direction. She talked about burning her thumb on a hot glass tube, the proper sweetness of corn bread, an encounter last week with a family of voles who'd made big plans for her garage. Nadine laughed readily, an undervalued quality. Kate had been the opposite—she was annoyed by slow drivers, slow waiters, slow sentences that took a while to reach their destinations. A snag in the carpeting could undo her happiness.

Nadine let her laughter subside. "Bjorn says you're off-loading the vault."

I told her about Fergus Flint who might call any day, knock wood. I told her the Empress was for sale.

"You're getting ready," she said brightly.

I hadn't considered it in those words—*getting ready*. I'd been thinking in terms of *getting out*, which cast me inevitably as a refugee. *Getting ready* was better. It sounded youthful. Youth had crept away from me but perhaps was still in sight. "Nadine," said my voice. "You know how people daydream about the Bahamas, with the beaches and palm trees? I don't know if they really do, no doubt it's mostly advertising, but you're the island I think about."

She'd been leaning gently against me but stepped back at this and looked at me straight on. I'd only been saying what was on my mind—just cruising along, no major declarations in mind. Now I recognized the tightrope onto which I had stepped.

"Go ahead then," Nadine said.

"All right," I said. "Great, all right. Since the accident I am stupid. You've seen it yourself. Words come and go. My timing is off. I see things and then they aren't there. Loud noises bother me."

I could've kept going—it was a long list. Nadine had turned her face and wouldn't look at me. "Any of this might be permanent," I went on. "Nobody knows. But I think about you every day, and have almost forever. Even when I was seeing Kate I thought about you. Even before Alec flew away. You've been in my mind so long it's like you were always there. I can't remember when you weren't. I know you aren't really like an island. It's a bad comparison. I understand if you are tired of men with stupid old torches. I'm sorry this became such a speech."

There was a quite lengthy silence.

"I understand restraint," she said, clearly exercising some, "but ten years, Virgil. This isn't *Remains of the Day*."

I said, "It would've felt disloyal," only to realize this statement, my guiding star and default position, had not been true in years. "There was so much competition," I added—which likewise, spoken, became silly and beside the point. Burdens accrue in isolation. Pride, fear, stupidity, lassitude build up like layers of paint. I tried once more to get underneath and peel them all away. "I didn't think you'd like me back."

With her face still turned she said, "Is this why you're so good to Bjorn?"

"Maybe it was at first."

She turned to me. Her face looked soft and her eyes dark and canny. Desire and curiosity seized me.

"I always wondered what you thought," I confessed, "about that time in the post office, years ago."

She looked away seeming not to remember, so I briefly recapped standing in line, my mind adrift until I sort of woke up and realized I was holding her hand, had reached for it without even thinking. "How disorienting that must have been for you," I concluded, "and what you must've thought of me—inconsiderate, tactless, infantile, presumptuous . . ." I was so relieved to have this out in the open that I'd achieved a spontaneous adjective roll, but Nadine stiffened noticeably.

"I hope you didn't torment yourself about that."

"Less so recently," I conceded.

She said, "Virgil, you have been more stupid than you know, and for a longer time. You never took my hand that day." She looked fierce and angry. "Idiot—I took yours."

Words deserted me. Nadine's expression grew small and hard. She looked so mad I felt myself tumbling into a pit of new and formidable torments, involving missed chances and peak years wasted; I glimpsed an alternative time line in which I wasn't alone, thus never acquired the lonely habit of photographing storms, thus never drove over the cliff. But I didn't plunge far in this miserable vortex because Nadine's tough hands were all tangled up in my hair and she was pulling me in for the sort of nourishing, soft yet forceful, escalating kiss the movies only now and then get right.

"To be clear," she said, long moments later, "this means I like you back."

It's possible to perceive what is coming and still be dumbfounded when it happens. Even now I don't remember a precise chain of events, only Nadine's low voice, an awareness of her neck, its long smooth shadows, and a sense of things hidden and turning, as if the gears and springs that ease us forward hadn't been suspended but were always ticking patiently behind the scenes. I guess after a while you stop expecting to be at home with another person. Fully home at last. It starts to seem not just against the odds but against physics. Yet for the moment we were clear as water, plain as yes and no. She hung on and anchored me when vertigo returned. There was very much to talk about, yet nothing needed saying—all the ground was new, yet none of it was strange. She kept looking away then back to me, as though at a nice surprise. This was maybe best of all. I never once expected to be someone's nice surprise.

When Bjorn called, her head was on my chest. She'd been talking in a soft voice and cleared her throat to reclaim her usual tone before answering the phone.

I heard him say, "Mom? Is Virgil with you?"

"Yes."

"Can I talk to him?"

She handed me the phone.

"Hey, Mr. Wander." Bjorn's voice echoed slightly—he was in the auditorium. I could hear him pushing the clattery bucket down front. "I don't want to spring anything on you, but can I take a couple of evenings off?"

"What's up, Bjorn?"

"Job opportunity," he said. "Nothing permanent, just a little painting. Probably take less than a week. But it pays pretty good."

Nadine still had her head on my chest. I could feel her smile. I said, "Are you jockeying for a raise, Bjorn? Because we can discuss this."

"No, just seeing if you can spare me pretty soon."

"What's the job?"

"It's for Mr. Leer," Bjorn said. "He came to the movie tonight and stayed around after. He needs a few rooms painted in his house. He really liked the work I did in here."

Nadine heard him say *Mr. Leer* and sat up straight. I said, "Is he there now, Bjorn?"

"He left when I had to start cleaning up."

"I think you'll want to run this past your mom."

"Right—just thought I'd ask you for the time off, first."

"We'll talk about it."

I set the phone down. Just like that Nadine was apart from me—pulling her hair back, assembling herself. She moved fast. Her woolen coat was on a hook; she slid into it like armor. She pulled on leather boots. Her movements were aggressive and primitive. She might've been looking around for a crossbow.

"Where are you going?"

"To Leer's. Right now. Want to come?"

"Yes." I was confused but felt strong and not dizzy at all. I didn't understand what had got hold of Nadine, but I trusted her. Maybe she was further down a road I'd just discovered.

9

HERE'S THE SHORT HISTORY AS I RECEIVED IT, ON THE ROAD TO ADAM Leer's.

Leer had done a brief stint in the torchlight brigade, as I already knew. His mode was overkill—champagne, live lobsters flown in from Maine. It was exciting after track coaches, but Nadine kept alert. She read his long-ago *Esquire* interview, watched his disquieting movie. In person he was appealing and hard to deter. She declined his presents, and her rebuff amused him. She said to slow down or at least to call first; he cheerfully refused to do either. He'd sit on the porch doing magic for Bjorn, spinning coins that twirled forever, plucking cards from the air. He was a dazzling mimic with dead-on impressions of frantic old Mrs. Bloom next door and Bjorn's fourth-grade teacher Mr. Saddiq. Bjorn laughed himself limp while Leer watched Nadine for clues. But she was conflicted. Leer seemed incomplete. She admitted his charm but where was his tragedy? He'd outlived his family and two wives, yet didn't seem bowed in the slightest. He had full lips for a man of his age, his waist was still narrow, his hair wavy and thick. He wore his shirts open and his shoes without socks. *He thinks he's Lord Byron*, she said to a friend, who replied, *Then send him to me*.

In the thick of all this Nadine began dreaming, the images vivid but far away, blurred at the edges as if through a telescope. What tied the dreams together was Bjorn.

He died in every one.

He broke through the ice, he fell out of a window. He got an infection and shivered to death. Whether Nadine was awake or asleep the vignettes played at their own will—Bjorn crushed by a rockslide, stung by a bee so his throat buttoned up. In one striking episode his bones dissolved in rapid succession and he slid to the floor like a jellyfish.

Then Leer departed for several months—to consult on a movie, he said. In his absence Bjorn regained poise, if not really strength. Nadine found she could rest. Her mind recharged. She ceased being ambushed by death tableaux. She planted a garden, took a management class at UMD. In time she put the siege out of her mind as though forgetting the worst of an illness.

Life spun along until midsummer when she woke from a scene of Bjorn running. He was tall in the dream, with an easy long stride. Then he tripped and went down, rose, and bent panting over his knees. Color gathered at his lips like a bruise. She heard his striving lungs. "Mom," he said quietly. She woke wrung out and couldn't shake it. That afternoon the buzzer rang. Adam Leer stood on the porch—fresh from Mexico, brown as a penny, woven huaraches on his feet. He'd brought her a case of silver tequila and a live tarantula for Bjorn. She spoke to him through the screen—there's nothing for you here, thanks for the effort, stay away from my boy. Leer was silent and patient. He seemed unmoved by her rejection. His face settled into the weeds. He drove off leaving the gifts. Bjorn would be home from school in ten minutes. She watered the grass with tequila and crushed the frantic spider in its box.

We got to Leer's after eleven. Nadine drove up through his yard full of boulders and parked well back from the house. She turned off the headlights but left the car running. We were in a hard spot. We both knew we were proceeding upon nothing actionable in the adult world. Leer hadn't threatened anyone. He wasn't punching faces or boiling pets. As we climbed the porch steps I think we recognized the creaky limb onto which we'd crept, the limb of hearsay and folklore, and distressing but transitory dreams.

Nadine paused with her knuckles an inch from the door. "Are you with me?"

"You know I am."

She rapped hard five times.

Silence, then the light came on. The door opened. "Nadine," Leer said. "Virgil. Goodness."

He had on pajama pants and a dark blue bathrobe tied at the waist. His television was on.

He said, "Is there something I can do for you?"

Nadine stood there in her boots. "Yes. Stay away from Bjorn."

Leer did not seem taken aback but leaned against the doorframe with yellow light streaming out behind him.

"Is this because I offered him work? Like Virgil did? Have I transgressed some boundary?"

Nadine didn't give. Her voice was low and clear. "I said this years ago. I'm saying it again. You stay away from Bjorn. Don't approach him. Don't ask him to paint your house or shovel your steps. You see him coming, turn away."

She spun and descended the steps and walked toward the car, leaving me on the porch with Leer.

He didn't look the same. Normally in the cast of his face you saw a proud shine—a man admiring himself among the primitives. The shine was gone. His eyes looked small and dark and dry.

"Where does this come from?" he asked. "Virgil, what do you have to say?"

"She just said it. This seems pretty simple. Keep your distance from Bjorn, and all is well."

He didn't seem to have a reply. I walked away. Nadine stood at the Jeep with the engine running and the door open. I could feel Leer up on the porch behind me, staring out.

great wide open

1

SLEEP REFUSED ME—THE BLOOD IN MY VEINS WAS FULLY AWAKE. IT raced along at what felt like uncatchable speed.

I rose and turned on the light and stood in front of the mirror. The figure I cut was not imposing. Earlier, in the sweet soft part of the evening, Nadine had made a tender remark about my ribs.

In the kitchen I made toast with cheese, knocking around so Rune would wake up and come out, which he didn't. Why choose now to sleep so soundly? I wanted to tell him about Nadine and me. Part of what made my pulse so swift was surely the shock of returned affection. There must be a right next thing to do, but I couldn't think what it was.

And Nadine and I had celebrated our mutual discovery by going out in the night and goading a serpent. At least that's the premise we were working under, that Leer was at bottom an inveterate predator incapable of doing a kindness, for example, offering odd jobs to Bjorn without there being harm in the enterprise.

As the night crawled on this seemed less certain. Yes, his life appeared littered with accidents and assorted grisly conclusions—but wasn't that all of Greenstone when you thought about it? Maybe we all looked culpable from the proper angle; maybe I looked responsible for my parents, and Nadine for losing Alec. Maybe we'd been overly impulsive, or even threatening. Maybe my blood was racing because war seemed imminent.

I made a fist and held it out. It didn't look like much—not like a fist anyone would count on for protection. If war came seeking a person I loved, that undernourished fist was not going to be enough. I would have to put my whole body in the way.

In the morning I tried to call Nadine. When she didn't answer I went down to the Agate for breakfast. The place was nearly empty. Julie beamed when I ordered extra hash browns.

Someone had left a disheveled Duluth newspaper on the counter. I started in the middle and worked toward the front page. When I reached it I saw a photo of the pretty barista from the coffee shop in Duluth I had visited after seeing Koskinen, she of the colorful tattoos and scarf and merry outlook.

I got a cold feeling.

The caption below the photograph said *Missing*.

Her name was Josephine Sayles. Twenty-nine, single, an indebted graduate of Hamline Law pulling espressos in the Twin Ports. She lived alone and her absence had not been noticed until she failed to appear for a shift. A coworker described her as a generous person with a fondness for chamber music and a history of depression.

The photograph showed her smiling on a sunny day in Canal Park, the lake benign in the background, her incomplete ship tattoo like a story half told.

Julie came over to refill my coffee but stopped when she saw my face.

"I met this Josephine," I said.

"The missing girl? I heard about that. Terrible. I hope she can be brave," Julie said. "Oh. Oh Virgil. Here you are, honey," handing me an extra napkin before topping off my cup and trundling away.

She was surprised by my tears, as I was myself. Why this wrenching melancholy? Why did it seem as though a friend was lost, and not a stranger met one time? Then I recalled being lost myself, caught in that dream of drowning and decay, the illusion so powerful that the café upholstery became the spongy seat of my doomed Pontiac. I escaped the dream only when the barista walked up and dispelled it like a flag snapping in the wind.

I paid for breakfast and walked home and tried Nadine again. No answer, but immediately my phone rang back and I swept it up. "Nadine?"

"No such luck, it's Fergus Flint," said my Hollywood lawyer. "I'll call back, if it's a bad time."

He sounded tired, as he had in our previous conversation. His voice was still hoarse and craggy.

"No, it's all right."

Fergus reported having sent inquiries to all the studios on the list, "or their surviving entities." About half had responded. None so far seemed angry or vengeful. None had uttered the phrase "make an example."

"In fact," he said, "there have been several remarks indicating gratitude. Gratitude, I specify, to yourself—assuming your careful stewardship of their property. It's important you comprehend both how much and how little this means."

"I don't."

"Pardon?"

"I don't comprehend."

No doubt I sounded short-fused. Fergus took a cautious tone. "In other sectors of the economy," he explained, "gratitude might take the form of pecuniary reward, in-kind compensation, public credit. In the entertainment sphere the word is redefined. For example, overwhelming gratitude might mean you are somewhat less likely to be sued for punitive damages."

"Ah."

"Yes. Let's proceed to remove the prints from your location. I'll arrange transport if you are amenable. There's a facility here that stores old films in a climate-controlled environment until they can be properly reclaimed. It's agreed to receive your shipment, if you haven't changed your mind."

"Shipping won't be cheap. It's a lot of reels."

"I'm working on a couple of the studios for that. Those with most to gain. You have several desirables in that collection, you know. Not to mention the Cassidy outtake—from my conversations with a coy archivist, I believe you may be in possession of the last extant copy." Worry crept into the lawyer's voice. "I hope to God you aren't running it through your projector."

I was quiet.

He took a breath. "Surely this is a needless warning, but let me caution you against further showings of any of these films. It would constitute irresponsible handling. They are cultural artifacts. They are sensitive and vulnerable pieces of history." Fergus paused and I heard him sigh—clearly the phrases bored him hollow.

"I know it."

"More to the point, people are aware of them now."

"I understand."

"No more special occasions," said Fergus Flint.

"What's next?"

"I'll arrange for the truck. How's January?"

"Cold and dark. Have you learned anything about William Plate?" I hadn't stopped wondering about the man who had sold the Empress to Edgar Poe before dashing off to the Krishnas.

Fergus said he'd spoken with a studio rep involved with past "recoveries." While details were hazy, he did learn that one Destin Plate, cousin of William, erstwhile of Greenstone, had worked as a projectionist in the late 1960s, mostly in Brentwood and Bel Air. This was fifteen years before videocassettes. There was a class of entertainers, investors, and legal big shots who had screening rooms in their homes and threw parties at which Destin made extra money projecting whatever films had been procured—sometimes new films not yet released, often older ones of shady provenance, blue movies, specimens "misplaced" or set aside for studio executives, sometimes damaged copies slated for incineration. The parties ranged from intellectual gatherings to forthright bacchanalia. Destin, said Fergus, was one of a number of quick-fingered projectionists who ended up with impressive private collections, but he left LA in the mid-seventies when he was sought on charges of soliciting minors. It was easy to imagine Destin as a sweaty Turturro, loading reels into a station wagon under a fugitive moon, driving through mountain passes, deserts, endless wheat fields, hoping to find sanctuary in Minnesota with his intense and mentally declining cousin Bill.

"Thanks, Fergus."

"You're welcome. If you speak to Orry, greet her for me."

I hung up and paid the north closet a visit. There they were, a hundred seventy reels. I'd put them in order by studio while compiling the list Fergus required. I looked them over. A change had been wrought. Their presence had always infused me with an insider's pleasure, a low-key sense of providence. Now, nothing. The canisters shone dully. No life or brio emerged from them. I used to imagine this evocative compilation was the work of a rakish black marketeer, a Captain Blood of alleyway cinema. Now that vibrant image was gone. In its place flickered Destin Plate, solicitor of minors, small-time cad, and studio thief. I wished I didn't know—even though I *didn't* know, not really. The vault felt different; that was all I knew. The canisters looked wary and mortally tired. Some of their taped labels were peeling. Their new home had to be better than this.

Next time the phone rang it *was* Nadine. She said, "I had a note this morning—guess who from."

"You're kidding."

"Sealed envelope, taped to my door," she said. "I didn't hear anyone, but there it was. Listen." I heard the paper rattling in front of her. She read, "Nadine, fair enough. Distance kept. Adam."

"That's it?"

"Every word." She sounded more than relieved. She sounded cautiously exultant. I felt that way too. It made me wonder what we had expected.

"Did you talk to Bjorn?"

"About Adam, or about you?"

"Either one."

"He'll get over not painting the Leer house."

"What about the other?"

"We didn't talk about you," she said, her voice low and lively. "But he's spent some time around you lately—he might not be as thunderstruck as you expect. Virgil," she added.

"Yes."

"Tell me what you're thinking right now."

"You are my favorite person in Greenstone."

"Whoa, that was right on top," said her nearly laughing voice. "I can feel this going to my head. Let's have dinner tonight."

"Yes! Wait, there's something I have to do."

"Does it get in the way of dinner?"

"I told Lily Pea I'd check on Galen. He's been going after that sturgeon. She's afraid it'll pull him in if he hooks it."

"Send Bjorn. He likes Galen. You and I can do projection. I'll bring dinner. Courage, Virgil. You can wear those lame headphones if you need to."

We talked a few more minutes, during which there was a commotion on the stairs and Rune and Lucy thumped into the kitchen. Their coats and hats shed clumps of snow. There was a slight desperation about them because Lucy was leaving shortly to spend Christmas with her kids in California. They had a box of bakery doughnuts and were playing some undignified game with each other. Seeing me on the phone they shushed and opened the box and commenced eating the doughnuts, laughing quietly over cups of coffee. The raven tapped at the window, Rune let it in, and they devised a contest that involved lobbing bits of doughnut across the room to the bird, who caught and swallowed with athletic composure. The doughnuts disappeared. By the time I got off the phone Rune had retrieved a pair of light-wind kites and the two of them eased out and down the stairs.

The apartment fell still. The raven tucked its beak. I set the cups in the sink, then lit the blue candle on its shelf.

The flame swayed. My mind went to Nadine, her easy wish to have dinner tonight; and to Bjorn, who would not be thunderstruck. The raven tutted into its feathers, and I was glad for Rune, with life enough for more than just his vanished son. I thought of Marcus Jetty, who'd saved me from the lake, and Josephine the barista who had pulled me from a dream. I realized since my accident I had not prayed at all—neither to understand God's plan, nor to ease my sense of onus in my parents' awful deaths. At the arrival of gratitude, theology slid away, like a heavy coat. But now I prayed. Let her be safe in a warm dry room. Let her be brave, but more than that be stubborn. Sometimes the missing did return. Maybe tomorrow she would be back in the newspaper, home from wherever she had been.

2

NADINE STOOD IN THE LOBBY WITH HER HOOD THROWN BACK. SHE had a shoebox under one arm, a wayward red smile on her lips, and a movie ticket in her fingers. She'd bought the ticket from Bjorn, his hands full at the counter just now with a line of kids. We had the new romance featuring moody and beautiful vampires. The kids jabbered while four or five adults peered around avoiding each other's eyes.

"A crowd," Nadine said, nodding at the line. "That's nice."

I had to agree. It's good to have a line in the lobby—so what if I was tired of vampires? It was a merry winter evening and Nadine retained her happy mood until Bjorn went down to introduce the picture. He opened with hello, then halted abruptly. He cleared his throat and again fell silent. It was like a chain slipping off. A swell of apprehension and sympathy rose out of the seats. Light touched Nadine's brow as she peeked through the tiny square window. She hugged her elbows.

"Ellen isn't here," she whispered.

Eventually Bjorn made a half recovery to relieved applause and soon we heard his step upon the stairs. Nadine caught my eye, but slipping into the booth Bjorn seemed to have regained himself. His fingers flew over the console, he dimmed the house lights, the projector shuddered into its rhythm. I felt unreasonably proud of him. While the previews ran he smiled, cautioned me that the Simplex had been a little slippy, and asked Nadine for the Wagoneer key so he could drive to the riverbank and check on Galen Pea.

"Thanks for doing this," she told him.

"No problem. Enjoy the shoebox. Stay out of trouble, you two." He shot Nadine the dead-eye, which made her smile at me, which made me grin quite stupidly at Bjorn, which drove him ducking out of the booth.

As for the shoebox, it leaned toward tangy. Clearly the dangerous side of Nadine had assembled this haphazard picnic she referred to as "tapas," in this case olives stuffed with garlic and almonds and pimientos, asparagus wrapped in paper-thin ham, four kinds of cheese in foil packets, crackers encrusted with black pepper, an apologetic sack of prunes rolled in chili powder, and a golden tin of tasty small fish from Portugal. She even smuggled in a bottle of Argentinian wine, a thrilling transgression. It was my theater. We didn't see much of the picture. We didn't even talk much. The film boasts gales of pop music which kept knocking me off balance, but it was good to be running the booth again, especially in Nadine's company. The kids yelped and cheered, seats creaked and settled. It was only when the last of them were shuffling out that Nadine's cell phone buzzed.

"Bjorn," she answered, her face turning distant. "All right—one second." She touched the screen and he was on speaker.

"I'm headed into Duluth with Galen."

We heard Galen's hoarse voice delivering abuse over whistling road noise.

"He got bit, down at the river," Bjorn said.

"Did you say bit?" Nadine paled. "What bit him? The sturgeon?"

"No," Bjorn said. "A raccoon. It's a pretty bad bite. Shut up—get that seat belt on," he added to Galen, then explained that a skinny old raccoon came down the riverbank in the dark. It wore a ratty old collar and was almost certainly what remained of Genghis. The raccoon was making chickeny noises, squawking and sneezing. Galen grabbed his bike and pointed its headlight at the gaunt patchwork-looking animal, which spasmed at the mouth and gnawed its own spine. Ten feet away things broke fast. Galen attempted an end run, keeping the bike between himself and the coon, but it sprang between the wheels and caught him above the ankle. There it hung quivering, sneezing in a muffled way with its fangs in Galen's leg. Bjorn booted Genghis free and they sprinted away. Reaching the Wagoneer Galen was crying and furious. He slung tears off his face saying *Ima get rabies. They'll strap down my head and my hands*. Bjorn steered onto the highway and put his foot down. He didn't stop in Greenstone but sped southeast toward Duluth where the lit outskirts were just now coming into view.

In the depths of the Wagoneer we heard Galen say, "That old bus driver got rabies, you know what happened to him."

"Be still," Bjorn told him.

"He died on a twenty-foot chain is what happened."

"No he didn't."

I said, "Does Lily know?"

"Couldn't reach her," Bjorn said. "Left a message. We're just about there."

"Get to the ER. We're on our way," Nadine said, although Bjorn had the Wagoneer and I had no car at all.

"Okay."

"My shoe's full of blood," said Galen's distant voice.

"It's okay," Bjorn said. "You'll be okay."

"Ima get rabies."

"You aren't either. They can stop it. They give you a couple of injections and you're all right. You won't get it. This happens all the time to people. It does. Stay on your side."

We could hear road noise from the Wagoneer, the metallic click of a seat belt engaging.

"How many injections," Galen said in a rising voice.

"Not many," Bjorn told him.

"Liar, it's like a hundred. I read about it before. It's a needle this big and they stick it right in your belly button."

"I have to go, we're here," Bjorn said.

Galen made a gnashing sound.

"Be careful," said Nadine.

The last thing we heard as Bjorn hung up was Galen pounding the dashboard—from his panicked shrieks it was obvious rabies seemed less scary to him than a hundred needle stabs.

As it turned out he needed only five injections—they gave him the first right away, in the arm not the belly button, to everyone's relief. By the time we arrived at Rune's camper van things were fairly tranquil. Lily came straight from night class. Galen was cleaned up and glassy-eyed. He was impressed by his hospital bracelet and the warm cotton blankets delivered by nurses. Two separate doctors stepped in and looked at his chart and pointed lights in his eyes—they both assured him he wouldn't get rabies. This and the fact of only four remaining shots, as opposed to ninety-nine, freed Galen to see the upside. Other kids in his class had broken their arms or had their appendixes out, but he, Galen Pea, got a *rabies bite*. Nothing was worse except maybe quicksand. The second doctor described what would happen if he wound up with rabies full-on. You're a lucky man, the doctor told him. If you hadn't got in right away there'd be nothing we could do. You'd get thirsty but wouldn't be able to swallow. You'd snap your jaws and claw yourself. Four or five days of torment, then the end.

Galen was overjoyed. Everyone who visited heard the electrifying news. "Five days," he said, hunched on his bed like a vulture. "That's how it goes if you don't catch it fast. Five days of torture, then you die!"

"A doctor told you this?" said Rune, aghast.

"I'm a lucky man," Galen said darkly.

The event was adequate reason to keep Galen away from the river, and Lily laid down the law. He'd been attacked and bitten and rushed to the hospital. Enough. Galen folded at last. The doctors had warned him the shots would make him sick. He felt it coming on. The weather was getting cold anyway. Galen agreed to stay home and quit sturgeon hunting for now. He would take the winter off. The sturgeon would still be around in the spring.

No one felt worse about the incident than Beeman. He wrote an *Observer* piece about Galen's courage and Bjorn's heroism, then a self-flagellating editorial about Genghis and the hubris of subjugating wild creatures. After Galen's release he began dropping in regularly to bring the boy comics, flashlights, steel pulleys, rolls of parachute cord, survival candles, a Zippo lighter. He watched superhero DVDs with Galen so Lily could get back to her accounting class. Despite his efforts, Galen got discouraged—that vaccine is no seaside vacation. His face swelled painfully. Puffy red hives broke out on his limbs. Beeman's spirits dived as well. He dropped his asking price for the newspaper another ten thousand. He was quiet when we met at the Shipwreck for pints. I asked whether he was still seeing Connie Swale and he said she'd been spiritually awakened and didn't want to know him anymore.

To cheer him up I suggested one final Empress after-party. We'd pick a worthy movie, maybe two. I promised raisin pie. Beeman laughed and rightly so. Pie and a couple of rickety classics won't lift anyone for very long. Beeman knew the truth—I wanted one more evening with my corpus of illegals, before the truck rolled in next month and took them all away.

3

WE HELD THE PARTY CHRISTMAS EVE, ON THE TAIL OF THE NEW SHER-lock Holmes. Abandoning secrecy we invited the fourteen paying customers to hang around for a bonus flick, and three or four of them did.

Nadine had at first discouraged the idea, reminding me of Fergus Flint's admonition. I employed the last-chance argument—the finale for my illicit vault, the end of my outlaw career. No one in Hollywood would know.

First to appear were the usuals—Lily and Galen, Don Lean and Marcie, Ellen Tripp who kissed Bjorn on the mouth then departed for a dread family holiday. Jerry Fandeen drifted in but left straightaway, and just before showtime Ann arrived in sweatpants and a white-wine smile.

We also drew people I didn't expect. Dr. Koskinen drove up from Duluth with his wife Celeste—I'd mentioned it to him at my appointment the previous week. Marcus Jetty appeared, the first time in all these years I'd seen him at the Empress; even Julie and Margaret from the Agate Café came over, having shut down for the holiday.

Moments before the lights dimmed Jerry Fandeen returned from the Hoshaver carrying a pair of men's leather boots in a small size. "For the kid," he told me, meaning Galen Pea—it was hard not to notice Galen's delaminating footgear, which resembled heavy felt slippers. The boots had been left in Jerry's brother's hunting shack years earlier. "Probably won't fit," Jerry said, but they did—high-test boots, too,

barely used Red Wings with flexible soles and the speed-laces that snap
into place. Jerry waited for Galen to see him, then handed them over
without explanation. Galen stepped out of the slippers and the Red
Wings were his. "You want the right shoes for the job," said Jerry, and
that was the whole transaction.

The movie was *We're No Angels*, the 1955 Bogart about escaped
convicts, a covetous businessman, and a viper in a box. There was plenty
of laughter during the show, some of it from the comedy and some
from people catching up with each other. In the dark Nadine took
my hand and moved her fingers up and down my arm. So it seemed a
decent Christmas—maybe even a kind of pinnacle, given the realities
of a place like the Empress; and it didn't escape me that this little group
belonged in a movie itself, the fatigued ragtag ensemble unlikely to win
the day. Of course in the movies they generally *do* win the day—in the
final scene of *We're No Angels*, the viper bites the businessman and is
rewarded with sainthood and halo.

Not that we got to see it.

The projector suddenly quit. Light died off the screen. The sound
track ground to a silence so total somebody laughed with nerves.

It was the stillness that told me what was wrong, even before I
felt my way to the lobby and saw no lights there either, no LEDs, no
glow coming in off the streetlamps. The electricity had failed. People
crunched popcorn or half-stood, whispering. Blinding little smartphone
lights bounded here and there. I think everyone expected the power to
return, and when it didn't people started blundering into their coats,
scouring seats for gloves and hats. Already the temperature was falling.
Soon a slow parade of tiny beams ensued until everyone was in the lobby,
then finally out the door. Nadine stood in the diffuse moonlight coming
through the glass, trying to call the power company.

Bjorn was on his phone too, with Ellen Tripp. He said, "I don't
know. I don't see him. Here, ask Mr. Wander," and he handed me the
phone.

I said, "Ellen?"

She said, "Hi—is Rune with you at the theater?"

I realized I hadn't seen him in the confusion.

"My mom's an EMT, you know? They called her after the outage. I got a text from her, like a minute ago. She's with the ambulance."

"What's happened, Ellen?"

She was reluctant to say it. "Mom says an old man flew a kite into a power line. That's why everything got dark."

Some time must have passed because she said, "Mr. Wander, are you there?"

"Is he alive?" I asked.

She said, "A minute ago he was."

4

ATTACHMENTS ARE EASY TO SPOT IN THE MOVIES—THE FOND GLANCE
through a clouded window, the nod returned from across the room.
In reality I never saw my own attachment forming, nor recognized its
symptoms. I found myself thinking sometimes of Rune and sometimes
of my dad. There was a physical ache, novel yet dreadfully familiar. It
was like scraping, like the lining of my stomach being flensed with a
blade. Waking at night I could hear it.

When Beeman's father was dying back in North Dakota, Beeman
phoned me in varying states of distress from the hospital waiting room.
His anguish surprised me. Beeman never said much about his family.
I knew he used to call the old man Saturday mornings to talk baseball
or politics, trying to keep him from sinking into the marsh of incuri-
ous disapproval that swallows so many ancients. For all their amusing
battles Beeman had never thought to imagine a life without his dad.
I on the other hand had never stopped imagining a life *with* mine, so
that Beeman's fulsome suffering seemed a luxury to me. What I'd have
given for a similar chance!

Now I sat in a waiting room myself, sometimes with Nadine,
sometimes with Bjorn, while the snow slid streaming down the windows.

These were Rune's wounds: two blackened burns on the second
and third fingers of his right hand, where he'd held the string and
been unable to let go. A similar burn on the thumb of his left, this one

marked by what resembled an exit wound, as though the current tearing through his body had arrived at the end of that unlucky digit and holed his thumbnail to escape. There was a third burn on his left side, halfway up the rib cage—it looked like a furious mouth. Though his vision was unimpaired, the whites of his eyes were entirely crimson.

Despite all this his heart was steady. He didn't exhibit the arrhythmia common with electrocuted persons. The nurse gave him a sedative so he'd sleep a good long time. No one knew what he'd be like when he came to. At noon Nadine remembered it was Christmas Day and insisted that she, Bjorn, and I walk out into the swirling flakes. We found an open café with no customers and a "banquet special" of roast turkey and dressing with candied yams and corn pudding and red velvet cake. The waitress delivered us a tale of boyfriend woe in installments while refilling our coffees. It was a good meal and the waitress was funny. The boyfriend didn't know what he had. Afterward we wrapped up and went down the Lakewalk ankle-deep in snow. The wind was shifty and cold. Waves came ashore with hardening spray. The dark clouds moved like shoulders. At a spot where the wind had blown the beach clear, Bjorn and I spent a little time flinging stones at a deadhead log floating twenty yards out. I was more accurate but Bjorn had Alec's powerful arm. The rocks zipped out like bullets but the target was never in danger. Nadine caught my eye and smiled. A woman in a white parka with a big white sled dog passed us on the walk and said to Nadine, *What a lovely family you have*. Nadine thanked her. I didn't say anything. I felt unreasonably pleased and shy. That remark was Christmas enough for me.

When we got back to the hospital Rune was still sleeping. He slept until early the next morning when he woke suddenly and began to speak, sliding without warning into moments of private history. As green lights flashed and a nurse took his blood pressure, Rune described in detail the expression on Sofie's face while they were riding a Lofoten express ferry a decade ago. The boat was a new fast one and Sofie's silver hair whipped in the wind, and she leaned sparkling over the rail as if into the future itself. Hardly pausing for breath Rune ran down a short list of names he and Sofie liked for the newborn girl whose adoption they never achieved: Birgit, Gunda, Else, Jorunn, also Dusty, after Springfield whom Sofie adored. Rune rolled his red eyes and continued his scattershot monologue. He told about a city inhabited by the drowned, an ancient metropolis filled with fishermen, women who'd hurled themselves into the sea, Argonauts, master-race submariners, P-51 pilots, Vikings, Rune's father and two of his uncles, people pulled in by wights and fishes, children who fell through the ice. You'd think it a saturated place of muted colors and indistinct booming sounds but no, the city was bright and warm. It lay on the shore of a benign and stormless sea in which you couldn't sink. On the beach walked beautiful drowned girls with vivid scarves drifting behind them in the breeze. The old men, sailors, longboatsmen with braided beards, gathered at plank tables over glasses of whiskey and mead. The sun shone as if through stained glass. Tiny drowned children crouched in the shallows feeding pieces of bread to huge speckled fish as friendly as dogs.

By the third day the present seeped into him. He remembered our names and stopped retelling chance memories. This should've been encouraging, yet it seemed to me as the present gained purchase Rune also retreated. For example, by this time I'd brought in three or four of his liveliest kites and hung them here and there in his room—an idea of Nadine's, who thought of bright colors as restorative stimulants. When we arrived the next day the kites were gone. A nurse informed us he'd found them disturbing. He slept a great deal and I suspect feigned sleep to avoid our conversation. He didn't laugh at words or ideas that might've pleased him before. Beeman came and told funny stories, trying to coax out Rune's high-pitched laugh. But Rune was impassive behind the Ray-Bans he fumbled on whenever people visited, so as not to horrify them with his crimson eyes.

Out in the hall, Beeman was unnerved. "He used to laugh if I just said *yawp*."

"We're bringing him home tomorrow. At least it's supposed to be sunny—maybe that will help."

And sunny it was, late the next morning, when Rune was released. He wore the sunglasses when the nurse wheeled him out to the Wagoneer, then shaded his eyes with bandaged fingers while Nadine drove north. Her cheerful monologue soon ran dry. I couldn't think of a thing to say. First we ran out of talk, then we ran out of sun. Clouds mustered above. They appeared as the usual benign lambs but quickly turned to steel wool. Sure enough, a mile from the Greenstone city limits, snow began to fall.

That night at Rune's behest I took down the kites that had hung from trim boards and doorknobs since his arrival. They hurt his eyes he said. I stacked them in the north closet along with the illegals. The apartment looked clean and boring without them. Rune took off his sunglasses and it took all my will not to look away. You don't get used to bloody whites.

Nadine came in the morning to cook. No doubt she suspected I would feed Rune irresponsibly. Bjorn may have revealed to her the Guinness breakfast theory. She cracked eggs into a bowl, toasted up a good local sourdough, fried sausages, and made a blueberry coffee cake. The kitchen got steamy and rich-scented. How could it fail? Hadn't my own appetite returned, thanks to her? Yet Rune wasn't much cheered by her efforts. Electrocution had flattened his palate. In fact not much cheered him until the shaggy old raven flumped onto the snow-covered sill and pecked at the glass to come in. At this Nadine said, "You are not serious," but Rune's expression was so hopeful she opened the window. The bird soon developed a low sort of chatter like an AM radio or a sidewalk café half a block off. It perched on the coffee table, muttering and playing with nickels and quarters and kroner that lay in the bottom of a turned wood bowl. The raven tolerated the rest of us but treated Rune like a brother. If he was sleeping on the couch it would keep its voice down. It glared if you laughed or got loud. If Rune slept too long the bird would get nervous. Then it would hop over and peck him lightly, just to watch his eyes open, or to drop a bright coin into his palm.

As word of what happened went around, Rune attracted a stream of visitors. Don Lean puffed up the stairs with snow on his hat and big stripy Roger in the crook of his arm. Marcus Jetty came with a 1945 issue of *Life* about the heroic liberation of Finnmark. Lily Pea brought Galen whose stoic ferocity made Rune smile.

I hoped the flow of company would trail off. Instead it intensified. Some days I returned from City Hall to find strangers standing around the apartment. They were like pilgrims after the source of something, some of them tongue-tied, some scanning the apartment as if performing reconnaissance. "They're looking for the kites," Nadine informed me. One woman confided she had conquered a lifelong fear after flying two times with Rune. She never said what she was scared of. She offered to stay and nurse him full-time.

I appreciated these pilgrims' concern but confess to an introvert's desperation. Would the influx never stop? Would no one ever say, *Why, this is your home! What were we thinking, to drop by uninvited, and stay so long?* Still, I let it continue. Rune liked people in a palpable way. They warmed to him easily, and he seemed to enjoy them even as they wearied him terribly.

Those early days he asked often for Bjorn, but Bjorn had returned to the water. Along with the snow and low heavy clouds came a spate of northeasterlies with tall curling waves. Nadine begged him in vain to stay ashore. Several times I walked or cycled down and watched him hunting over the breaks. Ice gathered at his elbows and eyebrows. His board was a yellow dart across the hard blue waves. The weather came in so dark and low I couldn't tell where lake and sky parted until Bjorn appeared on his feet coming out of a cloud. Evenings he arrived at the Empress dressed in two or three sweaters, having risked hypothermia earlier. He made the little speech, climbed into projection, and essentially ran the Empress, while Nadine and I looked after Rune, and changed his nasty dressings, and tried to hold fast against defeat.

On a bleak night in early January, Rune emerged from bed where he had been all day and asked for akevitt. I poured some, and he told me what happened on Christmas Eve, when he left that final after-party to be alone with the sky.

He wasn't feeling melancholy, as I had assumed—he missed Lucy, yes, but he also missed the wind. It was one of the rare days when he'd failed to fly; as the movie droned on, dropping its hints about the avaricious villain and the viper in the box, Rune thought of the wind outside, and wondered how strong or light it was, and what it might be saying.

Finally he sneaked out.

Because it was calm he chose a wide white wing that would fly on a rumor. He walked south out of town on the highway, curving inland past the city limits. There's a place where the trees clear and the lake is a distant black line. He stepped down into the ditch, crossed an abandoned rail line, and set out through a field of stunted spruce where none of the trees reached past his waist. The quarter moon came and went in the dense high clouds.

The spruces gave out as he neared the lake. A grove of pines stood black to the south, then a line of boulders or upthrust crags and a dead tree trunk that bent toward the lake as if it had kept watch for years. Rune tied the wing to a reel of the lightest string he owned.

I pictured him calling up a breeze. It seemed to me the wind loved Rune Eliassen, and rose from nothing when he asked, and other days calmed its violence to give his kites free passage. The wing moved up and out like a messenger. It was gone from sight in a minute. The night was slap cold. It smelled of snow though none was falling. With height the kite got traction. The line tautened in his gloved fingers.

Twenty minutes he flew, half an hour, letting out line, the wing seeking farther and farther abroad. At a quarter mile out it reached the end of the line. This was when, as Rune described it, the bent tree overlooking the water straightened as though fixing a crick in its neck.

It shook itself and moved toward him. "My veins slowed down— they became very cold," Rune told me. "Is that the expression?"

As the tree approached it acquired limbs and a smile.

"How long have you been here?" Rune asked.

"Not the question I expected," replied Adam Leer, for now it was plainly he.

"You were here when I arrived. I thought you were a tree, you stood so still."

"Cold doesn't bother me. Neither does waiting."

"What were you waiting for?"

"That is not the question either."

"What question do you want?"

"You know. Surely you know. You've practiced it on everyone but me."

Rune was silent.

"You've forgotten. I'll remind you. Ask me if I knew your son."

Rune felt the string in his fingers. The kite dodged and shivered. The wind had come out of the west to begin with, but clocked around and came off the water. Soon the line pointed nearly straight inland.

Leer said, "If you won't ask, then I have one for you. Why do this? Fly these kites?"

"I like to fly."

"You more than like to. You need to. I drive past the lookout, there you are. Come down to watch the sea in peace, here you come to fly. I can't picture you another way. At first I thought discipline but as time passes lunacy seems more likely. I don't understand it."

"Why do you need to understand?"

"Because I'm curious. I'm a long time in this world now. People are simpler than they let on. Tell me what this gives you that you pay it such regard."

Rune didn't reply. Instead he offered Leer the string.

Leer waved it away.

Rune said, "The only way to understand flying is to fly."

"Then I pass. I don't know why anyone would play this game of yours."

Leer stood a long time without speaking, so long he seemed to bend and stiffen—even up close he looked a little like a tree again.

"I knew Alec," he said at last. "I knew him just a little—in other words, exactly as well I wished to. Tell me, did Nadine really say to you he was an honest man?"

"Honest how?" asked Rune.

"A man whose word would hold. One who wouldn't abandon a woman or a child."

Rune replied that he hadn't asked the question in precisely this way, but yes—she said Alec was honest.

Leer nodded and started walking toward the water. "I see that is enough for you. I'll say no more about it. Good night."

Rune watched him go. At the same time he felt the loss of resistance in his fingers. The wing went into a long swoon as the wind died entirely. He hauled in string by arm's lengths, it fell in heaps beside him. Soon the line was a thin trail on the snow leading inland. He followed it hand over hand. Through the tree farm it went, over the abandoned railroad. Reaching the highway he saw the slight glow of the city of Greenstone against cold moist clouds to the north. He crossed the pavement following the string until it rose static before him. He imagined it caught in a tree. He pulled. There was give so he pulled harder. A faint crackling erupted. Later he realized the crackling came from inside his head. He went down as though clubbed. The crackling turned to a grotesque buzz and a frying smell. Snow hissed on his burned tongue. His ribs knocked together and he threw up in the snow. His fingertips seemed to whistle. The glow over Greenstone faded slowly to black, then his own lights went out as well.

We sat in the living room with only the reflected light coming in off the roof. Rune held his side. His face had fallen. He flailed a little getting to his feet.

"Are you all right?" I said. He'd taken more akevitt than was strictly recommended for an electrocuted man on bed rest.

"When I was a boy a fever swept through," he said wearily. "Neighbor girl died. One of my friends lost the sight in one eye, my sister was frail for a year."

"And you?"

"Inside my fever I walked in the mountains. A man approached who was not a man. His eyes were flat and his hands were fire. He touched my face and it began to die." Rune shrugged. "When the fever departed my face was still changed. It changes now when I am tired, or afraid, or losing one fight or another."

"You can rest as long as you need to," I said.

The door opened and Bjorn came in. He turned on the kitchen light and stood squinting. He'd screened a film and swept the auditorium.

Rune was trying to unfasten his side bandage which needed changing. This was usually my job or Nadine's because Rune's hands still had their own ungainly wrappings, but Rune hated to have us do it—his injury embarrassed him.

Without a word Bjorn stepped in and peeled away the cotton. He set it aside and went to the kitchen and put warm water in a basin with antiseptic. He found a washcloth and dipped it and cleaned the wound. It was still an ugly hole. Rune looked away while his grandson daubed on antibiotic, folded gauze to the size of his palm, and placed it over the hole. Bjorn patted dry the clean skin. He found the white tape and tore off four strips and taped the gauze down neatly.

"Thank you, Bjorn," Rune said.

"You ought to sleep," Bjorn replied. "Mr. Wander, there were new leaks tonight. Three or four of them. Lanie Plume took one down the back of her neck. I found more buckets in the basement so we're all right for now, but if we don't get some snow off that roof we'll have to start handing out ponchos."

5

I'D WONDERED HOW LONG IT WOULD BE UNTIL THE LEAKS FORCED action at the Empress. I meant to do something about it the next day, but an important commitment took priority—the truck was coming in from LA to possess my bottle imps.

The driver phoned from ten miles out. The snow didn't alarm him as much as the midday gloom—"You guys got some medieval-type darkness here," he said, adding heartily, "Oh well, bring it on," as if propping up his courage. I had a weather map open before me. He was going to arrive between fronts.

Bjorn and I went down to the lobby to watch for the truck. Street-lights blinked on. Betsy Shane came out of the bakery and looked around and up at the sky and went back in. Two cars went through south to north, then two pickups. The cars had skis strapped to their roofs. The pickups were full of sled dogs.

Beeman arrived just before the truck. He wanted to document the event. I've never been a journalist but once the truck arrived anyone could see a feature story looming. The driver called himself a "relic courier." He was a raffish lout in a long coat and scarf. Besides repatriated films he told us he'd transported cabernet salvaged from the *Titanic*; slivers of the True Cross; the fossilized eggs of a *Saltoposuchus*, swift small predator of the late Triassic; and molars from a talkative French aristocrat whose guillotined head had briefly kept chatting. With him was a black-eyed, wiry man speaking continuously to himself in a language I didn't recognize. His glance darted everywhere and he waved in annoyance at the little shocked cloud of his breath. He handled the reels like an acrobat—they slid from the closet shelves to his long limber arms to a stand-up dolly and down the steps to arrive at the truck unruffled as a wedding cake.

In under an hour the reels were stowed and strapped in. The day was cold in a way that made your teeth creak yet the cargo hold felt like a greenhouse. Beeman and Bjorn stood on the twilit sidewalk. Nadine arrived looking nostalgic, but I felt nothing of the kind—in fact when the driver waved and the acrobat nodded and said *Bye-bye*, I could only grin. The truck pulled away. It was a murky afternoon, but I felt light and pleasantly shriven.

As it happened, the films were only the first purge of the day.

I'd seen Rune that morning retrieving his piles of kites from the film closet. I thought he was just getting them out of the way, but then he began to organize, brushing off the more weathered individuals and setting them out in some order sensible to him.

Light steps climbed the staircase and hesitated on the landing. There came a shy knock at the door.

"Hello, yes," Rune called, and Amanda Nelson poked her head in. I knew Amanda—she taught second grade at Greenstone Elementary, though she looked barely out of high school herself. Apparently she was a regular flyer.

"What can I do for you, Amanda?" I said.

"Oh—didn't you know? I'm here because of what Rune is doing." And she picked up the kite nearest her, which looked like a stone fireplace, and waved it about so the orange flame whickered with a sound close to actual fire. "Oh, it's beautiful!"

"Thank you," Rune told her. He didn't look my direction.

Amanda lifted the kite at arm's length and trotted in a tiny circle around the kitchen, the kite following agreeably. She went to Rune and gave him a hug. He looked at me dolefully over her shoulder.

It came to this: he couldn't face kites for a while. Though his burns were healing, his hands still hurt badly; the thought of all that sketching and cutting and folding, not to mention the lively tug of a finished kite in the air, was painful. There was more to it than that, I suspected—he seemed to regard his creations reproachfully, as if they'd let him down in some way. When Amanda stopped by the previous week, he'd offered the kites to her second graders. She agreed to take the lot of them. Later I learned she hung them overlapping around the classroom like a mythic parade. The catfish alone took up half of one wall. The kids wrote Rune letters saying *Thank you Mr. Eliassen. Please get well. Please come see us when you do.*

"I miss them, though," I admitted to Rune—the apartment looked clean and vast; the walls were dull and cold to the touch. The maple floor was a glacier. "I miss you working on them."

He nodded and went in his room and emerged with the one kite held back from Amanda. It was the big cinnamon hound, the one that first got my attention when I looked from the roof-deck after the fire.

"I saved you this one—you always liked it," Rune said, handing it over.

We finally got the roof cleared off—Bjorn came over, Beeman too, and they managed it in a couple of hard shifts, pushing the snow into a berm along the alley-side cornice, then heaving it over with shovels. They came in winded, chaffing me about faking a ruined shoulder.

"Almost forgot," Beeman said, digging into a pocket of his insulated jacket, "I got something for you, Rune." He handed over another cassette. "It's not much. A little compilation. Interviews with your boy Alec, back in his pitching days." Beeman looked apologetic. "We probably did fifty or sixty short hits like this, after ball games, but it was all analog then, we had to recycle our tapes. These were all I could round up. Nothing brilliant here—I just thought you'd like to hear his voice."

Rune stood looking ambushed but happy. He performed a small bow. "Thank you, Tom. Stay, sit down. Listen with us."

"Not a chance," Beeman said. "I'm on one of Ann's dread committees—I've got to prep for a meeting, or concoct an alibi." And he fled down the steps like an avalanche.

Rune clicked the tape into the player. The first thing we heard was Alec's laugh—it was high-pitched and easy as ever, and Rune rose an inch off the floor. Alec was talking about a game he'd just blown. He'd lost control of the Mad Mouse, filling the bases, then walking in two before a relief could be summoned.

"Couldn't keep her in the zone," Alec said. "I tell her where to go, but she rarely complies."

A significantly younger Beeman said, "The Mad Mouse is a girl?"

"I guess she is," Alec mused. "Does it surprise you?"

"Not all all," Beeman said, and they laughed. I hardly dared look at Rune but he was simply alight. There wasn't a line on his face. Why would there be? This was his first time hearing his son, and he liked him awfully well.

I soon learned those few brief interviews by heart. Rune played them whenever there were no visitors around, and Nadine wasn't here—he feared that hearing Alec would make her grieve. Bjorn had never heard the interviews either; he didn't say much, but seemed to lean toward the lighthearted voice of the dad he had mostly forgotten. Beeman had rescued only four short Q and A's, maybe six minutes of Alec on tape. Alec wasn't hard on himself. He didn't like losing, but this was Single-A baseball in Duluth, Minnesota. He wasn't delusional. He complained about the cold, joked about the monkey, and praised his teammates. "Did you see Hambone's sliding catch? Whoever knew?"

The one time Alec seemed pensive was moments after the perfecto. Of course a lot was on his mind—career performance aside, before the sun rose he'd be rushing Nadine to maternity. "Nothing seems the same, now," he told Beeman. "Whoever knew?" he said, again. This time the expression had an undertone, a gravity lacking earlier. Bjorn caught it too. "Listen to him," he said. "You hear that? This was just before I was born. Like *hours*. It's landing on him now, like bricks," he added wistfully. "*I'm* landing on him, that's what I think—those bricks are me."

6

ALL IT TOOK TO END THE FLOW OF PILGRIMS WAS THE RETURN OF Lucy DuFrayne.

The day she got back from California there were seven people I didn't know in the apartment. They meant well. The raven regarded them with hatred. Both Nadine and I had talked with Lucy on the phone—she knew what to expect, yet the sight of Rune's ebbing self drained the tan from her face. She transmuted her alarm into efficiency. She was so kind and sly that in five minutes the pilgrims were gone. People found their coats on and themselves on the street. They had the illusion they'd left of their own choosing. Lucy was air traffic control.

To celebrate her return we had a quiet dinner which ended early when Rune fell asleep at the table. He was so pleased to have Lucy back that his energy at first seemed a miracle, only to slur and fade. In front of our eyes he bent slowly forward until his head came to rest adjacent to a twice-baked potato. When Lucy placed a hand on his shoulder he opened his eyes muttering *Na ga over vinden*, which means something like "Now go over the wind." She got him to his feet and led him blinking to his room.

In the evenings we changed his dressings—more accurately, Bjorn did. It seemed no one else had the proper technique. I was too rough with the tape. How could anything heal with such crude handling? Was that a washcloth or sandpaper?

Even Nadine was not up to standard; with Lucy he affected a prim self-consciousness about his wounded skin. Obviously he wanted Bjorn to do it.

Thankfully Bjorn didn't mind. He wasn't squeamish. His hands, so deft at splicing celluloid, were equally adept with gauze and tape. "My dad was good at bandages," he said, with pride. "He'd say, Don't worry, kid, Dr. Sandstrom's here."

"Now you are Dr. Sandstrom," Rune said.

"You got that right. Now suck it up."

Every day the snow kept falling. The days got longer but no brighter. The raven kept Rune company and listened to Beeman's tapes with him. At night Bjorn screened the films, then came up late to change dressings. Despite his efforts the tear in Rune's side remained open and painful. I wondered if it would become a permanent aperture, as with the nineteenth-century patient whose stomach let doctors peer firsthand at grotesque digestive wonders.

While Bjorn attended him, Rune used the opportunity to impart family history. It was Bjorn's family too after all. He began with twin sister Gretchen, whose short poetry career an Oslo critic had called "a Roman candle fizzing and snapping above the Arctic Circle." Gretchen had died three years ago of a stroke. She was talking to students on the library steps when she appeared puzzled. *Hva kaldt vann!* she exclaimed, meaning *What cold water!* Then she slumped down in the shrubbery while the alarmed students mistook her words for a request and sprinted off to get her a drink.

"Geez," Bjorn said. "Sorry to hear it."

Rune's father Søren was a fisherman and sometime ferryboat captain now residing in the city of the drowned. His crew were sleeping when he vanished so details were scarce, but Rune imagined Søren leaning over the rail, black stocking cap, horned-rimmed glasses blurry with spray, enjoying the cranky weather just before Death eased him over the side.

"What cold water," was Bjorn's cautiously wry remark. "What about your mom?"

"Her sanity was sporadic. She thought she was a seal or porpoise. She accused the neighbors of being Nazi cryptographers. She believed my father had returned to life as a clock, always a few minutes behind."

If these were dark stories they did not bother Bjorn. He seemed to appreciate the practical mortality of his newfound forebears. They fished or farmed or taught, then they died. Rune spoke of Death not as an abstraction but as a corporeal being likely to show up sooner than we wish. Bjorn was curious what this personage might look like and Rune described the covetous robed skeleton of medieval woodcuts.

One day I arrived home unexpectedly early from City Hall. Climbing the steps I heard the raven chattering. That bird sounded more human all the time. Rune didn't hear me come in. He sat at the table with his bandage off and his lower lip between his teeth. His fingers picked at the wound. The skin had begun to heal, but he was pulling it apart.

The raven said something—nearly a word. It sounded like "hurry." Rune looked up and saw me.

"Oh," he said. I could see him wondering whether I'd realized what he was up to.

"I don't think that's necessary," I said.

"What do you mean?"

He was terrible at obfuscation. In fairness it's probably hard to obfuscate convincingly in your second language.

I said, "Bjorn seems glad to spend time with you. He might actually like it better without the bandage routine."

Relief crossed his face. "That would be nice—ouch, fy," he said, taping the gauze back in place. Thereafter the wound healed quickly.

7

I WAS TAKING NOTES IN ANN'S DREAD COMMITTEE. BEEMAN MUST'VE found himself that alibi—in fact the only people who showed for this festival update were Ann herself, Lydia, Don Lean, and declining councilman Barrett Becker. This was less than half the committee but Ann was undiscouraged. She had news—the band she'd been pursuing, Storm Warning, had agreed to open their tour with a performance on Main Street. No question this leveled us up. We'd need to cordon things off, hire security, commission a stage, and nail down the beer situation, also sausage and fry bread and glow sticks. When Ann veered into detail about the hiring of a carnival midway company I found myself hung up on the memory of a ride called the Gravitron, a round enclosure with slanted walls. You enter, and as the ride spins faster you are held against the wall by speed itself. Centrifugal force holds you tight to the sides. All around you the world is flying apart—you know it is, yet you can barely lift your arms.

Don was supposed to talk about the county's role in keeping Hard Luck Days under control—now that we'd got a famous band it seemed likely there'd be an actual crowd, our first in decades, in Greenstone. But when Ann opened the floor for questions or remarks, Don stayed quiet in his folding chair. His eyes were open but not alert. He sat at a slight tilt, and I found myself tilting the opposite way, silently willing him upright.

"Took a short nap in there," he confessed afterward. The meeting had gone long and he stopped at the Empress on his way home. Bjorn was up in projection, the movie ten minutes in. Don and I hung out in the lobby eating popcorn and drinking gritty cocoa out of the machine. "I just can't keep up," Don said. "I'll admit, I'm sick of the job."

He was talking about the recent spree of thefts, which came in the wake of a sizable pot bust he made a few weeks ago in the northern wastes of the county. He'd got a call from a man claiming the loss of a hundred grow-lights and four gas heaters from his nursery operation. Don drove out to investigate. The man came to the door sleepy and startled. His head, including his eyebrows, was shaved and his bare feet were thick and fungoid. He wore what looked like a sleeping bag with holes for his arms and head. With a despondent air, he led Don to what had once been a pig barn. Hundreds of lightweight chains dangled from the ceiling. Under the empty chains stood cafeteria tables containing four thousand marijuana seedlings. The seedlings had once been robust but now looked stricken and peaky. Clearly the tipster had also been the thief, boosting his own operation while thinning the competition.

Don said, "I'm guessing it wasn't you who called, about the stolen lights."

The arrest won Don a few accolades, then things began to fly off. While DEA agents and deputies packed up the pig barn, Don got a call from a rural-supply store reporting a robbery. The thieves loaded up four Quonset-hut kits, a Knipco heater, and two cases of Nut Goodies. Two nights later someone stole fifteen rolls of camo netting from Northland Unclaimed Freight, and the night after that he heard back from the greenhouse man—the one who'd lost his wind chimes, earlier. The greenhouse fellow had just returned for spring inventory and wished to amend his report: besides the chimes, he was missing a long-handled spade, six hundred feet of garden hose, and half a pallet of high-quality fertilizer.

"What kind of a person goes out, dead of winter, to steal fertilizer and *wind chimes?*" Don asked, annoyed.

"Large tomatoes and inner tranquillity are a bewitching combination."

"What's happening," he complained, "is someone's getting a jump on the next big cannabis ranch. This county's the size of an eastern state. They plant in the woods and between corn rows. There's no money for staff. I'm tired of this."

"At least the rabies outbreak is over," I said.

"Sure, but the vole plague is only beginning—now that's another thing," he said. The wet autumn had displaced thousands of meadow voles that promptly established new homes all over Greenstone. Voles don't hibernate but multiply year-round. Now spring was coming. Beeman had reported a flood of voles spreading like an oil spill down Ladder Street in the moonlight. On the school football field they tunneled so hard the snow collapsed, revealing capillaries in a thousand directions.

"We need more foxes," I said. "Foxes enjoy a vole."

"We have tons of foxes—the foxes can't keep up," was Don's dark reply. "These foxes are as tired as I am. We got a crowd coming in for the Bad Luck deal and they're going to be treading on voles. Ann's in my face about it. She thinks I have time to be a vole trapper along with cannabis and rock bands and carnies. There's too much going on," he said. "I got a defective disk in my spine. It's starting to slip. Everything is slipping. It's out of hand."

"It's centrifugal," I said.

"It sure is." Don finished his cocoa and peered at the bottom of his cup as though a forecast lay in the sediment. "I used to be a banker," he added.

"You hated it and were bad at it."

"Those things are true."

He gazed off though the glass lobby door. Jerry had gotten tired of people craning in at the showroom window, so he'd taped sheets of tan paper across it. Probably sensing impatience with his progress, he'd painted ALMOST on the paper in enormous block letters.

"I wish he'd take that down," Don said.

Poor Jerry—the sign described him exactly. He was almost a husband to Ann but not quite. He almost got promoted, then almost went to prison. He almost had the tools for the job.

From the auditorium we heard a few distant, desperate laughs. For a while there it was all bleak comedies.

Rune's side wound had healed, and his hands had also improved, though they sometimes still pained him and at other times were numb, so he often dropped bread on the floor. One Saturday afternoon I noticed him sitting in a kitchen chair out on the deck. It was a dream of a March Saturday, the sun twice its usual size and thermals shimmering off the rooftops. An eight-knot breeze pushed ripples up the shoreline. I poured two cups of coffee and carried them out along with a stale doughnut for the raven who sat on the balustrade practicing its English. Rune accepted a cup. I followed his gaze into the sky where several bright paint chips danced on the breeze. They were kites, recognizably Rune's. As the raven broke the doughnut in pieces and decided which to eat first, I retrieved a cheesy old spotting scope with which I watched passing ships. The bicycle was flying above the water tower. The black anvil rose out behind the Slake plant, the bowler-hatted man over the ore dock, the fireplace above the deserted swimming beach, and the giant catfish up at the lookout. In all we counted eleven of Rune's kites in the air. Amanda Nelson had distributed them to her second graders as academic rewards and they all agreed to go out that afternoon and fly if weather permitted. For a minute or two I was careful not to look at Rune. When I did he was suffused with color. He watched the kites fly, murmuring hums of approval. When we went inside he got out some lightweight paper and began to sketch at the table.

Bjorn too continued his upswing. His movie introductions got tighter and funnier. He helped me tarp over a section of roof to reduce auditorium leaks. The Empress didn't fill but got gradually less empty. If this continued into the summer I'd be at risk of turning a profit.

I don't know precisely when those two began to seem like men of the same family. Across the weeks Bjorn began to appropriate certain of Rune's facial expressions, especially a widening of the eyes signifying delight; as for Rune, a quickness reentered his limbs, and one night I arrived upstairs to find him at the table surrounded by scraps of paper and thread, designing a kite the size of his hand. This one was the simplest delta of wrapping tissue, its leading edges kept from collapse by a reinforcing fold over a strip of glue. He set it aside to dry. In the morning I found him flat on his back—after a moment of panic I spied the tiny yellow sail adrift near the ceiling on a barely visible thread. It circled and shifted at an altitude of seven feet. It paused for long moments. When inevitably it stalled and began to slip backward, Rune moved his wrist in short quick tugs and the kite regained movement and height. I made a good breakfast that day, eggs and sausage with fried potatoes. Rune ate it, and wanted more.

Bjorn also discovered the source of my dust volcanoes. They were from something called a powder-post beetle, which had got in somehow and bored microscopic tunnels through one of the lobby's exposed beams. Edgar Poe had installed the beams in a brief 1980s decorating spasm. Bjorn said the best way to evict the beetles was to extract the beam whole, so I walked over to the Hoshaver and hired Jerry to help. It didn't go well—Jerry seemed stilted and incapable, his gaunt serifed frame perplexed on the ladder, asking for screwdrivers and chisels and other wrong tools for the job. At last the old timber dislodged and crashed down while we leaped away. It made a big gash on the wall. We dragged the beam out the front and around to the alley. The wall looked bad and the ceiling worse. I called Marcus Jetty who had a big stack of reclaimed timbers to choose from.

Bjorn drove me to the Salvage & Tinker. Marcus was watching a *Match Game* rerun on a snowy TV, drinking a bottle of Rolling Rock. He walked us out back where the timbers were stacked under a patchwork of rusting shed roofs like the mottled slums of Mumbai. There were light oak beams, a warped crimson one, several in architectural white, and a few scorched numbers rescued from fire. One was the color of honey just starting to crystallize—that's the one I was after.

"Give a hand here, Bjorn," I said, but Bjorn wasn't there. He was out in the yard in a patch of sun, scratching his neck, looking down at Marcus's homemade wheelbarrow. It was full of the handsome clay roofing tiles you see in the southwest. He called out, "Mr. Jetty?"

"Yeah, son."

"Where'd you get the wheelbarrow?"

Marcus said he whacked it together from yard parts.

"Where'd you get the parts?"

Marcus's memory was well-known but even he couldn't recall the specific origins of the scrummy homebuilt barrow bits. He'd welded the big steel tub from odd pieces lying around. The varnished handles he'd probably cannibalized from another old wheelbarrow—they were standard barrow handles, anyway.

"I mean the wheel," Bjorn said. His voice wasn't usual. It was in retreat somehow.

The wheel Marcus *did* remember. He'd got it years ago off a Texan passing through after visiting his sister in Ontario. The Texan had picked up the tire on the rocky shoreline near his sister's home in Rossport. Marcus gave him a golf bag for it. The tire was a practical size.

"Bjorn," I said.

He had that deadpan expression but this time it didn't look like a way of joking or hiding out. His eyes were glazed. "I'm pretty sure it's from the plane," he said.

"What plane is that?" said Marcus.

And Bjorn said: "Mr. Chandler's plane. The one my dad flew out."

What Bjorn recalled was the name TUNDRA SLICK which was embossed in white letters on the smooth puffy tire. It connected with one of the rare memories Bjorn had of his dad as a pilot, specifically a day when they'd landed the plane in a hummocky pasture—they'd eaten a picnic lunch there, watched by Highland cattle. Alec ate standing while little Bjorn sat on the tire tracing the upraised capitals with his fingers. He remembered asking his dad, "What's tundra?" and Alec grinning and saying, "This right here," tapping the soft lumpy turf with his toe.

We don't have actual tundra in Minnesota, but close enough.

Nadine met us at the Empress. She carried a curling glossy of Alec beside the plane. At that time the tires were new. With a magnifying glass you could read the sidewall lettering, in a gentle arc beside Alec's left ankle. Nadine knelt to look at the faded old tire which Marcus had removed from the barrow. Waves and currents would have carried it up the shore, perhaps between Isle Royale and the mainland, taking who knew what loops and detours, past lighthouses at Lamb and Battle Islands, past caribou coming down to drink, past Canadian bays called Thunder and Black and Nipigon, washing up finally near the hamlet of Rossport.

Of course there was no proving the tire was part of the Taylorcraft's landing gear. Don Lean did take a serial number off it, which eventually established its manufacture in Anchorage in 1992, but beyond that no record existed. Lou Chandler had a look at it but could only confirm that Tundra Slicks are a specialty tire favored by backcountry pilots, himself included. It's fair to say not many end up in Minnesota, let alone floating in Lake Superior.

The discovery seemed to make Nadine weary, rather than sorrowful—Rune was the one who went to pieces when we told him of Bjorn's find. He looked at the photo of Alec, wearing his Dukes baseball jacket and a Hemingway grin, one foot propped on the tire of that plucky sparrow of a plane. Nadine wrapped Rune in her arms while his shoulders heaved. He didn't make a sound. Nadine rubbed his back but did not cry herself.

None of us had much to say for a while. Eventually Bjorn went home with Nadine. Rune shut himself in his room. I had a bottomless, hollowed-out feeling, as when Orry and I first saw one another after our parents had died. I slung on a jacket, then saw the big kite, the cinnamon hound, leaning against the living room wall. It didn't look like any sort of answer but it looked upbeat and ready to go. I disassembled it and rolled it up and rubber-banded it to the driftwood staff and rode the Schwinn to the lookout.

I'll confess to nerves—this was my first solo flight if you will. I was never sure how much of the magic of flying was the old Norwegian, how much was the kite itself, how much my minor trauma. The moment the dog slid out of my hand I knew that none of it mattered. Up it went in a bright southwesterly. Straightaway the string began to whine. I gave it whatever it wanted. In moments I seemed to shift angles on the sun and earth, looking down over the blue-green water and brushy slopes and foamy talus shoreline. I flew for quite a while. The day was warm but the wind cool and it got up under my shirt. I thought of Nadine who was taking new sights, adjusting her navigation. She'd said once she would get along better with Alec dead than alive. If he were alive then he still got up in the morning, considered his options, and made the choice to stay gone.

A shape appeared by the cliffside. A man stood out of the tall dead grass and stood wavering in his sleeves. It was Adam Leer. He'd been sitting there silent since before I arrived, it was jarring to realize.

"Mr. Leer," I said, as he approached.

"Poor Rune must not be recovered. Is that it? He seems to have passed the baton."

"He's all right."

The wind gained urgency. There was a turbulent stream at five hundred feet where the dog spun around and began to shake. I fed it line; it climbed out of the rough air and relaxed. Leer stood watching and I wondered would he wax eloquent now about our evolving selves, or high ceilings. Whatever his subject I was indifferent. In fact I resolved not to listen. But, strangely for him, Leer seemed discomfited. He blinked as though at sand in his eyes; he seemed for once not the master of his surroundings. He did muster a wisecrack about men who play with children's toys, as though a kite were beneath him.

"Would you care to take a spin?" I asked.

With an arch expression Leer accepted the string.

The big dog pulled him off balance and he stumbled a few steps forward. His lack of finesse surprised me. On a gusty day with that much sail you need finesse above all, whereas Adam Leer seemed to fly with a sense of opposition. He moved in odd stabs and lunges, held the reel in both hands and sawed it back and forth. The kite groaned and shivered and backed away. Leer fought it when no fight was needed. My heart leapt to realize the kite was fighting back. At some point it would refuse him. Leer jerked the string around until sweat popped on his brow. His mouth was a nasty crease. I offered to take the string but he snarled and slashed the reel to and fro as the kite bent shuddering to a slow sideways dive.

I knew what would happen before it did. When the kite descended to five hundred feet, that powerful stream of air seized it and bent it nearly double. Leer didn't have the hands for it. "Give it line," I urged him, but with an impetuous pout he leaned back holding tight. The kite bent in the middle until it was a shivering column.

Then the string snapped. The kite sprang to shape. It lost momentum and swooped forward fifty or sixty feet; but instead of tumbling to earth it stabilized, found purchase on the breeze, and moved out over the water. Leer flung the reel away in disgust. The kite, glinting, caught another brisk layer of air. It began to gain altitude. In moments it became a beautiful bladelike sail on the sky. It got smaller every second, then faded into a skein of cloud moving toward Michigan in no particular hurry.

Adam Leer squinted after it. A car came rambling in and parked. Jerry Fandeen opened the door and got out and stood by the old Audi wagon. I lifted a hand but he didn't wave back. He seemed to be waiting for Leer who said, "Oof, we have a meeting. Wouldn't you know it, now he's the one keeping *me* to a schedule." He gave me a grim look. "Never save anyone, Virgil, unless you wish to be at the mercy of their potential." And with that he walked to the Audi and slid into the passenger seat. The car stalled briefly when Jerry put it in reverse but he got it going with a minor backfire and they left the lookout trailing gray smoke.

I loved that kite, that cinnamon hound. We were old friends. I had soared and laughed with that kite. It got me out on the perimeter. I felt I had failed it somehow, and Rune too, even though he would've offered the string to Leer, just as I had. Thinking it over I became a bit less angry, and more proud of the kite itself: it had refused to be flown by Leer one moment longer. It broke the line and caught the next gust out of town. A perilous beautiful move, choosing to throw yourself at the future, even if it means one day coming down in the sea.

8

IN EARLY APRIL A LETTER CAME BY CERTIFIED MAIL FROM THE LEGAL department at a major movie studio, never mind which. Fergus Flint told me it was coming. It was my first communiqué from any of the studios.

> *Mr. Wander,*
> *Received the print(s) as arranged and wish to express gratitude for returning our property, even though it took twenty-five years to do so. As you are aware it is a crime to possess a film or any part thereof belonging to studios or their subsidiaries.*
> *The industry faces many challenges. Thank you for your interest. We have no openings at the current time but will keep your information on file. Best of luck in your job search!*

I got a huge bang out of the letter, which seemed written by two people on different continents, or by one person on opposite ends of a medical event; a few days later came a second missive from a Hollywood legal department, this one more coherent. It began by reminding me of the studio's largesse and humanity, also its essential mightiness and power in allowing me, a small-time projectionist and insect of low destiny, to buzz off and live out my rube life unpunished, unless of course they had a change of heart and decided to squash me after all, which they might do, come to think of it, the squash might still happen, mayfly that I was, no doubt at a moment when I felt safe and was looking in the other direction.

Somehow this letter made me even happier. Nadine came over and we took turns reading it aloud, and got delirious doing it—Nadine employed a brilliant faux-Russian accent, like a cartoon Natasha.

Mockery aside, the letter seemed fair. It's not as if I *didn't* keep all those movies all those years; Fergus however found it high-handed, and weeks later the trade magazine *Cinematique* called me to say it'd got wind of the struggling Empress, shadowy Destin Plate, the biggest film-cache repatriation in twenty years. I said too much to that reporter, Frida LaPlant, who was warm and a bit too familiar—for example, I admitted we'd opened the vault for a Christmas event after being warned against it by my attorney. Later Fergus would upbraid me for that. "You're a careless person," he observed, and he's certainly right. I *am* more careless than I was before. Tomorrow I might be more careless still, one of the fools God allegedly protects.

Meantime my city work hours spiked as Hard Luck Days came together. Ann had got word out that Greenstone was owning its status. She organized a parade where the idea was to dress up as the water tower that rolled through town, or a frog from the fabled monsoon, "or a person with rabies," she said, though I entreated her for Galen's sake not to encourage this. I'd rented four disaster movies including *Volcano* (1997) and *Earthquake* (1974) which I recommend as deeply silly. The muni liquor store chartered a twenty-six-foot reefer hoping to profitably anesthetize the all-class reunion. Ann struck a bargain with the tenth-grade shop class to build the music stage—a sturdy platform of dimensional lumber spanning the pavement between the Empress and the Hoshaver Building.

Though, for jinx-related reasons, no one would say so, it seemed our luck might be turning. Storm Warning's new album, releasing in days, was stacking up buzzy reviews in the music press. They'd "been in the abyss and clawed their way out." They had a tall weedy front man whose personal tragedy "adds a blue tint to every quavering note," and a female lead whose leathery voice was "a midnight raid that leaves your heart a smoking ruin." They had an accordionist and a prancing rock tubist, not to mention a stained-glass artist who occupied one end of the stage and improvised bold designs during the songs, stacking shapes of many colors on a parabolic scaffold evoking European cathedrals. Ann's hipster niece revealed the band would close the show with a new single called "Jesus Wept"; she said when they played the new number, and lit the stained glass, there would absolutely be weeping, as well as laughter, and abrupt revelations, and heart rates would spike, and babies be conceived, and distant Republicans grow suddenly agitated by inklings of heartfelt compassion. "It's gonna skid the paradigm," the hipster niece predicted. After Greenstone, Storm Warning was heading straight to Los Angeles to appear on Jimmy Kimmel. "You know what?" I said to Ann, breaking or perhaps just not caring about unwritten jinx law. "I think the stars are aligning."

"Utshay upway," Ann hissed, and her eyes were watery moons.

The day before the festival was cool and bright with a light south wind. I was on the streets early, double-checking everything. The city crew had managed a thorough park cleanup, repairing electrical hookups, replacing spent lightbulbs, and trimming the campsites. Carnival trucks had arrived with trailers of folded airborne teacups and spidery Ferris wheel trusses. The grass was mowed around early drifts of daffodils. Song sparrows lit up in the shrubbery. I did a circuit of the carnival, then of Main Street. At one end of the block the beer tent was taking shape; at the other, high-school sophomores marked the pavement with chalk, getting ready to set up the stage. Despite empty storefronts the downtown did not look terrible. The Agate Café had plumped for some sidewalk tables shaded by blue canvas umbrellas. I was about to knock at the door of the Hoshaver and attempt talking Jerry into removing ALMOST when I spied Ann moving at command stride and chose to get scarce. I strolled to the marina, then turned past the pier, past the Shipwreck, which had opened early to serve a glut of carnival workers, down the public beach toward the ore dock.

I was nearly to Slake when I saw the man on the water.

The sea was a little confused, the waves kicked up by the southerly wind colliding with residual swells from the east. He stood nearer shore this time—a lot nearer, it suddenly seemed. For the first time I had a good look at his face. It wasn't all that portentous; in fact it was fairly pedestrian. He looked pale and temperate, was roughly my size, with large hands you'd call capable despite their clammy whiteness. He watched me in silence and I him; and suddenly I got it back. I remembered, that is, the first time I saw him.

The actual first time.

The slushy road, "Mysterious Ways," the big wet flakes swarming up in the lights—all these memories had already returned. Now the event spooled forth like a continuous dream: the safety rail tearing away, the airbag's attack pinning me to the seat with my face turned right—and there next to me, completely at home, the man on the water, only then he was in the passenger seat. Though not belted in, he was fully composed. His fingertips lightly touched the dash. His face wore a weathered gratitude as though I had asked for his company. To see him was to realize I'd thought of him often. He was always known but never met. I didn't exactly plan to steer over the edge—it was more an impulse, born of long yearning. Maybe that is what called him. I don't know. Maybe that's how it works, or worked that day. In any case we endured that snowy arc together. He smiled, and I calmed myself. He had eye bags and crow's-feet and his teeth were slightly crooked. He wasn't what I thought Death would look like—he was not so different from myself—but then maybe he is no one's Death but mine. Maybe I'm his only charge, and yours will look like you. What I'm saying, he was there to assist. If it were mine to die in the lake, then into the lake he would go. Snow struck the windshield, the spinning wheels made a rising disconnected whine. As we neared the water concern crossed his face. I saw that I had become his responsibility. Then we hit.

The next thing I noticed was Marcus, choking the bejeebers out of my neck while water burbled up all around.

Watching the man on the water now, he didn't frighten me. He didn't curl his lip, or peer at my soul, or seem to resent my having thrown rocks at him that one time. He stood there invitingly. Looking down I was knee-deep in the lake. I couldn't feel the water or my feet. I looked up. He put his hands in his pockets and stood ever so slightly contrapposto. The wavelets brushed the hem of his pants. He looked ready to accept my company at last and take us forward. He knew the way. I'd been thinking of him all these months as threat or harbinger but that was wrong. He was an attendant. When Marcus intervened, he simply stepped aside and waited patiently. Eventually he would guide me on.

A voice said, "Mr. Wander, geez."

I looked round. Bjorn was onshore in his scabby wetsuit, board under his arm.

"Hi, Bjorn."

"What are you doing?"

I didn't answer.

"You all right?" he said.

"Sure." I was listening to Bjorn, but watching the man on the water. I don't mean to portray the event as one in which I had a choice—for example, to stay or go. Something would happen and a decision be made, but I didn't feel part of it or have a preference one way or the other.

Bjorn said, "Are you having some kind of a deal?"

Some kind of a *deal*. I had to smile. I glanced down and noticed water up to my waist.

The man out there was sure serene. I've always admired the unhurried. How kind of the attendant to come in a form that puts the attended at ease, like a guest from far off who comes to visit, but learns your language first.

"Listen, Mom said you should come for supper. She said she invited you already, but to remind you if I saw you. She wishes you'd get a cell phone again."

"Ah," I said—that's right, I was invited. Nadine had invited me.

I turned from the man to Bjorn. There was resistance. Part of me wanted to stay in the water. I was up to my chest but felt light, not cold. There was Bjorn, though, watching with what looked like growing discomfort. Abruptly I remembered the particulars of Nadine's invitation.

"Oh," I said. "Oh yes—how could I forget? Happy birthday, Bjorn!"

"Thanks," he replied. He peered around as though not wishing to be seen accepting birthday wishes from a cheerful moron up to his chin in the freezing sea.

"Eighteen!" I exclaimed. "An important year! A very big one indeed!"

"That's what they say," Bjorn replied, cautiously. "Maybe you want to come in now," he added.

And with that I turned to Bjorn and started wading back to shore. Halfway in I lost my balance and cracked my shin on a sharp boulder, which brought some feeling back and made me laugh and swear a couple of times. I felt goofy and hungry. I did want supper, and I wanted it with Bjorn and Nadine and Rune, Lucy too if she was around. I wanted to be in on Bjorn's eighteenth, which it seemed I knew something about—I'd got him a present, I suddenly recalled. What a relief, the thought of a warm kitchen, the giving of gifts, the awkward singing and generational strain. How gorgeous and lush and difficult. When I came out of the water and started to shake, Bjorn said, "Is something really large wrong with you, Virgil, or just something small, do you think?"

It was the first time he called me Virgil instead of Mr. Wander. I liked it. I said, "I'm guessing small," but then had to quit talking because the shakes got hold of me, and together we walked up the beach, the turtle-like stones shifting under our feet. At some point I realized Bjorn had his arm around my shoulders and was keeping me upright. He was strong, it was easy to miss that. What a strange world. In a movie I would take a quick glance back and the man on the water would be gone—there would just be the waves, and the hard sun looking down, and a little mist or sea smoke drifting along. You know that's how it would go. But this wasn't a movie. I didn't turn around.

9

BJORN WALKED ME HOME AND WAITED IN THE KITCHEN WHILE I
turned up the steam and showered some vigor back into my limbs.
I knew he was worried about me—he hadn't let go of my shoulder
until we reached the stairway. He was probably calling his mom that
moment with news of this oddball episode. I felt foolish but then I am
foolish, sometimes.

When we arrived for his birthday supper Ellen Tripp was already
there, at her sunniest and most affectionate, helping Nadine prepare short
ribs and potatoes and roasted brussels sprouts with a hot-honey glaze.
Rune pulled from his pocket a small box in plain tissue and set it on the
counter by the chocolate cake. Lucy DuFrayne soon appeared, which is
always like someone throwing confetti—she'd liked Bjorn the moment
she met him, and seemed to want him to think of her as a sort of wild
auntie with something up her sleeve. You'd have to say the party skewed
old, but Bjorn was a good sport and things balanced a little when Lily
Pea came by with Galen, to whom Bjorn was a god among men since
the rabies event. It was an early dinner because despite his birthday Bjorn
insisted on screening that night's movie, and I had a few last-minute odd-
ments to hang in the lobby in advance of Hard Luck Days. We therefore
did the feast efficient justice and got right down to presents.

Nadine—well, she gave Bjorn a car, which sounds more indul-
gent than it was. The 1996 Ford Escort boasted 127 horsepower at its

upper range, but this specimen had endured a quarter of a million miles. Clearly most of the horses were no longer in the corral. Bjorn was deeply pleased and gave Nadine a searching look—I suspect he understood that she'd sold most of her upstairs furniture in order to buy it. Lucy's present was a puck-shaped container of a surfboard embellishment proudly labeled Sex Wax, which made Bjorn bark with laughter, and Nadine cover her eyes. As for me I'd ordered him a surfboard rack, which we later installed on the roof of the Ford with medium twisting and agony; Nadine had told me about the car, and I figured anywhere he drove it he'd want that board along. Rune gave him an Opinel knife he'd got from a French sailor in the Tromsø harbor when he was ten years old.

"But it's your kite-making knife," Bjorn objected.

"It was already yours," Rune replied. Seeing Bjorn's puzzled expression he said, "Well, you're my grandson. Except for you, I would be the last post in the fence. Therefore all I have is yours already. There isn't a thing I can do about it."

"Oh—all right then," Bjorn said, "I'll use it right away," and opening the knife he went for the cake, and that was pretty much that.

That night Jerry Fandeen swung into the Empress lobby. His face was lined and he stank of petroleum and asked if I had any Gojo.

"Gojo."

"You know, the strong soap. My bulk tank leaked, spilled fuel oil all over the basement. Got it cleaned up but I'm out of Gojo."

I had none, only a bar of grainy soap that wanted to take your skin off. Jerry used the men's room a long time and came out with pink sore hands. He still smelled like fuel oil because of the long dark stripe of it on his shirtfront.

He stood looking at the candy display. "Can I have some of them Milk Duds?"

I reached down and tossed him a box.

"How much?"

"They're on me, Jerry."

"Hey! Thanks, Virgil."

His pleasure at free Milk Duds made me heartsick. His sadness seemed complete. It had left him nothing, no proper enjoyment, no Saturday mornings. Sadness wore him like a tailored suit.

I said, "You probably shouldn't stay there tonight."

"Stay where?"

"The Hoshaver. Because of the fumes."

"It's fine. I can't even smell it."

"It's more dangerous if you can't smell it," I pointed out. "You want me to step over there and check it out?"

Jerry had thrown a handful of Milk Duds into his mouth. He had to work mostly through them before he could answer. Eventually he swallowed and said, "Virgil, you got to stop looking out for me."

Next morning I went to the office. I felt slightly anxious. It was festival day—any number of shoes might drop. We might get a shoe monsoon. There were notes from Lydia and from Ann Fandeen. The carnival had hooked up to city power and blew a bunch of fuses. Two food vendors, corn dog and snow cone, had been promised the same prime location. I did not have the wisdom of Solomon.

By noon I slipped the civic leash. The day was warming and Greenstone was nearing capacity. The all-class reunion was at full tilt. Streams of middle-agers and old-agers and a few millennials strolled into and out of the school. I blended in long enough to hear remembrance of specific football games, blizzards, and squatting hairy meat loaves in the school cafeteria. I went to a school reunion once—people start with polite fondness, then recall how overjoyed they were to leave in the first place. The inevitable beer garden looms up quickly. I went into Betsy Shane's and bought two rhubarb tarts. The carnival midway rumbled, with fried smells and dappled light and jubilant dogs tearing around amid the doinky music. When I spied Nadine it was nearly two. She was sitting under a parasol at the face-painting booth. A bony-armed youngster with thick glasses and the smile of a human shark dabbed at her cheeks with a long brush. He was painting, of all things, constellations—not bunny whiskers or skeleton teeth, just a spray of tiny golden stars across her cheekbones. She paid the surprisingly restrained artist and turned up her face to me.

"I'm going as the night sky," she declared, maybe the sexiest thing a person can say. "Is that a rhubarb tart?"

Her cell rang. It was Bjorn, calling with the scantest of signals from the side of a county road.

"The car what?" Nadine said, pressing the phone to her left ear while blocking her right with her hand. "It quit? Where are you?" She kept shaking her head while Bjorn gave her spotty directions.

It took us a while to find them. We took 61 northeast four miles, then turned left on County 7 for another six. When you cross the range of hills like small mountains guarding the lake, the land levels off and descends to bog and tamarack. What I didn't mention to Nadine was the famous make-out spot for which we seemed to be heading. It's a wildflower meadow surrounded by poplars that make a soft sound in the wind.

Soon a dark outline appeared on the long straight road and up loomed the dispirited hatchback with Bjorn and Ellen standing beside it. Bjorn looked sheepish and Ellen practical. Nadine eased past and did a three-point turn and parked nose to nose. She had a set of jumper cables, never used. I hooked them up and Bjorn tried starting the Ford. It moaned to no avail. The cables were terribly cheap, with jaws of light bendy copper that kept slipping off the batteries.

Nadine was about to call Beeman when a car appeared—a slouchy old station wagon, the only car in Greenstone looking worse than Bjorn's. It chugged up and coasted to a stop on the centerline. I couldn't imagine what would bring Jerry out here but it was our good luck. Without a word he opened the back and rummaged under a tarp and came up with heavy cables. I clamped them appropriately. Bjorn started the Ford and Ellen got in beside him. Jerry collected the cables and wound them around his arm. As he did so the Audi stalled.

I said, "Do *you* need a jump start now?"

Jerry shook his head. He was used to the Audi. He looked straight forward in silence. In a minute or two he tried the ignition. The car started with a massive backfire that raised the rear end on its goner shocks and made a thready black cloud in the air. Jerry rolled up his window and drove away with his back bumper an inch off the ground. The oily cloud remained behind. It looked like a virus under a microscope, or the cruising soul of someone wicked who had died.

Bjorn and Ellen seemed suddenly in a hurry, nodding to us and heading back to town. Nadine and I stood alone on the road.

"There's a kind of notorious meadow down this way, if you know where to look," I said.

"Is *that* where that is?" she said.

The meadow was unoccupied when we got there. I don't honestly know how much traffic it gets anymore, but Don Lean used to run over at least once a week in his sheriff cruiser and rap on steamy windows. There was a fire pit full of ashes and the rims of burned beer cans, and there were colorful bits of paper where firecrackers had gone off. It was early for the real zoo of wildflowers but we walked around a little until the sky changed—a gust came in over the poplars and the air got cool in a hurry.

We got back in the car. The sunny day darkened before us. A cloud front that looked like huge belligerent knuckles appeared over the trees heading for Lake Superior.

"Should we go?" Nadine asked.

"Let's sit tight a minute."

The enormous dark knuckles took over the immediate sky. They were low and fast. Behind them came a long sweeping veil of rain. By the time it reached us it was snow. It peppered the Jeep and stuck to the poplar leaves and the heads of grass still standing. Wherever it stuck, it glowed. A beautiful, five-minute, mid-May blizzard.

"What's that sound?" Nadine asked—she heard it before I did.

At first it was like a distant train whistle, but of deeper timbre. A low note held by an organ. It held and held—that note had all kinds of sustain. Sometimes the note seemed to fracture or separate in the wind and become a droning chord.

"I think it's wind chimes," Nadine said—though it sounded deeper than that to me. It was impossible not to think of some madman working the pedals of a magnificent pipe organ, miles away, perhaps underground, the notes reverberating up through layers of stone until they rang in the open air. It was mournful and lovely. Then the wind subsided. The front passed. Melting snow dripped from the trees. The sun came out, and the music vanished.

10

WE GOT BACK TO GREENSTONE AS THE PARADE WAS LAUNCHING.

Parades always made me cringe—the sight of so many people lockstepping along, chests out, elbows pumping, seemed to denote an unearned pride or a humiliating need for attention. I have generally found something else to do, if any parades were nearby.

This time around it felt different. Under Ann's direction the Hard Luck Parade was at once daft and clever. There was only one marching band, a grubby-looking troupe procured at short notice from a high school up the shore—and they played a mournful foot-dragging dirge that upshifted suddenly to ragtime, like the funeral jazz of New Orleans. Behind the band came a hundred grade-schoolers in green frog suits, flinging themselves around out of time to the music, and after them a quartet of 4-H girls on horseback, trying to keep their fitful animals in check. This was difficult because twenty feet behind the horses was a fire truck that kept hitting the siren in bursts every time they started settling down. Last came a flood of reunionites and Storm Warning groupies who'd bought into the Hard Luck theme and dressed as unfortunates of every stripe: chained ghosts and zombies, shipwrecked mariners, a Stevie Ray Vaughan complete with sombrero, some cheerful fellow with a bear trap closed over his head, and a huge extended family of the damned who'd done up their skin in a crackly finish and gone for the red contact lenses. That was the whole strangely joyous brief parade, roughly following the four-block path taken by the runaway water tower, funneling everyone down to Main where there was street food and tent beer, as well as the Empress whose marquee was lit up with the titles of terrible movies.

It was a long messy night at the theater, and lucrative for once; people came and went throughout, getting swallowed by the trickier seats and extricating themselves, slipping out for corn dogs and returning to find their places filled by others. Sometimes the crowd drowned out the sound track; I wore the hermetic headphones, which amused Nadine. Afterward Bjorn despliced the films and took off with Ellen while Nadine vacuumed the aisles and I mopped up a cola pool of horrifying viscosity.

As the night assumed a stunned torpor we strolled through town, ending up on the waterfront. A slight swell touched the beach; the ore dock breathed against the sky. At the marina a handful of sailboats stood leaning around in their slips. A few of these were lit below and several had people decompressing in their cockpits—a zombie and a couple of frogs murmured hello and we nodded back, then stopped to greet a rumpled codger sitting on his foredeck eating spaghetti from a dented pan. His boat was an old pocket cruiser with wood spars and a long curved tiller tied off to the side. It had no electricity and the only light came from two paraffin lanterns shackled in the rigging. The codger looked happy and tired. He was leaving the next day. He waved us aboard, pointing at the sky which had a slight green wash of borealis. Tomorrow promised a brisk westerly. He would cross to the Apostles and from there to the Keweenaw Peninsula, after that the Soo, Georgian Bay, the Thousand Islands. I asked when he expected to return and he replied probably never. The world was mammoth and he had yet to see most of it. Telling us to hold still he disappeared down the companionway. We heard him clinking around in the dark. Soon he emerged holding three teacups and poured each of us a tot of something. It tasted like smoke and went straight to my fingertips. We toasted his voyage and stepped onto the dock. We were halfway to shore when he called quietly to Nadine, "If I had one like you, I'd stay."

At her front door she put her arms around me for a while. "What happened to you, anyway, Virgil?"

"Bump on the head," I said.

She reached up for a kiss.

"You know what you're getting here," I said. "I'm still fairly far reduced. I may never be unabridged again."

"None of us are unabridged, as you are well aware." She leaned back and looked me in the face. "Worthy adjective, by the way."

"Thanks, I was saving it."

I walked home. The city campground was full of trailers and fifth-wheel campers with a few tents scattered among them. Some kids crouched around glowing coals, roasting the night's last marshmallows. The air smelled lakey and fresh.

It was three in the morning. I couldn't sleep. After rolling and flipping my pillow for an hour I turned on public radio where a recorded newscast announced a body had been recovered from the Duluth harbor. It was Josephine Sayles. Her car had been located in a lot near the waterfront. Divers found her drifting on the bottom. Her pockets were full of stones.

Slowly I came up out of a dream in which people were dancing on the Empress stage. They wore costumes and swayed to music, and the song was the long low breaking chord Nadine and I heard during the five-minute blizzard. Coming fully awake I remembered Nadine saying *wind chimes*. I thought of Bjorn and Ellen stopped by the road, of Jerry arriving like a somber angel to jump-start the Ford. The memory urged me from bed.

It was past noon.

In the kitchen I poured cold coffee, then went to my bookshelves. I got down a county plat book, pages of maps with the landowners' names written in on their holdings. Every nosy person should have one. I ran my finger along County 7 as it straightened through the boglands. Here was where Bjorn and Ellen got stalled; a bit farther on, the necking meadow; just past that, a gravel road cut north along an eighty-acre parcel.

The name on the parcel was Owen Fandeen.

So that's what Jerry was doing out there.

I dressed quickly, feeling the vague dismay of hours lost—after hearing about Josephine I'd found Rune's bottle of akevitt and finally got to sleep. Grabbing notebook and pen I went out on the roof-deck. The midway was at full crush, its mishmash of music clearly insane. At the top of the hour the Lutheran church added its bells to the racket. The bells had long sustained tones. Again I thought of what Nadine and I heard in the meadow. They chimed two o'clock and stopped.

I opened the notebook and started a list.

hardware
fuel oil
wind chimes

I remembered Don Lean's question: what kind of person goes out in the winter to steal wind chimes and fertilizer? I'd answered him with a joke at the time, but now I thought maybe I knew.

I had a question for Ann Fandeen, but she didn't answer her phone. When I'd filled a notebook page with everything that seemed even slightly germane I dialed Don Lean. He was at the campground, sounding annoyed—many of the campers had complained about rodents wriggling under their tents in the small hours. Hadn't he predicted this?

"I think there's a larger problem than voles," I said.

"What's going on, Virgil?"

I said, "You understand I am often wrong . . ."

"That is true and I have always said so—"

"So I'm not trying to alarm you. Or cause trouble, or make anyone panic. Especially now I shouldn't be trusted, plus I prefer not to rat on a man whose luck has been rotten forever. In other words, use your discretion. It's probably only what I think."

After a pause he said, "Well that's a marathon disclaimer. I hope you are comfortable now."

"Not really."

"What is it you think, Virgil?"

"Jerry Fandeen is building a bomb."

11

DITCHING THE VOLE COMPLAINANTS, DON GOT TO THE EMPRESS IN minutes—he sounded like six men coming up the stairs.

We stood in the kitchen while I read him the first couple of points on my list.

And they sounded—well, amateur, really they did, now that the sheriff was there, breathing hard, expecting a damning recital. Don was unimpressed by my inductions. He sure seemed more the elected official and less my friend and ally. Earlier, when I was alone with my cold coffee, the list had seemed unassailable indeed.

He first affirmed that the stolen chimes, so far not recovered, were the deep-voiced variety. "I figured Brandon was inflating for insurance," he said. "Who pays six hundred for garden decor? But these aren't your tinkly porch chimes. They're 'Basilica Classics.' They're supposed to sound like a pipe organ."

He also affirmed that the fertilizer, stolen alongside the chimes, was based on ammonium nitrate—the common ingredient preferred by terrorists from Brussels to Bali, not to mention our homegrown bedlamites in Oklahoma City. More recently a Kansas fertilizer factory blew up, killing sixteen and startling a wistful space-station astronaut gazing down from above.

He then gently reminded me of the scope of my assumptions. "The sound you heard might not have been those chimes. If it was, it doesn't mean Jerry stole the fertilizer too. And if he did, he probably didn't build a bomb." Don stretched out his shoulders and arms. "Have you considered that Jerry might just want to fertilize something? He might be planning a large pumpkin patch. Corn or tomatoes. Marijuana's a popular option. You asked for my discretion," he added.

Having led with what I felt were the high cards, I reluctantly went down the list. Jerry's spillage of fuel oil in the Hoshaver. His years of explosives experience. His collection of screws and bolts and hinges, "hundreds of pounds of shrapnel," I lamely explained—at the risk of receiving a knock at the door, I'd researched bomb-building on Google. Don kept his own counsel but it showed in his eyes. I finished with some halfhearted observations about Jerry's mental state, his loneliness and confusion, his envy of the dead.

"His mental state seems fine to me," Don replied. "Look, Virgil—he's only now sort of got things together. He's kept himself clean—I wouldn't mind losing weight like he's done. He's making a wage and not drinking it all, doing that Hoshaver project for Leer. I'm trying to see the sense."

"He isn't himself."

"An overall improvement."

"You buy that Leer is helping Jerry, giving him some purpose," I said bitterly.

"What pokes you so hard about Adam Leer?" Don asked.

And what could I say to that?

What poked me couldn't be proved or measured.

You can't convict a man of a vibe—can't talk about the feeling you get that something is trying your door. Yet Leer spoke into Shad Pea's ear, his last day on this earth. He appeared to Rune who was nearly killed; spoke to me and I saw my death; took the hand of Josephine Sayles, and she gave herself to the lake.

Someone was climbing the stairs. Bjorn knocked and entered, the raven riding his shoulder.

"Morning, Bjorn—who's your friend?" Don said.

"I think he got lost," Bjorn replied. He'd awakened to find the bird on his windowsill—it drifted to his shoulder when he went outside, and hadn't left him all day.

Don said, "Friend in high school tamed a crow. Looked real sinister, and knew a couple of incendiary phrases. Does your bird talk as well?"

"Whoever knew?" said the raven.

"Not me, no matter what they say," Don replied. "Listen, Bjorn— have you seen Mr. Fandeen today?"

"Nope, what's going on?"

"Need his assistance," said Don.

At this I remembered an item I should've put on the list. "Bjorn, tell how Jerry solved that septic issue, out at Adam Leer's."

"Blasting cap," Bjorn said with a grin. "He was trying to clear the toilet with one of those sewer snakes, but it broke. Jerry was mad—he had some blasting caps in his truck and fed one down on a wire."

At *blasting cap* Don looked at my eyes. He said, "Well, you guys have a fine afternoon. I'll just pop down to the Hoshaver and see if old Jerry's around."

12

HE WASN'T AROUND, OR AT LEAST DIDN'T ANSWER THE DOOR. DON had to go back to his office for the security key vouchsafed him by the previous owner.

When he finally got in, the Hoshaver stank of fuel and rodents.

The fuel reek came from a fifty-gallon tank with a floor of congealing slurry. In the stockroom he found fourteen empty fertilizer sacks and two full ones. He looked for the crates of bolts and hinges and other trash hardware I'd told him about. The crates were gone. Don opened some windows. He called one of his deputies, Stumbo, and they drove to the Fandeen hunting shack. Still no Jerry. Blasting caps and alligator clips lay in disarray on a coffee table alongside two spools of coated wire.

While they were searching, the wind picked up. Low tones reached out of the trees. Stumbo, who preferred classical, said, "Sounds like the Canon in D."

Don called me from outside the shack. He had a bad cell signal which gave his voice an airless urgency. He asked what I'd noticed about Jerry's car, the day before, when he stopped to jump-start the Ford.

I told him the Audi was riding low, chassis bottoming out in the dips.

"You said that earlier. You didn't notice the payload he had in the back, to make it ride so low?"

"No—we were just glad for the help."

He said, "I got some calls to make."

Here's who Don had already called by the time he got back to town: Homeland Security, the FBI, the state patrol, two more part-time deputies, three volunteer fire departments from up- and down-shore, two sets of ambulance personnel, and a game warden.

Defending himself against unleveled charges of overkill, Don laid it out: from what they had found (empty sacks, drained oil tank, electronic supplies) and also from Stumbo's estimated payload of putrefied station wagons, Jerry Fandeen was believed to be tooling around with a thousand-pound bomb.

Don and Stumbo and Lydia and I were in Lydia's City Hall office. From her window we could see hundreds of people, a back corner of the beer tent, a slice of the stage with its overhung canopy, and the top of the Ferris wheel.

I'd never seen this many people in Greenstone. No doubt there used to be more on occasion, back in the heyday of mining and construction, but certainly not in my time.

If only we could've enjoyed it.

As we watched, a silver bus eased up behind the stage—its air brakes hissed, a few onlookers whooped.

"How about that, the band is here," Don said. "Excellent." His collar glistened with sweat; all of him was extremely damp and pale as a big summer squash.

"People need to know," said Lydia.

Don stood up, seemed about to say something, and sat down again. "Thing could be anyplace," he said at last.

"Anyplace you can hide an Audi wagon," Stumbo helpfully added.

Don squeezed the cell phone in his palm. Officers were watching the two roads into and out of Greenstone—61 going north and south, and Green Street, which becomes County 12 beyond the city limits. Two fire departments had arrived and were scouting alleys and back streets. Stumbo had drafted a public statement and was eager to set it free. Don had no such zeal. He had been sheriff six years. He dreaded questions until he had answers.

"What we have to do," said Lydia urgently, "is we have to send people home."

Stumbo opened a file and badgered Don to select a photo of Jerry for media use.

"Good grief. That one." Don pointed. It was the only recent picture, showing Jerry as he presently looked—skinny, gray, oddly shocked. I hadn't noticed before how his neck had got thin and long, like some turtles' necks that keep stretching and stretching out from their shells. His eyes were dismayed and surprised—arched brows above and blue bags below. If you didn't know Jerry it might make you laugh. It made me see I had failed him.

"Get it ready, but don't make it public. Not yet," Don said. "Anybody got a picture of the car? We need the car—hang on," he added, his cell phone barking.

It was Homeland. The Duluth agent was on his way, whistling up 61 behind a pair of state troopers, talking so noisily Don held the phone away. The excited agent seemed to be arguing for a general evacuation of Greenstone. Don wanted to issue what he kept calling a "shelter in place" bulletin. He dreaded a panic. The two did not seem near agreement.

Hard Luck Days was earning its name. Slipping out of Lydia's office and over to my own, I called Nadine on the landline.

She said, "I saw Jerry not an hour ago—he drove past my house, then drove past again in the other direction. Moving slowly, Virgil. That old car of his was scraping the pavement, even worse than yesterday. He looked more bewildered than violent, to me."

"Where's Bjorn?"

"Off with Ellen someplace—I'll try his phone but doubt he'll answer. What are you doing?"

"Whatever gets asked."

My stout quarterstaff was propped by the window—I'd been doing without it lately, but now it seemed like a good thing to have. I tucked it under my arm and left the office to find City Hall empty. I didn't know what Don and the agent from Homeland had decided, or where any of them had gone.

I locked up and walked down to Main. The festival rolled on without apprehension. The street was stuffed with kids in bright jackets, glow sticks circling their necks. Some had dogs on tangled leashes and others had freed their dogs to gather near sausage vendors. I smelled fry bread and mini doughnuts and almonds roasted with cinnamon. The Ferris wheel turned, its long spokes lit with bulbs in primary colors. I passed the beer tent and headed toward the stage where musicians or roadies were building a stack of speakers. Main was so crowded I had to thread a path sideways. I spied Rune with Lucy at a bakery stand. He waved. Lucy took a step toward me only to stop abruptly and dig down into her handbag.

Here and there people reached simultaneously for their phones.

The mood changed. Electronic devices rippled downstreet, digital layers of shudder and yip. An alert had been issued. Blocks off, a siren ascended and died; kids looked for their friends and zigzagged through the crowd. People laughed in disbelief, saying *What the hell* or *Is this a joke* until a tall yellow fire truck turned off the highway and came swaying down toward us. Harsh lights bounced off homes and façades. I looked past the stage to the campground. People were standing still and alert, interpreting facts and gauging their sense of alarm—then as I watched, a tall young woman lunged at her tent, tore it down in under a minute, and stuffed it loose into the back of a car. Engines woke, headlights bloomed and queued. Rides were still twirling on the midway as the first cars crept out and away. The beer tent swelled and then emptied; some of the vendors simply shut off their grills and hustled away.

"Look at all that unguarded bratwurst," Beeman remarked—he'd found me in the thinning crowd. "What gives, Virgil? Are we finished at last?" He was reading his phone as he talked.

About this time we saw the first runners. They were dodging a motorcycle that wove in and out, its rider jerking forward in bursts. The Ferris wheel slowed and stopped—the last rider took off his jacket and waved it around in the breeze. Downtown drivers lost patience and tore through the ropes of the temporary parking lot. The ropes caught on bumpers, dragging weighted posts behind them.

Half a block west the troopers arrived. Don bent over talking to one of them through the window of his cruiser. A four-wheel-drive pickup wheeled out of the campground and bounced through front yards as a shortcut. Two more trucks followed its path before a subcompact tried it and got hung up on the curb. People swore at cell phones. An ambulance crept up onto the sidewalk, its driver talking into a headset.

Past the stage I glimpsed Bjorn talking to a trooper, the man shaking his head, talking on his radio, waving Bjorn away.

Beeman said, "Hey Virgil, I found Lydia." He held up his phone. "She's talking to Anderson Cooper." He then took a call himself. The news online was mushrooming; #greenstonebomber had liftoff, along with #hardluckjerry.

I hated to think about Jerry this way. He didn't want notoriety or Internet fame. What he wanted was already lost. Wife, job, self-regard, whatever his name was worth—those things were gone.

The Ferris wheel was empty, its lights doused. The sun was low and the street was shady blue and hazy with the exhaust of inching traffic. Bjorn came trotting up looking bothered and excited. "Maybe he's at Leer's."

"Jerry?"

"He might be, right? Leer gave him his job. He practically lived there—come on." Without waiting he turned and headed up the street toward his house.

13

RUNE JOINED ME AS I RUSHED TO CATCH UP WITH BJORN. HE WAS full of breathless questions. While filling him in I failed to detect an approaching curb and cartwheeled harmlessly onto the boulevard. By the time we reached Nadine's, Bjorn was backing the Jeep out of the garage.

It took a few minutes to escape town since everyone else was escaping too. A hundred yards from the highway Bjorn pulled off into the ditch and four-wheeled us past a storm of shouts and honks. He turned north as the sun fell between two high hills to the west.

We climbed 61 past the lookout. Bjorn slowed and turned into Leer's drive. Boulders loomed around us, an early owl hunting among them. Leer's house drew near looking flat in the gloom. Jerry's car was not visible, but there was light in the house—movement too.

I knocked hard once, then opened the door and Leer looked up unsurprised. I called out that we were looking for Jerry and Leer went wordlessly out the back door. We shouted his name. He did not stop. He seemed not to rush yet stayed well in front. We reeled along fast but he was already at the edge of the trees. Then Bjorn flat-out ran, to keep Leer in sight, and I staggered along with my staff. Inside the woods it was dark and dreamlike. Sometimes I felt Rune's hand at my elbow and tree limbs brushing my face. I glimpsed Leer in the shadows ahead. His stride betrayed no anxiety. He even turned and might have smiled, dropping something behind him. Bjorn bent down and lifted Leer's suit jacket and flung it back to the ground. Forward we struggled and stumbled and ran, and forward Leer strolled before us. He tossed another shape over a branch: his cotton shirt. Now he was visible only for his white undershirt drifting ahead in the trees. Water burbled near—I remembered the river that crossed his property running down to the lake. A melody fragment reached my ears. Was Leer now singing a madman song, losing his clothes and mind? Bjorn tripped and rolled in the dead winter leaves and came up holding a shoe. The river came closer. Leer stood naked in the moving shallows. He seemed to sink. The water curled. We raced to the river's edge.

It is not deep there or especially swift except for a little waterfall where it drops over a shelf and pools and swirls before continuing. Rune took my shoulder and said *There* in my ear, pointing down into the pool.

Not ten feet away a great long fish lay swinging its fins on the bottom. It had a spine like a person's spine. Its long jagged face was mottled gray and it watched with a glimmering eye. Bjorn didn't see it but trotted upstream, hunting for a place to cross. I felt something going to happen and took a tight hold on the quarterstaff. The fish turned slowly about and finned itself downstream. What leisure it seemed to have. A fish that size fears nothing.

Bjorn thought my wits had flown, because while he peered over the water trying to glimpse Leer skulking among the trees I bounded into the shallows. I flailed the staff wildly. Bjorn laughed from shock. Something large was the matter with me, bashing the water as if driving out devils. But Rune was moving along the bank, tracking the surface, and at last the fish slid over a pebbly spot, so all of us saw its darkling spine break through in a slick of fast water. Then Bjorn leaped in after me and downriver we went, the fish out in front of us, leading us on, searching out places with depth for concealment, then being driven out as we crashed to our knees and our waists and one sudden drop-off over my head. Far off there were sirens. At a bend of the river we came out of the trees into a pasture. There was very little sunlight left and it threw a lemony warmth over the heavy grasses and two horses who stood watching us plow downstream. The staff helped me keep my feet in the river,

Bjorn splashing next to me, Rune on the bank. I lost sight of the fish, then caught it again, slicing along a steep cutbank—having an easier time of it now as the river hastened away. Lunging forward onto my face I got a hand on its tail but it twisted away. The lunge cost me badly. I lost the staff. Strength left my body. Bjorn got out front and took control of the chase. The landscape changed to tall grass and saplings. The Green Street Bridge was somewhere in front. Past it the river narrowed and sped. The fish would be down to the sea in minutes and lost to us forever.

Bjorn shouted then. I could hear no words, only noise and joy. I took my eyes off the fish and looked up. Galen Pea stood on the Green Street Bridge. We were some ways off but I knew it was Galen. Nobody else had hair that white. God knows the days he'd haunted this river—always from the bridge, against sense and instruction, but as Galen had told me long before, a fish can't look up. The sturgeon powered forth with confidence, attaining speed, water surging along its sides. It couldn't see what we saw, which was Galen Pea dropping like a stone dislodged.

It was a nervy leap. He timed it well. He made a *thack* instead of a splash. *Thack* is the sound of a boy in Red Wing boots landing on the back of his enemy.

I don't remember a struggle—not really. The fish was stunned, as you would be if ninety pounds jumped from a height onto your spinal column. When I panted up the fish lay on the surface. Its gills worked arrhythmically. Galen stood in the thigh-deep river. He had mud on his cheekbones like war paint and the fish's tail in his hands. He leaned back hard but the sturgeon was three times his weight. Just as it seemed to regather its wits Bjorn joined Galen and took hold too. Between them they dragged it over the mud and up onto the grass.

"Don't let go," Galen warned, then ran stooping to the foot of the bridge and came back with an oval rock the size of my two fists together.

With Bjorn holding the tail Galen knelt down in the dying glow and looked the sturgeon full in the face. It looked straight back. In the day's last sun its gills opened wide. A gust of wind hit Galen then and his hair was a storm at sea. He brought the rock down like the great Hiawatha and cratered the top of its head.

The fish lay quivering in the grass. I was breathing hard and sank onto a hummock beside it. Rune joined us, at the end of his strength. He sat down beside the fish. It was still trembling—it trembled quite a while.

I wasn't entirely sure what just happened. Bjorn slumped down a little confused. Galen bent over the fish, taking its measure with a piece of waxed thread he carried in his pocket. Finally Rune chuckled lightly. "Well my friend. You took him. You said you would take him and you took him."

Galen grinned; he danced with every step. Few are allowed the revenge of their dreams and this was also the fish of his life, bigger than himself and his dad together. He'd taken it with only his hands and his feet and a stone that he found on the bank.

The air chilled, fog rose out of the grass. Dark was urgently upon us, and I thought of Jerry Fandeen out in it somewhere, parked alone with his colossal firecracker, more frightened, it seemed certain, than all those he had frightened out of town.

Galen said, "I got to get this home somehow."

None of us mentioned Adam Leer.

I rose unsteadily. The hard fall earlier had spoiled my balance. I stuck out my arms like a ropewalker. My stout quarterstaff had slipped downstream—it was driftwood again.

14

WE DROPPED GALEN OFF AT HIS SISTER'S. HE STAMPED A LITTLE because we couldn't take the sturgeon, but it wouldn't fit in the Jeep. We had to leave it there in the weeds. Lily thought he was downtown during the mad outward rush and was angry and crying to see him.

Don Lean stood beside the vacant music stage with a couple of troopers. There was yellow tape around the Hoshaver Building and the loose tape lifted and bent on the breeze. A third trooper knelt looking up into the wheel well of the Storm Warning bus which was parked behind the stage. As we neared I saw that the bus had a flat tire.

"No Jerry?" I asked.

Don shook his head no, frowning at my soaked clothes. "Virgil, what, did you drive in the lake again? Who dragged you out this time?"

I explained we'd helped Galen Pea land his big sturgeon. Annoyance flitted across Don's face, quickly replaced by appreciation.

"No kidding. He caught the bastard? You take a picture?"

"Didn't think of it. What's next here?"

Don said there was an "all points" out on Jerry but that no one had seen him or the Audi in hours. It was full dark and a half-moon had risen. Even with the streetlights on, certain stars looked swollen and close.

"He's got to have holed up, that's what I think," Don said. "That old wagon isn't going far. Tomorrow we'll put some eyes in the air and see what we can see."

At the far end of Main a slender stooped figure came walking out of the night. He had his hands in his pockets and walked in a familiar shuffle.

"Well now," Don said.

No one ran toward him, they just let him come. He stopped at an abandoned stall and took a bratwurst off the grill and poked around and found a bottle of mustard and then reached into a serving tub with his fingers and pinched up some kraut. He draped it over the sausage and walked toward us eating it.

Don was laughing quietly.

The trooper said, "Wait—is that Fandeen?"

"Yes."

A trooper reached to unsnap the holster on his belt, but Don put a hand on his arm. "Hold tight a second here, Dale."

Jerry continued up Main. There was another vacated stand, fry bread at this one. Jerry stopped and picked a couple of rounds off the rack and helped himself to some napkins and came toward us eating one of the fry breads and holding the other in his free hand. When he saw the little group of us standing together next to the Storm Warning bus, he smiled and held up the fry bread in greeting.

"Don," he called, "I'm glad to see you—can we talk?"

"Stay where you are," the trooper ordered.

"Dale, relax—I'm glad too, Jerry."

When Jerry got close there was a sudden tight scuffle—Dale and the other troopers lunged in and got hold of his arms and yanked them back so he dropped the fry bread, and they put him on the ground on his face. I felt sick to watch with his shirt riding up showing the saggy white skin on his back. I understand the troopers needed to lay hands on him but come on. What stuck for me was Jerry's shock, the humiliation in his eyes, and fear and pain when Dale knelt down with his knee jammed up between Jerry's flappy shoulder blades. I tried to crouch near him so he could see someone friendly but a trooper kept shoving me away.

The whole time Jerry kept saying *I never, I never*.

Eventually of course they had to let him up and then he wouldn't look in anybody's face, not mine, not Don's. If Don was aghast at the troopers' intensity he didn't let it show. He spoke gently to Jerry, asking where the bomb was, and Jerry looked down at the pavement where his fry bread was lying along with some nickels and dimes from his pockets and said it was parked up at Slake.

"You're telling me the truth now Jerry?"

Jerry nodded and glanced up a moment. You could see he was afraid they would put him on the ground again. His chin was bloody and his cheek embossed with gravel. He said, "I got a dumb idea, Don. I had forgot about things, but I remembered myself—do you see?"

Don said, "I see it. I do. You want to go sit down in my office?"

"I guess," Jerry said.

One of the troopers was already talking on his radio and now Don unhooked his own radio from his belt. A bomb squad had been assembled and was evidently arriving from Duluth or Minneapolis. I heard Don issuing directions to the taconite plant.

A calm settled. A flock of low-flying geese went overhead, the undersides of their wings gently illuminated by streetlights. People began to come out from where they had been. Music came on somewhere, a door slid open, somebody laughed. Don took Jerry's upper arm and headed toward his cruiser which was parked in front of the Empress.

Then the air got white and flashbulb filthy. We turned in time to take the concussion on our chests and faces. A column of smoke ballooned upward and part of it caught fire. The sound of the world returned in cotton. The sky was shreds and flinders.

15

PEOPLE SWEAR IT RAINED HARDWARE—A CLOUDBURST OF LAG SCREWS
and bolts. This was no doubt true near the blast itself, but downtown it
mainly sprinkled dirt and chaff. You felt it against your face. My chief
impression was of trash in the air, rags and plastic, fly ash, smoke stink,
gnats rushing by. You expect a carnage tableau, but no. There was a
general freeze, then a scurry, the stirring sight of an ambulance crew.
People stood in clumps looking up at the smoke which remained its lit
self, turning and swelling, glowing inside like a hot summer cloud. A
horror, yes, but overall what you saw was relief. The worst arrives and
you are still whole.

Jerry's statement was somber and scattered. He attempted no defense
but described in rueful terms the explosive, his knack for ignition, the
fuel at hand. Asked the big *why*, he struggled to speak. When he did,
it was as if he were describing someone else. He'd felt for years that his
edges were dull. Like Greenstone itself, he was largely past. An empty
room. He got lost in his days, his thoughts didn't hold.

    That changed when he went to work for Mr. Leer.

    Leer welcomed Jerry. After one day working for him, Jerry
already felt different. He began to like mornings, and the feeling of
purpose he got the moment he turned onto Leer's scrubby drive. He

mowed and pruned, he painted walls. Around Mr. Leer Jerry didn't feel lost—he felt refilled, and even prized. Soon he required no guidance whatever. He put his hand to the task before him. When one job was finished, another appeared.

Leer was the first ever to shake Jerry's hand and say he had maximum ceiling.

A few weeks into his time with Leer, an idea came into his bones. It weaseled inside and took hold of the levers. The concept was simple: everything ends. Work, people, football, dogs, *The Bachelor*, towns, money. They outlived themselves, they came to an end. Jerry felt stirred with private knowledge. Something that seemed to be his alone. He'd hit the intelligence, struck the vein. A conviction developed. As a boy he had worried that the world would end. Even the Bible said it would. Now it was coming, and was nothing to fear. He felt free. He might be a prophet born for this. The day he moved into the Hoshaver Building he knew what to do, and how.

The neglected Hoshaver stood in the center of town. It had been everything, during its life—dime store, dealership, grocery store, café. Always a hub. He walked through it, lovingly. The idea came to him clean and complete. Hard Luck Days was coming. Like Jerry himself, the Hoshaver would be useful once more.

He accumulated bit by bit—scrap-iron shrapnel, dynamite caps. Little homebuilt igniter to set the thing off. The fuel oil was already on-site, in a bulk tank down in the basement. At last he lacked only the fertilizer and got badly lost, seeking that greenhouse. Mile on mile of one-lane road, a webby tangle of tamarack swamp. Increasingly roads confounded Jerry. But he found the place after all, on a Saturday evening, unprotected. Not even a barking dog. As a bonus he spied those pretty wind chimes, and took them as a present for Ann.

He briefly panicked when the sheriff showed up—banging on his door, on the very day! When Don quit knocking, Jerry piled the crates of scrap-metal shards into the back seat. He opened the alley slider and eased on out. Went north first, toward his brother Owen's shack, then realized people would look for him there. He got shaky then—he didn't want to be found, but also couldn't bear to be lost.

To get out of sight he turned around and drove back to Slake. The gate was locked but the hardware was old. Simple to lift the gate off its hinges, drive through, and lift it back on. He crept the wagon around to the rear and backed in under a loading ramp.

He stayed with the car all afternoon. He napped and thought of the end of things and got out and stretched his legs. Peering round the southeast corner he could see Greenstone—the water tower, the Hoshaver façade, the Ferris wheel, some sailboat masts. It looked long past. It looked like a picture in a museum or a book about how people lived once. He heard the distant midway rides. Mostly he watched the ore dock. He remembered the ships that used to load, the long chutes lowering, their drawbridge grace, rivers of taconite pouring out.

By late afternoon he knew they were looking for him. County vehicles kept going past. State police. An ambulance. Once he heard the voice of a trooper who'd parked by the gate talking on his radio. The trooper signed off and stayed there to eat. He sat on the bumper enjoying a bratwurst, then a second. The trooper kept waving to cars driving past. He ate a maddening third bratwurst, then leaned back on the trunk and turned his face to the sun. He dozed like this until his radio crackled. Then he drove away.

Jerry was hungry. He'd eaten little for months and didn't care, but now an end was coming. After the trooper he smelled bratwurst everywhere—on wisps of breeze, on the swells of beach waves and far-off laughter. He felt himself fading. Cheese came to mind, and strawberry milk. A long-ago picnic with Ann when she was unexpectedly generous.

It was pleasant and painful, thinking of Ann. She might not want him any longer, but he was still proud of her. Look what she'd done, making everything click down at City Hall. She always hoped to be big and successful. Now she had made it—a person had only to look at that carnival, smell all the food. A wave of noise reached him, a roar of gladness from a thrilling ride.

The last ray of the sun struck the water tower. For half a minute it was the radiant pale inside of an orange. A breeze came up and Jerry felt it go straight through him. It seemed to throw open the first window of spring, all the stale air swept out in a moment, replaced with fresh and sweet.

Jerry's throat lumped.

His Greenstone was over, but Ann's was not.

The kids on that ride still had Greenstone in front of them.

He'd got off track. He didn't mean to—he'd only been doing what came next to hand, glad for a purpose, doing his job, so pleased inside his private knowledge he'd forgot that the world was large.

I was mistaken, Jerry thought.

But the blasting-cap switch wasn't yet wired in; he'd waited on that critical, final step. He could leave the car there—the half-ton project, the end of it all. He'd walk back and talk to the sheriff. Don was an understanding man. Maybe he'd go and get Mr. Leer. They'd sit down together and sort all this out. Maybe start something new.

He slipped through the gate and walked into town. Cars drove past him and nobody stopped. Greenstone was spilling people fast. The music had ended. He walked past the carousel, empty of children—fun house and swing ride, nobody there. Hunger absorbed him—he smelled roasting almonds, the slight burned aroma twinged in his jaw. When he got to the vendors they'd all disappeared. Some had left food right out for grabs.

Jerry still won't talk about being dogpiled onto the pavement, except to say that he didn't expect it, walking up as he had of his own volition, grateful for his returned self and some nice fry bread. Maybe his pride is hurt, or maybe his mind jumps past it to the way the ground thumped, and everything was silenced. In his memory it's not the glaring whiteness that lingers, but the fine black dust that began to descend.

NOBODY DIED FROM JERRY'S BOMB.

To this day he insists it should not have gone off. Alarm still rises in his face when you mention it; he turns blotchy, like a child near tears. He swears on his life that his *little igniter* wasn't even connected. In his defense, an investigator did point out the car's battery placement beneath the back seat, not under the hood as is common. More than one such car has blazed up when overloaded seat-springs touched against battery posts.

None of which matters. The explosion hit like a meteor on the outskirts of Greenstone and burned us a deep new scar.

Groups still meet at the school to talk about it. Lanie Plume wrote a fine college-entrance essay about the experience which resulted in scholarship offers. Beeman published the essay in the *Observer*. She used the word *propulsive*.

After nearly a year we prevailed on Slake International to clear away the gnarled hulk that once was Greenstone's bread. It was an empty eyesore for decades, but people still felt mournful to lose it. Losing it proved for good we were no more a mining town.

In a gesture of goodwill, Slake sold us the land lease for a dollar. Ann wrote a grant, and we turned the site into a grassy park, our cheapest and prettiest option, with a picnic-table overlook and one of those interpretive historical markers your aunt reads aloud while nobody listens. Standing there—standing anywhere in town—you really notice how the sky has changed. When that looming trapezoid came down, the sky got wide. The light is vast. The lake is clean and the hills look blue and hazy. Ellen Tripp said, "You just see way farther now, and what you see is way better."

Last year a shop opened that rents bikes and kayaks in the summer, skis in the winter—no one expected it to succeed, but the place is usually busy. A microbrewery opened on Main. The beer is expensive but made right there, and they hired Nadine for the neon. In the fall the Department of Natural Resources announced plans to build that expensive breakwater after all, and designate a Harbor of Refuge.

It's hardly a renaissance, but it's a start.

And Hard Luck Days itself has thrived—Ann's idea was strong. A year after the blast, Storm Warning returned and played a beautiful set dedicated to resilience and high hopes. I don't know if it skidded the paradigm, but those were some pretty songs. Greenstone is riding a little wave, it seems. Every year the festival lands another improbable act. People like an underdog. Last spring Bob Dylan overcame his wariness and played our Main Street stage. I missed it, but Lydia went with a lemon pie, and ate it with Dylan after the show. She reports he said little, but his eyes were expressive. He called the pie "better than the Nobel."

We retain our proud affliction tales, our rotating hit parade. New ones dominate the repertoire. The Slake explosion, the Christmas Eve Blackout. Shad Pea and Galen—death by sturgeon and bold revenge. We struggled to contain our voles for months, the creatures laying waste to gardens, scrabbling up drainpipes, using superior numbers to overwhelm confident tomcats. It seemed they might actually drive us out until the following January, when a record irruption of great gray owls drifted down out of the north to swallow them whole.

Alec Sandstrom's vanishment has almost entirely dropped from the playlist, supplanted by Adam Leer's. There are theories—Leer drowned in the lake, or he fled to escape his fraud, his vague promises to our town having had no basis in reality. He was never in touch with a beer magnate or any other kind. The chopstick factory was a figment. Investigators combing his house found nothing to suggest any conversation about the reinvigoration of Greenstone. What they did find were artifacts, some incriminating and some only creepy, among them a hand-carved fishing lure of Shad's and a woman's bright Mexican scarf. Also a set of small vintage binoculars that fold into a tin box—the same, we're fairly sure, that Alec used in the Taylorcraft. Some posited that Leer sabotaged the plane. Shad Pea's wild story supports this, Leer showing up near the Wise Old the morning Alec flew out. So do some of Rune's sea-creature tales, if you credit such things. Unlikely? Well of course. What in Greenstone has not been unlikely? Maybe the world isn't small, as we constantly say, but expanding all the time.

In his absence Leer's home was locked down tight. The aspens returned. The yard went to pigweed and thistles and woodchucks. Siding and shingles began to flake off. Eventually some kids went out on a Friday night, drank deeply of life, and burned it down, an act of vandalism that failed to raise the usual indignation.

Let him be a phantom now. I think he won't be back.

Not long ago I stopped to see Lily Pea, to drop off a card of congratulations for becoming a public accountant. She wasn't home, but Galen was. He's still got the head of that massive fish. In the end it was all he managed to save, sawing it off with the French sailor's knife Bjorn had in his pocket. He keeps the head on a bookshelf, where it stares out with ancient, malignant eyes. It looks like an eater of worlds.

When the *Cinematique* article came out, I was surprised to see that the reporter, Frida LaPlant, had been in touch with most of the studios whose movies I'd returned. Because of my status as a man of no prospects, and perhaps because she owed Fergus a favor, she made me a primitive folk hero, a boonies Quixote or man of the people, as though I were baking bread in my kitchen and handing it out to the urchins. It was absurd but I rode it out. Of interest to me was Frida's exchange with a studio publicist who had gushed about the "exquisite condition" of one of the films. Frida asked if the film might be useful in a planned reissue of the movie; and if so, she pressed, whether the studio intended to reward me for my "humble stewardship and conscience." The publicist, caught off guard, said the studio intended to make an "in-kind contribution" to the Empress. I heard nothing more of this until Fergus called me one day.

"Anything you need?" Fergus asked me. "Digital projection?" He didn't sound tired now—he sounded like a man rubbing his hands together.

"I don't know."

"Ye have not because ye ask not," said Fergus.

"Don't really want it," I had to admit. I'm very foolish but it's tough to get excited about hard drives.

"I don't even know what to say to you."

"We could use a new roof."

"How much would that be?"

"Ten or twelve thou."

"I'll be in touch," said Fergus.

A few weeks later came a sweet cool Saturday up on the lookout. High clouds, birdsong, a slight offshore breeze, the sea sprouting columns of smoke that drifted lazily outward. Don Lean met us there, not in his uniform but in a dark blue suit from his banker days. He looked dapper and chubby and pleased—he happens to be an ordained minister along with everything else.

Bjorn had left early and fetched Nadine's parents. I'd met them only a few weeks before. What accepting people. Orry flew in from Colorado, a lot of white hair now infiltrating the red. She whispered the white hairs were "incorrigible," but she just looked more like herself. She had a small new tattoo of a smiling skull—I don't completely get it, but I like it. Rune stood up with us, and Bjorn, and Beeman, and that was the whole little tribe.

Or it was at first. People kept pulling over—the lookout's no secret and we kind of stood out, Nadine in her creamy cotton, a rose-bud crown in her hair. Drivers slowed their cars for a look, coming up the hill; they pulled in, then rolled down their windows and tried not to make themselves obvious. Soon there were a dozen cars lined up. Inside them were people important to us—Julie from the Agate, and

Lydia, and Ann Fandeen; Marcus came, and Lily Pea arrived with Galen. They all hung back until Nadine walked down through the twisting grasses. She spoke to them laughingly, teased them out of their cars so they followed her back with sheepish looks. By the time we said the important words they were twenty-five or thirty, dressed in their everydays, glad to be witnesses, wishing us well. Your tribe is always bigger than you think.

I'd like to give Jerry Fandeen a happy ending, but no. Jerry's in the penitentiary south of St. Cloud having a terrible time. I go see him sometimes. He enters the visitors' room looking heavy and pale—he tried to get strong, as in prisoner movies, where it's all weight lifting and yard fights, but prison's not that dramatic for Jerry. He says it's more like a long wait for something never to come. It's a bad time to be the man who built the bomb. He says it's as though he were being filled with despair, trickling in, day upon day, despair building up in his organs like mercury in certain big fish. He says the despair is now under control. He takes medication, but you glimpse the old trouble crossing his brow. Lost among strangers, that's how he looks.

Ann on the other hand thrives in the world.

After the bombing she divorced Jerry in sixteen seconds. He'd stolen those wind chimes for her, hoping their beautiful low tones would make her love him again. He'd hung them in a tree by her house where they bonged all night until she shrieked. In the end he took them away.

"How was I supposed to know they were stolen?" Ann asked Beeman, who was writing it up.

"It was in the paper," he said mildly.

"Like I read it all the way through," was her retort.

I admire Ann, though; she might be the only person on whom Leer had no ill effect. Maybe he even had a good one—maybe she touched that spinning flywheel and glanced off toward joy and fulfillment. I thought she might leave town and start over. Instead she stayed and ran for mayor, winning easily. Ann has ideas for Greenstone. She believes things are breaking our way. Maybe she's right. I'd love to see her preside over a renewal of our misty, blinking town. Yes and amen. That said, I'm not working for her—at present I'm busy with theater stewardship, making improvements that seem worthwhile, now that the roof is repaired. Ann wants me back as city clerk when my leave of absence is over, but I don't know. I did that job a long time. The previous tenant might've done it forever, but he seems on extended leave. Really, I doubt his return.

It took many months to afford and arrange, but we took Rune up on his invitation. We arrived in Tromsø in late November—just before sundown, for the long blue night. Against expectations it's not very cold. I like the noon twilight, the way snow is welcomed, the clean vivid ferries tonking away down by the swooping bridge. Maybe my name is really a calling. When insomnia strikes I go outside. Three in the morning and people are walking—locals and tourists, come for the borealis. We nod to each other, this league of insomniacs. All of us look up.

In our absence Bjorn is running the Empress, although we won't have him long. Finished with two years at the U of M, he leaves in the spring for Long Beach and Cal State's oceanography program. My guess is, he'll surf a bit too. In the meantime he's helping us evaluate offers—that's correct, for the Empress. Two offers came as a result of the magazine article and its follow-ups. In the insular movie-house world, the Empress is fleetingly famous. A bid also came over the transom from a California retiree who would be frankly rich in the Midwest, and another from a pair of St. Paul attorneys who believe in the "Greenstone Renewal." The offers are fair, but we're undecided. We rise in the morning and sometimes—just laugh. Stay and be part of whatever comes next, or sell and step out the door? Livings get made in all sorts of ways. There's not a bad option, as Beeman says.

For now we're catching our breath, in Tromsø.

Rune and some friends are planning a party—that's what they do when the sun reappears. Lucy is coming, which has Rune keyed up. We'll gather to wait for the sun. They say it unsticks from the jagged Lofotens, shines half an hour, and settles again. It's morning, it's evening—the very first day. There'll be music and fried cod and no doubt some akevitt. The event starts early and gets fairly loud, but a reverent silence is said to arrive in the final minutes of night. Some people weep and others cheer softly. Some blow out candles kept lit through the dark, and the smoke drifts away in the sun.

Down in the harbor a sailboat is docked with a crazy American couple aboard—Rune claimed he saw some semblance of us, and took us down to meet them. He's some sort of a vagabond writer, she an elfin creature aging in reverse. One night they both dreamed that they lived in the dark, in a boat all covered with snow; they provisioned their vessel and now here they are. Their plan is to sail farther north in the spring, to Svalbard they say, with its sluggish walruses and stark merry puffins. They invited us down to their tight little craft which is cold at the edges but snug where it counts.

"What's next for you two?" the old sailor wonders.

We've seen them a lot. He asks every time.

But all I can say is our future is airborne. I never saw a winter so blue. We all dream of finding but what's wrong with looking? When the sun rises we'll know what to do.

Acknowledgments

Thanks to Molly Friedrich for representing this novel with vigor and wit, and to Morgan Entrekin for giving it a home.

I'm grateful to my editor, Elisabeth Schmitz, who along with Katie Raissian helped to get Virgil ready, stand him up straight, and prod him to make his short declaratives. The best copy editors protect you from yourself, and Kirsten Giebutowski performed this job heroically.

Lee Enger started me early on the lifelong discipline of kite-flying, and briefly parked an antique Taylorcraft in Dad's garage; Lin Enger read an early draft and delivered a hopeful verdict on a cold Saturday morning.

Liz and Mike Towers gave steadfast friendship and encouragement, cinnamon rolls, even their Spare Oom in our time of need.

Thanks to Paul and Paula for calm anchorage, as well as Dean and Sara. Ty and John are lifelines of humor and perspective. There's nothing better than being resoundingly surpassed by your own.

And I'm indebted still to Robin, champion of line and color, who somehow continues to suspend her disbelief.